Look what people are saying about this talented author...

"Tawny Weber is—and will remain— on my Must-Read list. No, I'll top that, she is on my Must-Preorder list!"
—*Night Owl Reviews*

"Tawny Weber certainly knows how to pen delicious stories, filled with heat, humor and lovable characters."
—*CataRomance*

"Tawny Weber mixes sizzling sex, strong characters and suspense into an exciting, satisfying book."
—*RT Book Reviews*

"Another winner from Ms. Weber, who seems to never disappoint her readers."
—*Fresh Fiction* on *Wild Thing*

"Ms. Weber writes satisfying romance with kick that also makes you laugh and want to come back for more."
—*Long and Short Reviews*

"*Wild Thing* ended as it began, with a grin. Ms. Weber consistently shares her sense of humor with readers through the antics of her characters and she's succeeded again. I was thoroughly entertained from beginning to end."
—*Long and Short Reviews*

Dear Reader,

One of the things I love about reading is revisiting characters I've enjoyed in past stories. I'm always wondering what happened after The End, and how their Happily Ever After is going.

That's why this story has been so much fun for me. First of all, I was able to give Hunter his own romance (he's always been one of my favorite secondary characters from my Undercover Operatives series). But also, Hunter's book is paired with *Coming On Strong,* which features another of my favorite couples, Belle and Mitch.

I hope you have as much fun reading the stories as I had writing them. You'll have to let me know.

If you're on the web, I hope you'll stop by and visit! I've written an extra epilogue for readers featuring the entire Undercover Operatives clan in Black Oak. There are also insider peeks into *Midnight Special, Coming On Strong* and many of my other stories. Stop by my website at www.TawnyWeber.com or find me on Facebook at https://www.facebook.com/TawnyWeber.RomanceAuthor.

Happy reading!

Tawny Weber

Midnight Special
&
Coming on Strong

Tawny Weber

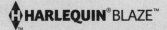

If you purchased this book without a cover you should be aware that this book is stolen property. It was reported as "unsold and destroyed" to the publisher, and neither the author nor the publisher has received any payment for this "stripped book."

ISBN-13: 978-0-373-79754-7

MIDNIGHT SPECIAL

Copyright © 2013 by Harlequin Books S.A.

The publisher acknowledges the copyright holder of the individual works as follows:

MIDNIGHT SPECIAL
Copyright © 2013 by Tawny Weber

COMING ON STRONG
Copyright © 2009 by Tawny Weber

Recycling programs for this product may not exist in your area.

All rights reserved. Except for use in any review, the reproduction or utilization of this work in whole or in part in any form by any electronic, mechanical or other means, now known or hereafter invented, including xerography, photocopying and recording, or in any information storage or retrieval system, is forbidden without the written permission of the publisher, Harlequin Enterprises Limited, 225 Duncan Mill Road, Don Mills, Ontario, Canada M3B 3K9.

This is a work of fiction. Names, characters, places and incidents are either the product of the author's imagination or are used fictitiously, and any resemblance to actual persons, living or dead, business establishments, events or locales is entirely coincidental.

This edition published by arrangement with Harlequin Books S.A.

For questions and comments about the quality of this book, please contact us at CustomerService@Harlequin.com.

® and TM are trademarks of Harlequin Enterprises Limited or its corporate affiliates. Trademarks indicated with ® are registered in the United States Patent and Trademark Office, the Canadian Trade Marks Office and in other countries.

www.Harlequin.com

Printed in U.S.A.

CONTENTS

MIDNIGHT SPECIAL 7

COMING ON STRONG 223

ABOUT THE AUTHOR

Tawny Weber has been writing sassy, sexy romances for the Harlequin Blaze line since her first book hit the shelves in 2007. A fan of Johnny Depp, cupcakes and color coordinating, Tawny spends a lot of her time shopping for cute shoes, scrapbooking and hanging out on Facebook. Come by and visit her on the web at www.tawnyweber.com.

Books by Tawny Weber

HARLEQUIN BLAZE

324—DOUBLE DARE
372—DOES SHE DARE?
418—RISQUÉ BUSINESS
462—COMING ON STRONG
468—GOING DOWN HARD
492—FEELS LIKE THE FIRST TIME
513—BLAZING BEDTIME STORIES, VOLUME III
    "You Have to Kiss a Lot of Frogs..."
564—RIDING THE WAVES
579—IT MUST HAVE BEEN THE MISTLETOE...
    "A Babe in Toyland"
592—BREAKING THE RULES
612—JUST FOR THE NIGHT
656—SEX, LIES AND MISTLETOE
660—SEX, LIES AND MIDNIGHT
688—BLAZING BEDTIME STORIES, VOLUME VII
    "Wild Thing"
726—NICE & NAUGHTY
738—A SEAL'S SEDUCTION
739—A SEAL'S SURRENDER

To get the inside scoop on Harlequin Blaze and its talented writers, be sure to check out blazeauthors.com.

Other titles by this author available in ebook format.
Don't miss any of our special offers. Write to us at the following address for information on our newest releases.

Harlequin Reader Service
U.S.: 3010 Walden Ave., P.O. Box 1325, Buffalo, NY 14269
Canadian: P.O. Box 609, Fort Erie, Ont. L2A 5X3

TAWNY WEBER

MIDNIGHT SPECIAL

To everyone who asked for Hunter's story.

Prologue

HE COULD HAVE BEEN WRAPPED around a sexy redhead, letting her use his body to fulfill any number of her kinkiest desires. He could be playing pirate and the captive wench at that very moment, stripping off his eye patch while singing "Love Machine."

But, _no_.

FBI Special Agent in Charge Hunter had figured he'd wrap up the last hour of the day by picking up a low-level criminal reputed to be fencing hot art. Find the guy, work a little intimidation, figure out who he was schlepping bronze nudes for. Easy as one-two-three, done in plenty of time to grab a shower before his date.

Except the dumb-ass fence must've had something hot going down, because after finally tracking him down in that skeezy bar in Hoboken ten minutes ago, the guy had taken one look at Hunter's face, run to his rusty Tempo and peeled out.

Adrenaline racing, he'd chased the idiot over the bridge back into Manhattan. Now, his hands gripping the steering wheel, Hunter stayed glued to the guy's bumper. He eyed the speedometer. One-twenty heading into a residential district. Probably not a good idea.

As chill as if he were on a Sunday drive, he mentally mapped the area, then pressed down a little harder on the gas so his front fender was level with the Ford's rear tires. He feinted to the right, as if he was going to ram the guy. He grinned at the wild-eyed stare in the rearview mirror, quickly followed by a look of desperation. The dumb-ass cranked the wheel, taking the first right on two tires.

Hunter smirked, easing back on the gas and letting dumb-ass think he was getting away instead of falling into a trap.

"Special Agent Hunter, in pursuit of suspect in Ford Tempo." He reeled off the license number and their current location. "Requesting backup at Pier 57. ETA, three minutes."

Just then, the Ford lost control. The guy bounced his fender off three cars, and then he got stupid. Hunter saw the Ford's rear glass shatter just in time to duck before the bullet came through his own windshield.

Son of a bitch. This was going to screw up his ETA. To say nothing of his date.

Pissed now, he set his jaw, wrenched hard on the steering wheel and used the momentum of the car ricocheting off the curb to slam into the back end of the other car.

Hunter hated being late.

He didn't bother pulling his own gun. He just rammed into the back of the idiot's car. The damned thing exploded. Hunter flinched as the flames lit the night sky, not sure if he was glad or not when the dumb-ass rolled out of the car just before it went kaboom.

The impact of the blast sent his own ride spinning.

He flipped three times, each one sending his brand-new, government-issue vehicle bouncing like a beach ball across the pavement. The seat belt cut viciously across his chest before the air bag deployed with the impact of a fist to the face. Hunter's head snapped back, his ears ringing like the Liberty Bell.

Freaking A.

As his car slid to a stop, his head kept on spinning like the tires that were whirling in the air. With a growl, Hunter decided that, yeah, he was glad the idiot had been thrown clear. Now he could kick his ass.

Climbing out through the window, he grimaced as his palms met a carpet of broken glass. Pain ripped through his head. Muscles, clenched tight during his little loop-de-loop, seized up painfully.

"Sir?"

Knees drawn up, the back of his head resting against his wrecked car, Hunter opened one eye.

"Ferris." Figured. The beat cop was Hunter's age, but gleamed like a bright new penny. Bright, hopeful and so damned young.

"Are you okay?"

"I'm breathing, aren't I?" As long as the air was hitting his lungs, Hunter was on the job and doing fine. "You get my guy?"

"Layton is rounding him up now. An ambulance is on its way."

"He needs an ambulance?" Hunter opened both eyes now, squinting across the dock to the other squad car, the cop and the puny idiot who didn't know how to drive.

"The ambulance is for you."

Hunter sneered. Then, figuring it'd have more impact if he wasn't sitting on his ass, he pushed to his feet and shook his head. He regretted the move when the sky did a slow three-sixty. "I'm fine."

"Uh-huh. Sir, I gotta say, I've worked with a handful of feds over the years. Most of them, they're total paper pushers. But you?" Ferris shook his head, giving Hunter a doleful once-over. "This is the second time in as many weeks I've answered a call with you on the other end. Running out of exploding buildings, high-speed car chases… You might want to sit behind your desk once in a while. Push those papers. Give your body time to recover."

"Desks are for wimps," he said with a dismissive smirk. Desk jockeys meandered up the ladder. Hunter planned to vault his way up. Eight years on the job and he was a special agent in charge. So far, he was doing pretty damned good, about two years ahead of where his old man had been at his age. Not surprising, since his father had wasted time and energy on marriage and a kid. Of course, as the kid in question, Hunter figured the old man's choice had worked out fine. But losing his wife when his kid was six had unquestionably put yet another crimp in the career climb. So, while Hunter was more than willing to follow his father's footsteps as far as his career was concerned, that was as far as it went.

No wife.

No kid.

Just the job.

It'd be nice to quit getting blown up or set on fire, though.

He lifted his hand to the wet patch on his cheek, noted the blood and sighed. Yeah. A break wouldn't be a bad thing.

"Aren't you, like, a boss?" Ferris matched his steps to Hunter's limping stride as they made their way toward the EMTs. "You don't *have* to have the crap trashed out of you on a regular basis, right? You could opt out once in a while."

Well, that was one way of looking at it. Hunter glanced down, saw his new jeans were ripped at the knee, and cussed a mental streak. Dammit. The deputy director wasn't gonna spring to pay for two pairs of pants in a single month. And the shoes were toast, too.

Behind them, a huge explosion was followed by a gust of fiery air. Bits of metal flew through the air, followed by the sound of the firefighters rushing to contain the conflagration.

There went his car.

"Holy shit." Ferris turned to watch the blaze.

Hunter didn't bother looking back.

Not that he'd admit it to anyone, but suddenly the idea of cozying up to a desk for a few days was sounding pretty damned good right this second.

1

A SMART WOMAN KNEW WHAT she wanted, and how to get it.

Marni Clare considered herself damned smart.

Every step she'd taken up the career ladder had been weighed, calculated and carefully thought through. From starting her first newspaper in second grade, to choosing to work as a reporter at smaller papers instead of larger for a chance to build a stronger criminal-reporting portfolio. Right up to her move last year to shift from papers to *Optimum,* a renowned national magazine that'd give her a stronger gravitas.

Everything she wanted always boiled down to her career. And what she wanted right now was information on a patient who'd been admitted here a week ago. The huge explosion of a derelict warehouse owned by reputed mobster and current FBI prisoner Charles Burns had been all over the news.

What hadn't been on the news, but Marni had managed to ferret out using her super-reporter insider info, was that someone had been injured, requiring an ambulance ride to this very emergency room.

She wanted to know who that someone was. Everyone was focused on Burns. On the trial, on the odds of a conviction. Marni had the feeling that whatever had gone down in that explosion, whoever had been involved, was the bigger story, though.

And she wanted it.

But sneaking patient information out of a very ethical nurse wasn't an easy task. It required stealth. A gift with reading people. A little bit of finesse.

And, of course, a bribe.

"I brought you cupcakes. Your favorite, chocolate with raspberry frosting," Marni said, setting a cute little purple basket on the counter and giving her cousin a bright smile.

"You brought me cupcakes?" Sammi Clare-Warren gave Marni a suspicious look. "Why?"

"Why would I bring my favorite cousin cupcakes?"

"You're up to something," Sammi declared knowingly. Still, she did slide the basket closer and sniff at the cupcakes. She gave a hungry little sound, as if she was sniffing at pure temptation, then pushed them back and gave her cousin a narrow look. "What do you want?"

Marni debated. She could tell the truth, that Meghan, Sammi's sister, said her twin had come home eight days ago raving about the drool-worthy, too-sexy-for-words FBI guy who'd been admitted to Emergency after a building exploded.

Or she could just throw herself out now, muttering a lecture on the sanctity of patient privacy and abuse of family ties.

"Wait…" Sammi gleefully drew the word out like she'd just discovered where Marni kept her secret stash of girly toys. "I know why you're here."

"Do you?" Marni wasn't sure if she should pull on an abashed look or go for guilty. It was hard to tell what Sammi suspected.

"You're hoping to meet someone." Sammi's grin was

pure triumph. And now that she'd divined her cousin's ne-
farious scheme, she pulled the basket of cupcakes across
the counter.

"Seriously? You think I'm trolling the emergency room
for a date?" What was wrong with her family? Did they
not know her, not at all?

"Why else would you be here at nine o'clock on a Friday night?"

Marni pushed her hand through her hair. Oh, now that
was just pathetic. Just because she was the only one of her
thirteen cousins still uncommitted didn't mean she was
looking to change that status. Especially not like this. She
didn't figure it conceited to acknowledge that she was a
good-looking, intelligent, fun woman. If she wanted a guy,
there were plenty of better places than this to find one.
But she didn't want a guy. She wanted a career. A fabulous, famous, reporting-on-big stories career.

Which she'd told her family over and over and *over*.

"You think I'm here looking for, what?" She gestured
to encompass the sterile, run-down room. "An old man
with pneumonia and a fat inheritance he's looking to be-
queath? Or a single, male accident victim with a good-
paying job that doesn't live with his mother?"

Sammi peered around the glass partition toward the
waiting room, as if checking to see if either of those potential dates had come in. Then she squinted at Marni.

"You make it sound like the only guys we get in here
are all messed up."

"That's because other than the doctors, whom you've
already deemed not worth setting me up with—" *thank
God* "—the only guys you get in here *are* all messed up."

Choosing the cupcake with the most frosting, Sammi
peeled back the paper liner and took a big bite.

"Then why are you here looking for a date?" she asked around her mouthful of chocolate.

Marni buried her face in her hands and groaned.

"Hey, some of those messed-up guys are pretty good-looking. There's a car accident victim in room five right now even you would drool over. He has that smoldering, sexy thing going on. And muscles. Talk about hot. His shoulders are to die for."

Sammi sighed so deep, she sent the papers on her nursing station fluttering. Marni wasn't sure any man was worth that much oxygen. Not even the one she was after.

Then again, what she wanted from him had nothing to do with the size of his...shoulders. And everything to do with the Charles Burns case. Indicted on SEC fraud and money laundering, the wealthy CEO was on his way to trial. After his dockside warehouse had exploded last week, rumors had started flying that the feds were going to bring new charges.

If she could get a handle on what they were, even an inkling about what had gone down with that explosion, she could write the article of her life. The one that would launch her out of the questionable fluff as the senior editor of Style and Entertainment and into the nitty-gritty of real reporting. Investigative reporting.

Marni gave a mental shiver of delight.

All she needed was a break. And that break was standing in front of her, licking frosting off her knuckles.

"You've had *one* sexy guy in here in the entire month, yet you think this is the place I should look for eligible bachelors?"

"You're the one who came in here looking for a guy."

Touché.

"If I wanted a guy—" which she wasn't saying she did "—I wouldn't want one who was sick. I want a guy who's healthy. One who's strong, with a brilliant mind and an intense personality. Sexy and fit, with a body that you can tell he takes care of. Running, swimming, I'm not picky. As long as he's got a sweet ass and some solid biceps. Oh, and washboard abs. There's nothing sexier than a guy with a flat stomach in tight jeans and a T-shirt."

Whew. Marni almost had to fan herself over that image. Not that she wanted a guy. She really didn't. But the fantasy was pretty sweet to entertain, all the same.

"We get guys like that," Sammi assured her. "The hottie that's in here right now? He's all of that and more. I mean, not too many guys can look gorgeous after almost being blown to pieces. But this guy is hot, and not just because his hair was singed."

"Hair straightener gone wrong?" Marni joked with watchful eyes.

"Building gone boom."

Bingo.

"So what's his name?"

A name would tell her if he was really with the FBI. Marni's pulse raced. A name might, with the right research, even tell her what the case was that'd resulted in an exploding building.

"I nicknamed him tall, dark and sexy." Sammi shrugged. "But really, I just know him as 'ruptured inner ear and broken rib.'"

Tall, dark and sexy? What good did that do her?

Well, Marni considered, it might do her good if she was open to getting naked and wild with a guy. But hot sex was on page two of her goal list, something she could get to later. After she'd reached her career goals.

"How can you stand it?" She tilted her head toward the computer. "You claim the sexiest guy you've ever seen was in here, you have his vital statistics, home address, heck, even where he works all there in the computer. You're telling me you don't peek?"

How had she cornered all of the nosiness in her entire family?

"Peeking wouldn't be ethical," Sammi said, her lips a prim bow.

"What fun is your job if you can't peek?"

"Oh, and your job is better? Why don't you get to bring home all those fashions you're always writing about?"

Because the magazine had a strict policy against their reporters accepting products, figuring any gifts would result in a story bias.

Okay, fine. Ethics were a good thing.

But they weren't going to help her get that name.

"There's tons of intrigue and excitement in Style to make up for the lack of perks. You should see how crazy it is during fashion week." Marni didn't add that most of the craziness stemmed from her chafing over always being stuck covering fluff stories. She'd been thrilled to get on with a magazine like *Optimum*. An award-winning periodical with national distribution, covering everything from politics to human interest to entertainment with a little crime and world news thrown in, too. It was a dream job. Originally hired for her gift with human-interest pieces, Marni had quickly realized that wasn't going to get her any big attention. So she'd taken the only senior editorial spot and became the head of Style. But now nobody took her seriously. She was the pretty little blonde with an eye for spotting the next hot trend and a gift for schmoozing with the hoitiest of the toity. But not a real journalist.

This story was it, she vowed. The one that'd make them see her as more than a curvy Kewpie doll with a trivial byline. But first she had to get that name.

"I guess you're right, though." Marni put a heavy pout

into her tone, adding a sigh for good measure. "The magazine really is a lousy place to meet single, heterosexual guys. So maybe you can help me out. Tell me more about the one with the singed hair. He sounds dreamy. Maybe I could meet him."

Marni wanted to cringe, to yell, *Hey, doesn't anyone know me well enough to realize that's total B.S.?* But she knew better. It didn't matter how often she claimed her career was her life, twenty-six was old-maid status in her family.

"Really?" Sammi did a little dance in place, jiggling with enough excitement to dislodge the pencil from behind her ear. "You want to meet tall, dark and sexy? He's in exam room five, and has to walk right past us when he leaves. You can check him out yourself."

Was it the FBI agent? Was he working the same case? Grilling her cousin and trying to sneak out a name was one thing. But actually seeing the guy herself, being able to follow him, maybe even meet him? *Holy cow.* Marni almost did a little dance herself right there on the faded linoleum. It took all her control not to rush down the hall, trying to find the fifth exam room.

"Nurse Clare-Warren?"

The women both turned, Sammi coming to subtle attention for the approaching doctor. "Hang back," she muttered to her cousin with a subtle shooing motion of her fingers.

Using patience she only expended on the job, Marni gave a cheerful nod and stepped aside. All the while pretending she didn't see the doctor trying to catch her eye.

This was it. Her shot. If she pulled off this article, they'd give her a slot as an investigative reporter. Working the crime beat. Digging for details, breaking the big stories. In a world where most reports in the papers and magazines were fed via carefully controlled press releases and media manipulation, she wanted to stand out. To be like the big reporters in the heyday of newspapers. The ones who squirreled out information, who were often as instrumental as cops in stopping crime. The ones who weren't afraid to expose ugliness.

She wanted to be like her aunt Robin. A Pulitzer Prize–winning reporter, she'd given the cold shoulder to traditions, diving into the men's milieu when women were still chained to the oven by their apron strings. She'd jumped right in and made their world her own. She'd interviewed global leaders, had waded into war zones and broken stories on topics as varied as criminal justice and corrupt politicians. Her career was amazing.

Exactly the path Marni wanted for herself. She just needed her break.

And this FBI case, with the exploding building, art theft and rumored mob connections, was going to give it to her. She'd write a huge story exposing the truths, the reality of how the FBI had busted a bigwig CEO, and she'd get the inside scoop on the real crimes of Charles Burns before the trial got going. Fame, fortune, accolades…they were right around the corner.

"Marni." Sammi's impatient tone interrupted Marni's daydream. "This is Dr. Green. Maybe he could show you through the E.R."

Huh?

Shaking off the dream of glory, Marni pulled her attention away from her ambitions and focused on the eager man standing next to her cousin. Forty, balding with bad plugs and a hint of garlic on his breath, he was looking at her as if she was his favorite centerfold come to life.

"Hello, it's nice to meet you," she offered formally, hoping the distant tone would clue him in to her disinterest.

"It's great to meet you," he said, shaking her hand just long enough to make her want to grab the antibacterial lotion off the nurses' station. "Nurse Clare-Warren explained that you're writing an article on our hospital?"

Again, huh?

At Marni's questioning look, Sammi shrugged, then tilted her head toward the no-personal-visitors notice taped on the file cabinet. Then she held up five fingers and tilted her head toward the exam rooms.

Ooooh. Marni offered her cousin, and the good doctor, a big smile.

"You were interested in a tour of our emergency facilities?" he queried, making it sound as though he was extending an invitation to see the backseat of his Lexus. "I'll fill you in on the details of what I do here."

Sammi was now mouthing *married* behind his back and making faces.

Figured.

Still, he could get her in closer eavesdropping range of exam room five, so she might as well take advantage of his interest. In the fake article, and in her body.

When a girl looked like Marni did, the choices were limited. Fight to be taken seriously, courting frustration and disappointment on a regular basis. Or accept that her curvaceous figure, Kewpie doll face, flaxen hair and big blue eyes were the stuff fantasies were made of, and use it to her advantage. Marni wasn't big on frustration, disappointment or losing. So she was all about the advantage.

"Sure. I'd love a tour, especially of the exam areas. That's the focus of the article," she lied. Smiling, she pulled out her ever-present notebook, making sure her elbows angled out so as to keep at least a foot between them. Noting exam rooms one and two to her left, she turned in the opposite direction.

And was pretty sure she heard her cousin giggle as she went. It was hard to tell, though, with the doctor rambling on about his qualifications. A few of them even applied to his job.

"Excuse me, Dr. Green?" An exhausted-looking guy in scrubs stepped out of one of the exam rooms and gestured for help. "A minute?"

The good doctor gave a frustrated huff, then asked Marni to wait.

Her gaze angled one door away, labeled five.

"Oh, sure." She bit her lip, then made a show of making a few notes. "I'll be fine here. I'll just get everything you said written down before I forget."

Giving the doctor a big smile, Marni stepped just a smidge to the left and let her eyes slide past the balding head to the open door of exam room five.

Her heart raced. Her pulse skipped. Her mouth went dry.

Oh, baby.

Those were definitely some sexy shoulders. Right there, above a very nice ass. The shoulders were bare, and Marni was pretty sure it was a crime that the ass was covered.

She'd never wanted anything more than her career.

Until now.

"I don't have time for this crap."

Hunter glared at the doctor, then shifted the same threatening look at his boss.

"You should have thought of that before you messed yourself up again. What were you doing chasing some low-level art fence? It has nothing to do with the Burns case, dammit." Looking as frustrated as Hunter felt, Deputy Director Murray took the clipboard from the doctor's hands and flipped through the chart. As if he could change the diagnosis by reading it himself. "You should have taken the time off like I ordered."

"That was an order? I thought it was a suggestion," Hunter countered with a grin. At least, it was supposed to be a grin. But the good doctor, his hands now free of the clipboard, was poking at Hunter's ribs again like some kind of sadist. They were cracked again, dammit. He knew it, the doctor knew it, Murray knew it. Poking wasn't gonna change that fact any more than Murray glaring at the chart was going to change the diagnosis of further damage to Hunter's inner ear.

"You're supposed to be on the West Coast to testify in a week," Murray snapped, shoving the metal file at Hunter in accusation. "How are you planning to make that happen now that you're on the injured hero's no-fly list?"

"Seriously?" Hunter asked the doctor. "I can't fly at all?"

"Not unless you want to risk losing your hearing, collapsing in the air or possibly bleeding from the brain." The doctor offered a cheery smile to go with that dire prognosis before stepping out of the room and closing the door behind him.

Well, none of that sounded appealing.

Hunter's brain, still thankfully not bleeding, raced. He had to get to California for that trial.

Charles Burns was a nasty piece of work who thought he was going to skate on the current charges. He'd already won the first round by having the case tried in California, claiming that was his main residence and corporate headquarters. His defense team was the best dirty money could buy and the crooked CEO knew that the worst he'd do was a couple of years and a fistful of fines.

Unless the FBI could pull together all the pieces that had exploded in their lap last week. Pieces that would add racketeering and, if Murray had his way, attempted murder to the list of charges. Burns was so sure that he'd gotten away with murder. The creep had no idea that Hunter had rescued the victim he'd left for dead just before the building exploded. It was up to Hunter to turn a botched homicide into enough evidence to not only put Burns behind bars for life, but take down his entire operation for good.

He had an ace in the hole to make that happen. By hauling Burns's victim out of the explosion last week, before she was blown into tiny bits, he'd secured the devotion— and a huge amount of insider information—from the rumored late Mrs. Burns. In return, he'd promised that she'd stay dead.

"Beverly Burns only agreed to hand over her husband's books, files and passwords in exchange for not being brought into the trial."

Murray waved that away.

"And she's yet to hand it all over. At this point, she's offered up maybe, what? Seventy percent of what she said she would? She's holding out the rest for a cushy life of luxury in witness protection. To hell with that. I don't care if she's interested in testifying or not. We have ways of making people talk."

His eyes narrow with dislike, Hunter asked, "Don't you need a heavy accent and a flashlight when you say shit like that?"

Murray sneered. Hunter's flippant remarks were just one more thing the deputy director didn't like about the man he saw as his subordinate.

"Look, I want this guy put away. We have a witness who can guarantee that. Just because you're all comfy cozy with criminals doesn't mean we should coddle her at the expense of the case."

"Comfy cozy?"

"Black Oak, California," Murray shot back. "Three known criminal elements, and you let them go. Hell, you were best man at one of their weddings last year, weren't you?"

"Caleb Black was DEA and is now the sheriff of Black Oak. Hardly a criminal element."

"And the rest of his family?"

"Well, I did walk Danita down the aisle when she married Gabriel. But I wasn't best man at that one, even though Danita's FBI, too. Maya married an FBI agent as well and I caught the bouquet at their wedding. Is that too cozy?" Hunter made a show of shaking his head in disgust. "Yeah, they're all major criminal elements, all right. Good thing each is assigned their own personal law-enforcement babysitter."

"You think it's funny?"

Yeah, pretty much. Murray was one of those guys who operated in black-and-white. Us and them. Good and bad. Hunter saw life in shades of gray.

He didn't say that, though. Instead, he pointed out, "You're just pissed that you'd have arrested the wrong person."

"I'd have arrested a criminal."

"Tobias Black wasn't behind the crimes in question. Arresting him would have been a grave miscarriage of justice. Just as it will be if you force Beverly Burns to testify against her husband, jettisoning the illusion that she died in that explosion. If Burns knows she's alive, he'll have her killed. He knows she's alive and cooperating with the feds, he'll have her killed faster. She won't make it to the trial."

"She's under FBI protection. She'll make it to testify."

Hunter just stared. Unspoken, but clear, was the truth

that if she testified against her husband, her life expectancy would thereafter be on par with that of a fruit fly.

"This is my case." Ignoring the pained scream from his rib, Hunter got to his feet and gave Murray a look of cold determination. "I've already cleared the plan through all appropriate channels."

"I spoke with the director myself. Unless you can show you've nailed Burns without his wife's testimony, she's taking the stand. You have a week into the trial. Good luck with that." He waited a beat, then with a smile filled with malice, added, "Oh, by the way. How are you getting to California? Driving? You're gonna have a great time building a case from behind the wheel."

That Hunter's car currently resembled tin foil went unspoken. Not because the deputy director was playing nice. But because the man knew the value of leaving the worst unsaid. It lingered there, floating above them like a vile stench.

Hunter debated his options.

"Fine, I'll take a train."

"Train?"

"Sure. There has to be a train going from New York to San Francisco." Despite the fact that the room was spinning in three directions at once, Hunter shifted into intimidation mode, using his four-inch advantage to loom over his boss. "Bottom line, we're not bringing Beverly Burns into this trial. I made a promise. She gave us ample information to indict Burns on twice as many charges as we already had. Enough to shut down his entire operation. In exchange, we not only tuck her away in the hidden depths of WitSec, but make sure everyone believes she died in that explosion."

"The trial is in a week. And we're still desperately sifting through all of that *ample information*. It's not like the pieces we need are just sitting there waiting to be used to nail him to the wall."

"I know the Burns operation inside out. I'll find every single piece," Hunter vowed.

"This case hinges on you, then, doesn't it? Now there's a damned good chance this guy will walk free because you couldn't resist hotdogging it down the pier on the hood of your car."

Hunter gritted his teeth. Asshole or not, Murray was right.

"I can work the case while I'm on the train just as well as I could here in my office. I'll just take it with me."

"Those files are classified."

"I've got clearance. You need more, I'll make a couple of phone calls and get it for you."

Hunter didn't pull the connection card out very often. He didn't need to. His father's legacy at the FBI was the stuff legends were made of. The bureau chief was Hunter's godfather. And his own record wasn't just shiny, it glittered. So while he never played the prima donna, it was pretty rare that he heard the word *no*.

And he wasn't about to hear it now. Murray offered a sour smile. The man knew Hunter was going to vault right over his position on his climb up the ladder. He didn't like it, but there wasn't a damned thing he could do about it.

The doctor stepped back into the room. Face blank now, Murray turned away to make a phone call.

"Here's your prescription, filled. I wrote up a list of dos and don'ts for you to ignore, as well."

"Add the drugs to the list because I'm not taking them." Hunter grimaced as he shrugged into his shirt. Every muscle in his body was screaming.

"You don't take two of these before you go to sleep tonight, you won't be moving tomorrow." He held out the pills and list with a patient smile.

He had a job to do, one he couldn't accomplish doped up. Hunter's eyes cut to Murray's back, then he started buttoning his shirt. The tips of his fingers whimpered their protest.

He wouldn't get it done if he was laid out, either.

"Fine." He stuffed the bottle and paper in the pocket of his leather jacket just as his boss ended his call.

"I pulled some strings and found a vintage rail car heading west. New York to Chicago, Chicago to San Francisco. You've got a private sleeper car on the Midnight Special. It leaves tonight at nine forty-five. An agent will meet you in Chicago with the files, a secured laptop and luggage."

Hunter didn't gloat. Why would he? He'd known he'd win all along.

"Midnight Special?" It sounded like something offered by a discount prostitute.

"It's a restored luxury train owned by a private rail company. This is some kind of themed trip. Passengers are required to participate."

"I don't play dress up."

"You do if you want on this train."

Hunter just stared, his gaze steely and his jaw set.

"You want to find something else, feel free. You want to go now, the train leaves at nine forty-five," Murray said again, his smile just this side of gloating.

He could ignore the participation requirement once he was there. But he just had to get on that train. Hunter glanced at his watch.

"It's quarter of eight now."

"Guess you'd better hurry, then."

2

ALL MARNI COULD HEAR from the exam room were murmurs. Words like *expert witness, new information* and *vital testimony.* There had been mention of studying the case, of classified documents and secrets to protect.

It was all so juicy.

And she had the inside scoop.

The *Midnight Special.*

Her fingers flying across the screen of her phone, Marni called in her excellent research skills to find as much about the train as she could while hurrying back to the nurses' station.

Owned by an eccentric movie director, the fully restored passenger car was a dedication to opulence and luxury. Crossing the country only six times a year, each tour was dedicated to a particular theme. She squinted at the screen and winced. This one was film noir. Ah, well, at least the fashions had rocked in the forties.

She wasn't sure what excuse she'd babbled at Sammi as she raced out of the hospital. She vaguely remembered muttering something about a story, vintage clothes and sexy shoulders.

She flew across the hospital parking lot as fast as her

high heels could carry her, diving into the driver's seat of her Mini Cooper and giving a little scream of triumph.

This was it. Her big break.

She was going to follow him.

Marni glanced at the dashboard clock. Eight o'clock, a half hour to the train station and she didn't have a ticket. Thinking fast, she pressed the phone button on her steering wheel, then chose her roommate's number.

"I need a favor," she said over the top of Carrie's cheerful hello. "I'll be swinging by in about ten minutes. Can you meet me out front with a suitcase?"

The stunned silence on the other end made Marni wince.

"You want me to pack for you?" Carrie asked, sounding equal parts thrilled and terrified. As if she'd just been asked to play opposite Johnny Depp in a love scene.

Film noir meant forties crime melodrama. She'd read that the entire trip was one of those mystery events where everyone dressed up.

"Think vintage fashion, the forties era," Marni instructed her cousin. "Cocktail dresses, pencil skirts, my floral cotton dress and maybe the wool suit if you can find a wide belt. Oh, can I borrow your fedora? And don't forget to pack my black leather T-strap pumps. They're perfect."

"You want me to pack anything vintage, in less than ten minutes?"

"You can't do it?"

"Are you kidding? This is awesome. What's the deal? Where are you going? With who and for how long?"

Marni cringed, then tried to pretend that the sound of drawers and doors flinging open was reassuring.

"Put together enough for a week—no, make it two weeks, just in case there isn't laundry on the train. I'm catching the Midnight Special tonight to San Francisco and I'll miss it if I don't hurry."

"Ooh?" From the beginning of the syllable to the end, Carrie went from excited to curious to suspicious. The banging and slamming stopped. "Why? What are you doing?"

"I'm chasing a guy." Hoping that didn't sound as silly to Carrie as it did to her, Marni bit her lip.

"A man…?" The last word was offered in a juicy whisper, with just a hint of *as if* thrown in. The skepticism didn't just come from the fact that Carrie and Marni had been favorite cousins since they were babies, or that she'd heard Marni vow over and over that she wanted to be just like their aunt. It was that Carrie, like everyone else in the family, figured that Marni was just biding her time with this career until the right man came along. Oh, she could keep her job. The family considered themselves evolved enough to believe women could and should have careers outside the home. As long as the home in question included a husband and at least one darling tot. Which meant the careers had to lend themselves to taking good care of said husband and requisite tot.

Carrie had listened often enough to Marni railing against that family creed, sympathizing with her vow to someday, somehow, find the perfect guy. A sexy stud who'd be available when she wanted him, able to cater to all her sexual needs and happily slide back into obscurity when she was busy with her career.

"You found a boy toy like you're always talking about?" Carrie asked in hushed awe. "A hot, gorgeous guy who will provide your every sexual desire, know where the G-spot is and why foreplay is vital, then quietly leave you alone in the morning?"

"I wish," Marni muttered.

That was her ideal man. There to scratch that G-spot itch, dispose of ugly spiders, to be able to laugh at himself and, oh, if only, know his way around a dance floor. So, pretty much nonexistent.

But that wasn't going to get her cousin packing any faster.

"Well, maybe," she corrected more loudly. "I mean, I don't know how good he is in bed or anything. But he's got shoulders to die for, a body that won't quit and oh, baby, his butt is so nice."

Stopped at a red light, she squirmed a little in the seat of her car at the memory of the FBI guy's back. A guy like that, sexy and strong, dedicated and focused? That kind of guy was dangerous. Not because he carried a gun. But because he was the only kind of guy she could ever imagine herself giving up her dream for.

Lucky for her, she was sure he didn't have the rest of her fantasy guy requirements.

Great shoulders or not, no guy was that perfect.

Which made it easy to tell Carrie, "I'm going to chase him down and see, though. I mean, why not, right? I'm supposed to be on the great manhunt, putting every effort into pulling myself out of this shameful single life."

"You saw a guy for the first time, what? Tonight? And suddenly you're so hot for him, you're hopping a train to chase him across the country?"

Marni scrunched her nose, wondering if that sarcasm was going to ooze some ugly substance out through the car's Bluetooth speakers.

"Didn't you chase Robert to Virginia?" she countered.

Carrie had followed her army paratrooper all the way to the altar. When he'd been deployed to the Middle East a couple of months after their wedding, she'd chosen to move back to New York to be close to family, with plans for Robert to put in for a transfer to Fort Hamilton when his tour was finished.

"You're thinking marriage?"

Marni cringed.

"I never said that."

"You compared chasing this guy to my chasing Robert. That means marriage."

Maybe that'd been the wrong argument. Too late to change it now, though.

"Look, I've got to call the train station and make sure I can get a berth. Will you have my bag ready when I get there?"

"I'll be on the front stoop in five minutes," Carrie promised.

With a quick thanks, Marni gratefully ended the call.

Her gratitude, and good humor, were gone when she pulled up in front of the apartment building twelve minutes later.

"I'm late," she said through the open window. "I've got to hurry."

"I added a few extras from my closet, and borrowed some from Liza across the hall. She has better evening wear than either of us," Carrie said before she hefted two suitcases and a satchel. "I wish you had a bigger car, though. I don't think this is going to fit in your trunk."

Before Marni could lift her chin off her chest, her cousin rounded the car, pulled open the passenger seat and started hefting bags into the back.

"How could you pack so much in such a short time?" And where was she supposed to put it? Didn't trains have dinky berths?

"Hey, don't let it be said that I didn't do my part to help my cousin launch a major offensive on the Great Clare Marriage Quest."

An offensive in defeating it, maybe. If she knew the truth, though, Carrie would likely grab the bags back out of the car, then throw herself across the hood to keep Marni from leaving. So she kept that to herself.

"Thanks," she said instead. And knowing her cousin tended to worry, she added, "I'll check in tomorrow."

She only caught a glimpse of Carrie's smile before the other woman wrapped her arms around Marni's neck and whispered "good luck" in her hair. Then, with a glance at the clock on the dash, she scooted back out of the car, slammed the door and made an *onward* gesture by waving her arm forward.

Her stomach doing a crazy interpretive dance of nervous excitement, Marni grinned and waved.

This was it, time to make her dreams come true.

Thirty minutes later, she was ready to scream. Every second was tiptoeing closer to a nightmare than a dream.

"What do you mean, I can't get a berth? I called I was told there were three available."

"Those are the overflow berths," the porter said with an apologetic smile. He gestured, moving Marni off to the side and out of the way of the ticketed passengers boarding the train. "You shouldn't have been offered one. The train is actually fully booked. I'm sorry for the mix-up."

"Can't I just get a seat instead, then?" Pretending she loved the idea of crossing the country sitting uncomfortably upright, Marni offered her sweetest smile. The one that flashed not only a dimple, but included a flutter of her lashes, as well.

The porter, a distinguished-looking gentleman in his forties, blushed. But he still shook his head and gave her a regretful look.

"I'm sorry. We're not a commuter train. There is no sleeping in the public cars."

"But—"

"Excuse me, Porter Jones, there's a passenger situation that needs your attention."

The porter and Marni both turned to the younger man, also dressed in the blue serge uniform and cap to indicate he was a part of the train crew.

"Of course. Porter Simpson, could you finish up with Ms. Clare for me please?"

"Sure," the younger man said with an enthusiastic grin. After a sharp look from his superior, he brought it down a few watts, plastering on a serious look and nodding. "I'd be happy to help."

After a warning look, Porter Jones excused himself.

"So what can I do for you?"

"According to Mr. Jones, there's nothing that can be done." Marni pushed a frustrated hand through her hair, then lifted it in a helpless gesture. "I called forty-five minutes ago, and thought I'd booked space on the train, but apparently I was wrong."

"What? No way. I took that call. You asked me to reserve you a berth, so I logged it in." He opened his vintage brass-and-leather folder to reveal a very modern computer tablet, using his finger to pull up a registration page.

"Marni Clare, right?"

At her nod, he tilted the screen toward her.

"See, here. I reserved the last berth for you. I just need your credit card to finish the booking."

"Thank you so much." Excited, Marni plucked her wallet from her clutch and slid out her credit card for him.

He ran her card through a little handheld device, then waited. He ran it again, then frowned.

"Okay, well I must have done something wrong." His face crumpled a little and he looked down the platform as if searching for help. Not seeing anyone, he gave Marni a rueful grimace. "This is my first trip. I'll figure it out, though. I mean, most of our training is in service, you know? Bookings are usually done by the senior porters."

Not sure if she should be worried or not, Marni took her credit card back. "Is this going to be a problem?"

"Nah. I mean, I put your name on the berth registration, see?" He held up the tablet and pointed. Marni noticed the small icon at the bottom of the screen labeled Apply was still lit. As if it hadn't been pushed, or the registration information hadn't been sent through. "And it has your credit card number right here so it recorded your payment information. So it's all good."

"But—"

Before she could ask him about the apply icon, the train's whistle blew loud and strong.

"All aboard," he said with a grin. Closing the tablet back in its case, he lifted her suitcases and angled his head toward the steps. "Right this way, ma'am."

But...

Her hand on the handle of her satchel, Marni hesitated. She was pretty sure he hadn't actually completed the reservation. Which meant that she might not have a berth when she got on the train.

Of course, it wasn't as though they were going to toss her out the window once they were in transit. Worst-case scenario, she spent the night in a lounge or dining car sitting up, and they'd put her off in Chicago the next day. Plenty of time for her to work the train, schmooze her way through the passenger list and see what she could find.

Even if she did get the berth, this was a gamble.

Less than twenty-four hours to find a guy who, given his injuries, would definitely be sleeping for the next eight or ten of them. She didn't know his name, his voice was a husky blur. All she had to go on was a set of gorgeous shoulders and a very nice butt. The chances of getting all of the male passengers with dark hair to strip off their shirts and turn their backs was probably on the slim side.

Still, it was a chance.

"Coming," she said with a big smile. She swung her satchel over her shoulder, tucked her purse tighter under her arm and hurried after him. Excitement swirled as she looked around, taking in all of the details. The train was a crisp red, the windows glistening like crystal against the harsh neon lights of the station. Holding the brass rail, she climbed the steps after the porter, then gave a soft gasp.

"Oh, my," she breathed. It was like stepping into the past. Lantern-style lights lined the damask-covered walls of the narrow aisle. Instead of utilitarian grays, metal and plastic, everything she could see was pure luxury. Rosewood gleamed. Brass shone. Each berth door was heavy, polished wood with a discreet brass number.

It wasn't going to be easy to find her FBI guy in this setup, she realized. When they reached the door marked seventeen, the porter stopped and, using a key from the huge ring at his waist, he opened the door.

He set her bags at the foot of the comfortable-looking full-size bed before pulling a second set of keys out of his pocket and choosing one.

Holding the two up to the light, he compared the key to the one on his ring, gave a satisfied nod, then handed it to her. He settled her suitcases into a cubby at the foot of the bunk-style bed, twisted the blinds to let in the bright station lights, then stepped over and turned on the light in the tiny bathroom.

"Breakfast is served in the dining car from six to eleven. The schedule of movie events is here," he indicated, pointing to a brochure on the little dresser. "Tomorrow I'll deliver your information packet. It will describe the rules and suggest strategies, as well as detailing your role for the Mystery Murder event."

"Thank you so much," Marni said, tucking a tip into his gloved hand. "I appreciate this, a lot."

His boyish grin flashed again before he wiped it clean and gave her a sedate nod.

"If you require anything, just call the porter's desk. It's star four on the intercom."

With that and one last look around as if completing a mental checklist of his duties, he gave her a nod and left.

"Well, then," Marni muttered to herself as she peered around the sleeper car. It was bigger than she'd expect on a train, and just as luxurious as everything else she'd seen so far. Way more luxurious than her credit card would probably like, she realized.

Were all the berths this fancy? Was there anything cheaper? Holy cow. She dropped into one of the plush club chairs and took a deep breath. The magazine was generous with her expense account. Mingling with the rich and famous of the fashion world didn't come cheap, after all. But they weren't going to reimburse her for this since she wasn't on a legitimate assignment.

Unless she broke the story.

Ambition stirred, intense and edgy in her belly. Big breaks were few and far between. This one had fallen into her lap. This was meant to happen.

The story was hers.

Excited again, Marni jumped to her feet and pulled one of the suitcases out, setting it on the crisply made berth, and flipped it open.

"Oh, Carrie." She sighed.

No wonder she'd looked so smug. She hadn't packed for Marni to travel across the country to the theme of film noir. She'd packed for Marni to manhunt her way into hot-and-sexy's bed.

All of Marni's best lingerie, silkiest underthings and most provocative clothes were tucked in here. Fitting in was one thing. Looking as if she was on the forties stroll was another.

Suddenly exhausted as the chasing-a-hot-story adrenaline drained from her body, she decided to worry about it in the morning. Right now, she just wanted sleep. With that in mind, she showered in the itsy-bitsy excuse of a bathroom, then slid into an even ittier and bittier excuse of a nightie. Her face freshly scrubbed, her hair tidily brushed, she slid the suitcase under the berth and pulled her own tablet out of her purse. Read, or sleep? Realizing she wouldn't manage to read two pages, she set the tablet aside and turned off the lights.

She cued up her tiny MP3 player to her favorite subliminal recording, "Ambition Made Real" set to relaxing music. Tucking her earbuds in, she scooted down under six-hundred-thread-count sheets and moaned in delight.

A good night's sleep filled with subconscious messaging and she'd be in prime investigative reporting mode first thing in the morning. Time to make her dreams come true.

WHAT A FREAKING NIGHTMARE.

As he got on the train, just before the departure whistle blew, Hunter cursed. Every cell in his body throbbed in painful unison, from his hair follicles to his toenails.

Hunter cursed as he made his way painfully through the train's corridor, looking for the dining car. He needed food. Food, a shot of whiskey and about thirty hours of shut-eye.

He'd settle for the food, though.

"Are you still serving meals?" he asked the tuxedo-clad host who met him at the door of the dining car. "Can I get a burger?"

"Of course, sir. Right this way."

It was a sad state of affairs that Hunter wanted to ask for a table near the door just so he didn't have to cross the room. Instead, he gritted his teeth and followed the guy. Always alert, he scoped out the other diners. A dozen people in the high-income range from the bling and quality of their clothes. Couples, except one lone woman who was looking at him as if he might be more tasty than the piece of prime rib on her plate.

Now that he had a gauge on the room, Hunter ignored them all. Including the hungry-looking brunette.

"Burger," he repeated as he dropped into a chair, his back to the wall and the room in full view. "Medium, along with whatever you put on the side. Add a bowl of that beef soup, rolls and a Cobb salad. In whatever order they cook fastest."

Rolling a car tended to make him hungry.

"And to drink?"

He debated.

Technically, he was off duty. He was also under doctor's orders to take the next twenty-four hours off and recuperate. He couldn't work the case until they reached Chicago and he got the files.

"Whiskey, neat."

While he waited, he'd go through his own notes and list a few priorities. He barely had time to pull out his notebook before his drink arrived, quickly followed by the rolls and his soup. Hunter dove into the meal with gusto, jotting down notes between bites.

Saving Beverly Burns had been a godsend. For the FBI as much as her, probably. A trophy wife with a brain, she'd made the fatal mistake of telling her husband off for having an affair. Charles Burns, figuring divorce proceedings might be headed his way, had thumped her over the head and tossed her into one of his warehouses, then set the damned thing on fire.

Hunter read over his outline of events, jotting down notes here and there as he ate. By the time he wiped the last crumb from his lips, he was comfortable with his plans for the case, full and totally exhausted.

"Can I get the bill?" he asked the waiter who was clearing his plate.

"No charge, sir. Meals are included in the cost of your trip. I just need to note down your berth number."

He hadn't seen the berth yet, hadn't even checked to see where it was. Hunter pulled out the train ticket from his pocket to check, impressed despite himself. He hadn't figured Murray for the type to book a luxury trip. The guy doubtless had no choice, though. The cattle cars were probably all full.

"I'm in seventeen."

"Very good." The man made a note before asking if Hunter wanted anything else.

"Just some sleep."

It wasn't until he stood up that Hunter realized his aches were gone. He blinked a couple times to bring the room back into focus and wondered what the hell kind of whiskey they served here.

Then he winced. Hell, the doc had poked him with a needle or two, probably some kind of painkillers. Too bad he hadn't remembered that before he'd thrown back a couple fingers of alcohol.

He wasn't impaired. Just a little foggy.

No problem. He wasn't driving, wasn't working the case. His only objective for the rest of tonight was to get some damned sleep. He'd walk a little slower to compensate for the slight haze the room had taken on. Hunter never let anything stand in his way.

Sleeping berth seventeen was easy enough to find. Not bothering with lights, he stripped naked, tossing his clothes over the back of a chair. Thankfully, Murray had had someone deliver a change of clothes to the hospital, but it was all Hunter had until his luggage was delivered, along with the case files.

Soft fingers of moonbeams peeked through the window, lighting the bed curtain enough for him to find the opening. The bed was turned down, welcoming as he sank into its comfort.

His last thought before he dived into sleep was a mild feeling of regret. He'd really been looking forward to his naked romp with the redhead. So much that he could smell that rich, floral temptation that was pure feminine delight.

Not a bad thing to go to sleep with.

3

Hunter wasn't sure what woke him up.

One second, he was down so deep, even his subconscious was sawing logs. The next, he was floating on a sea of pleasure, his entire body stirring with passion more intense than anything he'd ever felt while awake.

Gotta love the dream life.

And he was loving it enough that he didn't even try to surface. Instead, even as his conscious mind nagged and poked at him to deal with…something? A problem? An issue? He didn't know. He didn't care. He was feeling way too good.

It was rare that he mixed painkillers and alcohol. He didn't know if it was the quality of the hooch or the fact that his meds had been injected, but this was all new. Instead of fuzzy and zoned, he was horny and hard.

He liked this experience a hell of a lot better, he decided as his hands curved over some sexy imaginary ass.

Might as well ride with it. A smart man knew better than to try and wake himself from an erotic dream. A smarter man took control of the dream and dived in for all he was worth.

So Hunter grabbed on to the fantasy—by the sweet

cheeks, no less—and dived in. He buried his face in the soft cloud of hair, breathing deep the floral scent. Then he slid lower, until his lips encountered warm flesh.

Soft, silky warm flesh. His mouth skimmed a slender throat with hot, openmouthed kisses. One hand still cupping a lushly curved butt, his other slid upward. Over a deliciously curving hip, along the sweet indentation of her waist covered in a slippery satin fabric, and up to the full—oh, baby so full—round flesh of her breast. For one delightful second, he simply held her. Then he brushed his thumb once over the satin-covered nipple.

It hardened with gratifying speed.

God, he loved a responsive woman.

Reveled in the instant pleasure her body offered when it reacted to his touch.

Fingers, as soft and light as a breath of air, skimmed over his shoulders, leaving a trail of pleasure everywhere they touched. So delicate, so tempting.

His body, so miserable the night before, was awash with passion. It was like floating on a sea of pure sensation, every breath, every touch feeling better than the last.

Hard, throbbing and ready to rock, his dick signaled its approval of the fantasy.

Now, this was how a guy should recover from almost being blown up.

MARNI'S HEAD SPUN with delight, falling back against the pillow as she sank deeper into the best dream of her life. Had she ever felt this good? She didn't need to do a body check to know the answer. The delight, the power of desire, they tangled and swirled through her sleep-heavy mind. She'd fallen asleep to her subliminal messaging and the gentle rocking of the train, exhausted by nerves and adrenaline.

And this, she was sure, was her body's way of thanking her for a wonderful night's sleep. By giving her a hot, juicy wake-up fantasy.

Her dream lover's lips trailed over the sensitive curve of her throat with hot, openmouthed kisses. She shivered when he buried his face in the curve of her shoulder, reaching up to comb her fingers through his hair. The strands fell like silk over her flesh.

His hand, firm, yet tender, cupped her butt, squeezing the full flesh. The other was doing magical things to her nipple, teasing and tweaking. Spiraling around, then pinching. Pleasure pooled, hot and wet, between her thighs. Marni shifted, sliding one leg up her dream lover's rougher one. The friction added an edgy delight to the already incredible feelings swirling low in her belly.

He moved lower, sliding his lips over her chest. His mouth was wet on the satin of her nightie, leaving a damp trail until he reached her aching nipple. His fingers worked the other one with skillful precision, keeping time with the swirl of his tongue, the scrape of his teeth.

Marni shifted, pulling his thigh between hers, pressing the throbbing, swollen wet heat of her clitoris against his leg, trying to relieve the building pressure.

His teeth nipped, then he pulled back to blow a puff of air over the tip of her breast.

Marni's body exploded. It was a pop of an orgasm. Quick and intense, a prelude to the banquet of delight yet to come. She shuddered, her fingers digging into his hair as she held his mouth close, wanting more.

So much more.

Her dream lover moaned.

Out loud.

So loud, so real, the sound reverberated against her nipple. It felt so good.

Except, dream lovers didn't do that.

Alarmed out of her delightful reverie, Marni forced her eyelids open.

Her dream lover was solid.

Real, even.

Black hair swirled like silk over a head—a real, live head—currently snuggled up against her breast.

"What the hell?" she gasped, both hands releasing their passionate grasp of his shoulders to shove at him. "What do you think you're doing?"

Dream lover's head shot up, his dark blue eyes snapping with emotions so intense, so violent, Marni recoiled against the wall. Terror pounded in her head as her fingers scrambled to find her nightie's straps and pull them into place. To cover her nakedness, even though her body was still clamoring for more.

As quick as the fury had flashed, his eyes mellowed. Turned calculating, assessing. Not cold. A blue that rich could never be cold. She didn't know why, but the feeling of threatened terror eased, drained away. The embarrassed shock was still there, though, along with a huge dose of what-the-hell?

She pushed again, her hands tingling as they slid over shoulders as hard as iron but smooth as silk. Whiskers shadowed a strong jaw, and midnight hair, mussed from her very own fingers, fell over sharp brows to emphasize the tiny line between them.

Her eyes skimmed lower, taking in the breadth of his shoulders, the skin golden even in the dim light filtering through the shaded window. His chest was a work of art. Her fingers itched to touch it again, to comb through that light dusting of midnight-dark hair and see if it was as smooth as it looked.

Still on tour, her gaze continued south, following the

tempting path of hair. His belly was flat, lightly dusted so the hair emphasized, rather than hid, the sexy six-pack.

Feminine curiosity, and her body's craving to know if it was as big as it felt against her thigh, tempted her eyes to wander just a little lower.

Whoa. She yanked her gaze back to his face. Strange man in her bed. Ogling him topped her stupid-things-to-do list.

"I know this train is all about luxury and indulgence, but I don't think this is the wake-up call I expected," she finally said. She'd hoped for humorous sophistication. She had to settle for a breathless squeak.

WELL, THIS WAS ONE HELL of a way to wake up.

All traces of sleep, painkillers and whiskey cleared from his head with a blink. Hunter was left with surprise and an overwhelming degree of passion.

Waking up horny was one of the perks of being a guy, like peeing standing up. But in all his years of appreciating his masculine advantages, Hunter couldn't recall waking up quite this horny.

Then again, this was the first time he'd ever had a fantasy come to life.

As still as a cat gauging its prey, Hunter inspected the woman next to him. She looked like a cross between a porcelain doll and a sex kitten.

Flaxen blond curls waved around her face, floating to pale white shoulders. Her eyes were huge, the color of a cloudless sky and surrounded by a lush fringe of dark lashes. Heavy with passion, clouded with dazed shock, they had an intelligence in their depths that warned Hunter not to underestimate her. The rounded cheeks, flushed pink, and cupid's bow mouth completed the picture of adorable confusion.

Figuring it was only fair since she'd taken her own visual tour, he shifted back a little to take in the rest of the view.

Damn.

She was as deliciously curvaceous as she felt. Perfectly rounded breasts pressed against the glistening satin of her nightgown, her skin so pale it almost glowed in the morning light. The fabric clung to her, emphasizing her tiny waist before disappearing beneath their shared blankets.

He should get up, give her some space. But he liked it here. Liked the warmth still radiating off her lush form. Liked to think his large body, his intimidating presence, were putting her on the defensive.

Except she didn't look very defensive.

Amusement danced in her pale blue eyes. Her full lips curved now, as if she knew he was trying to intimidate her and she wasn't impressed so far.

Well, then.

Time to be impressive.

"You don't make a bad wake-up call yourself. What have you got on tap for Snooze?"

She arched one perfect brow, then shifted back toward the wall. For some women, that might look like a retreat. Others, an escape. On Blondie, it just looked like she was getting a better view of the situation, so to speak.

"I'm not much of a snooze kind of gal." She slid into a sitting position, taking the blankets with her as if to emphasize her point.

Well, it seemed the fun was over.

Which meant it was time to find out what the hell was going on. That sort of figuring was his specialty, but he'd never had to use his deductive skills and analytical talents to figure out why a gorgeous woman was in his bed before.

This should be interesting.

Not caring that he was nude, Hunter tossed the blankets aside and slid from the bunk. His lips twitched at Blondie's appreciative gasp. He met her eyes, liking the heat there. This was a woman unafraid of her own passions, eager to embrace and explore life and avail herself to its sensual offerings.

And he wasn't just thinking that because she was looking at him as though he was a hot fudge sundae, topped with extra whipped cream. Or because her nipples were once again stiff peaks beneath the satin of her nightgown.

He was too busy taking in the rest of her body, exposed by the blankets he'd tossed aside, to care if she was liking what she saw. Because he was *loving* the view himself.

The tiny nightgown was a rich berry shade. The same color as her nipples? He couldn't tell through the satin, even though the wet fabric still clung to her hardened peaks.

"Do you mind?" she protested, holding one hand up as if to block the view of his dick. Hunter gauged the size of her palm, then his own impressive erection and shook his head. She was going to need a few more hands to block the sight of this baby.

"Sweetheart, you sneak into a guy's bed, you have to expect to see a few things you wouldn't catch sight of over drinks and dinner."

MARNI SHOULD BE OUTRAGED. Shocked, even.

But she was too busy visually gobbling up the delicious view.

Oh, sweet baby. What a body.

"I didn't sneak into your bed," she finally responded, her tone more absent and offhand than angry and dismissive.

"No? My bed." He pointed to the bunk, then shifted

his finger to her. "You. Since I didn't invite you in, I'd say *sneaked in* is a good term."

That cut right through Marni's foggy passion. Irritation chased back desire. Not away. There was no chance of not feeling desire when a guy as gorgeous as this one stood naked in front of her. But her brain was starting to override her body. Or, at least, trying to.

"Let's think about this," she said, sitting up straighter and offering a chilly smile. "When I arrived in this cabin last night, mine was the only luggage here. There was no sign of anyone else using the room. When I climbed into bed, it was empty. You weren't here. I'd say that makes you the one sneaking around, don't you think?"

His laugh was as appreciative as it was sardonic.

Then he turned his back toward her. She couldn't quiet her approving moan at the site of his perfect—not just great, but perfect—butt. Her gaze slowly meandered up the golden planes of his back, and since he wasn't looking, she wiped her lower lip to make sure there was no evidence of drool.

Then her eyes landed on his shoulders.

His shoulders!

Her drool dried up, the lust in her belly replaced with a different kind of excitement.

It was him.

Those were the shoulders.

Marni shifted to her knees, ignoring the blanket that fell back to the mattress, and narrowed her eyes. Then she squinted, blurring her vision a little, as if she was seeing that broad muscled wonderfulness from farther away. Like, from a hallway peering into an exam room.

She took in the hairstyle, shorter in back and longer on top. The taper of his waist and the sharply defined muscles of his back. Then her gaze returned to those shoulders.

Oh, yeah, it was him.

She'd had a little early-morning delight with the very man she'd told her cousin she was chasing down for a hot, sexy time.

Funny how those things worked out.

"Do you have your ticket?" he asked, turning to face her and buttoning his jeans at the same time. "We'll take them to the porter, see where they made a mistake."

Wincing, Marni dropped down to sit flat on the bed.

Uh-oh.

Cute porter boy hadn't given her a ticket.

Which meant he probably hadn't finished booking the berth, either.

Think fast.

"I'm not sure where my ticket is. I know I had it when I got on board," she lied, pushing her hand through her hair and heaving her most frustrated sigh. "Tell you what, why don't we get breakfast. After a cup or three of coffee, I'm sure I'll remember where it is."

Her brain scrambled from scheme to idea to plan, but none of them seemed viable. She'd come too far to lose this story now. Fate wasn't putting everything in her lap just to toss her off the train, was it? She just needed a little time. She'd come up with a plan, make contact, establish a rapport and be well on her way to getting an inside scoop on the hottest criminal case of the year.

Cool your jets there, hotshot, she reminded herself. *Gotta get past step one before celebrating a Pulitzer.*

Hadn't the senior porter said something about overflow berths? Maybe one of those was unclaimed and she could book it. In the meantime, she just had to keep from getting kicked out.

How the hell was she going to do that?

Her eyes dropped back to the bed.

Oh, no, her mind screamed.

Please, yes, her body clamored.

"We can eat after we sort this out. I'll go get the porter, see what happened," hottie said, interrupting her internal struggle. She watched him shrug into his shirt, noting his slight wince, as if whatever had sent him to Emergency was still hurting.

"I'm not dressed," she protested.

"You have five minutes." He pulled on boots, then stood to tuck his shirt into his jeans. "I'll bring coffee along with someone who can sort this out."

Marni stared at the closed door for thirty precious seconds, then vaulted from the bed to grab her suitcase.

She didn't waste time with underwear, not trusting that he wouldn't be back any second. Instead she shimmied into a rich charcoal pencil skirt and a pale pink angora sweater. Not bothering with a brush, she scooped her hair up and anchored it with a large clip, then stuffed her feet into her highest pair of black leather pumps. When a girl topped five-four on tiptoes, high heels were a must for facing down bullyboys.

Needing all the advantages she could get, and knowing that she'd think naked orgasms every time she looked at it otherwise, she quickly tugged and pulled at the blankets to make the bed.

She'd just plumped the pillows when the door reopened.

Hottie walked through, followed by—oh, bless him— her favorite porter friend. And quickly moving him up the list of her favorite people, the porter was carrying a silver tray with an elegant coffee set and two porcelain cups.

He set it on the small table, then gave Marni a distant smile.

Her heart sank.

"There appears to be an issue with the berth?" he said,

addressing both her and Hunter. "Miss Clare, it seems you and Mr. Hunter have both booked the same space."

The worry in Marni's gut was so strong, not even the delicious aroma of rich coffee could distract her.

"We both booked it?" Hottie, aka Mr. Hunter, frowned and crossed his arms over his chest.

"I'm sorry, sir. It looks like someone made a mistake. Both bookings came in at the last minute, well after our usual deadline. Sometimes mix-ups happen with last-minute reservations."

"Fine. Just move one of us to a different berth."

"Again, I can't apologize enough. But there are no other berths. Every overflow sleeper has been claimed."

Nooo. Barely managing to keep her protest silent, Marni's stomach sank.

"This is the only berth available?" Hunter confirmed in a chilly tone.

"This one is booked, as well, sir. By both you and the lady."

Heart racing, Marni waited for him to ask who'd booked first. Or to dig out his government credentials and pull rank.

"Fine. We'll figure it out." With a quick tip for the coffee and a nod, Hunter dismissed the man.

Marni wasn't sure who looked more relieved, her or the porter. She knew he hid it faster, though, because she was still smiling when he gave a quick nod. With a murmured goodbye, he hurried from the room, leaving Marni to finish spinning this out.

"Look, I know how special this train trip is. I mean, film noir on a restored vintage train is a once in a lifetime thing, right?" Ignoring his baffled look, she made a show of tapping one finger against her lips in consideration. "Oh, I know…"

"I'll bet you do," he said, his smile just as sarcastic as his tone. He settled into the club chair, crossed one ankle over a knee and gestured for her to go ahead.

"We can share."

"What?" Sarcasm fled, shock taking its place. Marni's lips twitched. Obviously that wasn't the answer he'd been so sure she had.

"I'll share the cabin with you. You'll have to take the top bunk, of course," she said, gesturing to the discreet notice on the wall that indicated another bed could be pulled down. "And we'd need a few privacy rules, just to keep things from getting messy."

She paused, wetting her lip and trying to get a gauge on his reaction. Clearly the guy had gone to the stoic school of FBI training, though. Other than losing the sarcasm, his facial expression hadn't changed.

Should she be worried that she was pretty sure she could stare at that face for hours, losing herself in those deep blue eyes, and never tire of seeing that same considering expression?

"You want to share? This cabin." His hand circled to indicate the space. It was a very small circle, fitting since it was a very small space. "With me. A total stranger, and a man whom you met for the first time, almost naked, less than an hour ago?"

Doubts, tiny ones, started creeping under Marni's cheerful demeanor. It wasn't as if she'd share with just anyone. He was FBI, for crying out loud. But she wasn't supposed to know that. Still, she didn't like looking like a naive idiot.

"Well, I do want your name, and you'll have to give that nice porter a character reference so he can check on you for me," she said with a saccharine smile. "I'll take your picture with my cell phone and share it with my entire family, too, so they know exactly who to look for if anything happens to me. Oh, and from now on, I'll be sleeping with pepper spray under my pillow."

"That a girl." Instead of looking offended, he gave her an approving smile. Then he sucked in a breath and shook his head. "Still, smart as you're being, I don't think sharing a berth for a week is my idea of fun."

Sharing a berth?

Or sharing one with her?

Feminine ire prickling, Marni gave him a hard look.

"Did you have any other ideas?"

For just a second, his eyes flicked from her face, to the no longer rumpled bed, then back again. When he met her gaze again, there was a heat in his dark blue depths. Sexual, intense, powerful. Her mouth went dry and her stomach dove into her toes as Marni wet her lips.

This wasn't about sex.

No matter how many ideas he had in that direction.

"Nope," he finally said. She blinked a couple of times. Had he read her mind, and was denying her the comfort of that no-sex lie? She replayed the conversation to try to figure out what he was noping.

He wasn't going to argue about sharing the space?

This was awesome, right?

Immediate and ongoing access to the key source for her story. A chance to sneak in hard-hitting newsworthy questions, maybe cull together some major points to write another article. This one on the mystique of the FBI agent.

She gave a delighted little shiver at the idea of delving deeper into his…mystique.

This was it. Her chance of a lifetime. She could get the hottest story of her career, indulge in her love for writing in-depth character studies and put the polishing touches on her very own launching pad to career success. All at the same time.

"So," she said with a bright, cheery smile. "Looks like we're roommates."

4

HUNTER WATCHED THE PRETTY little blonde pretend that she was perfectly comfortable with his staring.

He figured a few hours of this friendly roommate farce and she'd not only welcome but be falling all over herself grateful for his offer to refund her full ticket cost and put her off the train in Chicago.

In the meantime, he'd just kick it here in this cozy club chair and enjoy the view.

A view that was currently sitting at the small desk, typing away. Waves of gold flowed around a round, dimpled face. A milkmaid complexion combined with thick lashes and big sky-blue eyes completed the picture of all-American beauty. She was too lush to qualify as the girl next door, though. More along the lines of Marilyn Monroe than Jennifer Aniston.

Not that he was paying any attention to that overt sex appeal, even though it was wrapped in a deliciously tight-fitting, fuzzy pink sweater that cupped full breasts and a perfectly fitted, hip-skimming gunmetal-gray skirt. The packaging was pure feminine heat. The kind that made him think of long nights sliding over her body while she moaned in appreciation.

Not that he was affected by lush curves or pretty blue eyes.

At least, not while on the job.

Right now those eyes, partially obscured by black-rimmed rectangular glasses, were fixed on the screen of her laptop as she typed away. He was pretty sure if he tried to read over her shoulder, he'd see nothing but gobbledygook.

Because if there was one thing that Hunter was damned good at, it was intimidation.

Five minutes later, his frown was more irritated than menacing. She hadn't even looked up. Her expression was focused, her fingers still flying over the keyboard. Heck, her breathing and skin tone hadn't changed at all.

What the hell?

Hunter shifted in the chair.

He tapped his fingers on the slick fabric.

He crossed one leg over the other.

Then he uncrossed them.

He scared gangbangers and drug lords.

He sent crime bosses cringing behind their hired guns.

And this pretty little blonde barely noticed he was here. Was she immune to men? Had she gone to an all-girls school or something?

Suddenly, she looked up and gave him a bright smile.

"Oh, just remembered I'm here, did you," he muttered.

A tiny frown creasing her brow, she reached under all that thick hair and pulled a small, wireless earbud from her ear.

Hunter almost growled.

Half his intimidation was based on his ability to sit, silently staring. How would she know he was silent if she had noise blasting through her head?

"I'm sorry, did you say something?" she asked, pulling the other mini-earphone out and shaking both in her palm.

"Nothing."

"Oh."

After a couple of seconds of his death stare, her smile drooped, and then she bit her lip and looked away.

There. He still had it.

The ability to intimidate sweet women. He'd bet he could make babies cry and puppies whimper, too.

"You look grumpy."

Hunter scowled.

"Really grumpy," she decided, closing the lid of her laptop, setting it aside and getting to her feet. She glanced at the clock on the wall, then at her watch as if to verify the time. "I'll bet you're hungry. We haven't had anything but coffee in two hours. Want to get breakfast?"

"Look, you're going to have to let me have this berth," he said instead.

"I'm what?"

"I can't do this roommate thing. It was nice enough of you to offer to share, but it's just not going to work."

"So you're leaving?"

"No, you are."

Her cupid's bow mouth dropped open and she stared for so long, he wanted to blow on her face to make her blink.

"It's my berth. I was in it first. Out of the goodness of my heart, I offered to share it with you. So why would I give it up?"

Hunter considered flashing his FBI badge and going the national security route. But he was seriously tired. Tired and sore and empty. He needed a little downtime. He had a week to build a case that would put away the head of one of the biggest criminal organizations on the East Coast. He wasn't going to do that with people bugging him, asking FBI questions and passing him in the hallway muttering, "The truth is out there."

He could ask her to keep it a secret. But in his experience, women couldn't keep secrets. And she'd have no reason to want to once he'd booted her off the train.

"I was in an accident recently," he ventured, shifting his expression from intimidating to doleful. "I'm feeling some pain. I need space, privacy, so I can sleep when I feel like it, pace at night if I'm hurting too much. I need it if I'm going to recover properly."

Her pretty face creased in sympathetic lines and she poked out her lower lip in a sad pout.

"You poor thing."

"So you'll vacate the berth," he confirmed.

She patted his forearm. Hunter frowned at the heat he felt at her gentle touch. There, another reason to be glad she was leaving. A couple more touches like that and he wouldn't be thinking about the case, about catching up on sleep or about the miserable ache of his screaming muscles.

It was as if he was hardwired after their little wake-up games. She touched, he got hard.

"Sorry, but no." She even added a regretful smile to her refusal.

Hunter frowned, trying to pull some of the blood north to his brain so he could remember what she was refusing.

"You're kidding, right?"

"Look, this trip is important to me," she said, looking less like a china doll and more like an avenging angel all of a sudden. Her chin lifted, her eyes heated and she got that same stubborn my-way-or-else look his mother used to get. "I'm not giving it up."

"I need my rest."

"I need to get to California."

"So fly."

"You fly."

"I can't fly. I told you, I was in an accident. Ruptured my inner ear. I fly, I die." An exaggeration, but he was going for effect here.

"I fly, everyone on the plane dies," she shot back. Clearly she was better at exaggerating.

"Oh, please."

"They will all die. I know they will. I've had horrible dreams for years about crashing, of going down in flames. And my psychic agrees. If I get on a plane, it will crash. I owe it to those other people to not put their lives in danger." She gave a big, tearful sniffle before turning her back to him.

Hunter squinted. She'd played it pretty well, but that had to be a total bullshit act.

When she faced him again, her lower lip was trembling just a little and she'd raised her chin as if putting on a brave face. Hunter almost grinned.

She really was cute.

Until she heaved a big sigh and shook her head.

"I guess that settles it. Unless, of course, you're giving up the berth?" When he gave a scowling shake of his head, she shrugged, then walked over to the little table by the door. He wasn't sure whether to be relieved that she might be going, or wish she'd walk a little more so he could enjoy the view of her hips swaying.

She picked up a small leather folder.

"Breakfast?" She waved the menu in the air.

Hunter frowned. He was starting to get the feeling that she wasn't going to be easy to get rid of. Not willingly.

"How about we settle the room situation first." He folded his arms over his chest and leaned back in the chair, making it clear he wasn't moving until he'd gotten his way.

She gave an elaborate eye roll, leaned against the table and matched his crossed-armed stance.

"And what is it that you suggest?" She widened those gorgeous eyes, pure sweetness and light.

"I suggest you get off in Chicago. Take the next train. I'll cover your ticket and reimburse you for this one." There. Pure generosity. He offered his most reasonable smile to go with it. The one he used when he gave criminals the choice between jail and bodily harm.

"I have a better idea." Her smile took on an irritated edge, toning down the sweetness and dousing all that light. "Why don't you get off in Chicago instead? You're the one with the issue, you can take the next train."

"I have to be in San Francisco in seven days."

"I have to be in San Francisco as soon as possible," she countered.

"Then fly."

"I told you, if I fly, people will die." She gave a stubborn jut of her chin before adding, "Do you need to talk to my psychic? She'll tell you."

Hunter growled. His wannabe roommate didn't even blink. Instead, she waved the menu in the air again.

What the hell? Had he lost his mean-guy mojo in that car accident?

"I haven't eaten yet today," the not-at-all-intimidated blonde said with a wide-eyed look and a pat of one slender hand on her tummy. "And I promise you, the hungrier I get, the less reasonable I am."

When had she been reasonable before?

Hunter all but growled.

He wanted her out. He had a case to build. An explosion to recover from. And a general state of mental health to maintain.

He couldn't work on high-security material with a civilian in the room. He couldn't relax with a gorgeous blonde hovering around his libido. And his mental health was already taking a hit, thanks to her lack of respect for his dead-eye stare.

He could pull rank, flash his badge and boot her out of the berth.

Except for two things.

First, she'd been here first. Booking a ticket an hour before the train left didn't give him the right to steal a bed out from under her.

Second, and as much as he hated to admit it, Murray was right. Another few days without things exploding around him and he'd have been clear to fly. But he hadn't been able to resist hotdogging, trying to wrap up one more case, to tally one more arrest on his record before the big, career-breaking trial next week.

His innate fairness said he couldn't pull rank to get the cabin. It said nothing about not using every trick at his disposal to convince her to leave willingly, though.

"Actually, I'm hungry, too." He rose to his full height and offered a slow smile filled with as much sexual heat as he could muster. Which, given that he was still half-hard from waking to find her sexy little body in his arms, was quite a bit. "Marni, right? Why don't we visit the dining car."

Looking a little flushed all of a sudden, she blinked a few times, her lashes sweeping over those big eyes as if she were trying to refocus. She wet those full lips, sparking a sharp, deep regret in his belly that he hadn't tasted them before he'd been pulled out of the fantasy. Were they as delicious as they looked? As soft? Did they yield, or take control?

"You're hungry?" she repeated, her words a breathless rush.

"I'm starving." He let his voice drop just one decibel above a husky growl and let his gaze slide down her body. As though, if they didn't get out of here now, he wasn't going to be able to resist taking a big, juicy bite.

Hunter was gratified by her shaky breath, but his own libido took a hit at the amazing things that breath did for her fluffy pink sweater. She was like something sweet and sugary, swirled atop what promised to be a rich, decadent treat. But he was just as good at ignoring his sweet tooth as he was his sexual urges while on the job. All he had to do was remind himself of that. A few dozen times.

Hunter crossed the room, taking the menu from her suddenly lax fingers and tossing it on the table behind her. Marni's eyes never left him, her focus so intent on his every move. Beneath the suspicion—smart girl—and an intense curiosity—dangerous if she wasn't careful—there was just enough desire for him to use to his advantage.

With that in mind, Hunter initiated his Evict Blondie plan.

"Babe, here's the deal. You're a very beautiful, very sexy woman." He paused just long enough to enjoy the wash of color over her cheeks and the way her eyes softened. "I'm not a man who's big on denying himself pleasures. I like delicious food, a good Scotch and losing myself in the delights of a gorgeous woman."

He let that hang there between them, as heavy and intense as the erection hanging hard between his legs. His body craved the feel of hers, wanting nothing more than for him to press that hard-on against her curves, to feel her warm welcome. But this was Intimidation 101, not Advanced Sexual Harassment. Hell, if he couldn't scare her into getting off the train, he deserved to share her berth, and he'd have to attend all those stupid dress-up functions the train offered, too.

She wet her lips and looked away. Hunter let himself smile. No worries about tracking down a lame forties-style fedora, here.

Then she shifted her gaze, slowly lifting her lashes as her eyes traveled higher and higher up his body. It was as though she was reaching out and dragging her fingers along his thigh, caressing his throbbing dick, scraping her nails over his flat abs, smoothing her fingers through the hair on his chest, then oh-so-lightly skimming his face.

Finally, as if she'd tired of the torture, her gaze met his. Her eyes were heavy with desire, hot with the promise that the passion he'd tasted that morning was only the tip of the iceberg.

"That's fascinating, I'm sure," she told him in a breathy voice. "But I have every confidence that you're also a man of control. A man who understands the word *no*. A gentleman, through and through."

Shit.

Hunter's expression didn't change, but his admiration for her jumped up a couple notches. So did his determination.

He stepped closer.

She stepped backward.

He stepped again. So did she. Until her back was against the door.

Hunter's smile was wicked as he placed his hands on the door, one on either side of her head. He leaned close, just enough to make her aware of his body, but not touching anywhere.

"Is that what you think?" he challenged.

SHE THOUGHT SHE WAS totally in over her head and sinking fast.

Marni's body was on fire. Her nipples were craving

the touch of his fingers again. Her body melted, hooked after that teensy taste of orgasmic pleasure he'd showed her that morning.

Control, her mind screamed. *Get a grip.*

"So you're saying if I don't get off the train in Chicago and let you have this berth, you're going to…what?" She let her gaze drop, her mouth watering when she saw the impressive bulge pressing against his zipper. "Seduce me?"

And how would that go? she wanted to ask. Would he start at the top and work his way down her body? Or begin with her toes and lick his way up?

"I've never forced myself on a woman. Never had to, never been tempted to," he promised. "All you have to say is no."

It wasn't as much the smile accompanying his words that pulled Marni from her sexual reverie. It was the amusement in his tone, as if he was laughing over the idea of her refusing him.

Maybe he was right.

Maybe she wouldn't be able to resist the heat, the sexual energy between them for the entire week. Not if they were sharing this space. Sleeping in the same room, listening to each other breathe night after night. Aware of the other's body, so close, in touching distance.

Her pulse raced.

But she ignored it. Just as she ignored the rest of the possibilities she'd just listed.

This was a job. An important job, with a story that could launch her career. She wasn't going to be scared away from it by sex. Or more precisely, by the possibility of incredible, mind-blowing, body-melting, once-in-a-lifetime awesome sex.

She could resist.

For the story, for her career, she could resist.

Maybe.

"So?"

"So, what?" she repeated, her brow furrowing as she met his gaze again.

"So what do you say?"

She knew what her body wanted her to say. But her ambition was stronger. Determination, motivation and a few cold showers would keep her from doing anything stupid.

"I say…" She leaned closer, close enough that she could feel his breath warm on her skin. Then she reached up with one finger and tapped it gently on the soft curve of his mouth. "No."

Marni ducked under his arms, hurrying across the room as if racing against the possibility of him grabbing her back. Feeling as though she'd just run a marathon or through a horror movie to escape a horde of zombies determined to eat her for lunch, she blew out a heavy breath.

She didn't know if she was grateful or miserable when Hunter didn't follow. As soon as she realized he wasn't going to pursue her, her body sagged into a limp mass of unfulfilled desire against the dresser.

"Fine." He snapped out the word with the same intensity a starving panther would use to snap a slab of raw meat in half. "Let's go."

"Go?"

"Breakfast. We'll discuss this over food."

When she continued to lean on the dresser and stare, Hunter arched one mocking brow. That's all it took for Marni to force her body to move.

Get food. Coffee. Richly scented coffee, she thought as he yanked the door closed behind them. Thankfully, shutting away the view of the bed and the thought of temptation.

Or at least the view of the bed.

Ten minutes later, Marni was having second thoughts. Now that they were out of the bedroom, so to speak, she wasn't sure she could handle going back in there with him.

Maybe she should get off in Chicago, she thought as the waiter led them across the crowded dining car to a small table by the window.

She now had the name of the FBI agent in charge of the case, which was more than the FBI public relations liaison had offered before. She had enough information on the explosion to put together a decent story and, since Burns hadn't been implicated yet, if she got the story in by midnight, it might run before the trial next week. But the story would be speculation that he blew up his own building, without any facts to back it up. It'd be a decent story.

Maybe. If she found some way to build it into more than conjecture and supposition.

But it wasn't enough to be her breakout story.

It wouldn't launch her up the reporting ladder of success.

With a smile of thanks for the waiter holding the leather dining chair out for her, Marni settled down across from Hunter.

She bit her lip, pretending to read the menu while her brain swirled in a million directions at once.

She couldn't get off the train. She needed a big story, not a fair-to-middling one. Hunter was her hook. Her big break. Her provider of the sexiest, most delicious sleeping orgasm she'd ever had in her life.

"What can I get you?"

"Another org..." Horrified, Marni pressed her lips together, not daring to look at Hunter. She could feel his gaze on her, though. Like a laser peering into her soul, searching out secrets and sexual fantasies. "An organic fruit tray, if you have it," she corrected with a bright smile and a flutter of her lashes. They worked as distraction enough for the waiter, who blushed and wrote so hard on his pad that he broke the tip of his pencil.

"Sorry. Be right back," he muttered, hurrying away. But not without giving Marni one last effusive look.

"Do you do that often?"

Steeling herself, Marni shifted her smile to curiously innocent before she met Hunter's gaze.

"Do what?"

"The cute thing. Does it work all the time, or is it a fifty-fifty thing?"

More like seventy-thirty. And only with men. She'd never been called on it before, though. Which meant he was likely in that elusive, unreachable thirty percent who wouldn't see her as just a pretty face. He might expect something.

Like the truth. Her truth.

Something no man had ever looked past her face and figure to wonder about.

"Can I bring you anything else?" the waiter asked as he set the plate of fruit in front of Marni.

It took all her will to pull her gaze from Hunter's intense stare. Marni blinked at the waiter a couple of times, trying to focus her thoughts. Then, not bothering to look at the menu again, she handed it to him and ordered, "Coffee, two scrambled eggs, whole wheat toast and a side of potatoes."

"Right away." He offered an excited smile before turning away.

"Excuse me," she called before he could leave.

"Yes?"

Her lips twitched at his eager reply, and then she tilted her head toward Hunter. "My friend is hungry, too."

"You're something else," Hunter said after the blushing waiter had taken his order and hurried away. "Those eyelashes should be registered as lethal weapons."

Marni batted her lethal weapons.

"But they won't work on me."

She stopped batting.

What would work on him? What was it going to take for him to relax enough for her to sneak a story out of the guy?

Because she'd do it, whatever it was.

Except strip naked and beg him to take her.

Well, *maybe* whatever it took except that.

5

MARNI MENTALLY RECITED all of the reasons it was important to keep her clothes on as she considered the sexy FBI agent across from her while their waiter poured coffee.

There had to be a better—aka less dangerous to her mental and emotional well-being—way to get this story.

She'd spent a little time researching while he'd tried to stare her out of their cabin earlier. With a document opened, she used typing away at her aunt's life story as she knew it as her cover. It'd been a few years since she'd worked on a biography type profile, and she'd forgotten how much she loved it. Curiosity drove all of her writing, but there was an extra spark to a profile, the excitement of digging into the who and why of a person's life that she found fascinating.

She'd been so lost in the joy of writing, she'd had to force herself, between paragraphs, when she was sure he wouldn't jump up and grab her laptop to see what she was doing, to access the FBI media files.

Special Agent in Charge Hunter. No first name on public file. Second generation FBI with more commendations than she had shoes, he was based in New York but had worked out of D.C. and San Francisco over the years, too.

She'd emailed a few contacts, hoping they'd shed more light on the enigmatic FBI hottie before the end of the day. Not just because he was totally fascinating. But because she was going to need every bit of light, every shred of information she could get, if she was still going to be sleeping on this train tonight.

"So what kind of accident were you in?" she asked as soon as the waiter had finished arranging—and rearranging—the china cream and sugar containers. At Hunter's frown, she added, "You said you'd damaged your inner ear in an accident and couldn't fly. That sounds scary."

"I was in a car accident last night." His shrug suggested it was no big deal, but she saw the way his lips tightened a little in the corners at the movement. He must still be in a great deal of pain. All of a sudden, she felt horrible about keeping him from that rest and recovery he'd said he needed. She vowed that once she'd secured her place on the train and gotten a grip on her raging hormonal response to him, she'd do her best to help Hunter feel better. Well, almost her best.

"It must have been really bad to damage your ear," she observed, although she figured *re-damaged* was probably more precise. "I'm surprised you're able to travel so soon after something that devastating. I was rear-ended once and was laid up in bed, bruised and sore for three days afterward."

He shrugged again, either dismissing her concern, or her mini–sob story, she wasn't sure which.

"So what do you do?" he asked.

"I work in fashion, but I want to be a writer." A good lie was woven around the truth, her grandpa always said.

"A writer? What kind of a writer?" His deep blue stare sharpened, as if warning bells were ringing in his head.

"Biographical. I'm working on a wonderful profile right now," she said, thinking of the couple of pages she'd written that morning. Her excitement and love of writing bios almost made her words bounce. "It's about a groundbreaking, prizewinning feminist who flouted family expectations to build a career in a man's world."

The suspicion in his sexy eyes faded into what just might be boredom. Marni frowned. What was up with that? The handful of biographies she'd written were anything but boring. She'd even won awards for them. Her fascination with the bits and pieces that made up the lives of people who'd made a difference, who'd stepped outside the box and forged their own path, came through loud and clear.

She'd debated for a while about sticking with profile reporting. The process of digging into someone's history, of sharing their world and their story, was incredible.

Just not as incredible as being an ace investigative reporter. She straightened her shoulders, pulling her head out of the clouds and telling herself to focus. A biographer was all well and good, and maybe someday after she was rich and famous she'd try her hand at it. But for now, she was after bigger career kudos.

And she needed the man across from her to get them.

"So what do you do?" she asked, propping her elbow on the table and resting her chin on her fist. "Businessman? Big-time CEO of a million-dollar company? Engineer? Ladies lingerie salesman?"

His lips twitched.

"None of the above."

She waited.

He just leaned farther back into his seat and smiled.

"You know, to share the berth with you, I do need more information than just your name and a snapshot of you from my phone's camera," she chided, figuring going on the offense was always preferable to playing defense. Especially with a man like Hunter, who was clearly used to putting people on the defense.

"I still haven't agreed to share anything, though."

"Do you always play hard to get?"

Her laughter faded when his gaze heated, the intense look in his eyes making it clear that he was remembering just how hard he'd been earlier this morning, and just exactly what he'd been so close to getting.

Marni's breath caught in her throat. Her thighs melted, heat swirling low in her belly as the memories filled her head, too.

"Look," she said, leaning across the table and giving him her best don't-mess-with-me look. "We both know that neither of us is giving up that berth. We also know that if you had the power to kick me out, you'd have used it already. So you're stuck. I'm stuck. Let's quit being silly and deal with the reality of that, why don't we."

Hunter's eyes flashed with frustration for just one second, then turned mellow and amused again. She had to give him credit, this was a man in command of his emotions. A tendril of heat sparked again in her belly as she remembered how it'd felt when he'd almost lost control in her arms.

The idea of making a man, a strong, controlled man, forget himself and go wild… She gave a tiny shudder of delight. Oh, that was a sweet concept.

But one she was going to ignore, she reminded herself sternly. Career over sex had always been her mantra. Just because she was potentially sharing a cabin with the hottest guy she'd ever met didn't mean that mantra was going to change.

"How do you suggest we deal with being stuck together?" he asked in a tone she knew wasn't nearly as friendly as he made it sound.

"Let's start with getting to know each other." She countered his fake friendliness with saccharine sweetness. It was only fair. "I told you what I do. What do you do?"

He hesitated for a second, then reached over to snag one of the large, juicy red strawberries off her plate.

"I work for the government," he told her before nipping the berry in half with strong white teeth.

Marni watched his mouth as he chewed, her own watering for a taste. She licked her lips, trying to stay focused. This was definitely going to be a challenging week.

"Government? That's either hellishly boring or terribly exciting," she offered with a laugh, the flutter of her lashes inviting him to tell her which one.

He didn't take the invitation.

"So, what do you do for the government? Are you in politics? Or are you one of those regulatory inspectors, going from business to business, checking to see if they are following the rules?" She forked up a spear of fresh pineapple and nipped off a bite, letting the rich juice slide over her tongue as she waited to see how much he'd tell her.

"I'm in accounting."

"Sounds fascinating."

"Not really."

"Your accident, was that accounting related?" she asked, her eyes not leaving his as she popped the rest of the pineapple into her mouth.

"Accidents are unfortunate happenstance events that can often be tied to errors in numeric calculations."

"Clever." She gave him an exaggerated wide-eyed look of admiration.

Hunter grinned in response.

Then he leaned both elbows on the table and gave her a serious look. "Tell you what. I'll talk to the conductor, make sure he has all the vital information to vouch for me. You check with him, see if you feel comfortable. Sound fair?"

"Sure." Oh, that was smart. She could do the same, instructing the conductor to notify her family with all of that information if anything happened. That way she didn't have to tell them that she was pursuing a hot story instead of a hot guy. "Now that we've settled that, let's talk about the fun stuff."

"I'm on this train to work."

"I am, too," she insisted, honesty giving an extra weight to her words. "I'll admit, I'm excited about the film noir events they have planned, which is why no other train would do." Especially since she'd checked the trains leaving Chicago that'd put Hunter in San Francisco in time for the trial and this was the only one. "Still, it's important that I work this week. That I get this story done. My career, my future, depends on it."

"On this biography?" The skeptical look on Hunter's face made it clear that she'd lost a few points in her argument for them to share the berth. "I didn't realize publishing worked quite that fast."

She almost jumped up and kissed the waiter for choosing that moment to bring their breakfast. Her mind raced while he arranged their plates.

She lifted her fork, ready to use a mouthful of eggs as an excuse not to respond until she'd figured something out. But the look on Hunter's face, suspicious expectation, had her laying the fork right back down. What was it with this guy? Was it being with the FBI that made him so suspicious, or was he with the FBI because he was naturally distrustful? And wouldn't that make a fascinating biography?

"My aunt is in San Francisco," she blurted out, her mind one word ahead of her mouth. "It's her story I'm writing. She's not doing well. The family expects to lose her anytime."

Again, all truthful, given that the family had disowned her aunt when she'd run off to join a commune in order to write an insider view of the free-love movement. Marni had heard her grandparents say time and again that Robin was lost to them.

"I'm sorry." Looking as if he really was, Hunter reached across the narrow table to pat her hand. "Are you and your aunt close?"

"She's my hero." Marni's smile was bittersweet as she spoke that truth. What she didn't share was that because of the family rift, she'd never met the woman in person. Then and there, she vowed that once she reached San Francisco, she was going to remedy that. "I don't think she has any idea how much I admire her, want to be like her. She's lived this amazing life, and is such a strong woman. She deserves to have her story told. Have you ever known anyone like that?"

After a second of hesitation, Hunter nodded. "My father, I suppose. He always inspired me in a lot of ways. I always wanted to be like him when I was a kid. I guess he was a hero, you know?"

"Then you know what I mean. My aunt is so special to me. I need to do this. I need her to be proud of me."

Hunter grimaced, then gave a nod toward her plate as if to indicate she get to eating. Since he dug into his slab of fried ham and three eggs over easy, Marni slowly followed suit. But she didn't take her eyes off his face.

She didn't have to wait long.

"Here's the deal…"

"Yes?"

"We'll share, but there are a few rules." He looked about as enthusiastic as if the words were being forced out at gunpoint. She didn't mind. It wasn't as though she needed him to want to have her around. Not like she would if they were going to have another bout between the sheets. Or against the wall. She swallowed, trying to get past the sudden lump in her throat at the image of the two of them up against the door like they'd been just an hour ago. She imagined his body tight against hers, this time while the train's motion added a whole new level of erotic to their sexy dance.

"Rules?" she croaked, trying to banish that image.

So far, she sucked at this focus-on-business goal of hers.

"I need privacy to work. I'm preparing a classified financial report and can't have you in the room. We'll establish the hours, and during those hours each day, you clear out of the room. You can write in the lounge, or watch movies, or paint a picture for your aunt. Whatever you want to do. But during work hours, the room is mine."

Marni managed to contain her butt-wiggling happy chair dance, instead raising a single brow in inquiry.

"Anything else?"

"Yeah. You take the top bunk. I'm sore and don't want to have to climb into a tiny bed that's too short for my legs."

"And that's it, your last rule?" she asked, her heavy sigh making it clear she knew he was going to toss in another one.

She was right.

After a quick frown, he shook his head and leaned forward.

"Nope. One more. The minute you change your no to a yes, you be sure to let me know."

HUNTER LIKED THIS TRAIN. The old-world feel, harkening back to an easier time, it had a lot of charm. A man of the times, he didn't yearn for the days without 4G, Wi-Fi, instant records checks and string bikinis. But the gritty world of a gumshoe, the cut-and-dried appeal of simpler—though no less horrible—crimes, yeah. He could see why people would drop a pile of money to pretend they were a part of that era.

After he left Marni to finish her meal, he moved through the cars, from dining to lounge, past one renovated into a movie theater and back toward the caboose. He wasn't officially on duty, but he always found it handy when traveling to introduce himself to whoever was in charge, as well as to get a lay of the land. Or in this case, to memorize the layout of the train.

It was standard protocol.

Not as if he was avoiding his new roommate or anything.

That he'd chosen not to walk her back to the cabin had nothing to do with avoiding temptation. So the woman was hot. And sweet. And sexy as all hell. So she did fascinating things to her skirt when she walked.

That didn't mean jack.

Except that she was sexy and sweet and smart.

He'd worked with plenty of sexy women. They never distracted him from the job.

He knew a few sweet women. They rarely made enough impression on him to merit more than a kind word.

He was surrounded by smart women. They had a way of seeing things, an innate understanding of human nature that he appreciated.

So the sexy, sweet and smart blonde waiting in his bedroom shouldn't be a distraction. If he couldn't handle prepping a huge criminal case with a pretty little thing like her around, well, hey, he wasn't much of an FBI agent, then, was he.

Feeling as though he'd just gone the mental equivalent to whistling in the dark, Hunter gave a mental groan. Before he could decide which direction to take his mental lecture, though, his phone rang.

Saved by the cell.

Grateful, even after checking the call display, he answered.

"Hey, Murray."

"Any problems?"

"On a train dedicated to gritty detectives and dames in distress?" Hunter quipped, knowing the irony would go right over his boss's head. "I'm handling it just fine."

"You're going to have to dress the part. Participate."

"No, I'm not." Hunter climbed the steps to the open-air gondola car. Since most people were at lunch or down doing some silly movie thing, the platform was empty but for a dozen glossy benches for relaxing to enjoy the view.

"Yeah. You are. I told you that when I booked it. It's mandatory participation."

"I can ignore mandates just fine." Giving in to the aches in his body and the screaming pain of his cracked rib, Hunter dropped to one of the benches to give his body a time-out.

"Don't want to waste taxpayers money, now, do you?" Murray's words were light, but the edge beneath them was a direct attack on the habit of only turning in expense receipts if he figured they supported whatever official means he offered up in his case reports.

He had a habit of breaking cases his way, though, and

taking the financial hit rather than dinging Uncle Sam for payment. Like the case he'd broken the previous year in Black Oak, California.

Tobias Black, a notorious con artist and master criminal, had, in Murray's view, skated free thanks to Hunter's taking matters into his own hands instead of playing by the rules. Rather than use his own guys to infiltrate the crime ring and try to bust Tobias, Hunter had called on a buddy in the DEA who specialized in the many wicked ways of Tobias Black.

That the buddy was also Tobias's eldest son had been pretty damned handy. Caleb Black was Hunter's best friend since they'd been college roommates. Long after they'd graduated, the two men still had each other's back. Still stayed in touch, were still tight. Hunter had gambled on that friendship, pulling Caleb into the sting operation. Murray had called that a serious breach of protocol.

Then a month later, one of Hunter's own agents infiltrated the crime ring without permission, using Caleb's sister, Maya, as cover. The deputy director had been pissed enough to spit nails when, instead of busting the agent down to checking shipping manifests in the Gulf of Mexico, Hunter had promoted him. But hey, Simon had broken the case open and brought in vital information. Enough information for Hunter to make his next call to bring in Danita Cruz, his protégée at the agency, as a fake hooker. Danita had found the final key to not only close the case, but to bring yet another criminal off the streets in the form of Gabriel Black giving up his con artist ways to marry Danita.

Murray had thrown such a fit, his face had turned ten shades of purple. But the powers that be had done backflips over the busting of a statewide crime ring, the arrest of a dozen major criminals and the takedown of the town's dirty mayor.

Still, his unorthodox methods had guaranteed Hunter's spot on Murray's short list. But since he'd covered his own expenses, right down to the tux he'd worn as Caleb's best man, the deputy director hadn't been able to do more than lecture him on protocol.

"I'm not playing Sam Spade on a train," Hunter told his boss, who was gloating so hard on the other end of the line he was practically breathing heavy. "I'm here to work, remember."

"You can't do two things at once? Losing your edge?"

Hunter snorted. Was that the best he could do?

"I made sure the agent who's meeting you in Chicago in three hours packed a suitcase with just those events in mind. Be sure to get a picture or two. I'm going to want it with your report."

With those words and a cackle worthy of any cartoon villain, Murray ended the call.

This case was becoming a three-ring circus. In the center ring was a vicious criminal whose ass Hunter had vowed to put away. But he couldn't ignore the other two rings to do that. He didn't mind so much the sexy blonde in one of them, but the political posturing and jealous games in the other were annoying.

Irritated despite himself, Hunter contemplated the view for a few seconds. Then, like he did most things that irritated him, he shrugged it off.

MARNI SAT CURLED ON THE comfy club chair, her laptop on the table next to her, her cell phone in her hand as she juggled texts and emails with the skill of a teenager.

When Hunter had tromped off an hour ago to do whatever he'd muttered he was doing, she'd hurried back here for a little research time. He didn't have any luggage and hadn't left anything in the room other than a faint hint of his cologne. But now that she had his name she was able to tap into a few more sources than she'd had before. She was contacting everyone she knew, both official magazine sources, old friends and even family.

"Oho," she exclaimed when Meghan's text came through. Sammi might be tight-lipped about sharing official hospital business, but Meghan had ways of sliding information out of her sister that was nothing short of twin-tastic.

Hunter hadn't been admitted alone that first night.

Meghan's text read:

Watch it. Hottie you're so in lust over has a girlfriend. He was with her that first night in emergency, so says Sammi. She's worrying about you getting all gaga over someone who's already hooked.

Someone else had been in that explosion last week? A woman?

Marni's brain raced. She was so excited, she tossed her phone on the table and got up to do a fist-pumping happy dance.

This was it. This was a real break.

Oh, think of the story.

Hunter and someone else had been in that building.

Was the someone else another FBI agent? Had they survived? Were the rumored new charges connected somehow?

She had to find out. She just had to know.

Before she could do another butt-wiggling dance, there was a knock. She quickly shut down her email and exited her message app, then with a deep breath, pulled open the door.

It wasn't Hunter.

"Hi," she greeted with a warm smile. "Simpson, isn't it?"

The porter stepped into the room, hooking the door on a chain so it didn't close behind him while he fetched a covered tray of food from the cart in the hallway.

"Right, hi," he said with a big grin. He pushed his spiffy porter's cap back on his forehead, then gave a head tilt to indicate the room. "It looks like this worked out okay. You got the cabin, right?"

"Well, that's actually a problem," Marni said, closing her laptop and shrugging. "With no other berths available, and neither of us willing to leave the train, Mr. Hunter and I are actually sharing the cabin."

A knowing glint lit the young man's gaze. Before he could say anything, though, Marni walked over to the bed.

"Can you show me how to pull down the bunk? Since I'm shorter, I get the top bed," she said with a rueful smile.

"You get...?" The porter frowned, setting the lunch tray on the little table, then moving over to press a button next to the headboard of the main bed. A bed slid out of the wall like something out of a fifties sci-fi movie. Marni grinned, wondering if the bed was covered in Jetsons sheets.

The porter walked to the foot of the bed and opened a small panel, and out twisted a set of steps for easy bedtime access.

"We will set up the bed at nine each night and return it to its cubby during the morning cleaning. You have your own sleep light here." He indicated a small lamp on a wire gooseneck. "The blanket has temperature settings built into the lamp controls, as well."

"Oh, isn't that clever," Marni said, trying to pretend a light and blanket controls would be enough to keep her from wanting to slide into the bed below and have her way with Hunter's body. "Thanks so much."

"So, wow. This really isn't what you wanted?" Looking more upset for her than smarmy over the enforced roommate situation now, Simpson hefted the bunk back into place and latched it closed. "I feel bad. I wish there was something I could do."

Marni bit her lip. Rooming with Hunter was ideal on so many levels. Sure, he was a strange man. But he was a safe strange man. Everything she'd found out about him said he was completely trustworthy. As long as she wasn't a criminal, that was. And since lying wasn't actually a criminal act, she figured she was fine. And if he was serious about spending his days working in here, there were so many possibilities for ferreting out information.

But rooming with Hunter also meant no privacy.

It meant that every bit of time spent in the cabin would either be in his presence or with constant reminders of him. Like now, he wasn't here but his scent floated in the air, forest fresh and inviting.

How could she focus on writing the story of her career if she was spending every night lying awake above the sexiest body she'd ever felt? Wondering what he'd do if she climbed down that ladder and slid over his body in the dark, pressing hot, wet kisses to every inch of his skin?

Marni's pulse skipped a few beats and she was tempted to wave her hand in front of her face to cool off.

"Any chance another berth might become available?" she asked with a doleful smile.

His grimace was all the answer she needed. Not wanting him to feel any worse, Marni patted his arm. "Don't worry about it. I'll make do. But remember, if one does open up, I'd love first dibs."

With that, a big smile and a generous tip, she thanked him for bringing lunch. Looking relieved, the porter turned to the door.

"Oh, one last thing." Simpson all but smacked his palm against his forehead, grimacing as he turned back around to pull a sheaf of papers out of his handy leather portfolio. "This is your role for the Train Whodunit. You and Mr. Hunter are playing a gumshoe and his dame. Your character is one of the main suspects for the murder that will take place tomorrow night."

"Really?" Marni laughed, taking the pages with delight. "I've never been cast as a femme fatale before. I think this might be fun."

Then she saw the drawing. A slinky woman, in glittering spaghetti straps and seductively sweeping curls, draped all over a guy in a hat with six-foot-wide shoulders and a skinny tie.

Her pulse sped up. Hunter had shoulders like that. Wide, strong and sexy. The kind that made her fingers tingle with the need to touch. Broad enough to support the weight of the world, sturdy enough for a woman to hang on to while he took her on a wild, naked ride.

Whew, it was getting hot in here. Marni puffed out a breath, then gave the porter a doubtful look.

"I'm not sure how Hunter's going to feel about all of this," she said. She looked at the pencil sketch of the fedora-wearing gumshoe with the lantern jaw again, then flashed Simpson a big smile. "Is there any way to make mine a stand-alone character? Just in case. After all, for all we know, he hates solving mysteries. Or worse, that he's horrible at it."

"Oh, I think I can handle it."

It was anybody's guess who jumped higher, Marni or the porter. Her heart racing, she glared at the man standing in the doorway, gloating over their reactions. Did he specialize in sneakiness in FBI school?

"Sir, I've got your character dossier here," Simpson said, recovering first. "You're a hard-bitten gumshoe with a soft spot for your secretary."

"A soft spot, hmm?" Hunter took the papers, but didn't release Marni's gaze. His smile was slow, wicked and challenging. "I guess we'll see how well I can pull *that* off."

6

HUNTER HAD SPENT PLENTY of time undercover. It wasn't his specialty, but he was still pretty damned good at immersing himself in the part, losing himself in the role while still keeping his objective clear.

But it was always a job.

This, he thought as he snagged a stuffed mushroom cap from the roving waiter, was ridiculous.

Three lounge cars, one after another, had doors thrown open, giving the image of one very long room. Crystal chandeliers reflected the multitude of lit candles, even though it was only five in the evening. All of the blinds were pulled closed against the evening light, so as not to ruin the ambience.

Most of the people milling about were dressed in forties-era evening wear. Narrow suits, quite a few shoulder pads, and glitteringly slinky dresses filled the rooms. It was a costume jeweler's dream, with fat fake diamonds and strand upon strand of plastic pearls.

A bunch of adults, well-to-do if the cost of this event was anything to go by, all playing dress up on a train? Pretending to solve a fake crime that they all knew was coming?

Yeah.

Ridiculous.

Then his gaze fell on Marni as she wove her way across the room with the skill of a politician's wife. A smile here, a chatty word there, always moving but totally unrushed.

He popped the mushroom cap into his mouth and watched her, pretending she wasn't the sexiest woman he'd ever seen. And that he wasn't anticipating, even a little, how fun it'd be once she reached his side.

"What do you think?" she asked when she reached him. Her laugh was breathless as she looked around the room. "Isn't it great? I've never seen so many people outside a movie screen, theater stage or kindergarten classroom so into playing make-believe."

"You look like you're enjoying it."

She was, too. Artfully made up, her eyes glowed and her cheeks had a flush that went perfectly with the pale pink of her satin dress. Unlike the other women, she didn't glitter. She glowed. Long sleeves hugged her arms, but left her shoulders bare while the rest of her dress wrapped and draped over her curves. His hands itched to slide over that slick fabric, to feel those curves. To cup her hips. To curl over her luscious breasts.

She was so damned delicious. His body tightened, as if his brain needed that reminder that she was sweet sexiness wrapped in pink satin.

Because, yeah, his brain wasn't already imagining the various ways he'd like to strip that fabric off her body and rediscover the delicious treasure he'd held only that morning.

Hardening painfully, he shoved his fists in the pockets of his jeans, wishing he was wearing slacks. Or sweats. Anything roomier.

"When's the murder?" he asked, needing distraction.

A tiny frown creased her brow. Instead of answering, she accepted a flute of bubbling champagne and took a sip, staring at him over the rim.

"Didn't you read your assignment?"

"I skimmed it."

"You might want to update your skimming skills, then. It clearly outlined the timetable. Tonight is a meet and greet, costumes optional. Which is why you are here, in jeans, and nobody is suggesting you go shovel coal in the engine room."

"And the murder?" he asked again. Not because he cared. But it was fun to see her try to school him.

"Even though costume is optional, character isn't," she hissed, leaning closer as a group of women commandeered the chairs next to them. "We're not supposed to discuss the setup or details of the events except in our rooms."

"Don't you think you're taking this a little too seriously?"

"The winner gets a thousand dollars and a trophy," she pointed out.

"Ooh," he teased. Not that a grand was anything to toss away, but money wasn't one of his big motivators. And trophies? Those weren't even little motivators.

She giggled, lifting one shoulder as if in agreement.

"I think it'll be fun. I'd like to win, not so much for the prize, but because I think it'd be cool to figure out the mystery. Don't you enjoy putting together clues, pitting your intellect against others and figuring things out first?"

Hunter gave her a curious look. Her words were pretty passionate, her tone awfully excited for a woman whose life revolved around clothes and dead people. Because those were the things that came to his mind when he thought fashion or biographies. Maybe that's why these mystery events were such a big draw. Every accountant and housewife wanted to be a supersleuth.

"Mysteries are okay," he said with a shrug. Not that he wasn't a fan of piecing together the puzzle. But he got a bigger charge out of outsmarting dirtbags who thought they were above the rules. Who figured they were smarter than the law. Since he *was* the law, letting them know just how wrong they were was his ultimate pleasure.

"I'll bet you're more of a suspense kind of guy," she guessed, tilting her champagne glass his way and leaning close to whisper. "*Die Hard* instead of *Sherlock Holmes?* Blazing guns instead of a magnifying glass?"

"Sexy blonde instead of bespeckled old maid?"

He liked the way her eyes rounded, but she didn't look away even as her cheeks warmed with a soft flush.

"Don't you think Sherlock had something hot going on with Irene Adler?"

"Was she the brunette who drugged and stripped Robert Downey Jr.?"

He liked how she laughed. Full, deep, honest. This wasn't a woman afraid of enjoying life to the fullest. He remembered how she'd felt in his arms that morning, regretting just a little that she'd awoken before he'd found out if she would have enjoyed that to the fullest.

His thoughts must have shown on his face, because her laughter died, her smile faded. Heat, intense and curious, flared in her eyes. She bit her lip. His eyes narrowed. He wanted to step closer, to pull her up on her tiptoes and offer to nibble that lip for her.

She looked as though she'd be pretty cool with that, too.

"Hello, there."

Marni blinked, then shook her head as if her gaze was still fogged with sexual heat. She turned to face the person who'd joined them. Hunter took another second to watch her, not in any hurry to look away.

"Hi," Marni offered with a shaky breath.

Finally, Hunter looked to see who she was greeting.

The woman appeared to have stepped right off a movie set. Low budget and black-and-white.

"Hello," he offered disinterestedly. He wasn't on the job, and she wasn't the type he had any interest in on his own time. Maybe if he hurried her along, he could get back to seeing how hot things could get between him and Marni before one or both of them remembered why it was a really bad idea to stoke that sexual heat.

"Well, well, aren't you delicious." With a sultry smile, the brunette looked him up. Then she looked him down. He was surprised she didn't take a visual three-sixty around his body.

Hunter grinned at Marni's hiss.

"Nice to meet you," he added, more because it was fun to watch Marni's reaction than because it was the truth.

"My pleasure," the vamp greeted, leaning forward to offer her fingertips.

Hunter wasn't sure if she expected him to kiss them or shake them. Since her nails were as sharp as talons and her rings as big as his eyeball, he opted to shake.

"I'm Sugar Dish," she introduced, fluttering her lashes in a pale imitation of Marni's flirty move. "I'm traveling with my aged aunt, a wealthy art collector."

"Right. Sounds good." Hunter knew she was playing the role and expected him to play along. But while he'd vaguely heard of these mystery events, he had no idea what the rules were and hadn't bothered to read the ones the porter had given him.

"And why are you traveling across the country?" she

asked, shifting sideways as if blocking Marni from her view could cut her from the conversation.

"Business."

She blinked those spiky lashes again, then gave him an impatient look.

"What kind of business?"

"Personal business."

He watched Marni's eyes dance with amusement, even as she gave him a chiding look and shook her head.

"Care to have a drink later and share what kind of personal…business you do?" she offered, her proposition more genuine than her bustline.

"No."

"Well." In a huff worthy of any forties seductress, she tossed her chin, turned on one heel and stormed off. She did, however, give his ass a pat on her way across the room.

Marni's grin turned into a glare at the woman's departing back.

"You're not playing the game correctly," she said when they were left in the wake of the brunette's perfume.

"I don't play games." Especially not ones that involved getting his ass patted by strange women.

"Then you really should reconsider getting off the train." She got a stubborn, for-your-own-good sort of look on her face. "This is a themed event trip. Unless you're going to take the rest of your meals and spend all of your time in the room, you're a part of the event."

Hunter gritted his teeth. Damn Murray.

"You're supposed to share the basics of your character tonight," Marni explained. "We're laying the groundwork for tomorrow's big occurrence. The more information you get tonight, the further ahead you'll be when they kill someone."

Could he volunteer to be the corpse? Then he could stay in the cabin and play corpse for the rest of the week. Hunter sighed. If only Murray could hear this conversation. The guy would bust a gut laughing.

"Do you not understand how this works?" she asked quietly, laying her hand on his forearm in what she probably figured was a sympathetic gesture.

Hunter's body went on high alert, though, wanting more than sympathy from her touch. Desire heated his gaze before he could hide it. Those slender fingers tightened for just a second. But she didn't pull away.

"I understand just fine."

He understood that she was more temptation than he'd ever faced.

He understood that she was a complication that he didn't have time for.

And he understood that his resistance to that complicated temptation was hanging from a very thin, very frayed thread, ready to snap at any second.

"Why don't I go through it with you later," she suggested. "They allow people in the same cabin to share their character information. Kind of like working as partners."

He didn't work with partners.

Ever.

Hunter's goal was to reach the top of the FBI, eventually to be director of National Intelligence. An honor awarded to few, appointed by the president himself. He still had a lot of climbing to do to get there, and he moved faster alone.

"I know what I'm doing."

"Do you, now?" The skeptical arch of one eyebrow echoed the doubt in her tone.

"I'm confusing the masses. The less information I offer, the less they can pin on me when the crime happens."

"So you're just going to offer, what? Nothing?"

He considered, then pulled a face and nodded. "Yep."

"I'm not sure that's a winning strategy," she mused.

"I am." Especially since the only thing he planned to win was his privacy.

"I think my way is better."

Better? Than eight years' experience as a decorated FBI agent with an arrest record a mile long? Then Hunter forced himself to remember what this was about and shrugged instead. His methods had netted him plenty of bad guys. He didn't have anything to prove. Nor did he need to brag just to impress the pretty girl.

Especially since he wasn't interested in the pretty girl.

Marni shifted, turning to look around the room. The light glistened off her bare shoulders, making his fingers itch to touch, to see if her skin was as smooth as the satin of her dress.

Okay. So he didn't *want* to be interested in the pretty girl.

"Look, if you're serious about kicking me out of the cabin every day while you work, that means I'm out here." She waved her hand to indicate *out here* was the rest of the train, and all these people. "Since we're partners, so to speak, you'd better play along so you don't ruin my chances to figure out the mystery, okay? Otherwise I'm going to sit in that cabin and stare at you. All. Day. Long."

All. Day. Long.

He wasn't sure he could take her and him in that cabin with her complete and total attention focused on him for that long. The way he was feeling right now, he'd make it maybe a half hour, possibly forty-five minutes before he stripped himself naked and asked her what else she wanted to focus on.

"Well, hello."

Hunter barely resisted snarling as they were interrupted again. What was with these people trying to socialize?

"I'm Peter. Peter Principle. I've been watching you from across the room and simply had to come over and introduce myself."

Smirking at the overblown drama of the guy's words, Hunter tore his gaze off of Marni to see what kind of dress-up dork this one was.

Except he didn't look nearly as stupid as he sounded. His tux was custom, his haircut top dollar and his capped-tooth smile full of wealthy smarm. This guy might be pretending to be someone else, but he really lived the moneyed life represented in this little shindig.

"I'm a wealthy investor, traveling to California for the opening of my newest hotel," the guy lied. Or playacted, Hunter supposed Marni would claim. Hunter liked *lied* better.

"Indeed?"

Hunter frowned when Marni's smile shifted from curious to seductive. His gut clenched and his shoulders stiffened. He glared at the smarmy asshole, wondering how much effort it would take to toss the guy off the train.

"I'm Moira Mystery," Marni offered, introducing her character and letting him shake her hand for way too long.

"Would you like to take a walk? I'd be happy to show you the upper deck of the train and the lovely view in the moonlight."

"It's six-thirty. The moonlight is pretty wimpy with the sun still up," Hunter pointed out.

Irritation quickly chased confusion on the guy's surgically sculpted face.

"You'll have to forgive him," Marni said in a throaty voice, sliding closer to Hunter's side and patting his arm as if he was a crazed old man. "He's ever so jealous when men pay attention to me."

"Ahh, you're a couple?" Smarmy asked, still looking irked.

"He's my boss," Marni said, giving an exaggerated eye roll. "He hates anything that might keep me from focusing on the job, though."

Hunter looked down at her, all cozy and sweet.

Then, unable to resist, he chose stupid over smart, and wrapped his arm around her shoulder to pull her tight against the hard length of his body. She felt so damned good there. Too damned good. Still, he didn't let go.

"Her boss," he agreed. "And her lover."

Marni's body was on fire.

From the side of her forehead, where it was pressed against Hunter's chest, to the bare skin of her shoulder, where his fingers wrapped tight. The parts that weren't on fire were tingling with sexual sparks.

"So, what was your name again? Pete? Yeah, Pete, sorry. But she's not available for any fake midnight walks," Hunter said, giving a little shoo motion with his chin to indicate the guy be on his way.

"Well, that was interesting," she murmured two seconds later when the charming Peter had practically left a cloud of smoke in his hurried wake. "Lovers? Really?"

"Let's go." Hunter started toward the exit, not letting go of her shoulder.

Marni would have dug in her heels, but, big shock, stilettos weren't very sturdy. Instead, she shifted to the right, out from under Hunter's arm.

She didn't like being led, any more than she liked being played. And while she wasn't sure what his game was right now, she had not a single doubt that she was a pawn in it.

Marni wasn't against playing games, but she never played unless she had a firm handle on the rules. Or if the stakes were so high, she couldn't resist the odds.

"We're supposed to go in for dinner soon." Marni wasn't interested in food. But she figured it'd be better to stay in the crowd. Smarter would be to let Hunter leave alone. To put a little space between them until she got a grip on the crazy desires that were rushing through her body like hormones run amok.

"I'm not hungry." His words were flat. Matter-of-fact. But the look in his eyes, hot sensuality, said he had a voracious appetite for something other than food. Something like her, if his heated stare was anything to go by.

"We arrive in Chicago just after they serve dessert."

"Then we should have an hour to settle things, shouldn't we."

"What things?"

He just stared. A patient, calm look that said he knew she was smart enough to figure it out and had no problem waiting until she was brave enough to own up to it, too.

Marni gulped.

She was used to being dismissed.

To being considered fluff. Light and sweet. Her own family ignored half of what she said, all sure they knew her better than she knew herself.

And here was this man, looking at her as if he knew the real her. The her inside. The one that was strong and brave, with enough ambition to reach the stars. The one who knew her own mind, and had the gritty determination necessary to make all of her dreams into a solid reality.

He didn't say another word.

Just turned and walked toward the exit.

As if attached by a string, Marni was helpless to do anything but follow. She silently walked at his side as they made their way through the crowd, both ignoring the attempts here and there to engage their attention.

Shoulder to shoulder, they made their way down the narrow corridor to their berth.

"I'm pretty sure our roles are boss and secretary," she pointed out randomly as he shoved open the cabin door.

"Check the stats. I'll bet a lot of bosses and secretaries sideline as lovers."

"We don't."

"Sure we do," he said, dropping into the chair and giving her a smug look. "Especially if it keeps creeps like that off of you. Go ahead, you can thank me."

She gaped.

"Thank you?"

"Yes, thank me. If I hadn't gotten rid of him, you'd be shoving his lechy hand off your shoulder right now, side-stepping yet another of his tacky attempts to look down your dress and wishing like hell you were here with me, debating how long paint would take to dry if a train left New York traveling forty miles per hour, and the paintbrush left California traveling eighty miles per hour. Because, you know it'd be a lot more interesting than what Creepy had to say."

Marni hated that he had a sense of humor.

Gorgeous and sexy were bad enough.

But gorgeous, sexy and fun?

She was doomed.

"How do you know I wasn't interested in that creep—I mean, that gentleman," she corrected quickly, biting the inside of her lip to keep from laughing.

"Because you have better taste than that. You're not the kind of woman to be taken in by smarm."

It was as if he was wearing magic glasses.

As if she'd lived in a blind world all her life, and he was the first sighted person she'd ever met. It was so cool. And just a little scary. Because her tricks, her usual ways of getting around people and situations, they weren't going to work if he could see right inside her.

And getting around him, hiding her real intentions and keeping him off center were vital if she was going to accomplish the only reason she was on this train. To get that article.

Not, she scolded her body, to get laid.

Before her body could offer a rebuttal, Hunter looked at his watch, then got to his feet.

Her heart raced. Was he going to show her what he did think she'd be taken in by? He crossed the room, but not toward her. Instead, he headed for the door.

"I've got to meet someone at the station," he said, his hand on the doorknob. He gave her a long look over his shoulder before pulling it open. "You have a couple hours. You might want to use them to figure out how you're going to handle tonight."

"Tonight?"

"Yeah. Tonight. You need to decide if you're going to be camped out above me on that uncomfortable bunk. Or if you're going to rethink that no you gave this morning."

With that, and a look hot enough to remind her of every delight she'd felt in his arms that morning and to hint at how many more they had to offer, he left.

Marni stared at the closed door for a long time.

They'd been on the train less than a day. They had six more to go.

Maybe she should reconsider this case.

She'd always figured she'd risk anything for a big career break.

Her body, and the delights Hunter promised, wasn't a bad price to pay.

But her heart?

That was more than she was willing to invest.

7

MARNI BLINKED, TRYING to bring the room back into focus. Her eyes were blurry, her head ached and her body…oh, her poor body.

Lack of sleep bad enough.

But lack of sleep for three days added to an ongoing state of unfulfilled sexual arousal? That was straight-up abuse.

"Another espresso, Miss Mystery?" the waiter asked with a friendly smile.

Marni hesitated.

It wasn't that she had an issue with six espressos before noon. It was the worry that the lack of caffeine boost, combined with almost painful jitters, would be worse than falling asleep at the table.

"Maybe a cup of hot tea instead," she decided. "Earl Grey with a side of lemon wedges, please."

If nothing else, she could suck the lemons.

Maybe the citrus would add a little extra zing to her article.

Marni checked her email, excited to see a note from her editor. He was looking forward to seeing the article and, thankfully, had agreed to cover the expenses of her trip. Marni gave her laptop an affectionate look, all but patting its casing in pride.

Over the past three days, while banished from her cabin, she'd written a damned good article. She'd done in-depth research, not only on Charles Burns, but on the FBI, as well. She'd pulled together an incredible amount of facts, figures and information on Burns, his history, his organization, his marriages, right on down to his addiction to cherry licorice. What she didn't have, though, were the insights that would take this from an exposé to a hard-hitting piece of journalism. It might be a good follow-up for after the trial, buried somewhere in the middle of the magazine. But it still wouldn't net her the cover.

Frustratingly, neither would the pitifully small bit of information she'd been able to cull together on the man who'd arrested Burns in the first place. Because Hunter was still an active-duty FBI agent, there was almost no information to be found—including his darned first name, which had driven her crazy for an entire day. Then she'd shifted focus, spending almost as much time studying Hunter Sr. as she'd spent pulling together information on Charles Burns.

The man was amazing. The more she found out, the more she wanted—no, needed—to know.

She pulled up that document, noting that the word count was quickly heading toward a novel instead of an article. The man was fascinating, both in his adventures with the FBI and in the connections he had outside it. What must it be like to have a father who stood godfather to the child of a notorious con artist? Who'd headed up the FBI, had dinner with presidents and vacationed with foreign leaders? Rick Hunter's story enthralled her.

It'd been through studying his father that she'd garnered the most information on Hunter. She'd talked to people who were happy to share stories about the senior Mr. Hunter, and she had charmed out of them bits and pieces about Hunter's own talent for looking past the obvious and his habit of solving cases through unconventional methods.

"Your tea."

She mumbled a thanks to the waiter as she made more notes on her laptop. This profile of Rick Hunter was probably the best work she'd ever done.

"Well, you're bright-eyed and bushy-tailed this morning. And with a fake murderer on the loose." Sugar Dish, as the brunette had introduced herself three nights past, sidled into the chair opposite Marni with a big smile. Ever since the mystery murder had occurred, everyone had been sleuthing their hearts out. "I don't know how you do it. Must be rough, those all-nighters with your boss."

Marni sighed, and realizing she wasn't going to get any more writing done, shut her laptop cover and gave Sugar, or Carla as she was known outside the train, an impatient look.

"Again with the all-nighters jokes?" She sipped her tea while Sugar ordered a cup of coffee. "You know we're not really a thing."

"And you know I think that's a horrible shame." The brunette grinned and fanned herself. "Because your handsome roommate is worth losing sleep over."

Wasn't that the truth?

Most guys, after a couple of days of constant exposure, lost that initial oh-my-God-gorgeous appeal.

Hunter, though, just kept getting hotter. He was hot in the morning, with his blurry-eyed mumbles and stubbled chin. He was cute in the afternoon, during the one hour he'd designated that she was allowed in the room—as long as she brought a snack. He was freaking sexy as hell in the evening, when he wound down and relaxed, losing a little of that intense edge that always seemed to drive him the rest of the time. He was fascinating and so damned cute, the way he'd share stories about him and his father, the hero worship he'd mentioned once coming through loud and clear.

Was it any wonder she wasn't getting sleep?

Or that each passing night made her think there were much better ways to spend those endless waking minutes instead of staring into the dark, resisting her body's urges.

The other woman thanked the server, waiting for him to pour her coffee and leave the creamer. While doctoring her caffeine with that and enough sugar to give a diabetic a coma, she studied Marni's face.

"Of course, it looks like you're doing just fine on that lack of sleep already. Wouldn't it be better if you were having great sex to go with it?"

Marni snickered into her teacup. She'd been prepared to straight up dislike the other woman. Especially after she'd hit so hard on Hunter that first night. Jealousy wasn't a pretty thing, but it was powerful.

"We're not a couple," she said, trotting out her usual excuse. "We're strangers who happen to be sharing a berth. Just like this train would have seen in its heyday."

"Yeah, yeah." Sugar waved that away. "But you're a smart woman. You've got brains and looks, and enough savvy to know that the only reason the two of you are both lying awake all night in separate beds is because *you* are choosing to."

Something Hunter reminded her of each night.

Not in words.

But in the look in his eyes, the husky tone of his voice as he said good-night. He didn't tease, or play games like some guys would, like insisting he always slept naked and stripping down in front of her. Instead, he respected her no, kept his boxers on and tortured her with the wonder of what was underneath.

She was going crazy.

Just thinking about it got her hot, made her want to wiggle in her seat.

"I'm not a fling kind of gal," Marni demurred truthfully. She could be. She would be, if it wasn't for this article. She wanted to be, given how intensely her body reacted when Hunter was in the room. How her nipples beaded at the sound of his voice. How the few times they'd casually touched, her thighs melted.

She took a deep breath, reminding herself that, as always, career came first. It had to.

And she couldn't, in good conscience, use a guy for a story while riding his body to new heights of orgasmic pleasure.

"I'm hearing a lot of *are nots* out of you," Sugar said with a tilt of her head. "What about the *ares? What are* you?"

Horny.

Obsessed.

Quickly sliding toward infatuated.

What she was must have shown on her face, because Sugar reached over and gave Marni's hand a sympathetic pat.

"Sweetie, if you want something, you know perfectly well how to make it happen." With that, and a wink that was as natural as it was in character, coffee cup in hand, the brunette rose, tossed her hair over her shoulder and scanned the room. "Now, I'm off to find out who is allergic to red roses, but loves hot bubble baths before bed. Three days down, three left to find the killer."

She arched a look at Marni, who, figuring one good

turn deserved another, angled her head to the three crimson roses in the bud vase in front of her.

"Oh, good point." Scanning the room to see who had ditched their centerpiece, Sugar gave a little finger wave and was on her sleuthing way.

Marni gave the departing woman a grumpy glare.

She had no problem figuring out how to get what she wanted.

The problem she had was figuring out how to not take what she shouldn't want.

It was exhaustion. That had to be the problem. If she'd had sleep, she wouldn't be having these crazy ideas. Or, at least without the cloud of fatigue, she'd be mentally strong enough to shove them back in a dark corner of her mind where she could more easily ignore them.

That was it. She'd spent yesterday afternoon in the library car, dozing next to a corner bookcase. She'd awoken to the hissing whispers of six people, three of whom were sure Hunter was the murderer, and the other three just as sure he'd been murdered himself in a surprise twist they hadn't heard yet.

When they'd seen Marni was awake, they'd all plastered on their most innocent smiles and pumped her for information on her boss, Lex Lanternjaw.

"He can eat lunch out here," she decided in a grumpy mutter. Scooping her laptop into her messenger bag with a scowl, she left the dining car and stormed toward her cabin. Hunter was making her job harder, her fake job and her real one, by hiding out in their berth. He could get his tush out in public so people quit trying to pump her for information.

And while he did, she could take a nap.

A glorious, deep-sleep, cozied-under-the-covers nap.

It was all she could do not to melt into a puddle right there in the corridor.

With a big smile, her arguments all neatly lined up, she flung open the cabin door.

There, in the desk chair exactly where she'd expected to find him, was Hunter.

Sleeping.

She almost slammed the door shut, just to watch him jump.

Then she noticed the exhaustion on his face.

Looked as though the two of them had his-and-hers matching circles under their eyes.

She sighed, her entire body sagging under the weight of her shoulders. She was so tired, she felt as if her head was floating a foot over her body. She needed sleep.

Marni shut the door with a quiet snick, then laid her laptop on the small table next to it. Sliding off her shoes, she eyed the button that would release the bunk from hell.

If she pushed the button, it'd wake Hunter.

Then they'd have to have the argument over him leaving and her napping. And she was just too tired to argue.

Besides, three nights she'd lain on that bunk. For a piece of mattress-covered plywood, it wasn't too uncomfortable. If she hadn't been constantly struggling against the desperate need to climb down and jump the man beneath her, she might have actually slept okay.

But it wasn't as comfy as the bed. The bed was glorious. The bed was wide. The bed was sleepy-time heaven.

She was napping in the bed.

She stopped at Hunter's side, glancing at the work spread out around him. The laptop showed a lock screen. The papers sitting next to the multilock briefcase looked like they were in code. Even his notes were some form of weird shorthand she couldn't decipher. All she could make out were the initials B.B. here and there.

Snoop?

Or sleep?

No contest.

Silent as a mouse, Marni carefully, oh-so-slowly, pulled the duvet back. Her watchful gaze never left Hunter's face as she slipped under the plush cotton and slowly, as if the sound of the feathers compressing might wake him, lay her head on the pillow.

Oh, mercy.

It felt so good, she almost cried.

Breathing deep, she inhaled the rich scent of Hunter's cologne that permeated the bedding. It was like being wrapped in his arms. Hugged close.

Slowly, so slow she wasn't even sure when it happened, her eyes drifted closed. Her brain drifted into that glorious cloud that was a deep, dreamless sleep. Her last thought was how wonderful it felt, as if she was actually in bed with Hunter.

MARNI WAS FLOATING. Somewhere, high above the level that consciousness could currently reach—higher than she had any interest in checking out—something nagged. Like a thorn in her shoe, it poked at her, trying to get her attention.

She snuggled deeper into the pillow, easily ignoring everything except how wonderful she felt.

Wow. Sleep was awesome.

Warm, delicious and awesome.

And a total turn-on.

Not an unusual state for her these days. It was as if being around Hunter had flipped her desire meter from average to super-high, keeping her in a constant state of excitement.

This wasn't the usual sex dream, though.

Maybe it was four days in close proximity to the hottest guy she'd ever met. Hormones run amok. Constant awareness keeping her passions simmering. Heck, maybe it was just horny overload.

Whatever it was, Marni's body was on fire.

Curiosity pierced her sleepy cocoon.

She pulled herself out of sleep just enough to take stock of what was going on.

She could feel the rumbling motion. So she was on the train.

Warm sunshine glowed behind her closed lids. So it was early afternoon.

The duvet was light and comforting over her body, the mattress soft and giving beneath her. So she was still in bed.

And there was a hard body wrapped around her back, one arm thrown over her waist. Her body was awash in a lusty sort of awareness, her nipples aching and the damp heat between her thighs needy.

She wasn't dreaming.

Her eyes flew open and, without moving her head, she glanced down at the hand pressed against her belly. Just there, within inches of relieving that damp, hot need.

Holy shit.

She was in bed with Hunter.

Again.

How did this keep happening?

She should get up.

She should rip herself out of his arms, jump from the bed and throw a fit. Accuse him of taking advantage of her. Of sneaky napping practices. She should be outraged.

She snuggled deeper instead, breathing deep the scent of his skin, letting the warmth seep into her muscles, relaxing her even more.

Outrage?

She wasn't sure she could force herself out of his arms even if the train were on fire.

God, he felt good.

Hard and solid.

Warm and safe.

Comforting and, oh, yeah, she wiggled her butt just a little against his groin, he felt sexy.

"Do that one more time and you're going to have to deal with the results," he murmured sleepily against her hair.

Her breath caught in her throat. She was tempted. Oh, so very tempted.

And in this second, with Hunter's arms tight around her and his erection pressing its delicious length along her tush, she couldn't think of a single reason not to give in to that temptation.

At least, not a single reason she cared about.

HUNTER WAITED, EVERY FACET of his being hoping she'd wiggle her ass again. Just like he'd hoped, every night on this train, that she'd hang her head over the edge of that damned bunk and tell him she'd changed her mind.

That she wanted to strip them both naked and play a few rounds of count the climaxes.

He knew better.

Over the past few days, she'd been sweet. She'd been friendly. She'd been fun and entertaining and sexy as hell.

She'd also been sticking to her no.

Still, a guy woke from a dead sleep to find his fantasy woman in his bed, he was bound to hope.

Hunter was used to catnaps. His was a job of long hours

and odd sleeping arrangements, so he'd taught himself early on to snatch enough energy from fifteen, twenty minutes of shut-eye to let him power through.

He'd opened his eyes, and there she was, like a fairy-tale princess, waiting under the covers.

He hadn't been able to resist climbing in with her. Both to freak her out, because he loved that chiding look she gave him, and because he was weak. Yes, he admitted it to himself. He was weak enough to take whatever chance he could get to wrap his arms around the delicate blonde. To hold her, breathe in her scent, to tempt his body with the feel of her curves.

And yeah, to hope she'd be tempted right back.

Enough to change her no to a hell yes.

He'd been doing a damned good job of avoiding Marni so far.

Focusing on the case. Scouring the files his agents had taken from Charles Burns's secret safes. Delving into the computer drive they'd recovered from a house nobody realized he owned. The information Beverly Burns had turned over was a gold mine. So much so that Hunter was taking an extra careful pass to make sure it was all real. It wasn't that he didn't trust the woman's fury against her husband trying to blow her up along with his building. But Hunter had an innate wariness of gift horses who were angling for a deep cover in WitSec, and a fat payoff to continue the luxurious life they felt they deserved.

He'd be a lot further if he'd been getting sleep.

The first night, he'd blamed it on his body's aches. A taped rib wasn't comfortable to sleep on, and the constant motion of the train was doing weird things to his ruptured eardrum.

The second night, he decided it was that, plus the fact that the only time he slept with another person in the

room—unless they'd just had sex—was when he was undercover. So his senses were on automatic alert, keeping
him from anything but the most cursory of rest.

Last night, he'd dropped the bullshit excuses.

He'd lain here on this very bed, staring up at the bunk
above him, aching to touch Marni. To taste her. To feel
her in his arms again.

He wanted her like crazy.

And then she moved.

Just a little.

So little, his brain argued that she might have only
been breathing.

His dick argued right back that she'd just tossed aside
the no and opened the door to yes.

Hunter hesitated.

And she moved again.

This time, with the sweet pressure of her butt against
his erection, there was no mistaking her intention.

"Oh, yeah," he murmured, sliding the silky swathe of
her hair aside so he could plant his lips on her delicate
throat. He breathed in the soft floral scent of her hair and
groaned. "Oh, yeah, baby."

His mouth moved over her skin, sliding, kissing, caressing. One hand was anchored between their bodies, but the
other was free to roam. And roam it did. Up the rounded
curve of her hip, down the gentle slope of her waist and
along the glorious weight of her breast. He cupped the
weight, loving how her breath shuddered and her breath
quickened.

Needing to make sure this was a genuine yes, not
something she could dismiss later with a half-assed I-
was-asleep excuse, he swiftly shifted positions. So Marni
was flat on her back, staring up at him, those big blue eyes
rounded with shock and blurred with passion.

She was gorgeous.

Pale pink washed her skin, making it glow. Those cupid's bow lips were open, whether in shock or invitation, he didn't care. He took them anyway.

His gaze not releasing hers, he kept the kiss soft. Easy. Uncomplicated.

The way he usually liked his relationships.

The complete opposite of this.

Because as soft as she was, there was nothing easy or uncomplicated about Marni.

Her eyes didn't shift, didn't try to slide away. Instead, they challenged. They tempted. They dared him to take it further, to show her what he could do.

Hunter had never refused a dare in his life. But he'd never been as excited about meeting one as he was in this second.

His hands anchored on either side of her head, he took the kiss deeper. His tongue slid along her bottom lip, then traced the edge of her teeth. Passion flared in her eyes, but she didn't blink.

Instead, her tongue, delicate and cool, met his. Just the tip, as if she was testing the taste of him. Her breath was a soft, fluttering inhalation. Then she moaned.

Oh, yeah, baby.

She liked what she was tasting.

His tongue dove deep, pulling hers into an intense dance. Swirling, tangling, thrusting against each other. Hunter shifted, so his body weight was angled between his hip and one shoulder, so his hand was free to roam. And roam it did. His fingers skimmed, light and teasing, over her shoulder and down her chest. His palm hovered over her breast, then slid across the soft cotton fabric covering her stomach and down to her low belly where her shirt was tucked into another one of those sexy, hip-skimming, knee-hugging skirts. He didn't dip lower. Just skimmed. Teased. Reveled in the soft give of her body beneath his hand.

She had the most incredible body.

Welcoming, warm, gloriously feminine.

He wanted more. Needed more. Had been driving himself crazy wondering what more would be like.

Now he was going to find out.

Excitement surged, adding an urgency to Hunter's hunger.

His mouth delved deeper. He reveled in Marni's sweet, rich flavor, his fingers working their way back up her body button by button, freeing each from the fabric and revealing silky soft skin. When he reached her chest and that last button, he couldn't resist. He pulled his mouth from hers to look at the bounty he'd just uncovered.

Like Aphrodite rising from the foam, her breast was encased in frothy lace the color of the inside of a seashell. Lush and rounded, he could see the raspberry tip through the shimmery fabric. His finger traced, light as air, around that tip.

Marni gasped.

He ran his thumb across the pebbling flesh. Once, twice, then pinched.

Marni moaned.

His finger slid between the pale pink lace and her even paler skin, her nipple hardening to a gratifying peak beneath his knuckle.

Marni's fingers dug into him, one hand on the waistband of his jeans, the other gripping his shoulder as if deciding whether to pull him over her or shove him down so she could straddle his body.

Either position was fine with him.

Figuring he should help her decide, he gently tugged the

lace down, revealing one gorgeous breast. He closed his eyes for a second, so blown away at her perfection, then opened them again because, well, he just couldn't resist.

He took that raspberry-red, pouting tip between his lips, twirling his tongue around the sensitive flesh. Her cry of pleasure was almost lost in a pounding sound from somewhere behind them.

Hunter's body tensed, but he didn't stop.

The only threat he could sense was to the end of their pleasure. And he wasn't ready for that to happen.

Marni gasped, though, making as if to pull away.

"Ignore it," he advised against her nipple. To emphasize his point, he nipped at the bud with a gentle scrape of his teeth. Her body arched, shuddering as she pressed her breast closer to his mouth. Hunter sucked, hard, reveling in the taste, the texture, the deliciousness of her.

The knock came again.

Marni's body tensed. He could actually feel her desire seeping away, like a faucet shutting down.

If Hunter's mouth hadn't been full, he'd have clenched his teeth. *Ignore, ignore, ignore,* he mentally chanted. But he didn't say a word. This, like their sleeping arrangements, was her decision.

"You should get that," she finally breathed.

Hunter pulled away to stare at her, biting back the barrage of cusswords. Her eyes were blurry with passion, but her jaw was set. Hunter wanted to argue. He damned near wanted to beg. Instead, like the gentleman he hated himself for being at that moment, he ripped his body off hers and stormed across the room.

"What?" he snarled as he yanked the door open.

"Your, um, outfits for tonight," the porter stammered, his eyes flashing fear. "My instructions were to provide costuming for the big event, that you'd take part in the mystery skit tonight."

"Whose damned instructions are those?"

The kid, his hand trembling, shoved the hangers at Hunter, then started flipping through papers so fast, he tore a couple.

"Mr. Murray indicated when he booked the room that you'd take one of the roles this evening. We assumed—" The kid stopped to gulp so hard, his Adam's apple almost bounced. "We figured that meant both people in the room. You can skip it, though. I mean, I'll make—get someone else to take the parts. You don't have to do it."

Hunter had scared plenty of grown men in his day. But he'd never felt like this kind of jerk.

"No, I'm sorry. I didn't realize what was going on," he apologized. When the kid tried to take the hangers back, he shifted them, then dug into his still painfully tight jeans to find some cash. "Here, thanks."

"The, um, the instructions are pinned to the costumes."

"Okay." Hunter started to shut the door.

"The dinner dance starts in an hour."

"Right." Hunter glared.

The porter swallowed again, then turned heel and scurried away.

Dinner dance. In costumes.

Murray was definitely getting his revenge for Hunter pissing him off.

Shutting the door, Hunter took his time turning around to face the bed and its delightful occupant. He wasn't sure what he'd see on her face, but he was betting it wasn't going to be an invitation to finish what they'd started.

He tossed the costumes, hangers and all, over the back of a chair, then met Marni's eyes.

She looked like she'd been well loved.

Her hair tumbled in a tangled mass of curls over her shoulders. Her eyes were heavy with passion, makeup smudged and lips swollen. She'd tugged her clothes into place and now sat, prim as a schoolgirl, on the edge of the bed. Her feet were still bare, though. Hunter wanted to kneel between her thighs and lift one foot, cover her toes with hot kisses, then work his way up her leg.

"So?" He waited.

She swallowed hard, then lifted her chin. "So that was fun."

"Fun?"

Hunter couldn't help it. He laughed.

"Let me get this straight. You broke the rule by coming into the cabin during off-limit hours." While he had unsecured top secret material out in the open, no less.

"You climbed into my bed. Rubbed your sweet ass against me until I had a hard-on to rival a railroad spike. You drove me to the brink of what had promised to be the most incredible orgasm of my life. And then you forced me to answer the door."

He gave her an are-you-freaking-kidding-me stare.

Unfazed by his rant, Marni batted her eyelashes right back.

"What? And that isn't fun for you?"

8

It took every ounce of her will to keep the glib smile in place as Marni waited to see what Hunter would do. Heck, she still wasn't sure what *she* was doing.

Fun?

She had no idea why that'd popped out of her mouth. Her only defense was that her brain didn't function well on sexual overload.

Heck, one second, she'd been floating on a sea of incredible pleasure. The next, she'd been pounded back to earth. And not in the fun, sexual way she'd have enjoyed.

Her body felt as though it was going to splinter into tiny little pieces. Nerves wrapped around desire, tangling with excitement and overlaid by fear.

And Hunter just stood there, staring.

Unable to hold his gaze, she shifted her attention to the fancy clothes he'd tossed over the back of the chair.

Vividly aware that she was barefoot, as if the sight of her naked toes was the ultimate tease, she rubbed one arch against the other. Hunter's eyes shifted to her feet. Narrowed. Heated.

Marni gulped.

She jumped up from the bed, crossing to the outfit and

lifting the dress as if it were suddenly the most fascinating thing on earth.

All of her attention was focused on the man behind her.

She waited for Hunter to do something. To say anything.

But he didn't.

He just leaned against the wall, his arms crossed over his chest, and stared. She could feel his eyes on her back, like hot lasers equipped with tiny sexual fingers that teased and tempted everywhere they touched.

Her breath only a little labored, Marni pretended she didn't notice. Laying the dress back on the chair, she crossed to the tiny bathroom to get her brush, running it through her pillow-tangled hair. Then, realizing that this would just remind both of them why her hair had been getting tangled on the pillow, she tossed it on the table.

She looked around the room, her eyes flitting from this to that, landing everywhere but on him.

His briefcase and laptop were once again locked away.

The green landscape flew past the window like a blurred watercolor.

The bed—where just a few minutes ago he'd been inviting her to enjoy what was promising to be a pretty sweet orgasm—was mussed, with the duvet kicked to the bottom of the mattress.

Her pulse jumped ahead a few beats.

She wanted that orgasm.

She wanted it so badly, she was afraid she'd do something stupid. Something crazy. Something she'd regret, maybe not in the morning, but within a couple of days. Because she figured that was probably about how long it'd take to return from climactic pleasure la-la land.

"Are you attending the party tonight?" she asked, tossing random words out to try to defuse the tension. "It's the big event, where everyone gets to toss out their suspicions and make accusations. I think it was Peter. He had means, opportunity and motive. What do you think?"

"I'm not interested in games."

Well. Marni pressed her lips together. She was a smart girl. She didn't need an interpreter or a big flashing neon sign to pick up on the double entendre.

Her fingers dug into her palms as she stared at the dress. She wasn't trying to play a game. But she didn't know what she wanted, either. Well, that was a lie. She wanted him. But should she give in to that desire? What was going to happen if she did?

Was she strong enough to separate her physical needs and her emotional hopes? Was she smart enough to keep from hoping for something that she knew was impossible? Something guaranteed to demand more than she could give if she was going to achieve her career ambitions?

Finally, shoring up all her nerve, she looked at Hunter.

He didn't look pissed.

Or impatient, or irritated, or any other negative thing that she'd imagine most guys would feel after finding a willing woman in his bed—twice—only to be denied. And maybe he did feel all of those things, but he was too much a gentleman to show it.

That scored a lot of points in her book.

That, and the memory of his lips on her breast.

She sucked in a deep breath, pulling her gaze away again to finger the beaded fabric of the evening gown.

"So?"

"So?" she tossed back, still staring at the dress.

"So are you going to play dress-up?"

Marni tilted her head, taking in the entire gown. It was one of the prettiest she'd ever seen. The kind that made a girl want to play dress up, to put on her highest heels and fanciest jewelry. To pretend she was a princess.

A fair maiden.

The most desirable woman in the room.

Of course, Hunter made her feel that way, too.

Marni closed her eyes, and for the first time she could remember, decided not to weigh the consequences. Not to put her career, her ambition first.

For the first time, she was a woman first.

She blew out a deep breath, imagining she were letting go of all her fears, every worry and caution.

Then, because she'd gotten what she needed—the space and time to make sure she wouldn't regret her actions— she turned to Hunter with a smile.

It was her most seductive smile.

"Actually, I had a different sort of entertainment in mind," she told him quietly. "One that requires we stay here. Together."

Hunter straightened from the wall. His gaze, so intense she was sure he was peering into her soul, didn't leave her face.

"We keep ending up in bed together by accident," she pointed out, pretending nerves weren't clutching at her vocal cords and making it hard to speak. "Maybe we should see what it'd be like if we started out there together, on purpose."

His eyes flamed bright with the promise of a passion deeper than anything she'd experienced yet.

"You're sure?" His words were low, husky.

Marni's fingers trembled as she slid her hair behind one ear. She wanted to look away. It was so hard to think when he was staring at her. Hard to discern the right choice when she was looking directly into the face of temptation.

"Is it just sex?" she blurted out. She winced, but managed to resist slapping her hands over her mouth in embarrassment. She was equal parts horrified at the neediness of the question, and proud of herself. Hey, if a little honest talk before getting naked scared him away, then so be it. She'd be better off without him then.

She backed up that silent lie with a defiant lift of her chin.

"You're something else." He laughed. "Every time I think I've got you figured out, you change things up."

"Is that a problem?"

Walking toward her, he slowly shook his head. "Nope. I'm all for honesty. I'd rather we lay it all out now, before we get naked. Because as soon as the clothes come off, we're not going to be talking for a long, long time."

Marni's heart raced. Both at the image of them naked and unable to talk for long, sweaty hours. And at his mention of honesty. One excited her like crazy, the other scared the hell out of her.

She bit her lip, twining the fingers of one hand through the other as she struggled with the scary part. Did her being a reporter, here to do a story on his case, qualify as something she needed to confess to merit that honesty he mentioned?

Since the probable reward for that kind of honesty was her tush being tossed off the train, she figured she'd stick with sexual honesty. It wasn't as if she was sleeping with him for the story. She didn't expect him to moan the details of the Burns case while she kissed her way down his body.

Would he be pissed later?

Yes.

Could he claim she'd slept with him to get the story?

She didn't see how. And that wasn't just her horny side

talking. Even though the horny side was doing a few mental cartwheels now that it was sure it was getting its way.

"Finally got it all settled in there?"

"What?" She frowned, wondering when Hunter had moved. He was one step, maybe two, away. How had she not noticed? Heat spun around her like a whirlpool of energy. It was as though all of her nerve endings were standing on edge, waiting.

"Your mind is just as fascinating as your smile. Did you know that? It's like I can see you working through all of the options, debating with yourself and lining up your reasons. Pro and con."

Marni wrinkled her nose. It really was weird to have someone see her, know her, that well. People who'd spent their lives with her didn't see her nearly as clearly. She wasn't sure she liked it. But she wasn't sure she didn't, either.

"If you think you're so smart," she taunted in a flirtatious tone, "can you also see what I decided?"

He stepped closer. Close enough that she could feel the heat, the energy, off his body. Close enough that if she wanted, she'd just have to lift her fingers to touch him. And oh, how she wanted. His smile turned wicked, as if he'd just flipped the locks on a sensual prison and tossed the key out the window. Marni's pulse raced, nerves and desire tangling together in her belly. Excitement was a drug pounding through her system. She was helpless to resist it. She wanted more. She wanted everything.

"You decided to cover your butt," he said slowly, his words so low they were barely discernible over the sound of the train's wheels racing across the tracks. "You want this. Want to see what it's like between us. You probably figure it's a safe bet. We hit California in two days. If the sex sucks, you only have to avoid me for a few dozen hours. If it's incredible, you figure the few dozen hours are enough to immerse yourself in it, but not enough to get addicted."

She'd been addicted since that first morning, waking up to his mouth on her body. Feeling the edgy, needy fingers of desire gripping her as never before. But he didn't need to know that.

"Scary," she muttered, her smile a little shaky. "Do you read minds in that government accounting job of yours?"

For just a second, the heat in his gaze cooled. Shuttered. Like that part of him, the special agent man, had stepped aside. Like he was waiting. Judging. But not involved.

"I've spent a few days watching you. Learning you," he finally said. It didn't escape her that he was completely ignoring her question about where he'd learned his mind-reading tactics. Instead, he reached out, his fingers sliding through her hair. Marni shuddered, her mouth going dry at his touch. "I've spent even more time thinking about you."

Her ego wanted to know what he'd seen watching, what he'd learned. But the woman who was teetering on obsessing over him? All she cared about was that last part.

"And just what have you been thinking about me?" she asked, the words catching in her throat as his fingers skimmed her jaw, then slid under her hair to the back of her neck.

"My thinking has kind of gone like this." His mouth descended.

Mmm.

She really liked the way he thought.

And she really, really liked the way he kissed.

Her mouth opened to his, reveling in his taste. His tongue thrust, strong and hard. Marni welcomed him with a moan, anticipation so intense it was almost painful as she met each thrust with a welcoming glide of her own tongue along his.

His fingers were so warm, his body so hot. She skimmed her palms over his shoulders—oh, baby, she loved his shoulders—and reveled in their broad strength. His body was a work of art. One she wanted to study. To worship. To spend untold hours exploring in great, delicious detail.

"Mmm, now this is even more fun," she murmured as his mouth shifted so his lips whispered over her cheek and along her jaw.

"Fun, hmm?"

"Oh, yeah. Don't you think sex is fun?" she teased, her fingers tunneling into the silky thickness of his hair.

"I guess we're going to find out."

Even though she'd known where this was going from the second he kissed her, a powerful surge of excitement exploded deep in Marni's belly. Her thighs quivered, her nipples puckered. She was so ready to see just what they'd be finding out.

"Marni," Hunter rasped, his lips hovering just over hers.

"Yeah?" She forced her eyelids open, meeting his slumberous gaze.

"It's gonna be incredible."

HUNTER WASN'T A MAN afraid to make promises. He knew how to make things happen. But this was the first time he'd ever promised a woman incredible.

It was the first time he'd ever promised a woman anything.

He didn't know whether to be horrified or excited.

He settled for completely turned-on.

Wanting, needing to taste more, he sucked her lower lip between his teeth. Marni moaned.

"You like that?" he asked, his words a husky whisper as he shifted backward just a little, so he could see her face.

"I do," she breathed, her head falling back. Her hair fell like a soft curtain over his hands. Her eyes were closed, a rosy flush making her skin glow.

He gripped her hair in one hand, tugging gently to shift her head to one side, then took advantage of the move by skimming his lips down her now exposed throat. He nibbled the delicate flesh, reveling in her breathy moan. He reached the juncture of her collarbone, burying his face there for one second and breathing deep her enticing scent.

When he reached her blouse, his patience snapped. Through with the gentlemanly pretense—hell, all of the pretenses—he gave in to his own wants and ripped the fabric aside.

Her gasp, and the pinging of buttons, bounced off the walls. She pressed her hips tighter against his throbbing erection, which was all the proof he needed that she didn't have an issue with the damage.

He made quick work of the rest of her blouse, sending her bra flying along with the ruined clothing. Then he leaned back to take in the gorgeous bounty he'd been dreaming of.

Incredible.

Her skin was so pale, her nipples a rich raspberry. Tight and puckered. He couldn't resist tracing his forefinger over one generous areola. Her breasts were lush, perfectly round and so inviting. His mouth watered to taste her.

Marni's eyes were slumberously sensual as she watched his surveillance. She arched one brow, as if asking what was taking him so long.

Good question.

Hunter cupped both breasts in his hands, weighing their

bounty, lifting the delicious tips for his mouth. His tongue swirled around one, then the other. He sipped, delicate and sweet. Her fingers dug into the small of his back, her breath coming faster and faster.

His dick throbbed, tension spinning tighter and tighter through his body. Giving in to the desperation, he sucked hard on one nipple while his fingers plucked at the other. She cried out, then almost made him explode by wrapping one leg around his thigh and pressing herself tight against his dick.

Hunter dropped to his knees, yanking the zipper of her skirt down as he went. He shoved the fabric down over her hips, then took another second to appreciate the glorious view.

Clad only in a tiny pair of zebra-striped panties at odds with the vintage look she'd been sporting all week, she looked like a modern goddess, offering a glimpse of heaven to the mortal at her feet.

A heaven he was all too ready to enjoy.

His eyes hot, his body desperate, he snapped that black-and-white fabric with a quick twist, leaving her totally nude.

Marni flinched, as if she were going to modestly cover herself. Then, at the look in his eyes, she gave a shuddering sigh and stepped a little wider, as if inviting him to go ahead and look.

He did more than look.

He leaned in close, hitching one of her thighs over his shoulder. He waited just long enough for her to settle her shoulders against the wall for balance, then he dove in.

He ran his tongue over her clitoris.

She cried out, then grabbed on to his head as though she was afraid of losing her balance.

He sipped. He nipped. His fingers reveled in the delicate dance in and out of her hot, wet canal.

Her breath came faster and faster. When he sucked the throbbing pink flesh between his teeth, she cried out. Her body spasmed, contracting around his fingers as she came.

"Bed?" she gasped.

"I don't think so," he responded, quickly getting to his feet. "Every time we land in that bed, this ends."

Her laughter filled the room even as she made quick work of his shirt, seemingly caught in the maelstrom of his desperate hunger.

Hunter wasn't kidding, though.

Hell, he was barely thinking.

He shrugged off his shirt while her fingers reached for the zipper of his jeans. His brain was barely engaged, all of the blood in his body throbbing along with his erection. He had just enough foresight to kick off his shoes so he could rid himself of the denim, then grabbed his wallet out of his pocket to snag a condom.

He knew she was on the Pill. He'd shared a tiny cabin with her long enough that little things like that became obvious. But he owed it to her to make sure she was safe until they could talk. And talking was out of the question right now.

So he quickly sheathed himself, her hot stare making it a little harder to get the latex over his still growing erection. Hell, all it was going to take was a touch of one of her fingers at this point, and he'd blow.

"Now."

He pressed his body against hers, his hands skimming up and down her curves. She gripped his shoulders, her nails digging in tight as she wrapped one leg around his thigh.

He lifted her by the ass, holding her body flush against his. She used his support to anchor her other foot around him, both ankles locking at the small of his back.

When her wet core pressed tight against his straining cock, Hunter lost it. He shifted their bodies so she was caught between the narrow dresser and his hips, using the rounded edge of the wood to anchor her hips as he thrust.

Hard.

Intense.

Deep.

Holy freaking hell, so incredibly deep.

Hunter growled as more pleasure than he'd ever felt pounded through him, even as he pounded into Marni.

Her cries started low and deep, growing higher and keener with each thrust. Her breath came in quick pants.

"Oh! Oh, oh, oh," she chanted, each word more breathless than the last, each one a higher decibel as her voice and her body climbed pleasure's peak.

Hunter thrust again.

Her fingers clutched at his shoulders, nails digging into his flesh. He growled.

She tensed.

Her eyes flew open to meet his demanding stare.

Pupils so huge they drowned out her sky-blue irises, Marni stared right back. There was a demand in her gaze, insisting that he give her more than satisfaction. Insisting on more than just sexual fulfillment.

He didn't know what she needed, what she wanted.

He just knew that whatever it was, he wanted her to have it.

He wanted to give her everything.

Hunter thrust again, holding her gaze.

Then he smiled.

A wicked promise that said without words that he'd meet her demands, and push her for a few of his own.

With that in mind, he shifted her higher.

One hand still on the sweet curve of her ass, he skimmed the other up her silky skin to cup her breast.

He bent his head, sucking the full, pouting tip into his mouth. His tongue swirled, sipping at her sweetness. He nipped, wanting to eat her up, to take everything she had.

His eyes never left hers.

She flew over the edge.

Her body exploded beneath his. Her breath shuddered, her entire being shaking with the intensity of her orgasm.

Beneath the exquisite pleasure on her face, he saw shock. Like she'd never felt anything so powerful. So good.

Yeah.

He grinned, his ego battling his body over which was being stroked harder right at that moment. Then she shifted, moving closer so her mouth closed over his.

Hunter lost it.

His breath.

His control.

His mind.

He was pure instinct.

His body bucked hard, shaking with the power of his orgasm. It exploded, taking him to levels of pleasure he'd never experienced. Never imagined.

He poured and poured and poured into her.

The climax was like a rolling earthquake, it just kept coming.

Finally, so breathless he was seeing spots in front of his eyes, the orgasm retreated to tiny shudders.

His legs were water. His arms shook. He could barely breathe.

Damn.

Never in his entire life had he felt as incredible as he did in that moment.

9

HUNTER CONSIDERED HIS life damned good. He had a great career. He had excellent luck with the ladies. He was financially secure, had good friends and a great father.

He'd never claim to be a humble man, nor was he interested in false modesty. So he'd always been pretty comfortable with the fact that he was good at sex. Damned good.

But he'd never been—the *sex* had never been—this good.

He wasn't surprised, though.

Marni inspired him to new levels of greatness.

What was tripping him out, though, was how fabulous the nonsex was with her.

They sat across from each other at the small table in their cabin, Marni's hair a tumble of curls over her silky robe. The deep blue fabric clung to her full breasts, emphasizing nipples still peaked from his earlier ministrations.

"So who's your biggest life influence?" she asked, dipping her strawberry into a pot of warm chocolate, then nibbling. Hunter's mouth watered, his gaze locked on her mouth.

"Influence?" he repeated absently, shifting in his chair. His jeans, all he had on, tightened enough to make him glad he hadn't bothered to snap them.

"Yes. Influence. Mine is my aunt." Marni continued to eat her strawberries, alternating between the chocolate and fluffy whipped cream. As she nibbled, she talked about her huge family and how her aunt stood out from what sounded like a very intrusive crowd.

"How do you deal with that?" he asked, interrupting her description of a recent family outing that'd turned into a speed dating–style blind date, with four cousins bringing along their version of her perfect man. "The interference, the constant nagging. Isn't family a pain in the ass?"

Marni laughed and shrugged. The movement did delicious things to her robe, the fabric rippling over her breasts, baring a little more of that pale, silky flesh. Hunter shifted in the chair again.

"They're interfering, yes, but they love me. There's something incredibly comforting in knowing they are always there. The ties of family are like a safety net, you know? It's a lot easier to fly knowing they are there."

Hunter nodded before he realized he was agreeing.

"My dad's like that, I guess. He's always had this absolute belief in me. Even when I was a kid." Hunter gave a little laugh, remembering. "I was maybe four when I declared I wanted to be—" FBI. Hell, he was getting a little too relaxed here. To cover his wince, he reached over and stole one of Marni's strawberries. "I'd told him I wanted to be like him. He never laughed. He just sat my four-year-old self down and said if I wanted something, I had to work at it. Then he spent the next fifteen-to-twenty years showing me how."

Twirling the strawberry between his fingers, Hunter watched the juicy red fruit swirl as he remembered all the times, all the ways, his dad had been there. Had influenced him. Paving the way in his career, showing him overtly and silently his unstinting support.

"You really look up to him, don't you?" Marni asked quietly. "I mean, I love my family, but the only one I think I might want to be like is my aunt. But you and your father, that must be a pretty special relationship."

Hunter shrugged, a little abashed to realize just how much he did love his father. And how easy Marni made it for him to feel those emotions without feeling like a jerk. The only other person he'd ever talked about his family with was his best friend, Caleb.

Shifting his gaze from the strawberry to Marni, he noted the sweet warmth in her eyes, the softness in her expression as she looked at him. It was as if she was reaching into his heart and tugging at the strings there. As if she was testing to make sure he had enough depth, enough emotion, to match hers.

Damned if he didn't wonder that himself.

And suddenly, for the first time in his life, he hoped he did.

Like a slap upside the head, Hunter reeled at that insight.

Then, because he knew thinking about it would ruin what they had going here, that the minute he accepted that there was something emotional here, he'd slam the door shut. If he ignored the emotions, he could happily enjoy everything else between him and Marni.

The laughter.

The discussions.

The teasing.

And the sex.

Those emotions, though, kept pounding, pushing, trying to get his attention.

Determined to ignore them, Hunter went the only route he knew would work one hundred percent.

He stood and, ignoring Marni's surprised look, pulled her to her feet. Then he grabbed up the tray of chocolate and whipped cream.

"What are you doing?" she asked, following him to the bed.

"You ate all the strawberries," he pointed out, flicking the belt of her robe open with a quick twist of his fingers. The heavy satin slid down her body, leaving her gleaming, naked, in the dim lamplight. "So I'll have to eat my snack off your body."

MARNI LAY IN HUNTER'S ARMS, her body limp with satisfaction. Forty-eight or so hours of exploring each other's bodies, of playing out ever sexual fantasy that could be played on a moving train, and you'd think she'd be satiated.

She glanced at the floor next to the door, where the daily briefings of the train's murder mystery event had piled up since their first morning together when Hunter had insisted that Simpson slide them under the door instead of disturbing them.

The last one declared the murderer to be Peter Principle, and invited everyone to the final party that evening to celebrate the sleuthing successes.

Which was yet another reminder that the train was due in San Francisco in the morning.

A feeling of panic tried to take hold in Marni's stomach. This was almost over. She needed to get her fill of Hunter. To convince her body that it'd had enough to last the rest of her life.

"That was good," he murmured against the back of her neck. One hand released its gentle hold of her breast to slide down to her waist, but the other stayed, all cozy and tempting, in the warm, damp heat between her thighs. His fingers didn't move. Just set up camp, like an ongoing reminder that he could send her spiraling into a lovely orgasm anytime he wanted. "I think that was good enough to qualify for our top-ten list."

"Which position are you bumping to put it there?" she asked with a husky laugh.

"Hmm, I don't know," he teased, his warm laughter making her hair flutter across her ear. "I'm pretty sure they're all tied for first place."

"Nice answer," she said with a sleepy giggle.

And not one she'd argue with.

Every time they'd made love was a vivid memory. Every kiss, every touch stood out in her mind in bright, intense detail. It was a little scary how incredible they were together.

They'd had each other every way she could imagine, every way he'd suggested. At this point, they'd need to hit Google for position inspiration.

"You know, I think we need a tiebreaker." She reached behind her, her fingers trailing between their bodies to cup his growing erection. The man had the most amazing recovery powers. "What do you think it'll take to top all the other times? You on top? Me on top? Chocolate, whipped cream, scarves? What do you think?"

Hunter's laugh was just this side of wicked.

Seductive.

Marni melted at the sound. She should laugh, too. Make as if it was all in fun.

But he made her feel things inside, the most incredible things. She could handle the physical ones. The emotional ones, though? They were starting to scare the hell out of her.

"Why don't we give this a try," he suggested, his lips

skimming her shoulder before he shifted downward. Marni shivered, reluctantly releasing her hold on his hardening cock. She loved stroking his length, enjoying the power of his reaction to her tactile teasing. Still, she reveled in the feel of its rigid velvet slide as it pressed lower, over her butt cheeks and to her thigh as he kissed his way down her spine.

Marni moaned softly when he reached that delicate spot at the small of her back and nibbled soft, wet kisses over her sensitive flesh. She wrapped her arms around her pillow, curving her body into the mattress and rolling flat on her belly to give Hunter better access to play.

He seemed to have some special sense of when her thoughts were going too deep, of when she was freaking herself out.

Marni knew that part should freak her out, too.

But whenever she got her hand on the handle of that freak-out door, he pulled her back, distracted her with incredible sex.

Her eyes fluttered, the lights of the passing night flashing through the train window as his hands squeezed her breasts, his tongue skimming the curve of her back where it met her butt before continuing downward.

His hands scooped under her body, lifting her hips into the air as he wedged himself between her thighs so they parted wide. Heat, a combination of embarrassed delight and passion, washed over her cheeks—all four of them. He pressed one finger, then two, into her burning, wet passage. Marni whimpered. His tongue slid along her folds, sipping and flicking. She moaned.

He played her as if she was an instrument and he a master musician. Fingers and mouth worked in concert, building the tension in her body to a crescendo pitch. Marni's back arched. Passion tightened, curling like a taut spring between her legs.

All it took was one extra pluck of his finger, his teeth scraping over her aching bud. The climax swept through her body. Marni buried her face, her cries muffled by the soft pillow. Her body shook with the power of her orgasm, tiny tremors going on and on.

She felt Hunter move and tried to catch her breath, to prepare for the next round. Hands grasping her hips so she couldn't move, though. Then he plunged.

Hard.

Powerful.

Marni tried to meet his thrust, to intensify the driving friction.

But he held her captive, his fingers stabbing into the soft flesh of her hips like a vise.

She whimpered.

He slid in, then out.

Slow, wet, deep and hard. He was so big, so incredible. And totally in control.

Marni's fingers flexed, as if to reach back. But she didn't. She kept her hands on the pillow, her body at his mercy. This was a part of the game. To see how long she could last before trying to wrest back some portion of control.

She didn't make it more than a minute, maybe two, before the next orgasm exploded. Lights flashed behind her closed eyes, like fireworks matching the heat deep in her belly.

Before the scream had cleared her throat, he flipped her over. His hands gripped her thighs again, this time anchoring them high, so her ankles draped over his shoulders.

Through passion-blurred eyes, Marni stared at his face. Tight, controlled. And right there on the edge. She knew the signs now. The taut pull of the flesh around his eyes. The fire in his gaze as he demanded without words that she put it all out there, that she give over everything. Because he'd do the same.

The thought of that, the knowledge that he was willing to put everything he had into this connection between them, that it was so much more, bigger, deeper than just his very talented dick in her very well-pleasured body, flipped her trigger.

Marni arched, gasping.

She couldn't close her eyes. Couldn't tear her gaze from his. But she flew over the edge, soaring higher because he smiled, his look pure triumph.

Then, because she knew it drove him crazy, she called on the last vestiges of her own control and gave him a sultry smile and a flutter of her lashes.

His explosive climax sent her flying over one more time, her gasps mingling with his guttural cry.

Oh, yeah. The man was amazing.

THE TRAIN WAS STILL. They must have arrived in San Francisco, Marni realized when she awoke the next morning.

And she was still wrapped in Hunter's arms.

With a deep, satisfied sigh, she gave herself a moment to revel in how good it felt. Better than anything she'd ever experienced. Not just the sex, which was mind-blowing. But this, she realized, snuggling closer. Feeling so connected, so safe. So loved.

Her eyes flew open.

Her heart stopped for a quick, panicked second.

What had happened? Or a better question would be, What the hell had she been thinking? Or not thinking, clearly. If her brain had been engaged instead of her body reveling in indulgent pleasure for two days, she'd have seen this coming. She'd have been able to sidestep it.

Maybe.

But it was too late now.

Terror took hold in her belly.

She'd gone and done it. Brilliant, career-focused, got-her-shit-together and nobody-was-going-to-stop-her Marni Clare had absolutely gone and done it.

She watched as the room did a slow, murky spin, even as her mind grappled with the truth.

She'd fallen in love with Hunter.

Holy cow. How could she fall in love with him? She didn't even know his first name.

She shifted. Slowly, so as not to wake the man who she was suddenly terrified of. As if he were an explosive device that any quick move might set off, she put every bit of her concentration on getting away as fast as she could without waking him up.

And tried to pretend she wasn't turned on by the feel of his hair-roughed thigh sliding over hers, of the heavy weight of his arm as she carefully lifted it off her waist.

As she slid from the bed, he muttered something in his sleep, then rolled facedown into the pillow.

The urge to climb back between those sheets and cuddle against his warm body was stronger than anything Marni could remember feeling. Stronger than her desire to protect her heart. Stronger than her ambition and career goals.

It was like getting hit upside the head with a giant cartoon frying pan. Marni swore she could see little birdies flying in circles around her head, all singing to the demise of her dreams. Tweeting their goodbye to her career.

Terror buzzed in her ears, gripped her stomach in a tight fist.

She had to get out of here.

Not to protect her heart.

Hell, that was already guaranteed to be shattered. She'd have to deal with it no matter what.

But if she didn't leave now, didn't get away from the Novocain-like effect Hunter had on her ambition, she'd give it all up.

And end up hating herself.

She dressed in silence. Constantly reminding herself to pull on each item of clothing quietly, as if a single sound would waken not only Hunter, but waken a Hunter who would immediately start spouting off verbal demands that she wasn't prepared to meet. Questions.

She was the one supposed to be answering questions. To be searching for information, building a story.

Some ace reporter she was. The only prize she'd had her eye on for the past two days was the one between Hunter's thighs.

She wet her lips, her gaze sliding over his body with regret for the blanket covering that prize. One more peek, one more taste, was that too much to ask for?

God, she was ready to come again just thinking about his dick. She realized in the past couple of days, this gorgeous man had unknowingly provided her with years of sexual pleasure, whether he was present in the flesh or not.

As she held on to the table to steady herself while slipping into her boots, she averted her eyes, glancing at a sheaf of papers Hunter had forgotten to put away when she'd surprised him the previous night. As before, the writing was a bizarre mess, somewhere between Middle-earth runes and sloppy shorthand. Was that an FBI thing or just how he wrote? Smiling a little, she imagined Hunter as a schoolboy, explaining to his teacher that his report was illegible because he was gonna be a government agent when he grew up.

Even though she knew she couldn't read anything there, she flipped through the pages as if they were a fan. Then, frowning, she flipped back to one that'd caught her eye.

B.B.

Beverly Burns?

Beverly Burns had disappeared. Nobody knew what had happened to her. Rumors abounded, everything from a runaway wife to Burns locking her in a cellar somewhere.

Marni had talked to the doorman of their building right after the explosion. He'd told her that the couple had a major argument the night before, a screaming match right there in the middle of the lobby. It'd ended ugly, with the missus slapping her husband across the face, then storming out. When Marni had followed up with the same doorman four days later, he still hadn't seen the pretty young Beverly. Nor, he'd whispered, had someone come to get any of her treasured possessions. At least, not according to the maid who cleaned their apartment.

Marni actually knew Beverly Burns from her work in fashion circles. Using her husband's money, she'd launched her own designer line and was obsessed with being the next big name in fashion. The woman was a vain name-dropper who lived for her clothes and valued each button more than any single person in her life. She wouldn't have taken off without her fancy wardrobe.

Had Charles done something with her?

Or was she the woman Hunter had escaped the exploding building with? Had Burns left her for dead before blowing up his own building? Was she still alive? Meghan had said there was a woman, but not whether she survived or not.

Holy cow. That'd blow her original story idea out of

the water. Tying Burns to attempted murder? She could start working on her Pulitzer acceptance speech as soon as she turned that article in.

Trying to curb her excitement, Marni frowned at the notes again, but couldn't make heads or tails of more than the initials. Then she spotted the letters *SF* and the word *Paris*. She turned the paper over, noting it was a hotel receipt dated three days ago, again with the initials B.B. She glanced at the bed quickly to make sure Hunter was still sleeping, then shifted a couple of the papers covered in his unreadable handwriting to see if there was anything she could understand.

Did this have anything to do with the case? How? Burns was strictly U.S. From what Marni had been able to pull together, the guy had a major phobia of the ocean. He refused to fly over water, so hadn't ever left the continent.

So what was all the information on fashion and Paris for? Was Hunter looking into being transferred to Europe? Did they even have FBI operatives overseas? In the fashion industry? Her brain raced with possible answers, a million more questions and a ton of directions of inquiry. She wanted her laptop. She wanted her phone. Like a nagging, impossible-to-ignore need, she had to get to the bottom of this.

All of her excitement came to a painful, screeching halt in her mind. She sighed, feeling as if someone had just poured a vatful of misery over her head. Getting to the bottom of this meant using this information she'd just found. And that meant betraying Hunter.

Frowning, she looked over at sleeping beauty, his soft snores muted by the pillow cushioning his face. Marni's gaze softened as her eyes traced the strong lines of his back. Her fingers itched to touch, her mouth watered for another taste.

She'd never get enough of him.

Her stomach clenched, terror hitting her like a brick wall.

This was supposed to be a fun interlude. Great sex. A once-in-a-lifetime experience. Hot times with a sexy federal agent. That was the kind of thing that looked great in a fascinating biography looking back over the adventurous life of a prizewinning news reporter when she was, oh, say seventy or so. The sexy chapter, guaranteeing reader delight.

What this wasn't supposed to be was a way for Marni to ruin her life by falling in love.

She'd always said she was too smart to put her career behind some guy. Despite the fact that her entire family had always ignored her vow, she'd always said she wasn't marrying, because she wanted her career to come first.

And the best way to avoid the trap of marriage was to evade the complication of falling in love.

She knew that.

She'd vowed it.

Her knees went wonky.

And she'd gone and done it anyway.

If she wasn't afraid the sound would wake Hunter, she'd smack herself in the forehead.

Instead, she did the only thing she could think of.

The only thing that made any sense when faced with the huge, mind-blowing realization that she had just gone and fallen for a man so strong, so intense and so powerful he'd make her second-guess her every career decision. Hell, at this rate, if Hunter offered her six orgasms a week and a quickie on Mondays, she'd probably agree to don an apron and play housewife.

She shuddered at the terrifying image.

As quiet as a mouse under the nose of a starving cat, she packed her bags and gathered her things.

Then, after one last, desperate look at the man sleeping in a fog of sexual satisfaction, she ran away.

HUNTER WOKE SLOWLY, irritated before he'd even opened his eyes but not sure why.

He'd fallen into a sexual stupor, exhausted and satisfied, hours ago. Now? He forced his eyes open to a squint and gauged the light coming through the window. It was morning. Time to get up.

Alone, he realized as he rolled to the edge of the bed, looking for Marni's warm, soft body.

Suddenly alert, he shifted, looked around. Where the hell was she? The sliding bathroom door was open, and the rest of the room took less than a second to peruse.

One thing he'd learned from pre-awesome sex with Marni was that she wasn't a morning person. She didn't slide quietly and happily from bed. Nope, she arose in a grumpy state of clumsiness, banging into walls on her way to her shower.

So where was she, and why wasn't she here, sharing that endearing grumpiness?

He showered and threw clothes on in record time, determined to find Marni and haul her back into bed. He didn't care how much she needed her caffeine. He wanted morning wake-up sex, dammit. And he wanted her, there, where he could see her, touch her. Be with her.

As irritated with himself for that deep, intense need as he was with her because her absence forced him to admit it, he yanked open the door.

And stopped short.

"What the hell are you doing here?"

All of a sudden, Hunter realized the train was still.

He'd been so obsessed with finding Marni, with getting her back in bed, it'd totally escaped him that they'd already arrived in San Francisco.

"I'm here to make sure you didn't screw up the case," Murray said, his smile bland as he stepped around Hunter and into the cabin.

Hunter would have shot back a pithy remark about never screwing up anything. But there was something in his boss's stance and expression. A taunting sort of triumph that said the guy thought he had something embarrassing to gloat about.

Frowning, Hunter cast a fast look around the cabin, making sure Marni had all her stuff tucked away as usual. He relaxed. Other than her scent, there wasn't much sign of her.

"Screw up? Based on what? You weren't happy with the amount of info I got for you this week? Something wrong with me building enough evidence against Burns to add five more criminal counts to the charges? Including suspicion of murder."

That last one had been a major triumph, as far as Hunter was concerned. He'd dug deep enough into the email files Beverly had provided to find three instances he suspected were execution orders. He'd forwarded the information and his suspicions to the New York office for his guys to track down. He'd heard just last night that they'd found enough to tie Burns to one, possibly two of those murders. Hauling the guy up on murder one without bringing the wife he'd tried to blow to smithereens into it? Success in Hunter's book.

He waited to hear what it was in Murray's, though.

"You spent the·entire trip here in this cushy berth?" the deputy director asked, twirling his finger to indicate the cabin.

Hunter leaned one shoulder against the wall and shrugged the other.

"I thought participation in the events was mandatory," Murray continued, his smirk a reminder of why he'd booked Hunter on this particular train in the first place.

"I think we've established that I'm okay ignoring rules that get in my way," Hunter shot back.

Murray's smile was replaced by an irritated grimace. Then, saying the words as if they were painful, he told Hunter, "Looks like your refusal to follow directions paid off in this case."

"Because you didn't get any photos of me looking like an idiot?"

"Because I got a tip that there was a reporter on the train. She's been asking questions about the Burns case, digging around. I don't want this story broken on the cover of some magazine."

Hunter grimaced. Damn. Unlike Murray, he didn't begrudge them doing their job. Hell, there were a lot of times their job made his a lot easier. Still, this case was as sensitive as a teenage girl with self-esteem issues. The extra charges could fall apart over the slightest detail. The last thing the FBI needed was some half-assed article on the case to put a screw to the works.

"Who's the reporter?" Everyone he'd met had been using their mystery event pseudonym, so he probably wouldn't recognize the name. Still, it was good info to have.

"Marni Clare," Murray said, consulting his pocket computer. "Writes for *Optimum* magazine."

What the fuck?

Hunter's expression didn't change.

His body didn't shift from its casual stance leaning against the wall.

But his mind?

Well, it took a good ten seconds to get past the vicious swearing for his mind to engage.

Marni was a reporter?

A freaking reporter?

He mentally put his fist through the wall, cussed up a storm and heaved a chair out the window. In his mind, he threw a fit so ugly, hardened criminals would hide.

But, thanks to years of practice, on the surface he kept it casual.

He cast another glance around the cabin. This time he noticed that Marni hadn't tucked her bags away, keeping things neat. She'd tidied herself right out of there. Her suitcase wasn't under the bed. Her lotions weren't on the tiny bathroom shelf.

"Nope. Didn't meet anyone claiming to be a reporter, or anybody asking questions about the case," he said honestly. His brain raced, reviewing the week. She'd never mentioned the case, or even hinted that she knew anything about the Burns case. Either Marni was a hell of a lot better reporter—or actor—than any he'd ever met, or she had no clue that he was FBI.

"Figured you kept it under control, but I had to check. Wanna get coffee before the official debarking time?" Murray suggested, glancing at his watch.

A vat of it might kick-start his brain, pushing him past this mental stuttering shock that the woman he'd been falling for had used the hell out of him.

Hunter still kept his expression neutral, but his gut churned with fury.

He'd love nothing more than to get coffee and find his erstwhile roommate for a few words, except he was sure she was long gone. Which meant she wouldn't be outing him as an idiot to his boss.

Still, discretion and valor and all that crap deemed it smarter to just get the hell out of here.

"Let's just go. Meals in this place are a circus, complete with sideshows. We'll check into the hotel and load up on room service." To emphasize his choice, Hunter grabbed what little he'd unpacked and started tossing things into his suitcase.

His eyes fell on the bed, still rumpled from his and Marni's last mattress tussle. The image of her face, glowing and tight with passion, filled his mind.

Watching her fly over the edge, listening to her laughter, seeing her curled up asleep next to him… He'd finally understood how a guy could put his career in second place for a woman.

Damn, he was an idiot.

Murray poked around the cabin. Cozy when it'd just been Hunter and Marni, with two large men—one of whom was bristling with barely controlled fury—the space was more fitting to a dollhouse.

"Yeah, let's go. I'll bet you're tired of this cramped space, right? Done with the whole train experience?"

Packed bag, briefcase and laptop in hand, Hunter offered a bland smile.

"You have no idea how done I am with this entire affair"

10

SHE SHOULD BE EXCITED and filled with anticipation. She was about to make one of her dreams come true. Meet her hero, the woman who'd inspired her every career decision since the second grade.

Marni stared at the looming town house, as elegant as the rest on the steep San Francisco residential street. But the flowers flanking the steps were a blurry yellow, difficult to focus on through eyes that kept tearing up.

She'd done the right thing—for both of them—by leaving Hunter.

She'd done the right thing—for her career—by tracking down the information from that hotel receipt, pulling every string she had to find out who had been in that hotel suite in the week after the explosion. While she hadn't been able to get a photo or name confirmation, she had gotten a physical description from a room service waiter describing the temperamental redhead who'd thrown her chocolate cake at the back of the head of the guy who, as the waiter put it, looked like an extra from *Men in Black*. Marni was sure that redhead was Beverly Burns, and that the cake-splattered suit-wearer was FBI or someone from WitSec.

She'd spent two days writing an edgy, hard-hitting article that would break open not only the case against Charles Burns but also point to the games the FBI played.

She should be thrilled.

Instead, she felt ill.

She should be exploring the excellent San Francisco shopping venues to choose a perfect edgy reporter wardrobe.

Instead, she was wearing her oldest jeans and a T-shirt as black as her mood.

Telling herself to focus on now, instead of crying over then, Marni wiped a nervous hand on her hip. Taking a deep breath, she climbed the steps, raised her hand and knocked on the bright red door.

"Yes?" the woman answering greeted. Her hair was as blond as sunshine, the creases around her eyes deep and cheerful. Slender and stylish, she looked at least ten years younger than the forty-eight Marni knew her to be.

"Robin Clare?"

"That's me. You selling something? I hope it's cookies. I'm partial to those chocolate mint ones."

Marni answered with a smile and a shake of her head.

"Actually, I don't have anything to sell. I'm here to meet you."

"You a reporter?"

How cool was it to be recognized as a reporter by one of the best in the business? A tiny thrill tickled its way up Marni's spine, but was chased back down by a trickle of doubt. Because she wasn't sure she had what it took to deserve that recognition. Not yet. And for the first time since she was eight years old and had started the *Gradeschool Gazette,* she wasn't positive she had what it'd take to be a great reporter.

"I'm Marni Clare," she answered slowly, her words as

hesitant as her confidence in a warm reception. "Melinda and Jason's daughter."

Robin's eyes, the same blue as her own, rounded for a second before narrowing to inspect Marni.

"Are you, now? Did something happen? Last I checked, everyone was healthy, hearty and whole."

"You check on the family?" Marni asked in surprise. Didn't *estranged* mean you locked that part of your life in a dark closet somewhere, pretending it didn't exist except in middle-of-the-night-insomnia-induced memories?

"Course I do. Better to know all the facts, even when you don't plan to use them." After letting Marni mull that for a second, Robin waved her inside. "But I can see from your face they're all fine. So you must have some other reason for crossing the country to show up on my doorstep. C'mon in. We'll talk."

Marni followed her aunt into the chic condo. Red walls, white trim, stark black leather furnishings all made a vivid backdrop for... Marni squinted to be sure. Was that art? Tall and slender, short and squat, black metal sculptures dotted the room like scary shadows waiting to jump out and yell boo.

"Be comfortable," Robin suggested, pointing at a thin leather bench and taking the one opposite. Marni perched on the surprisingly comfortable seat, still looking around.

"This is an incredible space," she finally said. Incredibly scary, but that little clarification was probably too rude to mention during their first meeting.

Robin looked around with an assessing and indulgent eye before nodding. "It is incredible, isn't it. I'm about finished with it, though. I've got my eye on a Persian theme next. A lot of carpets, silk pillows, gilt and tassels."

"I beg your pardon?" Marni shook her head, confused.

"I get bored. Oh, the constant travel helps, but it's not

enough. I used to move every two years. But staying in one condo is financially smart given the real estate fluctuations. Instead, I redecorate. Well, not personally. I couldn't tell a Chippendale from a chifforobe. I hire a decorator. They send me a catalog each year, I choose a theme and by the time I get back from my next story, the entire place is redone. Right down to the sheets." She wrapped her hands around her upraised knee and gave a satisfied nod.

Marni could only stare.

It wasn't as though she came from an unsophisticated nowhereville. She lived in Manhattan, for crying out loud. But she'd never heard of anything like that. It was so, well, indulgent. So impersonal. She frowned, looking around again, wondering if it felt as empty as it seemed.

Marni's nails dug into the tender flesh of her palms as she tried to pull her emotions back where they belonged. This was crazy. She shouldn't be second-guessing her choices because her aunt had a bizarre decorating style. She should be excited, craving the same privileged life. That was her goal. Freedom, fame, the ability to create a life that was perfectly suited to her own particular tastes.

Still, all of a sudden, she missed her mother's china cabinet. The one that had been in the family since before Marni was born. The one her mother wished, time after time, that she could get rid of because it was so huge and ugly, but wouldn't for sentimental reasons.

"So. You'd be my niece. Marni, right? That makes you the fifth girl from the oldest."

Marni started to correct her since she was actually the eighth oldest of her thirteen cousins. Then she did a quick count of just the girls. Devon, Meghan, Sammi, Carrie, her. Then Kyra, Lannie, Sheila and Marla.

Wow.

"You really do keep up with the family, don't you?"

Was that because she missed it? Her heart a little heavy at the idea of her aunt being so shut out, Marni almost reached over to give the woman's arm a pat.

But Robin's shrug didn't seem sad. More...disinterested.

"You're not here to borrow money, are you?" Robin asked, her affable smile fading a little. "I've got a strong policy against lending."

Borrow money? Horrified, Marni opened her mouth to protest, then snapped it shut. Was that better or worse than asking for career advice?

Before she could decide, Robin wrinkled her nose and added, "But family is family, so I might be willing to reconsider once I hear your story."

Holding out one hand in dismayed denial, Marni shook her head so fast, she whipped herself in the face with her own hair. "Oh, no. Thank you, but no, I'm really not here for money."

Robin arched one perfectly groomed brow, leaned back on her own bench and waited.

"I'm here to ask about your life," Marni blurted inelegantly. She winced, pushed her hand through her hair. "I mean, I want to know more about you. About your career. What it's like, leaving the demands and expectations and, well, the burden of everything you grew up with and chasing your dream?"

"Exhilarating. Have you ever jumped from an airplane?"

"No. About the closest I've ever gotten was maybe jumping on a trampoline," Marni offered with a weak smile.

Robin dismissed that with a wave.

"The drop from the plane, knowing you're completely at the mercy of fate, it's fabulous. That you can depend on just yourself, your equipment and the elements… That's the life, Marni."

Marni didn't get it. What did willingly stepping out of a perfectly sound airplane to plummet to the earth, dependent only on a flimsy piece of fabric and the wind, have to do with being a reporter?

Her confusion must have shown.

Robin leaned forward, her hands hanging loose between her knees, the look on her face intense.

"That's what it's like walking away from family. Leaving behind the safety net and demands. It's like diving into the unknown. It's fabulous."

"Couldn't you be the same reporter, have the same drive and success if you hadn't walked away, though?"

"Not a chance. There's no way I'd have pushed as hard, or felt as free if I hadn't closed that door."

Marni bit her lip. Well, then. Maybe she could settle on a similar career, with half the success, and keep her family ties. Just sort of distance them a little. Like, from the opposite coast. California, from what she'd seen since getting off the train that morning, was pretty.

The train.

She sighed.

And Hunter.

She was standing in a tidal wave of misery. As if she'd just wrenched open that door and let all the pain she'd tucked away pour out. She'd left him there, sleeping. She hadn't said goodbye, hadn't left a note. Nothing.

He'd figure it out, she knew.

The man was FBI. All he had to do, if he cared enough, was run her name and he'd know she was a reporter. Would figure out that she was a liar.

That she was a heartbroken, miserable liar was still her own secret, though.

"Can I ask a personal question?" she blurted.

"All questions should be personal. Otherwise they're a waste of air," Robin declared.

Right. Marni grimaced.

"You want a drink?" Robin offered after a few seconds of pained silence as her niece tried to figure out how to word her nosy question so it didn't come out like a waste of air.

Tequila would be nice.

Marni settled for ice water.

And used the couple of minutes while her aunt was gone to pull herself together. She wasn't a sucky reporter, dammit. She was just an emotional mess after leaving the man she loved. She was pathetic, not talentless. There was a difference. This was an interview, not a desperate plea for some answer that would paint a clear path for her own life.

Treat it like a biography, she decided. She was writing Robin Clare's life story. What information did she need to tell it right?

With that perky little pep talk ringing in her head, Marni lifted her chin and offered a bright smile of thanks when her aunt returned.

"So, my question is about relationships. You've achieved so much with your career. The stories you've broken, the places you've traveled, they're remarkable for anyone, let alone a woman who began reporting when it was a completely male dominated field."

"World's still dominated by men, girly. Don't let anyone tell you different," Robin broke in.

Marni made a mental note that her aunt still faced gender bias, wondering if it was as strong now as in the past, or if her views were a by-product of years of fighting prejudice.

"Did you feel you had to choose between your career and your emotional life?" Grimacing, she wet her throat with her ice water, then reframed that. "What I mean is, did you ever have a man who wanted more from you? Who resented your career?"

That wasn't quite the same as asking if she'd ever screwed over the man she loved for a hot story. But Marni figured that was the kind of question you eased into.

From the knowing look on her aunt's face, she'd picked up the subtext without much trouble, though.

"I made a decision early on that my career was my priority," Robin said slowly. As if each word were a bomb she was carefully setting on the painted concrete floor between them. "Because of that, all of my relationships have been based on a framework of distance. On the knowledge that I'd need to pick up and go at a moment's notice. That when I'm focused on a story, it gets all of my attention. I've had plenty of wonderful men in my life. But none took precedence over the story."

Marni looked at her hero. In her forties, Robin had seen and done everything Marni dreamed of. Except maybe that jumping out of the airplane thing. And now she was facing the rest of her life without the emotional accomplishments the rest of the Clare clan deemed mandatory. Family, marriage, children.

She didn't seem to mind.

"Do you regret it?"

"Regret it?" Robin's eyes rounded in shock, as if Marni had just asked if she'd offered blow jobs in exchange for inside scoops. "Girly, I love my life. I have success, travel, money. I'm living in one of the most exciting cities in the world, I mingle with the famous. I have lovers when I want, and privacy when I'm through with them."

"I take it that's a no."

"Not just a no. That'd be a hell no."

Misery settled in Marni's stomach.

She wanted to hear that it sucked.

That the life of an ambitious reporter, totally focused on chasing stories, on climbing the career ladder, was empty. Was lonely. Heck, she'd been hoping for a little sorrow.

"Seriously? It's that great?" she asked.

"Seriously." Robin gave her a rueful smile. "I can tell that's exactly what you were hoping to hear."

Marni's own smile was a little weak around the edges.

"I guess I'd hoped you'd tell me that giving it all up was a mistake. That family, a relationship, love, that they all trump ambition."

"Can't tell you what I don't believe." Robin paused, watching Marni over the edge of her own glass as she sipped her drink. "But I can give you a little advice if you want it."

That's why she was there, wasn't it? Even as her shoulders sank despondently, Marni made a bring-it-on gesture with one hand.

"Your climb up the ladder is yours. Not mine. You get to choose your baggage. And you might be better at carrying certain things. A relationship, kids, all that stuff isn't at odds with a great career. I've interviewed plenty of people who have both. I've worked with a few, too."

Hope was like a tiny seed trying to sprout against all odds. Marni had never before thought it possible, but suddenly she wanted to believe she could do it all. That she was strong enough, clever enough, dedicated enough to balance the successful career of her dreams with other things. Things like kids, family. Love.

Hunter's love. She swallowed hard against the painful lump in her throat.

"Would you put a story aside if you knew it'd cause a problem for someone you cared about? Ever?"

Could she set aside this story, sit on the news that Beverly Burns was still alive, no thanks to her husband? Could she ignore the information she'd discovered that proved Charles Burns had tried to blow up his wife, along with that building? But that a sexy, dedicated FBI agent had dragged her out of there before she'd been decimated? Could she pretend the FBI wasn't hiding the rumored late Mrs. Burns away, in exchange for as much dirt as they could get on her husband?

Marni wanted to think she could.

For love.

But she wasn't sure.

"Set aside a story for a man?" Robin mused, her face screwed up as if she'd just tasted something nasty. "I've never met a man who made me ask myself that, girly. If I did, though, I have to think he'd make the question moot. Because if he was the man for me, he'd know I couldn't take that path. The story, the truth…it's everything."

Not for the first time in the past couple of days, Marni was beset by doubts. Her stomach churned, misery making her ill. What did it say about her ambition, her dedication, if she wasn't willing to break a story because it might upset someone?

Shoulders as heavy as concrete, she wondered if she'd been fooling herself all these years. Because now, when faced with a shot at the biggest story of her life, she didn't want to take it. Not because she was afraid of success. But because she didn't want to betray Hunter.

"You've got some big choices to make," Robin observed quietly.

Marni met her gaze with her own troubled one, comforted by the sympathy in her aunt's blue eyes.

"You make them while worrying about how others will live with your decision, and you'll never be happy." The older woman set her glass aside, then after a visible hesitation, got up and crossed the room to sit by Marni. "You make them by asking yourself if you can live with them. Then, whatever others think, you'll know you've done what's right for you."

"Even if it hurts someone?"

"Girly, we all get hurt. That's life."

HUNTER CLIMBED THE STEPS of the federal court building, his briefcase in one hand, coffee in the other.

His gut burned as he downed the dregs, and he found no satisfaction from crushing the cardboard cup and spiking it into the trash.

He was getting used to that dissatisfaction. Caffeine and fury had fueled his past forty-eight hours, and as far as he could tell, the rage roiling in his gut wasn't going to dissipate anytime soon.

It was a toss-up what had infuriated him more.

Waking to find the train had arrived in San Francisco and Marni had disappeared. Not a word, not a note, nothing.

Or finding out she was a reporter.

So far, she'd turned in jack, though. At least, his sources hadn't been able to dig up a whisper of any story, except for that initial call to her editor that Murray had filled him in on.

Didn't mean she wasn't writing one.

The question was, what did she have to fill the pages? Supposition? Public knowledge?

He hadn't said anything about the case.

She hadn't asked diddly.

But his instincts, those vital intuitive flashes that not

only saved him from disaster, but often gave him the brilliant insights that put his case close rate at the top…those instincts said she had plenty.

Hunter shoved the heavy glass door open with enough force to send the oak bouncing against the marble wall and earned himself a few glares. He ignored them as he stormed his way through security and to the courtroom.

He tried to argue down his instincts. There was not one exchange between them that involved what he called business. Not directly, not overtly, not discreetly. The only interest she'd shown was in his body. Not his job.

Stopping in front of an eight-foot oil painting of the East Bay, he gritted his teeth. Well, hell. Had he just crossed over into his-ego-doth-protest-too-much land? It wasn't as if he'd never been pursued for a case. Or as if he'd ever thought a woman was more interested in him than she really was.

He stared blindly at the blur of land beyond the Golden Gate, forcing himself to face reality. None of those times mattered. Not on the job, not off.

Because, dammit, this was the first time it'd hurt.

And if she broke that story, it'd hurt a hell of a lot more than his embarrassingly fragile emotions. It'd send his career into a tailspin, ruining everything he stood for. Everything he'd dreamed of, worked for, his entire life.

"Special Agent Hunter, good to see you."

Glad for the interruption, more than happy to sideline his obsessive mental circles, Hunter blinked the concern off his face and turned to greet the prosecuting attorney.

"Denton," he said to the dapper blond man with a nod. They'd worked together on a few cases, and Hunter knew that beneath the cordial smile and frat-boy looks was a shark with an ambition addiction. There was nobody he'd rather have arguing this case.

"The opposing counsel is meeting with the judge now. We'll know of their decision within the next fifteen minutes."

When presented with the extensive additional charges two days before, Burns's team had been faced with the option to take their chance trying the case with the new charges. Or call for a mistrial and let their guy stay in jail while they regrouped and gave the FBI enough time to keep digging through suspicious information until they found solid facts. Aka, searching for bodies that'd turn those suspicion of manslaughter charges to murder one. Either way posed a risk. To Burns, that was.

Hunter wanted this case moving. Now.

He was one hundred percent sure that the feds would get the proof they needed to take Burns down if it was put on hold.

What he wasn't one hundred percent on was what his sexy little roommate knew, or what damage she could inflict on the outcome of the case, or quite possibly the life of Beverly Burns.

Focus, he mentally snapped. Worry did no good. Second-guessing and prognosticating was a waste of time. *Set it aside and focus on the damned job.*

"What's the temp?" he asked the attorney, wanting to gauge the chances that the lawyers would choose to move forward with the trial.

"Burns isn't liking his current accommodations. He's cocky enough to know that suspicion of murder isn't proof." Denton shrugged, as did Hunter, his gaze locked on the courtroom door. "My money says we're eating crappy courtroom cafeteria lunch today."

It didn't take more than five minutes before they were called into the courtroom. Denton spoke with the leader of the pack of lawyers flanking Burns, then nodded. His face was passive, but Hunter could see the look in his eyes. Countdown to shark attack. Looked as though they'd be sticking around for cafeteria jello surprise.

Then, and only then, did Hunter let his eyes shift to the crime boss. Broad and badass, the guy sported an iron buzz cut, a sharp jaw and a suit that'd cost Hunter a month's pay. Cocky and confident, Charles Burns didn't show an ounce of concern.

Perfect.

More than ready to take on Burns, his fat-cat attorneys and, hell, the entire criminal justice system if necessary, Hunter dropped to his seat and gave the crime boss an ugly smirk.

Yeah. This was war.

Six hours later, after a hearty lunch of that jello surprise and a questionable burger, Hunter took the stand.

"State your name for the records."

"Special Agent Michael Hunter, FBI." With that, Hunter raised his hand, recited his oath and settled into the game.

The questions were softball at this stage. Establishing his authority, outlining his role in the investigation. The defense wasn't stupid enough to try and take a hatchet to his reputation. They were going to try to limit his effectiveness, make his testimony irrelevant.

At ease, his expression and body language making it clear he was as comfortable as if he were lounging in his own living room, Hunter rarely took his gaze off of Burns.

Finally, while Denton and Burns's head shark yammered over a point of procedure, Hunter let his gaze wander.

It landed on a pretty blonde in the back of the room, seated behind a huge mountain of a guy, seemingly trying to hide.

He should have kept looking at the crime boss.

It was as though the floodgates burst. All the fury, the anger and frustration that'd been dogging him for the past two days pounded through his system again.

His responses became clipped. His attention split.

The chilly distance that was his usual testimony style took a hit as that anger started sparking at the edges.

Burns shifted in his seat.

His attorneys started scribbling a lot faster.

Murray frowned.

Denton tried to hide his grin.

Hunter didn't give a damn about any of that. He met Marni's wide-eyed gaze across the courtroom.

He watched her gulp. But brave little reporter that she was, she stood her ground. Or given that she was seated on one of the hard wooden benches, sat her ground. Lifting her chin, she met his glare with a calm look of her own, then probably because she couldn't resist, she fluttered her lashes.

He was torn between fury and laughter.

Over the top of that, though, was the dueling need to storm across the courtroom, grab her curvy butt and toss her over his shoulder. Whether he'd verbally rip into her or physically dive into her when he got them to privacy was the only question.

11

MARNI GLANCED AT HER watch: 10:00 p.m. You'd think the terror-inspired headache she'd earned seeing Hunter in the courtroom that afternoon would have faded by now. She'd only managed to stick around for ten minutes, leaving before he was freed from the safe haven of the witness stand.

Her head throbbing worse now from the combination of self-disgust, a very loud restaurant and one glass past her limit of wine, she opened her hotel room door, tucking her key card into her purse. She stepped out of her heels right there in the doorway, not bothering with the lights.

She shouldn't have gone to dinner with her aunt. She hadn't been good company. She'd felt lousy after sneaking in to watch part of the trial. She'd expected to see Hunter, of course. But she'd figured she'd be staring at the back of his head. That he'd be facing the judge, not taking the stand. The shock of his eyes meeting hers still ricocheted through her body. It'd been all she could do to sit down and take notes instead of run from the courthouse in tears.

She'd learned more watching him on the stand than she'd learned in all her research. Not more than she'd learned by stripping him naked and nibbling her way down his body, but she didn't figure any of that knowledge was relevant to her job.

In the end, she'd hurried out of that courthouse confused, upset and overwhelmed.

But as miserable as she'd felt, she hadn't wanted to risk the tenuous new family bond with her aunt by canceling their dinner plans. So she'd popped a couple painkillers, slicked on her brightest lipstick and pretended that her life was peachy keen for three hours.

Now all she wanted was some relaxing music, a hot bubble bath and her pillow.

"You're out late."

Her scream ricocheted off the walls. So did her purse when she heaved it across the room. The responding grunt told her she'd aimed true. She spun toward the door, grabbing the handle and preparing to scream bloody murder.

"Aww, is that any way to greet me after all we've been through? All we've done with each other. To each other."

Marni's body went into a Pavlovian sexual meltdown at the sound of that voice coming through the dark. Even if she hadn't recognized the shadow across the room, her body recognized the husky laugh.

But even as her body was screaming at her to turn around and launch it onto that gorgeous body, her mind was whispering caution warnings, while her instincts danced around waving flashing danger signs.

All things considered, she figured her mind and instincts were the smarter choice right now. Her body, already warming, was obviously biased.

"Don't you want to stick around? There's so much we have to talk about. What you were doing at the courthouse today. What we do for a living. Why you ditched me on the train."

Wrapped around the door handle, her fingers spasmed.

For a second, she wanted to continue her flight out of the room. To run from this confrontation and her own heart's needs. She closed her eyes, trying to pull together her nerve to face Hunter for the second time that day. As long as he didn't know she was a reporter, she could pretend she'd snuck into the courthouse to see him one last time.

But if he knew...

She shifted closer to the door, halfway turning the handle. Her ears rang and black dots did a wispy dance in her vision. She was really, really sure that running away would be the smart move right now.

"I'll just come after you. I'm a stickler for taking care of unfinished business. You might have figured that out, though."

Marni sucked in a deep breath. Pretending her heart wasn't pounding so loud in her head that she could barely hear him, she plastered a serene look on her face and turned around.

"Why on earth would you think I'd figure that out?" she asked, making her tone both light and incredulous while sticking close to the exit. "I think I'd be more interested in figuring out how you ended up in my hotel room."

A dark, private hotel room. With walls thick enough that she could moan and whimper and scream her pleasure without worry of facing a trainful of smirking faces the next day.

Lust drowned out fear crazy fast.

Marni's thighs turned to water, her nipples beading beneath her simple white T-shirt. She felt as if she'd had a gallon of those eight-hour energy drinks, all at once. Her nerves stood on end, her body zinging as if it were going to fly apart any second. At the same time, a languid heat seeped through her veins, desire heavy and aching in her body.

This was just one more reason why Hunter was bad for her. He confused her body, her mind and her heart, dammit.

"Like I said." He moved away from the wall he'd been leaning on, his face shadowed but his gorgeous body vividly clear in the pale light filtering through the window. Marni's heart sped up again, this time spurred by passion rather than fear. "We have some unfinished business to take care of."

What business?

Her anxiety intensified.

She glanced at her laptop, neat and tidy on the desk across the room. Even if he'd poked through it, he wouldn't have found her Burns story or any notes. Once in college she'd had a breaking story about the various methods students used to cheat on their exams stolen from her computer. Losing that byline had taught her to keep everything close, that passwords were easy to crack and that when it came to breaking a story people would steal without compunction. She eyed her purse, where it lay in a sad heap on the floor, innocuously hiding a jump drive holding her story notes and the provocative draft she'd already written in a fake lipstick case.

She was sure he'd figured out she was a reporter. Was that why he was here? She bit her lip, wondering how fast she could run barefoot. Probably faster than if she were in heels, at least until she reached the pavement.

Or, her heart whispered, maybe he was here because he'd missed her. Maybe he'd disregarded her privacy, tracking her down because he couldn't let things end between them. Perhaps he was as crazy about her as she was about him.

Yep. And the tooth fairy could be real and Santa might be chilling at the pole. A girl could always hope.

Marni wet her lips, not sure what to do if she wasn't going to defend herself when he started flinging accusations.

So she did nothing, except wait.

"So?" he prompted, his smile on the wicked side of intimidating. As if he figured he just had to stand there and look sexy and she'd spill all of her secrets across his feet.

Marni lifted her chin, stubborn determination glossing over the ugly nerves.

"So, I'd think a man as sophisticated as you would have figured it out. Wake up, woman gone, affair over. One, two, three." She ticked the countdown off with fingers that only shook a tiny bit. "I'd say the business is all finished, wouldn't you?"

"Nah. I wouldn't say that. I might say sneaking out is cowardly. Or I could outline a few etiquette basics, such as waiting until a guy gets his pants back on before you call it quits." His words grew harder with each syllable, the smile gone as he leaned closer. Even with three feet separating them, Marni felt he was pushing right into her personal space.

She resisted the urge to back up. Instead, she dug her toes into the carpet, pretending they were holding her in place.

"I'm not playing this game," she decided with a dismissive sniff.

"Babe, you already anted up. You can't walk away now."

"I already walked away. Consider it me folding, if you'd like," she suggested with a stiff smile. She didn't care if she sounded like a chicken. Why shouldn't she? She was nervous enough to sprout feathers.

Then, in a move she'd never imagined from a man who held control with such a deft hand, Hunter lost it.

Before she could blink, he stormed across the room, kicking the chair out of the way. She didn't even have a chance to uncurl her toes and turn to run before he grabbed her by the arms and lifted her off her feet.

Marni squeaked. Now her toes were grabbing at air.

"We aren't finished yet," he growled, his minty breath washing over her face.

"Finished? With what? Were you shorted an orgasm or two? One more obscure sexual position suddenly occurred to you and you felt cheated by not getting to try it out?" The words tumbled past Marni's lips so fast, she sounded like she was stuttering. As if the faster she talked, the sooner she'd find solid ground. "We'd reached San Francisco, Hunter. The end of the line. What could you possibly think we still had to finish?"

Besides honesty, forthright truths about their jobs and the case he was currently testifying on, of course. But she swallowed those options along with a tiny whimper of pleasure as he pressed her back against the wall.

Frustration tightened his face, his eyes narrow and his jaw clenched. Fury flashed like a lightning storm, fast, intense and fascinating.

Her heart raced, and her body melted. Because even that sudden fear carried a sexual edge, deep and needy.

"What do we have to finish?" he repeated, his words so low she felt them rather than heard them. "This."

HUNTER TOOK MARNI'S mouth with vicious greed. He had to have her. And he'd be damned if he'd take no for an answer.

All of the frustrations, all of the fury and hurt and betrayal he felt was channeled into that meeting of their lips. It was too raw, too greedy to be called a kiss. It was too carnal to walk away from.

After a second of shocked hesitation, she moaned against his lips, then tunneled her fingers through his hair, holding tight. She tried to shift, wriggling her body between the hard—and getting harder by the second—body and the wall. Other than enjoying the hell out of the results on his own body, Hunter ignored her squirms. Then she slid one leg, still a half foot off the ground, along his. Her bare foot arched along his thigh, then wrapped around so her heel dug into his butt cheek.

He exploded, like gasoline being poured over a fire. He reached down to cup the warm, soft flesh of her thigh, then slid his hand up under her short denim skirt to grab her butt. She wiggled closer, anchoring the hot core of her passion against his throbbing erection.

He left her mouth to race his lips over her throat in huge, biting kisses. The scent of her, rich and floral, filled his head. Surrounded him in the memory of every bit of pleasure they'd brought to each other.

He was a proud man. A strong man.

But he was pretty sure that if he didn't have her, right now, he'd break down and beg.

The fragile softness of her T-shirt was no defense against his need. He simply tore it out of his way with one quick rip.

Her gasp echoed, bouncing off the walls as her fingernails now dug into his shoulders. Pain and pleasure twined, tight and powerful.

Her skirt was just as easy, short enough that he easily shoved the denim up her hips. He wrapped one finger around the fragile lace of her panties and yanked.

Bare to him, her body was hot and pulsing.

His fingers drove into her welcoming wetness.

Her gasp quickly turned to a moan, deep and throaty. Hunter took that as an *oh, yeah, c'mon.*

With a quick flick of his wrist, he had his jeans unzipped and the hell out of his way.

He gripped her butt, shifting back so her weight was balanced between the wall and his hands, and plunged.

Hard.

Intense.

It was like coming home.

Over and over again.

Marni's heels dug into his hips, anchoring her body to his as she met each thrust with a little undulation that sent his body soaring even higher.

"Michael," she breathed, her words a whisper that began in his ear and quickly sifted its way into his soul.

Michael.

That's all it took. One word that reached in and tore him to shreds.

With an eager growl, Hunter dove deeper. The edge was still razor-sharp. The need was still desperate. But his heart, closed and protected before, was wide-open and vulnerable for the first time in his life.

Marni's body convulsed, clenching around his cock. Her fingers bore holes in his back as she arched, wringing every drop of pleasure from her orgasm.

He watched her fly over the edge, the flush painting a pink glow to her skin, her eyes hazed with satisfied passion. Her delight flipped a switch, removing all restraints on his own.

Hunter exploded. His entire being poured into her in a pulsing stream. His growl turned to a groan, low and throaty. His body convulsed. Pumping, feeling more incredible than he'd ever felt before.

Instead of reveling in the power of his orgasm, though, a feeling he'd never felt before grabbed hold.

He stared at Marni's pretty face, flushed and damp

with proof of her own pleasure. He'd been shot at, blown up, chased by a bear and marked for death by a vengeful crime boss.

But this was the first time he'd ever been terrified.

It was like floating in a cloud. A pleasure-filled, mind-numbed, delight-induced cloud. All Marni could do was feel. Feel her breath, ragged and hot as it labored from a throat raw from screams of pleasure. Feel her pulse, pounding like a freight train, fast and out of control. Feel her heart, melting with more love than she'd ever felt for another person in her life.

She sighed. Her shoulders drooped against the wall, all of her fears, all of her worries sinking away. Whatever their differences, she and Hunter could work it out.

As if he heard her thoughts, and strenuously objected, Hunter released her butt so abruptly her feet slammed to the floor. He shifted, moving away from her body so fast she was chilled by the quick gust of air.

Her mouth dropped open. Shocked, she stared, but before she could ask what was going on, he'd stormed into the bathroom. The door shut with all the finality of an exclamation point.

She knew something had just gone horribly wrong, but she didn't know what. Her brain just wouldn't engage. On autopilot, she moved to her suitcase and found a shirt, pulling it on and tugging her skirt down to cover her still pulsating privates.

"How'd you know my given name?" Hunter asked when he stepped out of the bathroom.

Marni stared, her mind still numbed from the quick slide through a sexual fog.

"What?"

"You said my name. Just then." He gestured to the

wall where he'd just screwed her brains out. Without said brains, she wondered, how was she supposed to respond? Marni pushed her hands through her sweat-damp hair and shook her head.

"We spent a week on a train together, had more sex in that time than I had in my entire four years of college. You don't think I know your name?"

Tucking his shirt into his jeans, Hunter gave her a bland stare. And waited.

God, she hated the waiting.

It was even worse with this heavy expectation in the air. Hunter's unspoken demand. As if she were some recalcitrant child who'd easily fall in line with a wag of his finger and a disapproving look.

She'd be damned if she was going to cave to his tough-guy intimidation.

Marni lifted her chin and pressed her lips together.

He arched one brow, as if to say it was a little late for her to close her mouth, he'd already been there.

"So what'd you do? Use your contacts to dig into my FBI files? Poke into my college records? How deep did you go?" he snapped, his fury unabated by what had been— at least for her—a mind-blowing orgasm. "That's what a good reporter does when working a story, right? Opens every door, peeks into all the closets."

Marni caught her breath, trying to control the jolt that slammed through her body. As though she was standing on the edge of a high dive, knowing she was going to plunge at any second and trying to be prepared. Then having someone come up from behind to shove her right over the side.

Still, she reminded herself, she was a damned good swimmer.

So she waited a beat, using the time to steady her quivering nerves. She made a show of crossing one leg over the other and brushed a nonexistent piece of lint from her skirt. Then, her smile as chilly as his words, she shook her head. "I was in the courthouse when you gave testimony, remember. You were sworn in using your full name."

His face going blank, he stared. Calculating.

"And that's your excuse?"

"My excuse for what? Getting a little too emotional while you did me against the wall?"

"You know, I think I liked it better when you were doing that unobtrusive sweet act," he decided, crossing both arms over his chest and giving her a frustrated look.

She didn't bother to deny that it had been an act.

"Was that when you were pretending to be an unassuming government pencil pusher?" she asked instead, offering an arch smile. "How'd that budget go? Was your boss happy with the way you crunched the numbers?"

"Clever. I guess that comes in handy, your ability to play with words and craft shrewd questions."

"So you know I'm a reporter," she said with a shrug, making as if she didn't care. "And you are a big, bad FBI special agent. I guess we're even."

"Even?" He straightened, looking scary again. "You think so?"

Afraid he'd grab her for another round of wild sex, Marni jumped up from the bed. No point making it easy for him. She scurried—yes, she was ashamed to admit it to herself, but this quickstep was definitely a scurry—across the room.

"Yes, we're even. You lied, I lied. You hid truths, I hid truths. You aren't what you said…" She paused, then tapped her finger against her lips and shook her head. "Oh, wait, I'm exactly what I said. A writer. So I guess you're right. We're not even."

Suddenly she was tired of being scared.

Scared of Hunter's reaction.

Scared of her own emotions.

Scared of making a choice.

Enough was enough.

Marni didn't know what she was going to do about any of it. But she did know she wouldn't figure it out with Hunter looking over her in glaring fury, working his government-learned intimidation tactics.

"We have a few things to settle," he said, sidestepping her comparison of their job claims.

"Do we?" she asked, now crossing her own arms defensively over her chest. Hindsight said it'd been insane to sleep with the man central to the biggest article she'd ever written. Her judgment was compromised, her every decision biased by their relationship. Even now, when she knew damned well she'd written the biggest, strongest article of her career, she worried about turning it in. Worried that she'd hurt Hunter's career, jeopardize his case, make him look bad.

But even as she mentally screamed at herself for making such a huge mistake, she still couldn't regret it. Because her time, her relationship, her feelings for Hunter, they were once in a lifetime.

Even if they were, thanks to reality, now over.

He stepped closer, giving her a long, searching look.

"You've been asking questions about Beverly Burns," he accused quietly.

Marni blinked. Then, because she knew he was watching for it, she tried to keep her expression absolutely neutral. She couldn't stop her fingers from clasping around each other, though.

"So? We knew each other from the fashion circuit.

Maybe I was putting together a piece on her latest clothing line."

"And maybe you're digging into things that are none of your business."

"Hmm, isn't facts and stories that interest the public exactly the business of a reporter?" she mused, making a show of tapping her finger against her chin.

Hunter scowled.

"You've got nothing," he decided.

Marni didn't know why his assurance made her so angry. Maybe it was years of her family doubting her. Maybe it was her own questioning of her decision with this article. But it was as if he'd just blasted her in the face with a water balloon. She was drenched with irritation.

"I got the facts," she snapped back. "Facts like the FBI is covering up Beverly Burns's supposed death."

Reaching out as if to grab the words back, Marni winced. She'd never make it as a spy. Or secret keeper, for that matter. She was a reporter because she was nosy, not because she was good at keeping things quiet.

"Shit," he muttered, frustration, anger and regret all flashing across his face. Then, with a deep breath through his nose, Hunter straightened. As if he grew three extra inches, and not in a way that interested her, he was back to a menacing threat looming over her.

"Whatever you think you know, forget it," he suggested in a tone all the more formidable for its quiet. "You're risking lives if you keep digging. I'm not going to let you put an innocent woman in danger."

Let her? Marni couldn't tell which was stronger. Her anger at the idea that he'd *let her* do any damned thing. Or the sudden spurt of jealousy spinning through her system, green and toxic. From everything she'd found out, Hunter had made Beverly Burns his own personal pet project. Because he was just that kind of guy? Or because she was a sexy, gorgeous redhead?

"Oh, yeah. Such a poor, sweet, innocent woman." She gave a derisive scowl. "You're talking about the wife of a known mobster. Beverly Burns's own father was indicted on racketeering charges. She's got a reputation that's nearly as vicious as her husband's."

Something he should keep in mind while he was *protecting* her.

The look on Hunter's face wasn't possessive or affectionate, though. It was resolute. He stared long enough to make Marni want to squirm. Then, suddenly, he seemed to pull the plug on the scary aura. In the blink of an eye, he wasn't daunting FBI Agent Man anymore, he was the sexy guy she'd fallen in love with. But the sexy guy who looked crazy serious, determinedly grim.

"She's a dead woman if you let it be known that she didn't go down with that building," he said quietly, crossing his arms over his chest and frowning as if the weight of that was pressing down on his own shoulders.

Marni rolled her eyes, wanting to dismiss it as an exaggeration. But she knew Hunter didn't exaggerate.

"You're going to put Burns away. Between that and her family contacts, I'm sure she'd be safe enough," Marni hazarded.

"Her family is small potatoes compared to Burns. And you're not naive enough to think he won't have almost as much power behind bars as he would as a free man." The look Hunter gave her said if she was thinking in that direction, she should stick with reporting hemlines.

She had to suck in her lower lip to stop herself from pouting. It wasn't that she was naive. She just hadn't thought about it like that. So maybe she'd earned a few more articles on shoes, but definitely not hemlines.

"Just let it go," he ordered, as if he instinctively knew he'd made his point. Or, since she was such master spy material, he'd read it on her face.

"I'm not dropping anything," she shot back, shaking her head and reminding herself of everything she had on the line here.

"Marni…"

"What? What are you going to do?" she challenged. "Arrest me so I won't write the story?"

He gave her a long look, emotions swirling in the blue depths of his eyes. A shiver ran up Marni's spine as she realized that, yes, that had probably been his intention. If that story ran, she'd be jeopardizing his case. He was a man who worked outside the rules whenever it suited him, as comfortable using unconventional methods to close a case as he was calling the shots.

"You need to ask yourself this," he said, leaning in so close she could almost feel his heartbeat. "Are you willing to sentence a woman to death just to feed your own ambition?"

With that, and a look that clearly stated that if she was, she wasn't the woman he thought her to be, Hunter turned on his heel and strode out of the room.

His words echoed through the room.

He didn't look back.

Marni didn't know how long she stared at the closed door, not seeing a thing.

All she knew was that she couldn't face the mirror.

Because she couldn't handle what she'd see there yet.

12

HUNTER SAT IN THE CORNER of the dimly lit bar, glaring at his Scotch.

"You stare at it long enough, it might even be palatable."

He slid his gaze sideways, blinked in surprise to see his best friend standing there, then he shook his head.

"Not much makes rotgut palatable," he said, shrugging and pushing the glass aside. The rickety table wobbled. As appealing as it was, getting drunk wasn't a very good answer to his woes. But a better one might have just hitched himself onto the adjacent bar stool.

"This is a surprise," Hunter decided, keeping to his habit of understatement.

Caleb Black's eyes gleamed gold as he gave a wicked grin. "Consider it an early birthday present."

Hunter made a show of looking past his college roommate's shoulder, as if searching for a gift, then gave him a slow once-over. "You got a bow on you somewhere I don't see?"

"You asking about my package?" Caleb quipped. He looked as if he'd just dropped in for a drink and friendly hello, but Hunter knew him well enough to see the intensity in his oldest friend's eyes.

Hunter'd had enough rotgut to smirk, but not enough that he felt obligated to answer the questions in his old friend's eyes.

"You're a long ways from home. And my birthday is in November. So what's the deal?"

"San Francisco isn't that far from the Santa Cruz Mountains." In the years since they'd left college, Caleb had left an illustrious career with the DEA to settle in as sheriff of a small California town, but the two men were still tight. Probably tighter now, since Caleb wasn't spending half of each year undercover, and more likely to send Hunter dirty emails and regular texts. Or, like now, show up out of the blue. Caleb dragged the bowl of peanuts closer from the middle of the table.

"I heard you'd be here testifying, thought I'd come up and spend a day or so," he said. "I thought it'd be fun to watch you do the feebie dance, put a bad guy behind bars."

"He's not locked up yet."

And the case wasn't nearly as open and shut as Hunter had hoped. It wasn't that the feds' prosecutors weren't good. It was that Burns's money was paying for a top-notch team of sleazy sharks with the predatory skills of starving jackals.

The prosecution was winning. But it was taking a hell of a lot longer than any of them would like. Hunter knew from the increased frustration on Burns's face each day that he hadn't thought this would take more than a day or two, either.

Every day Hunter sat in that courthouse, ignoring the stink eye Murray kept throwing his way, trying to convince himself that keeping Beverly Burns in a safe house and out of the case wasn't a bad plan.

All the while he had this ticking time bomb in the form of a gorgeous, sexy blonde. He had no idea if she'd go off. No clue when. But the minute that story broke, the defense was going to call a mistrial, and very likely Burns would slide out from under the charges like the snake he was.

"So what's the deal? You're not usually the sleazy-bar drinking-alone type. Did the ferns die in all the preppie bars and this was your only option?"

"This case is getting to me," Hunter confessed, his words so low the tinny jukebox tunes almost drowned them out. "I called the strategy on it, and it's looking like it might blow up in my face."

Caleb pursed his lips, contemplating the far wall as if he could see the future in it. Maybe he could. His pretty little wife specialized in woo woo. Finally he slid his gaze back to Hunter.

"Worst-case scenario, you crap out at the FBI. I've got an opening for a deputy. You can come work for me."

After staring for one stunned second, Hunter threw back his head and laughed until his stomach hurt.

"Right. That's what I'm going to do if my career plunges into free fall. Plant myself in a tiny town, surrounded by known criminals."

"Suspected criminals," Caleb corrected with a grin, breaking open a peanut. "And given that two of them are married to FBI agents themselves, I'd say it's unlikely you'd have to worry about arresting anyone when you sat down to Sunday dinner with my family."

Now that was quite an image. Still grinning, Hunter let himself imagine a big, fancy Black meal with the guests lined up on either side of the table like cops and robbers. Paired off, boy, girl, boy, girl. And then there'd be him.

Alone.

No career, and no girl.

His grin slid away.

"What the hell is it with women?" Hunter finally asked. He peered at Caleb through eyes dimmed by enough rotgut to guarantee he'd feel like crap in the morning. "Why do they have to be so complicated? Or worse, so freaking obstinate."

"That's part of their appeal," Caleb mused, cracking open another peanut and popping the meat into his mouth. "Don't forget irritating, exasperating, confusing and, oh, yeah, sexy as hell."

Yep. That was Marni in a nutshell.

"You ever regret everything you gave up?"

"Gave up? For Pandora?"

Hunter nodded.

"I suppose you mean other than all the gorgeous women who'd constantly throw themselves at my feet?"

This time Hunter's nod was accompanied by a smirk.

Caleb lifted the basket of peanuts to poke through them, shook a couple into his hand and considered the question.

"It wasn't a matter of giving anything up. I'd already resigned the DEA, so the job wasn't in question. I might not have moved back to Black Oak if she wasn't there, but I've actually gained a lot from being there." Caleb chose a few more peanuts. "There are drawbacks. My father. Pandora's mother. They're more work than the criminals."

Hunter didn't doubt it. His own father had spent years trying to build a lock-tight case against Tobias Black, Caleb's dad. The man was a con extraordinaire. But a con with a heart of gold.

"What's her name?"

Caleb still had plenty of contacts in the DEA, and his own resources as a California sheriff. A name was all he needed to put together the entire story. Since Hunter was playing fast and loose with his stomach lining trying to decide if he'd done the right thing, he figured it was probably better not to offer up that information just yet.

He didn't insult either of them by playing stupid, though. He just shrugged.

"She tied to the Burns case?"

Hunter slanted a glare at his old roommate, wondering just how much digging Caleb had done before tracking him down.

"What's your interest in the case?" he asked instead.

"Not a whole lot other than wanting the trial to finish up quick enough that you still had time while you're on this coast to visit Black Oak."

"It should be this week. We've got him on the ropes, but his team is dancing fast. Still, unless something huge breaks, we'll be hearing closing arguments by Friday," Hunter hazarded, more open to discussing the realities of the case with Caleb than he'd be with any fellow FBI agents. Or even himself.

Especially since the biggest reality was that one juicy story hitting a national magazine could derail the entire thing.

He tossed back the Scotch with a pained grimace.

"You gonna come down this weekend, then? It'd be good timing. Maya and Gabriel are in town to celebrate the old man's birthday."

Once again numbed by the Scotch, Hunter smirked.

"You want me to attend your father's birthday party?"

Caleb matched his smirk with one of his own.

"Why not? Your dad will be there."

Shit.

Tension pounded.

"I'm not sure I'm up for seeing either one of them," he admitted.

Caleb didn't say a word. Just tossed back a few more

peanuts, then signaled the waitress for a beer. He gave Hunter's empty Scotch glass an assessing look, then lifted two fingers.

It seemed Caleb thought it was time to switch up his drinking preferences. Since he was swimming on a comfortable sea of booze already, Hunter didn't mind.

The scantily clad waitress, her hair a brassy shade that made Hunter miss Marni's soft flaxen curls all the more, dropped two steins on the table, held out her hand for Caleb's cash, then sauntered away.

Caleb took a drink, then pulled a face. Hunter probably should have warned him that what they had on tap in this place was a step up from horse piss. Then again, Caleb had been in enough dives to know that. He was just getting soft.

"It's never easy living up to certain reps, is it?" Caleb mused, referencing the comment about their fathers. "Or down to them."

Meaning their respective fathers.

Hunter shrugged like it didn't matter.

Then, Scotch-induced honesty forced him to admit, "I never figured living up to my old man was a problem. I mean, I had it figured out, you know? All the advantages he didn't have, a clear plan and a lot less holding me back."

"Like a wife and kid?"

"I'm not saying it was a bad idea for him," he shot back, grinning. "I think the results worked out pretty well. But for me? That kind of commitment would put a stranglehold on my trajectory."

"Or give you a nice cushion against your slightly obsessive drive to win."

Hunter frowned.

"Did you just call me obsessive?"

"Did you just claim you won't open your life to a wife

and the possibility of kids because they might slow down your climb up the FBI ladder?"

Hunter's head spun a few times clockwise, then once counterclockwise. Once it landed, he sighed.

"Okay, maybe I've been known to be obsessive. But that's what it takes, right? I want this career, and if I want it to shine, then I've gotta make sacrifices." Choices. Like letting the potential destroyer of his career move ahead with her story, just because he couldn't bring himself to play badass with her.

He'd listened to so many of her stories, watched how she lit up when she talked about writing, he knew how important her career was. But unlike him, she didn't have a strong family support system. Didn't have anyone who believed in her ability to make it happen.

No matter what it cost him, he couldn't be the one to crush those dreams. To intimidate the hell out of her so she was afraid to take a chance at them. Instead, he'd just cross his fingers and hope she didn't screw up his career on the way to making hers?

It was all Hunter could do not to drop his head into his hands and groan. He'd hit heretofore-unimagined levels of pathetic-ness.

"You're a mess," Caleb observed with his usual tact and diplomacy. "You never worried about trials before and usually take tough cases in stride. You want to talk it out?"

Hunter didn't know how to explain, even to himself, why he'd walked out and left Marni with the option to take her information public. He wasn't a do-gooder. Nor was he the kind of guy who left huge decisions up to other people, banking on his faith in humanity. Hell, he figured most of humanity was on the take, out to screw over the next guy.

Since he was clueless to explain the mess in his head, he shrugged instead.

"So you're saying I gotta go to your old man's birth-day bash this weekend if I'm gonna get my own birthday gift? Isn't that called dirty pool?"

"You'll actually get the gift in November," Caleb clar-ified. The only thing missing from his canary-eating grin were a few feathers. "I'm just giving you the official heads-up this weekend."

Hunter narrowed his Scotch-blurred gaze.

"You might want to spill it before you burst."

"You might want to wrap up this case before the end of the year." Caleb tossed another peanut into his mouth, crunched, then grinned. "Because we're gonna want you in Black Oak then. You know, since Pandora wants you to stand as godfather."

The Scotch blur faded from Hunter's brain in a flash.

"Pandora's having a baby?" He grinned, feeling good for the first time in a week. He clasped Caleb's hand in a hard shake. "Seriously? Congrats, man. That's great."

Caleb shrugged like it was no big deal, but his beam-ing smile screamed his joy.

Hunter reveled in his friend's happiness for a few sec-onds. Then the alcohol haze lured him back to his own black thoughts.

"How do you do it? Juggle the demands of your career, marriage and now a kid?"

"I'm not undercover anymore. I don't think I could do it if I was. You lose yourself. Lose your life."

Hunter nodded, having done enough undercover to know what Caleb meant.

"Otherwise, juggling is just like anything else. If it's something that matters, you make it work." Still straddling the chair, Caleb leaned forward, so it perched on two legs. It creaked in protest. "So, what're you thinking about?"

"I'm not thinking anything," Hunter dismissed.

"Right." Caleb ate a few more nuts, then let his chair drop flat to the floor. "Look, you've done me a few favors. Now, officially we're square since I did you one last year. But in the name of friendship, I'm going to spot you another."

"That favor, as you call it, was what snagged you the pretty little wife you're so crazy in love with. So I think we're even."

Caleb waited.

Finally, Hunter shrugged. "Yeah, okay fine. I'll owe you one."

It spoke to what a solid friend he was that Caleb didn't smirk. He just nodded, dropped his arms to the table and leaned forward.

"You got it bad for this woman. Bad enough that you're questioning things you've always seen as black-and-white."

Hunter didn't need to ask how Caleb knew.

"The thing is, relationships, women, they always dance in the gray. They aren't going to simply fall in line behind your career. At least, the right one won't." Caleb stared into his beer for a second, his big dorky grin back. Then he met Hunter's gaze and shrugged. "You just gotta ask yourself what matters. What's life like with this woman in it? And what's it like without her."

Hunter shook his head, wanting to dismiss the idea of anyone lining up ahead of his career with an easy smile.

But the image of Marni's face kept flashing in his brain.

"Then what?"

"Then you accept the inevitable. You're in love enough to ask the questions, you're in love enough to find a way to live with the answers."

MARNI PACED.

From the tall black statue shaped like a menacing umbrella, then back to the squat one resembling a demented rabbit. Back, forth, again and again.

She pushed her hand through her hair, her fingers tangling in the unbrushed curls. She was a mess. Three days of alternating between pacing, writing and crying hadn't left much room for grooming and tidiness.

"Well?" she finally asked, unable to stand the wait any longer. Or the view. These statues were getting uglier by the hour.

Robin didn't seem to care about her torment, though.

The older woman held up one finger and continued to read. Marni went back to pacing. She only made it to squat and ugly, though, before her aunt set the pages aside.

"Well?" Marni asked again. She sat on the black leather bench opposite Robin. Then, too worried to take the news sitting down, she jumped up and started pacing again.

"Well..." Robin gave the printed pages another look, then hummed.

Marni had only met her aunt five days ago, but she'd already figured out that while the woman was quick to ask questions, she was slow to answer them. She weighed each word like it was gold, and she was a miser. It was harder to use a quote against someone if the words went unsaid, she'd informed her niece over dinner the previous night.

Still, frustration surged through Marni's system. It was all she could do not to dig her fingers into her hair and tug.

Finally, Robin pushed the papers away and smiled.

"I think you've a great deal of talent. You have a spark in your writing, an edge and humor that are balanced by a depth of emotion that tugs the reader in before they realize it."

Oh. Eyes huge, Marni started to smile. That was nice.

"You need editing, of course. You're a little wordy in

places, meandering in others. But the core is here, and the impact is huge."

Marni's mouth opened, but no words came out.

Wordy and meandering were editable. Huge, with a core and impact? *Holy cow.* She wanted to dance with the tree. To throw her arms wide and embrace the entire weird room. To curl up on the leather bench and cry.

She'd spent three days working on that piece.

Three days of second-guessing every word, of lecturing herself five ways from Sunday over making a major mistake. She'd searched her soul and spent endless hours trying to decide if she was making a mistake.

"So you think I'm doing the right thing?"

Robin sighed, then, looking so much like her brother that Marni hunched her shoulders like she did when her father lectured, the older woman folded her hands in her lap.

"I think the right thing is a subjective question. You have to live with the results, girly. You're the one taking a huge step and quite possibly shifting your entire career." She unfolded her fingers to tap the pages again. "If this has the impact I think it will, you're going to see some huge career opportunities open. It's smart to be sure you want to accept those opportunities, and their repercussions, before you submit this."

As if her aunt had just pierced a balloon, the words sucked all the energy out of Marni in a shockingly fast swoosh. She dropped to the bench and wrapped the fingers of her left hand around the fingers of the right, trying to figure out what to do. She switched hands, staring at her manicure but not seeing the chipped pink polish.

"If I write this profile instead of the Burns article, I'm taking my career in a completely different direction. I love writing biographies, but they will never get the same kind of attention hard-hitting stories would." Marni pushed one hand through her hair, her fingers snagging on the snarls. "Am I doing it because I think it's the right thing? Or because of Hunter?"

"Only you can decide that. Life is made up of choices. And choosing is tough. Anyone who tells you different is lying, girly." Robin sighed and gave a jerk of one shoulder. "As for right or wrong, I don't know. I really don't. I've never met anyone who I cared about as much as my career. I've never had a lover I could imagine lasting as long as my career. I've never met a man who made me feel as special as being a reporter does."

Well, there ya go. As much as Marni had enjoyed weaving a fantasy around the idea of happy-ever-after with Hunter, she knew, really, that it was just that…a fantasy.

And just because she was feeling an overwhelming deep emotional onslaught that she wanted to call love, that didn't mean it really was. Nor that it would last. Nor, her gut clenched, did it mean that Hunter had any reciprocal interest.

Given how they'd left things—or rather, how he'd left things when he'd stormed out—she'd be tiptoeing along the edge of insanity to think there was something solid between them. Something strong enough to build the hopes of a future on.

Marni chewed on her thumbnail, the tiny flakes of polish leaving a nasty taste in her mouth. Giving up her career ambitions, making a serious one-eighty in her goals for the remote, so-slim-it-was-barely-existent possibility of a future between her and Hunter?

She'd have to be insane to do that.

Her fingers tightened around each other so hard, her wrists were numb.

Wouldn't she?

"I guess depending on a career is a lot smarter than banking on a relationship," she finally said, her words hoarse and painful. She cleared her throat, then met her aunt's gaze with her brightest, fakest smile. "Which is what I've always said. Always believed. That just confirms it."

As if she'd seen something painful in that smile, Robin grimaced. Then she sighed and lifted both palms to the heavens, as if asking for guidance.

"Look," she said, her words halting, as though she had to search for and weigh each one, "I'm not saying that's the right choice. It's the choice I made. But I made it based on the options in front of me. If I had a man who made my toes curl, who made me think and made me laugh? That'd be harder to resist. If he was a guy who understood me. Deep down, totally got me… I've never had that, Marni. But if I had, well, that'd be a hard choice to make."

With each word, Robin leaned closer, looked older.

Marni shoved her hand through her hair, trying to process all of that.

It was like laboring for years, pushing and climbing to get to the top of a mountain. Then breathlessly, painfully reaching the top, only to have the grand guru of all that was bright and shiny offer a shrug and a dismissive *Nah, it's not all it's cracked up to be.* She was torn between sympathy, pity and horrified tears.

"I told you once, I've told you a bunch of times, girly. You have to make your decisions based on your baggage. And sometimes that baggage looks pretty damned awesome in the beginning, but loses its appeal after living with it a few years. Or a few months." Her aunt waved a hand at the statues standing in stark relief against her bloodred walls, as if they were the perfect example.

Marni grimaced. She wasn't so sure of equating Hunter

with baggage or butt-ugly artwork, but she was sure he qualified as pretty damned awesome.

The risk was huge.

This wasn't a choice she could backtrack on. Whatever she did, regardless of the results, she was stuck with it.

"I want him," she murmured, finally looking up to meet her aunt's patient gaze. "Even if this doesn't work out, even if I'm making the wrong choice for my career, I still want Hunter."

Robin bit her lip, as if she was bursting to say something. But she settled on a nod.

"What?" Marni prodded. "Please? I came to you for advice, I'd really like to hear your honest thoughts."

"You don't know me that well, girly. And despite the fact we share blood and looks, I don't know you." Robin got to her feet. Now it was she who was pacing from ugly statue to ugly statue. Marni dropped her eyes back to her nails, preferring to see her mangled manicure to those monstrosities.

"Look, I hate giving advice. I'm a selfish woman. I live my life for me, for my goals. I've dedicated myself to my career on purpose. Not because I don't think a woman can't have it all. To hell with that kind of thinking. Women can have anything and everything they want, if they work their asses off."

Marni agreed, but didn't want to set Robin off on another rant about gender equality. So she settled for a silent nod.

"I chose to go it alone because that's who I am," Robin finally said. She dropped back onto the bench, making it safe for Marni to look at her again. "I am ambitious, selfish and lazy. I'm also terrified of failure."

Marni shook her head.

"Ambitious and selfish to make those ambitions a reality, maybe. But I don't buy the rest."

"Like I said, we don't really know each other yet."

Marni's lips twitched, and she gave a gracious nod, acknowledging the point.

"You've got a lot of me in you, girly. You're ambitious, too. Clever with words and you have an eye for seeing the story within the story. An eye that'll take an average piece to excellence."

"Do you think I'd be making the wrong decision?"

"Doesn't matter what I think. The question is can you live with making that particular decision?"

"As long as Hunter can, I can," she decided.

"And if he doesn't?"

Marni lifted her chin, pressing her lips tight together to keep them from trembling.

"I'll just have to convince him, then, won't I?"

"You think it's gonna be easy to convince a guy like that to accept you doing this to him?" Robin asked, waving the pages of Marni's story in the air.

"Nothing about him is easy. But I'll make it work," she vowed.

Because she wasn't taking no for an answer. She'd do whatever it took, use whatever tools were necessary to convince Hunter to forgive her. To give them a chance.

If he wouldn't listen to reason, she'd fall back on the one thing she knew he couldn't resist.

She'd strip naked and offer to show him her pole dancing skills.

13

IT'D BEEN A LOT OF YEARS since he'd been stupid enough to inflict a hangover on himself. The hotel room curtains still shut against the painful morning sunlight, Hunter squinted at the mirror as he knotted his tie.

He wasn't due in court until afternoon, but sitting here in the hotel room would just drive him crazy. He had other cases he could be working, could drop in the San Francisco offices and see a few old faces. He didn't want to socialize, though. He just wanted mental distractions to keep him from obsessing over Marni and the long list of what-ifs.

As if hearing his thoughts, someone pounded on the door.

Hunter clenched his teeth, the sound echoing hollowly in his head.

Murray? He was supposed to be heading back to Washington, having deemed the Burns case a failure since the lawyers hadn't hit it out of the park yet.

Caleb? He was probably already cuddled up with his sweet wife, having decided to drive home the previous night instead of waiting until morning.

Didn't matter who it was, Hunter didn't feel like talking to anyone.

He yanked open the door, ready to tell whoever it was to get lost.

Marni stared back at him, her big blue eyes assessing.

He had to work to keep his glare in place.

"I'm here to talk to you." She ducked under his arm and stepped into the room. When she'd reached the desk by the window, she set a leather messenger bag on the chair and faced him.

Damn, she looked good.

Her hair fell in a sweep of blond over one side of her face, a sexy reminder of the forties era the train trip had embraced. But her outfit was totally up-to-date. A blessedly short black skirt and matching tights, boots that ended at her ankles, and a flirty lace blouse in bubblegum-pink.

Her face was serene, her smile a friendly curve of those lush lips. He didn't see a hint of worry in her big blue eyes.

But her fingers were tangled together, twining and untwining, as if she was strangling them.

"What'd you want to talk about? I'm not giving you information on the Burns case," he said, putting the snarky words between them. More because he didn't think he could handle it if that was the only reason she was there, rather than because he wanted to be mean.

Marni's easy smile slipped for a second, hurt flashing in her eyes. Hunter cringed. Could he be a bigger jerk? Before he could apologize, though, she reached for the bag she'd set on the chair, unbuckled the flap and pulled out a file.

Holding it out toward him, she said, "I'd hoped to talk about something else first, but if you want to get the issues about the story and Burns out of the way first, here."

He wanted to toss the papers aside. He wanted to grab

her close, press her body against his and take her mouth in a God-it's-been-too-long kiss. He wanted to demand she tell him what that something else was she'd prefer to talk about, because it sounded like something he was going to much rather hear than anything to do with their respective jobs.

Instead, calling himself a wimp for the first time in his adult life, Hunter took the folder from her.

He didn't open it, though. He just kept staring at her.

She was gorgeous.

Sexy, sweet and so damned appealing.

He thought of Caleb's words the night before.

You're in love enough to ask the questions, you're in love enough to find a way to live with the answers.

Was he in love enough?

He'd lain awake most of the night, his head swimming in Scotch, asking that question over and over again. He hadn't come up with an answer, though. He'd never been in love. What did he know about those deeper emotions? And how could he know it was real, that it'd last?

Now, looking at Marni, the questions all fell away.

The worries, too.

He loved her. It was that simple.

And, he glanced at the file in his hands, that complicated.

"Go ahead," she insisted. "Look at it."

"What's this?" He riffled through the papers, his frown sinking deeper with each paragraph. By the time he'd reached the last one, his frown was fierce and furious. "Where'd you get this?"

Marni wet her lips, looking nervous for just a second before squaring her shoulders. She stepped forward and reached for the pages. Hunter almost didn't let them go, but figured he was between her and the door, so he'd have plenty of chance to tackle her to retrieve them if necessary. She didn't take them away, though. Instead, she shuffled through until she reached a particular one, then handed the stack back.

"In putting together the story about Beverly Burns, I talked to a lot of people. This guy here, he was her current lover until her disappearance. He doesn't know what's going on, of course. Figures she dumped him, so his ego is whining. He spilled all kinds of stuff, including that bank safety-deposit box he said she put files in under his name."

Hunter could only stare. Not at the name of their breakthrough on this case. But at Marni. She'd pulled off what he and a slew of trained FBI agents couldn't. She'd got what was very likely the final nail to pound into the coffin of a major crime boss.

"You checked the safe-deposit box yourself?"

Marni hesitated, then shrugged.

"I should have. That'd be the right thing to do, of course. But I didn't want to leave California." Didn't want to leave him, her expression said. Marni wrinkled her nose in a self-deprecating way, as if she knew she'd said more than she should, but wasn't going to take it back.

"So you sent some stranger to poke through vital information?" He'd heard a lot in his years with the FBI. You'd think he'd be immune. But sometimes he still wanted to drop his face into his hands and groan.

"Not a stranger, no. I sent my cousin."

Hunter gave in to frustration, rubbing at his forehead as if he could ease the aching throb between his eyes. She'd had her cousin do it.

"Marni, you know this is a federal investigation, right? The stakes are sky-high and you let a stranger, someone without any clearance at all, poke through the information? I know that might be okay for a story, but it's putting this case at major risk."

She nodded, looking totally unabashed at his words. Instead, she just looked calm. What the hell? He knew she cared about doing the right thing. She wouldn't be bringing him this otherwise. Did she not get the importance of confidentiality and timing in a case like this?

"Did I mention that my cousin goes by the name Sister Maria-Louisa with the Sisters of Charity?"

"Your cousin is a nun?"

Hunter cringed just a little, suddenly very aware of all the things he and Marni had done with, to and on top of each other. Was there some rule against that?

She didn't seem very intimidated, since she laughed with delight, clearly reading his discomfort.

"She is. And according to my mother, she still follows the family marriage dictate, as she's a bride of God." Marni pulled a face, then shook her head as if she were trying to shake off her irritation at that fact. "Maria-Louisa is also great at persuading gigolo wannabes to show her the contents of their safe-deposit boxes. She didn't read anything there herself, she just took pictures with her cell phone and sent them to me."

Hunter stared. Maybe it was the hangover. Or the fact that Marni was right here in front of him, close enough to pull close so he could bury his face in her hair. But his brain just couldn't wrap itself around what she was saying.

"Your cousin, the nun, has a cell phone? And she convinced a hood rat like Giuseppe Laredo to let her take photos of the goods he was hiding for his girlfriend, the wife of a known mobster?" He shook his head. "Seriously?"

"Well, yeah. Who better?" Marni shrugged, pulling another folder out of her magic messenger bag and handing it to him. He flipped the cover and saw a stack of eight-by-ten photos. "She's the queen of that spiritual guilt thing, but so sweet about it that you end up feeling guilty for being guilty, you know? She promised Giuseppe she wouldn't let the information become public, though. That's why I made you promise you wouldn't use it as evidence."

For the first time, she looked anxious.

"You won't, right? I mean, you'll keep my word?" Marni grimaced, then shoved her hand through her hair. "I know that's not fair, but, well, she's a nun. I can't lie to her, even after the fact."

Hunter stared at the photos.

Triumph surged. His grin was both excited and just a little vicious. They'd nail that son of a bitch to the wall with this. Listed right there on that photographed-by-a-nun page were the hit orders, the details of the deaths the prosecution wanted to bust Burns on. He didn't need to use these photos as evidence. With these names, he'd have the hit men, their girlfriends, hell, their mothers, all rounded up within an hour. It wouldn't take long before someone flipped on Burns. That's all he needed, one flip, and he had the guy solid on murder charges.

His hand was halfway to his pocket to grab his own cell phone when his gaze landed on the photo's date stamp.

"You had this when you came to the trial. When I—" *screwed you against the hotel room wall* sounded so tacky "—surprised you in your hotel room."

From the wash of pink coloring her cheeks, Marni got the subtext without a problem. She shrugged, then shook her head.

"Maria-Louisa went to the bank that same day and took the photos, yes. But I didn't receive them until the next morning."

After he'd guilted her over the danger to Beverly Burns.

"You said you're still writing the story?"

"I sent my story in yesterday," she confirmed, her smile a little shaky. Not out of nerves over his reaction, but with excitement.

He set the file aside, needing to have nothing between them for this next question.

"But you said you promised her the information wouldn't be made public. How can you do that and write the big-hitting story that's going to make your career soar?"

She took a deep breath, puffed it back out, then offered a cute shrug.

"I pivoted on my story," she confessed.

Pivoted.

For him? Because he'd guilted her into it? Because she didn't want to put a questionably innocent woman in danger? Why?

A million thoughts raced through his head. A million hopes took hold of his heart. But Hunter didn't show a single one. The same as he'd always done when he was in a position that put his life on the line, he kept his expression bland, his nerves on the catatonic side of mellow.

Even as he hoped beyond words that her answer would be the shot he wanted, he didn't bank on it.

Instead, he simply asked, "Why?"

MARNI'S MOUTH WATERED a little as she stared at the man who, the last time she'd seen him, had given her the strongest, most body-shaking orgasm of her life. The look in his eyes was so strong, so demanding, it was as if he was looking straight into her soul. Again. Maybe that's what made her so crazy for him, that he saw her. Beyond the hair and the clothes and the curves, he saw the real her. And demanded she be the real her.

"Marni?"

"Hmm?"

"Why?" he asked again.

Well, there's the million-dollar question. Marni's throat was so tight, she had to swallow three times to get the air past it and into her suddenly aching lungs.

"Why?" she repeated, buying time.

"Yeah." His voice as calm as his face, he leaned his hip against the dresser and gave her a look with about as much expectation as if he'd just asked her for the time. "Why'd you make a promise like that? What'd you pivot your story to? And what good is this information to you if you can't use it?"

Maybe he should be trying the Burns case instead of those fancy lawyers. Between those kinds of questions and his ability to see directly into her mind, he'd have already gotten the conviction. She bit her lip.

"I could have used it. I mean, I did make my initial promise to Maria-Louisa with the caveat that she couldn't hold me to it if the case involved murder. She agreed, since, you know, she's big on the commandments." Marni offered a shaky smile, waiting to see if he'd join in on the joke. He just stared. Okay, then. Her heart pounded. She almost pushed a nervous hand through her hair again, then reminded herself of how long she'd spent getting prettied up for this meeting. So she wrapped her fingers together instead and shrugged.

"If I break this story, it ruins your case. I know one lost case won't ruin your career or anything. Your reputation is too good, your record too impressive for that. Still, it felt, well, wrong."

"Why?"

"You keep asking that," she said in exasperation.

"Go ahead and keep answering."

Marni opened her mouth to tell him.

She tried to push the confession past her lips.

But she couldn't.

Not without having any idea if he'd reciprocate her feelings. Not without a clue if he cared about her, too.

"Why didn't you stop me? You knew I was working on the Burns angle and his wife being alive." Her nerves exhausted from the constant spin of emotions, Marni lifted her palms in question. "So why didn't you stop the story? Have me detained. Intimidate me into running back to hemlines and fashion shows."

There. She'd put the *why* right back in his corner.

From the look in Hunter's eyes, he didn't like it there very much. Frustration and something else, something deep and intense that made her stomach clench and her heart race, lurked in those blue depths.

Why? What didn't he want to tell her?

Marni held her breath, waiting to find out.

"I can't have you arrested for breaking a story. You know that."

"You could have made my life very difficult. You could have played the intimidation card," she countered.

"You don't think sneaking into your hotel room, slamming you against the wall and having wild-man sex with you wasn't intimidating?" he asked, the bitterness in his words clearly self-directed.

Marni frowned. Unable to help herself, she moved closer, reaching out to take both of his hands. His hard, strong fingers closed, warm and solid, over hers.

"I hate to break it to you, wild man, but I wasn't intimidated by that. Turned on, blown away, satisfied, yes. But scared and intimidated, no."

He arched one brow and waited.

Marni rolled her eyes.

"Okay, fine. Maybe I was overwhelmed, nervous and

a little freaked out. But not intimidated. Not enough to sideline my ambitions and sit on the biggest story of my as-yet-growing career." She bit her lip, and then, because she hated the idea of him turning what had been incredibly exciting and totally consensual sex into something he was ashamed of, she tightened her hands on his and shook her head. "But I never felt at risk, you know? I knew, no matter how angry you were and how important this case is to you, that you wouldn't cross any lines. I'm safe with you."

All of a sudden, the only real fear Marni had when it came to Hunter fell away. The fear that he'd break her heart. Tension poured from her body, leaving her feeling a little limp and teary-eyed. It didn't matter whether Hunter returned her feelings or not. Whether he was interested in a future together or separate.

Whatever happened today, she'd walk away knowing she'd be okay. That she had the priorities between her self, her heart and her career in an order she could live with.

Marni gave a silent sigh.

There. Now that she'd got all that touchy-feely stuff straight in her head, she squared her shoulders and prepared to make damned sure this went her way. Because she wasn't leaving this room until she'd got her man.

"You feel safe with me?" he repeated, clearly having spent a few seconds mulling that and, if his frown was any indication, not being thrilled by his conclusion.

"I didn't call you a harmless, fluffy bunny rabbit," Marni said with a soft laugh. "I just said I don't believe you're a bully. Not a physical bully, since I was right there enjoying that wall-banging with you. And not a mental bully, since you didn't play head games to try to intimidate me into falling in line on the story."

"The story." Hunter glanced at the desk, where he'd tossed the papers, then back at her. "So what's the deal on that, then? You claim I didn't influence your decision in writing the story. You also say you promised a nun, which is a big promise even if you did grow up together, that you'd keep this information from going public."

Marni took a deep breath and, because she needed to move to keep her thoughts from stuttering, slipped her hands out of his and stepped away.

She poked at the papers, then walked to the window to tweak the curtain open and let some light into the room.

"You okay?" she asked when Hunter winced. He nodded, then gave her an impatient look. *Hurry up with the details,* his eyes screamed. Okay. Time to get this over with.

"I actually did write a piece and submitted it yesterday. My editor contacted me this morning. He's blown away, really excited. He said they'd not only be running it, but he's moving me out of Style."

Hunter's eyes chilled.

He crossed his arms over his chest, steadied his feet as if he was bracing himself, and tilted his head for her to go ahead.

"It's not this article, though," she said, pointing at the deskful of papers. Starting to feel nervous again, she paced between the bed and the window. "Look, before I tell you about the piece I wrote, there's something I need to say."

Hunter waited.

Marni bit her lip, wishing he'd switch off the FBI face but knowing why he couldn't until he knew where the article situation stood.

"I did get on that train because of the Burns story," she confessed. "I knew through, well, a little sleuthing, that you would be working on the case prep. That you'd be a captive source, if you will."

She waited for his anger, but he kept staring, those blue

eyes calm and patient. Marni's stomach churned and she paced faster.

"I didn't poke into your files, though. I didn't search your luggage or try to hack into your laptop or listen to your phone calls, or anything like that."

Still, he stared.

Her pace increased.

"I didn't sleep with you to try to get information. I wouldn't use you like that, or cheapen this thing between us." She waved a hand back and forth between them, like the *thing* was right there, in all its three-dimensional glory. "I have high standards for myself, Hunter. I don't share myself with a man unless I have really strong feelings for him."

She hesitated, then, forcing her feet to stop running between the furnishings, she wrapped her fingers together and gave Hunter a shaky smile.

"I tried to resist this thing—" she gestured again "—between us. I knew it'd ruin my focus. Make me question my judgment in writing the story I was there to write. And worse, that it'd make it seem like I was sleeping my way to success."

He just kept staring.

She was tempted to kick him in the shin just to get a damned reaction.

Finally, he tilted his head as if acknowledging her point.

"I don't think the sex between us had anything to do with your story or my case," he said quietly. "I know you better than that."

Okay. Marni bounced a little in her boots. So far, so good. She could leave it at that, actually. Just clear the air, make sure things were copacetic and be on her way.

She swallowed hard, pretending her feet were nailed to the floor, and called on every bit of nerve she had.

"You know me better than anyone," she confessed. "I come from a huge family, a close family. But you're the first person who listens to me, who gets me. Who really sees me for who I am." She wet her lips, then shrugged. "But maybe that's just a by-product of your job?"

She held her breath, trying to keep her expectant look more interested than desperate.

"Are you asking about my feelings toward you?" he asked, narrowing his eyes. She hated that she couldn't tell what was going on behind them. He had that special agent face on.

Yes, she wanted to cry. Please, take over this conversation, grab the lead and pull the responsibility off her shoulders. She'd be happy to respond to his confession instead of making her own. That'd be so much easier.

She opened her mouth to say that. Then snapped her lips shut. Not because she changed her mind. But because she had no idea how the hell to put it into words without sounding ridiculous.

"I guess I'm trying to explain my own feelings toward you," she finally said, her words low and hesitant. "I wouldn't have slept with you on the train if they weren't strong. I could have resisted the physical attraction between us, but not the emotional one."

He closed his eyes, then reached up to rub two fingers against his temple. What? Was she giving him a headache? But when he opened his eyes again, they were glowing with a delighted kind of joy.

Enough to have her spilling out the rest of her confession.

"I admire you, Hunter. I admire your dedication to your job, and even more how you do the job your way. How you stand for people that others wouldn't. I'm in awe of your mind, at how you think." All of the energy that had made her need to pace, to bounce or move, seeped away. She stepped closer, once again taking his hands in hers as she met his penetrating gaze.

"You make me laugh. You make me think. You're pretty amazing in bed, or against the wall." She grinned when his lips twitched, and then she sighed deeply and confessed, "I love how you see the real me. And in seeing me, how you not only accept me, but encourage and celebrate who I am. You make me feel strong."

Hunter was shaking his head before she'd finished the final word.

"You don't give yourself nearly enough credit for your strength, Marni. I saw it before I knew what your job really was." She winced, but he kept going. "But after I looked into your record, saw the things you've done—and the odds you faced—I was even more impressed with your drive and focus on building the career you want."

Marni's heart melted, going as gooey soft as chocolate in the bright sunshine. She sighed, tilted her head to one side and gave him a tremulous smile.

"I love you," she murmured. "I really, really love you. I love your dedication, your strength, your smile and how you make me feel. Inside and out."

For a second, one miserably long second, Hunter's face went blank. His eyes dimmed. His smile faded. He seemed to freeze in place.

Marni's gooey heart froze, too. For that interminable second, she held her breath, trying to prepare herself for the easy letdown. Trying to convince herself that it wouldn't hurt nearly as much as she kept imagining.

Then, before she could call herself out for being a liar, Hunter pounced. He released her hands, grabbed her by the waist and spun her in a circle before pulling her tightly into his arms.

"I take it you think this is good news?" she asked, her words muffled against his chest.

"Good news?" He pulled back enough to give her the happiest grin she'd ever seen on his gorgeous face. "This is fabulous news. I love you, too. I never thought I'd feel this way. Never thought I'd care so much about anyone, let alone care so much more than I do about my career. I love you. Like I love nothing, no one, else in my life."

Delight and relief surged so strong, Marni almost cried. She managed to laugh instead, giving him the biggest, brightest smile and running her palm over his cheek in a gentle caress.

Her laughter died away at the look of intense passion in his eyes. His kiss was a promise. A bond. A pact that swore their love would not only get a chance, but that it'd flourish and grow. That it was now the most important thing in this powerful, committed man's life.

She didn't realize she'd actually started crying until he pulled away and wiped one tear from her cheek with his thumb.

"Happy tears," she mumbled.

His laugh was sweetly understanding. Then he glanced at the files again.

"I understand if you need to write that story, Marni. I respect people's right to know the truth. Even if I don't always like the timing and how it affects things. Don't put it aside just because of us."

"Oh." She wrinkled her nose, then figuring he wasn't going to take his love back once he heard what she'd done, she shifted out of his arms and offered a lash-fluttering smile. "Well, thanks. But I told you, I wrote a different sort of story."

Hunter sighed, leaned back against the desk and made a gimmee gesture with one hand. His smile stayed mellow, but his eyes were intense, not letting her look away. Marni puffed out a breath, then pulled the story file out of her bag and handed it to him.

"Just so you know, this isn't open for editorializing," she said, wiping her suddenly damp palm on her skirt. "I've already turned it in to my editor, he's already accepted it. It'll run in the next edition of *Optimum*."

He gave her a long, assessing look. As if he was debating whether or not he was okay with that. Then, with a contemplative look on his face, he flipped the folder open.

His eyes rounded with shock. Marni gnawed on her lower lip. His gaze narrowed as he read. Marni pressed a hand to her churning stomach. Not because she was worried he'd be mad. But because she wanted him to be proud.

After a minute or two, she wanted to rip the papers from his hands and read it aloud to him. Hurry, hurry, hurry.

Finally, just about the time she was sure her head was going to explode from nervous excitement, he flipped back to the first page, then closed the file.

"Still love me?" she asked with a shaky smile.

He gave a wordless shake of his head, lifting the file as if to say *wow*.

Good *wow* or bad *wow*?

"You are something else," he told her. "You wrote a profile on my father? You make him sound like, well, like the hero I always think of him as."

Hunter looked away and cleared his throat. Then he tossed the file on the desk, took her hands again and lifted them to his lips in the most romantic gesture of her life.

"I don't even have the words to thank you for writing such an incredible story. I've always been proud of my father, of his work. But I'm honored to see it laid out in such a remarkable way."

Relief surged so strong, Marni's knees almost gave out.

"I have to ask, though. Why did you change your focus? I know you talked a lot about biographies and stuff, but I thought that was just a cover."

"It was and it wasn't. The thing is, the more I talked about it, the more I worked on the profile of my aunt, just in case you happened to peek over my shoulder, the more I remembered how much I loved writing them. The more I researched for the Burns story, though, the more I dug into your history, and your father's. I was fascinated." She thought of those days with her aunt, their talks and the decisions Robin had helped her make. "I realized that while I might be good at hard-hitting news, it was the people in the news that captivated me. That's what I wanted to focus on."

She wet her lips, then touched the tips of her fingers to the folder before giving him a smile.

"I sent the piece on my aunt to my editor, too. He's excited to run it, as well. Instead of becoming one of the minor players in the news department, I'm being given my own segment each month. Profiles, by Marni Clare. And I couldn't, wouldn't have ever done it without you."

Just saying it made her shiver.

But not as much as the look of pride and delight on Hunter's face as he drew her closer. His fingers tangled in her hair while he gently took her lips in a tribute. Marni fell into the kiss, delighting in the passion flaming between them, the commitment whispered in that soft meeting of their mouths.

Slowly, so deliciously slow, Hunter pulled his mouth away from hers. She forced her eyes open, needing to see his face when she asked her last question.

"So, you're really happy about the story?"

"I'm really happy about the story," he assured her.

"Good. Because your biographical profile will run next month." When his mouth dropped, a horrified look skating through his gaze, she grinned and fluttered her lashes. "What can I say? I love you so much, I had to share how wonderful you are with the world."

Epilogue

MARNI HAD THOUGHT TELLING Hunter she loved him was scary. And she'd been crazy nervous over his reaction to her new career focus, and his special place at the center of it. But those nerves, that fear, had nothing on the acrobatics going on in her stomach at that very moment. It was like butterflies, bats and dragons were square-dancing.

"I really shouldn't be here," she murmured from her safe, cozy spot in the passenger side of the car, her seat belt still firmly in place despite the fact that Hunter had shut off the car and had one hand on the door latch.

"Of course you should. Besides the birthday bash, we need to celebrate you helping me put Burns away for life." Hunter gave her a knowing look, then reached over to unwrap her fingers from themselves, so her hand was twined with his instead. "This is my family. I want them to meet you. To know the woman I'm in love with. And I want you to meet them."

"I get that your father is family," she said, half turning in her seat to give him a curious look. "But I didn't realize you were related to the Black clan. I found a ton of information on them when I was researching the articles." A ton was an understatement. "I know you were college roommates with the oldest sibling, Caleb, right? Is that why you consider them family? Because of that?"

"The connections crisscross and bisect. My father spent half of his career trying to nail Tobias Black. Somewhere along the way, they became tight friends. But you know that. You wrote the profile." After giving her an appreciative smile, Hunter glanced at the house, a two-story Victorian complete with fancy gingerbread and a colorful garden. "And like you said, Caleb and I were roommates. His sister, Maya, is married to Simon. He's FBI and was one of my agents at one time."

"I thought the family, except for Caleb who was DEA, were all con artists," she interrupted, drawing her knee up and turning more fully. Her fingers itched for a pencil. This family was the stuff fiction was made of. Or seriously enthralling profiles.

"Yep. Well, officially, Tobias and Maya retired years ago. Gabriel was still on the take when I brought him in last year."

"You arrested your best friend's brother?"

"My protégée did. Danita Cruz. Or Danita Black now, I guess."

She hadn't found that out in her research. Marni knew her eyes were round to the point of falling out, but she couldn't help it.

"Gabriel Black, con extraordinaire, is married to an FBI agent? One who arrested him?"

Hunter laughed. "Be sure to use that phrase with him. He'll love it."

"One of the most notorious families of con artists, and each one is tied in some way to a federal agent?"

"Sure." Hunter shrugged. "You're going to love them. And the food. Pandora serves up some great eats. There are bound to be aphrodisiacs, so this will be fun."

Paying no attention to her jaw hanging on her chest, Hunter gave her fingers a squeeze, then let go and exited the car. Marni had no choice but to follow.

Aphrodisiacs?

Curiosity fought with nerves. They all sounded fascinating. And, she tried to swallow past the lump in her throat, totally intimidating.

Do-si-do, and here we go. She pressed one hand against her churning belly, then took a deep breath and plastered on her brightest smile, hoping the strength of it would shield her a little.

As she joined Hunter at the sidewalk, Marni started to head up the walk. But he caught her hand before she took a step and pulled her back into his arms.

Marni sank into the kiss, her nerves dissipating quickly as passion left no room for anything else in her body. But just as her lips were warming and her body heating, Hunter pulled away.

She murmured her protest, slowly opening her eyes and giving him a questioning smile.

"What was that for? Afraid to introduce a nervous mess to your family?"

"Maybe I just wanted to remind you that you love me before you face the craziness and question your choice," he teased. Then, his smile still in place, his eyes cooled. He glanced quickly toward the door, then, for the first time since she'd known him, looked a little worried.

Marni's earlier stomach churning do-si-do turned into a spastic jig as her nerves returned with a vengeance. Was he worried about his friends and family reacting to her? Nervous for her to meet them? Concerned over bringing a reporter into their midst?

Sucking in a deep breath, she pressed her palm against her stomach to try to calm the frantic dance.

"There's something I want to do before we go inside," Hunter said, his words so quiet they were almost carried away in the wind. "Something I want to say."

"Okay." Needing a little distance to brace herself, Marni stepped back just a bit.

And was instantly horrified when Hunter stepped back even farther. Could she just dive into the car and wait until this little birthday celebration was over? Then, after another quick glance toward the house, he puffed out a deep breath and grabbed her hands before she could make her dash for the safety of the car.

"I love you," he said.

That's all it took for Marni's nerves, fears and urge to flee to disappear. She gave him a bright smile, ready for whatever follow-up he was going to offer.

"I want to marry you."

Her brain stopped.

Hunter reached into his pocket and pulled out a small velvet box, flipping the lid and holding it out.

Her mouth dropped.

Her eyes shot from the ring, sparkling in the setting sunlight, to Hunter's implacable face, then back again.

She couldn't find the words.

She couldn't even find her breath.

Frowning, he shot a glance at the house again, then shook his head at her.

"You really should say yes. Avoid all of those what's-your-relationship-status, why-haven't-you-introduced-a-woman-to-the-family-before questions when we go inside," he suggested, sounding a little nervous.

Marni blinked.

"You want me to agree to marry you because you think it'll make your family behave better?"

That broke his stoic expression, making him bark with laughter.

"Hardly. I want you to marry me because I love you. Because I want us to spend our lives together, to build a future together. To celebrate this love every single day."

Her heart, already his, melted with love. All Marni could do was whisper yes, reaching one hand up to cup his cheek as she stood on tiptoe to brush a kiss over his mouth.

Hunter wasn't having any of that gentle, sweet stuff, though.

He grabbed her close, taking the kiss from gentle to intense with one swift thrust of his tongue. Marni's body joined her heart in the meltdown.

"Yes?" he clarified, shifting back just a little.

"Yes," she repeated, laughing.

As if afraid she'd change her answer, Hunter quickly slid the ring onto her finger.

Before she could even get a good look at it, though, he pulled her right back into the kiss.

When she finally eased back to beam up at him, Marni noticed there were at least a half-dozen faces pressed to the house's front window. Her laughter rang out, even as Hunter groaned.

Still laughing, Marni snuggled tight into his arms, then sighed with delight.

"Just so you know," she warned quietly, tilting her hand this way and that to watch the last of the day's sunbeams dance off the diamond, "our engagement is going to make my family crazy. And they aren't nice enough to wait behind a window. They'll grill you, nag you and drive you absolutely batty."

"They can't be that bad, can they?"

Marni brushed a kiss over his mouth, then, with her

hand snuggled in his, headed up the walkway to meet the people he loved.

"Oh, they can. You've been warned. But you can't get out of it," she said, curling her fist tight over the ring.

Hunter stopped to kiss her again, then shook his head.

"Sweetheart, I promise. We're in this together, forever."

* * * * *

TAWNY WEBER

COMING ON STRONG

Prologue

"I DON'T THINK I can go through with it," Belle Forsham said, one hand pressed to her chest. Beneath the beaded silk of her bodice, her heart raced like a terrified rabbit. "I mean, this is crazy, you know? What the hell was I thinking?"

"If I recall, you were thinking that Mitch Carter was the hottest piece of ass you'd ever seen," Sierra Donovan said absently, her attention focused on getting the fluffy white tulle arranged just so over Belle's blond curls.

"I said I *thought* he'd be the hottest piece of ass," Belle corrected, frowning at the image in the mirror. It was like watching herself through a Halloween filter. "I haven't been able to find out how hot he really is, though, have I? Which is why I'd be insane to go through with this, isn't it? Like, you know, buying a poked pig or something?"

"Pig in a poke?"

"Whatever."

Sierra just laughed and, with one last fluff of the veil, stepped back to gauge the results. "You look so...virginal."

Her best friend's tone said it all. Virginal was the last image Belle had ever aspired toward. Then again, she'd never figured on being a bride, either.

Wild and free, that was Belle's motto. Or it had been, right up until she'd met Mitch Carter. Then mottos had been nudged aside for her new obsession. Getting Mitch into bed.

Mitch was her daddy's new VP of Development. The man was gorgeous. Rich auburn hair, cinnamon-brown eyes and the tightest butt she'd ever ogled. He exuded an energy that fascinated Belle. Power, definitely, and drive. A kind of intense focus that promised a woman that once she had his attention, he'd give her the most incredible sex of her life.

And Belle wanted his attention. But while she'd practically panted at his feet, he'd barely acknowledged her. For a woman used to men drooling on her buffed and polished toes, he'd been a total challenge. She threw herself at him, he gave her polite acknowledgment. She flirted, he watched. She pursued, he evaded.

Hard to get? Hell, Mitch Carter was damn near impossible.

At least, to get into bed. For some bizarre reason, after about a month of chasing him, he'd turned the tables. To use his own words, he'd started courting her. She smothered a baffled laugh at the idea of it. They'd mostly attended business functions, family events with her father, the occasional romantic dinner.

Unable to pace in the voluminous dress, Belle fidgeted on the stool where she sat. Her fingers fiddled with her late mother's pearl necklace, so sweetly innocent as it circled with a heavy weight of expectation around her neck. Like the white dress and delicate veil, the pearls really didn't suit her. Of course, neither did marriage.

Three months of dating. A smoking-hot kiss at the end of the evening. A little touchy-feely to add to the thrill. But never more. God, she'd wanted more. Then he'd scared the hell out of her when, out of the blue, he'd popped the question. Marriage. He wanted to make an honest woman of her…which was just plain weird since he hadn't tried her dishonest ways first.

She'd been so hot for him, she'd agreed instantly. She'd rushed the wedding plans, pulled out all the stops and organized a ritzy society event in less than three months. Through all the planning, something she'd proven to be amazingly skilled at, she'd had one thought and one thought only.

Hurry it up so she could get to her wedding night.

But now, when faced with the actual nuptials, she wasn't sure it was the right thing to do.

"Sierra, am I crazy to marry Mitch after only knowing him six months? I mean, is this too fast?"

Her friend opened her mouth, most likely to offer some dumb platitude about bridal jitters. It wasn't nerves, though. Belle didn't know what it was, but the lead weight in her stomach made her feel trapped, terrified. She'd much rather feel jittery anxiety instead.

Then Sierra shrugged, her own worry clear.

"I don't know," she admitted, chewing off her lipstick as she started to pace the room. Her typical in-your-face honesty and her maid-of-honor duty to keep Belle from freaking out were obviously at odds.

"Does it matter, though? You've wanted Mitch since you first saw him and now you're getting him. Long-term, even. You'll have killer sex tonight and blow his mind. Happy-ever-after, all that crap—that'll come with time."

Crap, indeed. The last thing anyone would call Belle was naive, but compared with the cynical Sierra she was a wide-eyed romantic. Whenever she thought past the honeymoon, let herself focus on anything besides the killer sex she was anticipating, she felt ill. She understood honeymoons. They were all about indulging in decadent sex in as many ways, places and times as possible. But marriage? Oh, God. She pressed her hand to her stomach, hoping she didn't get sick all over her dress. Was she ready to get married?

Belle stared at her reflection. White satin, seed beads and tulle. It all went perfectly with the pearls. Sweet and innocent. Definitely not her style. Her first choice for a dress had been sexy and edgy, but she'd thought Mitch would like this better.

"I guess that establishes why I'm marrying him," she said slowly. She loved him. Or, at least, she thought she did. Or, at least, she figured what she felt was probably love. She was fascinated by his kisses and his mind. By the sexual energy that simmered just under the surface. She was willing to make a promise to Mitch and keep it. Add to that the fact that she was agreeing to tie herself to the guy before he'd given her a single orgasm…well, that had to be love.

So, yes, she was ready for marriage.

"But why is he marrying me?" she asked in a whisper.

"Why don't you find out?" Sierra prompted for, like, the millionth time. "Quit second-guessing yourself and trying to please him and just ask."

Confront him? Straight up ask for possible rejection? Hell no. One thing Belle had learned watching her late mother's bout with cancer was "what you don't know won't hurt you until later." She'd rather take her chances with the unknown.

"I'm just saying, if you want to know why Mitch is marrying you, he's the guy to ask," Sierra said, her tone making it obvious she knew she was wasting her breath. "He's marrying you because he loves you, of course."

"What?" Surprised, she and Sierra both spun around to see Belle's other bridesmaid, Mitch's sister, Lena.

Average height, average features, pale brown hair cut in an unfortunate bob that did nothing to hide her very high forehead, Lena looked nothing like her brother. Belle had first met her when the woman had flown in from Pennsylvania a week earlier. Where Mitch was dynamic, Lena was tepid. It was hard to believe the two of them were even related.

Belle wanted to like her, but it was a struggle. She'd first suggested Lena join the wedding party in an attempt to make nice with Mitch's family. But the other woman had a mocking, judgmental air about her that grated on Belle's nerves. She was trying to ignore it, though. After all, this was her new sister-in-law.

"He must be madly in love with you," Lena pointed out as she inched into the room. The pale rose bridesmaid dress that looked so sexy on Sierra made Lena look like a fluffy pink marshmallow. "Why else would he give up on his goals to get married?"

What goals was Mitch giving up? Belle gave Sierra a confused frown, then looked at Lena.

"Well, sure, partnership with your father is a huge incentive since Mitch had only planned on a short-term association with Forsham Hotels. It was the last step in his plan to take his construction company to the next level." She said all this while gliding an ugly shade of nutmeg lipstick over her thin lips. Then she met Belle's eyes in the mirror and shrugged. "His own development firm. He was counting on the experience and, you know, connections to help him out. Of course, I don't have to tell you how ambitious and determined to succeed he is."

"Partnership?" Belle frowned. What partnership?

"You didn't know?" Lena's mouth rounded to match

the oops look in her brown eyes. "I'm so sorry. Maybe he was saving the news as a wedding surprise."

"He's a vice president, not a partner," Sierra said, sounding as confused as Belle. "I thought he didn't have enough money or land to bring to the table for that kind of a deal."

"Well, yeah. But Uncle Danny said Mitch was given one of those offers he couldn't refuse. I guess your daddy's backing a risky land deal with the agreement that Mitch develop it for him. Aunt Edna said he saw a perfect opportunity and made the most of it." Lena gave a little who-knows shrug and a wide smile. Neither hid the malice peeking out from her simpering demeanor.

All those family names blurred in Belle's mind. She'd been so excited to be a part of a large family, for the first time since she was eight to have more than just her and her dad at the Thanksgiving table. But after meeting Mitch's relatives, she wasn't so sure. It was like coming up against a very large, very cohesive wall. And she was on the wrong side of it.

Lena babbled more family gossip and inane insights into Mitch's personality. Belle just stared, her mind numb.

A risky land development? Her father wouldn't go into a project like that with just anyone. It would require a family commitment. Had he offered to make Mitch family? Or had Mitch offered to marry her in order to get the deal? And what did that make her? The price he had to pay for success? An easy route to the top?

Recognition, denial and sharp pain twisted together in her stomach. She'd wanted to believe he was marrying her because he couldn't resist, because he was crazy for her. But she'd obviously been wrong.

It all made sense now. His reluctance for intimacy, his emotional distance. Her earlier bridal jitters turned to cramping nausea. He was marrying his way into a business deal.

Lena's overarched brows drew together above her gleaming eyes. "You look a little green. Are you feeling okay?"

"Of course she's not," Sierra snapped. "What are you thinking, coming in here and spewing ugly rumors like that? What kind of person goes around gossiping about her brother on his wedding day?"

"Stepbrother," Lena corrected with a pout. "My dad married his mom when we were teenagers. And you're the nasty one. I was just saying that Belle's lucky that Mitch loves her enough to give up his dreams of his own development firm to work for her father. I wasn't insinuating anything else."

Lena wasn't his real sister? Why hadn't he told her? Belle didn't know why, but that was the last straw. She stood, the stool pressing against her full skirt like the bars on a cage. She wanted to run, but where? To Mitch? Hardly.

"The hell you weren't trying to cause trouble," Sierra growled at Lena. Their voices seemed to be coming from a long way away, muffled by the buzzing in Belle's head. "You're intimating that Belle's father bought her a groom. Like she or Mitch would be that desperate."

"Desperate? No. But when you put it that way, the wedding does sound a little fishy, doesn't it?" Lena gave them a wounded look, then headed for the door. Once there, she glanced over her shoulder. "Of course, I'm sure Belle knows Mitch loves her more than any silly promotion. I mean, who gets married without hearing vows of love? And Mitch never lies, not even for a business deal."

Sierra's cusswords hit Lena's retreating back. The brunette stormed to the door.

"Sierra" was all Belle said.

"I'm taking her down. That bitch isn't getting away with ruining your day."

For just one second, Belle let herself imagine Sierra jumping Lena and pummeling the smirk off her face. For the first time in her life, she considered diving in to help instead of yelling encouragement from the sidelines. Unlike her friend, Belle hated arguments.

Before she could decide whether or not to encourage Sierra to chase the woman's passive-aggressive ass down, Belle's father strode through the door. Handsome as ever in his tux, he winked at Sierra, then gave his only child a doting smile.

"You're a beautiful bride, sweetheart. Mitch is a lucky man."

Lucky? Really. It sounded like Mitch and her dad were the lucky ones. After all, they'd made the deal between them. She felt like the booby prize. She sucked in a shuddering breath, trying to calm the nausea rolling through her system. It would be so easy to just go through with this. She wasn't stupid. She'd known Mitch didn't love her. She wasn't sure she loved him, although she'd been willing to convince herself she did. But, like this stupid schoolgirl wedding dress, she'd been trying to give him whatever he wanted. And he couldn't even give her the truth?

Tears stung her eyes as she mentally kissed happyever-after, *and all that crap,* goodbye. Which didn't suck nearly as much as being cheated out of her wedding night.

Belle swallowed hard and looked into the face of the only man she'd ever felt safe loving. "Daddy? Did you offer to make Mitch your partner?"

Oblivious as usual to his daughter's emotional state, Franklin Forsham shrugged and patted her shoulder. "Not to worry, sweetie. I won't work him too hard."

Belle's gaze met Sierra's. Sympathetic tears washed away the anger in her friend's vivid blue eyes.

Numb now, Belle looked past her father's broad shoulders through the open door to the archway leading to the chapel. She could see the swags of orchids and pink roses, hear the soft tones of the harp. Her storybook wedding awaited.

She couldn't do it. She wasn't a negotiating point or a piece of property to be acquired in a business deal.

"I can't go through with the wedding," she declared, gathering the slick folds of her white satin skirt in her fist. "I won't sell myself. I might be willing to change, to compromise, but I draw the line at being lied to and cheated."

"What are you talking about?" Franklin's face turned white, then red. Hands clenched, he looked like he wanted to hit someone. "Mitch cheated on you?"

Scared of the anger on her father's face, of the pain pouring through her, Belle just shrugged. Cheated on her, cheated her, what was the difference? Emotion choked her, heated tears washed down her cheeks. Unable to hold back her sobs, she threw herself into her father's arms.

This was the last time she'd ever let a man, or the promise of hot sex, mean a damned thing to her.

1

Six years later

"I FOUND A REPLACEMENT for Gloria, Mr. Carter. Everyone says this is the best event planner on the West Coast."

Unspoken was the understanding that Mitch would accept nothing less than the best. Which was difficult, considering his luxury resort was six weeks from opening to the public and had been beset by one problem after another. The most recent was the loss of the woman he'd contracted to handle all the resort events.

"Call me Mitch," he absently told his new assistant. He motioned to the vacant seat opposite his desk, but she shook her head, preferring to stand.

She'd been here a couple of weeks, but Diana was still jumpy and nervous. He knew he was demanding of his employees and it definitely made it easier to demand if they were on a first-name basis, so she'd better get over her timidity soon. They were almost at the end of his Mr. Nice Guy two-week break-in period.

He took the papers she handed him and in one glance was thrown back in time. Shocked, Mitch stared at the glossy dossier. The black-and-white photo didn't do justice to Belle Forsham's fairylike beauty. It didn't capture the gleam of her tousled blond curls, or the wicked tilt of her sea-green eyes. The shadows accented her sharp features, the light reflecting off her smile.

The best? Yeah, she was. Good enough to make a man stupid. He glared at that smile, irritated with his body's reaction. Belle Forsham was pure trouble. He knew she was, and still he got hard remembering the taste of her lips. He tried to dull his body's reaction by visualizing himself standing, alone, at the altar.

Yeah, the anger definitely dimmed his desire.

"Mr. Carter?" Diana interrupted his pathetic obsessing. "Do you want me to contact Eventfully Yours? They're perfect for the job given the scope of the resort's needs and what you are looking for in an event planner."

"I'd rather not work with this particular company," he said, making it sound like he'd put some thought into the decision. In reality, no thought was required. Despite how often she showed up in his dreams, usually nude, Belle was at the bottom of the list of women he wanted to see. And she was definitely the last one he'd consider depending on for any aspect of his success.

After all, who knew better just how undependable she was? He tossed the file onto the pile on his desk, the banner on her dossier catching his eye. He sneered. *Society's Planning Princess,* indeed.

"But…I don't understand. Everyone says they're the best. They've worked for a dozen A-list actors, some of the top musicians in the country and any number of politicians. They've arranged club openings, publisher parties, award-ceremony after-parties."

"They're not what I'm looking for," he snapped.

Diana's face fell, making her look like a sad chipmunk. Obviously sticking with her own version of the dress-for-success theory, she wore a tidy suit, stockings and ugly shoes. The overall image was serious efficiency, which was supported by the fact that she did a damned good job. Mitch wouldn't have hired her otherwise. He just wished she'd loosen up. He glanced down at his own jeans and work boots and gave a mental shrug. So she didn't have to loosen up to his level, but a little less formality wouldn't hurt.

"Let's look at the other event planners," Mitch instructed. "Sometimes a reputation is based on perception, rather than how good the firm actually is. I need more than gloss to make this work. If Lakeside is going to succeed, I'm going to need clever, resourceful and intuitive."

He pushed away from his overloaded desk and strode to the wide bank of windows that looked out to the lake. Almost completed, this resort was the culmination of all his dreams. Ten acres of verdant hills, lush gardens and what he secretly referred to as the enchanted forest, Lakeside was going to be the brightest jewel in his development crown and his first venture into hotels. So far he'd launched a half-dozen business parks, a mall and a couple of small restaurants. All of which he'd turned for a sweet profit.

But this resort was more than ambitious. For a guy who'd started out swinging a hammer, it was a huge coup. To kick this venture off here, in Southern California, was ballsy, given that he'd torched his bridges with the top hotelier on the West Coast six years ago.

"I need a creative wizard with killer contacts. Someone who gets what our clientele will want, who can make the resort a posh getaway for the wealthy. If I'm going to turn this into the most talked-about hot spot of the rich and famous, I'm going to need someone who kicks ass."

Diana's mouth worked for a second, then after an obvious internal struggle, she thrust out her chin and pointed to the abandoned dossier on his desk.

"But that's what I've been trying to tell you, *Mitch*. Belle Forsham is all of that. Her events are the most talked-about, the most outside-the-box successes of the last two years. She seems to know everyone, do everything. She…" Diana stopped, wrinkled her nose and took a deep breath before continuing. "She kicks ass."

Amazed she'd finally used his given name, Mitch gave a snort of laughter at the uptight way she said *ass*. Amusement faded as he glanced again at the photo of his ex-fiancée.

When had she gone into event planning? And how the hell had she stuck with it long enough to be such a success? He had to admit, though, she had the intelligence and creativity to make it happen; although she'd always tried to hide the brains behind a flirty flutter of her lashes. She was definitely a social butterfly. He recalled the guest list for their aborted wedding. It had read like the who's who of *People* magazine.

It was the memory of that damned wedding, the humiliation of standing alone in front of all those gawking and snickering witnesses, that cinched it. Mitch ground his teeth, long-simmering anger burning in his gut. Belle might have great ideas, be clever and well-connected. But when the chips were down, she couldn't be counted on.

"She's a flake," he finally said.

"She's the best." Diana held up a sheaf of papers, all recommending Eventfully Yours. "Everything I've heard, all the research I did says that Belle Forsham is the It Girl of events. She's the hottest thing on the West Coast."

Ambition fought with ego. The good of his company versus the biggest humiliation of his past. His need to see Belle again, to see if she was still that intriguing combination of sexy and sweet, battled with his desire to keep the door to that part of his history nailed shut.

Mitch looked over the resort grounds again, the gentle beauty of the sun-gilded lake beckoning him. Reminding him to do his best. A lot was riding on this deal. He'd sunk all his available resources into making this resort the most luxurious, the most welcoming. None of that would matter without guests with big enough wallets to indulge themselves.

He'd screwed himself into a corner once because of Belle Forsham. Or because of his desire to screw her, to be exact. He'd never wanted a woman the way he'd wanted Belle. But she'd been his boss's only child and off-limits. His old-fashioned upbringing and his worry that he'd be disrespecting Franklin if he had wild monkey sex with the guy's daughter had inspired him to the dumbest proposal of his life. Well, that and his idiotic belief that he'd fallen in love with her.

He'd handled it all wrong. He could see that now, but that didn't change the fact that she'd dumped him at the altar, and because of her he'd lost both his job and the respect of his mentor. Which bothered him almost as much as never having the wild Belle-against-the-wall sex he'd wanted so badly.

And he was supposed to welcome her back into his life? Was he willing to make a deal with the sexiest little devil he'd ever known in order to ensure his success?

He thought of his team. They were just as invested in the resort as he was. Because Mitch had little experience in the resort business, he'd brought in two managers—one to oversee the hotel, the other to run the three restaurants. He was the money man, the one with the vision, but he needed each of them on board to handle the hundred-plus employees and make sure the day to day of the operation ran smoothly while he made his vision a reality.

He glanced at the family picture behind his desk. He knew his family took great pride in his accomplishments, just as they had huge expectations for his success. Expectations that included supporting his grandmother and providing jobs for four of his cousins in his company. Those expectations were both a source of pride and a noose around his neck. He had to succeed.

The resort already had enough problems. On top of the usual construction glitches and startup issues, they'd been having a run of bad luck. Losing his event coordinator was just the last in a long string of unexplained setbacks. Could he afford to blow off the perfect planner out of pride?

Damn. He sighed and pushed the file on the desk toward Diana.

"Check her availability."

"THERE'S ONLY ONE MAN who'll satisfy you. Quit stalling and go for it, already."

Belle Forsham stopped pacing across the lush amethyst carpet of her office to roll her eyes at her best friend and business partner. The office was a quirky combination of trendy accessories, sexy textures and practical lines. Much like Belle herself.

"It's not like chasing some guy down for hot sex, Sierra. This is serious. We're talking business here. My father's business. Or should I say, the end of my father's business."

"Exactly. You want to save Forsham Hotels, you need to get help." Sierra flipped open the pink bakery box she'd brought in for their morning meeting and, after a careful perusal, chose a carrot-cheesecake muffin.

Not even looking at the other offerings, Belle automatically went for the fanciest muffin. Rich, chocolaty and decadent, just the way she liked it. Except she was so stressed, she put it down after one bite. Why waste the indulgence?

"I don't need help," she lied.

"Yes, you do. It's not like you and I can plan an event that will save your dad's butt," Sierra shot back, referring to their company, Eventfully Yours, as she licked cream-cheese icing from her thumb.

They were *the* elite event planners on the West Coast, catering to the rich and famous from Southern California up to Monterey. Combining Sierra's fearless attitude and Belle's knack for creative entertainment, the two women had hit the Hollywood scene hard and strong four years back. Eventfully Yours had grown from organizing themed playdates for sitcom divas' Pomeranians to arranging intimate soirees for A-list actors and five hundred of their closest friends.

"You know, now that I think about it, I really shouldn't be going behind my father's back," Belle stalled, sitting on the edge of her inlaid rosewood desk. "He'd be the first to say his heart attack is no reason to treat him like an invalid. If he wanted to make a deal to save the hotels, he'd do it himself."

Used to Belle's habit of squirreling out of anything that made her uncomfortable, Sierra just stared. It was that uncompromising, see-all-the-way-into-her-soul look that Belle hated. Whenever Sierra narrowed her blue eyes and shot her that look, Belle felt like a total wuss.

"Don't you think if my dad wanted to deal with Mitch Carter, he'd approach him himself?" she asked, playing her last excuse.

"Right. Your dad, upstanding guy that he is, is gonna go begging help from the man he fired from a dream VP position and partnership in one of the primo hotel conglomerates in the U.S. The same guy his daughter ditched at the altar."

"Exactly," Belle exclaimed, jumping up from her perch on the desk to throw her arms into the air. "Given our sucky history, why would you think Mitch wants anything to do with me?"

Sierra arched a brow, then gave a little shrug. Taking her time, she dusted the crumbs off her fingers, shifted in the plush chair and curled her long legs under her. Raising one brow, she tapped a manicured nail on her bare ankle.

"This is the guy who refused to have sex with you before marriage. I figure he has some twisted belief in things like honor."

Sierra rolled her eyes at her own words. Always the cynic, she didn't understand the concept of selfless honor. Of course, neither did Belle. But it sure sounded sweet.

"This would also be the same guy who, despite having the perfect opportunity to make your daddy's life a living hell when you ruined their deal, simply shook hands and walked away."

Walked away and left her daddy holding a piece of investment property that, because of zoning and development legalities, was now taking his business down the toilet. But considering what Belle had done, that wasn't really Mitch's fault. Was it?

"So he's freaking hero material," she muttered. "So what?"

Belle slid off her heels so she could pace faster. Nothing slowed down a good pace like four-inch Manolos. The way her luck was running, she'd stumble and break the heel. And she needed to move around and try to shake off the nasty feeling that had settled over her when she'd been reminded of how badly she'd treated Mitch. That he'd broken her heart was no excuse. She knew that now.

But knowing it and being willing to do something about it were definitely two different things.

"Exactly," Sierra agreed. "He's hero material. Which means he's hardwired to ride to the rescue. Even after all that crap went down, Mitch never bad-mouthed you or your father. If he knew how bad things are now, maybe he'd offer some advice. Or best case? He'll step in, checkbook at the ready, and save the company."

Belle grimaced.

Mitch definitely lived by his own code. Over the past six years he'd developed a reputation as the man with the magic touch. Mr. Money, a real estate developer with an eye for success, he was known in the industry as a fair man who played by his own rules, uncompromising, intense and dynamic. People appreciated his generous willingness to share his success, but behind the scenes there were whispers of ruthless payback to anyone who crossed him.

Which didn't bode well for Belle, since she was the one seen as most deserving of Mitch's revenge. Mutual acquaintances still joked that she'd better watch her back. She knew better, though. She'd never mattered enough to him to merit that much attention.

"He won't deal with me," she assured Sierra, playing her trump card.

"You don't know that." The way Sierra said it, as though she had some naughty little secret, made Belle nervous.

"Yes, I do." Belle took a deep breath and, with the air of one confessing a mortal sin, dropped her voice to a loud whisper. "I never told you, but I tried to see Mitch. Two years ago. Remember when I had that car wreck?"

Eyes huge with curiosity, Sierra nodded.

"I was shook up and had some weird idea that being hit in a head-on accident on a one-way street was a sign that I should make amends for all my wicked ways." She met her friend's snort of laughter with a glare. "I figured ditching Mitch topped my wicked list, so I sucked up my courage and went to apologize."

"No way," Sierra breathed. "And you didn't tell me?"

"There was nothing to tell. He was supposedly out of the country."

"Supposedly?"

"Well, I went back a couple weeks later and his assistant said he was out with the flu."

"So?"

"So isn't it obvious? He was avoiding me."

"He left the country and got the flu to avoid you?"

Belle rolled her eyes. "No, that was just B.S. He was probably there in his office telling his assistant to make something up so he didn't have to see me."

Sierra's expression clearly said "you've got to be kidding."

"Don't give me that look. It could be true."

"Only if the roles were reversed. You're the one afraid of confrontation, Belle. Not Mitch. If he were in the office, I'm sure he'd have taken five minutes to personally tell you to kiss his ass."

"And you want me to go chasing the guy for favors?" Belle ignored the confrontation issue. It was true, after all. "We both know he doesn't want anything to do with me."

Sierra hummed, then slid off the chair and crossed to the leather bag she'd tossed on the credenza. She pulled out a file folder with what looked like a printout of an email clipped to it.

Waving the file at Belle, she arched a brow and asked, "Wanna bet?"

"Spill," Belle demanded, making a grab for the folder. Sierra whipped it out of reach with a laugh.

"You really need to have more faith in your impact on people."

"According to you, people are only out for what they can get," Belle shot back.

"Exactly. So while Mitch might happily punish you when it's convenient, the tune changes when he needs something."

"And he needs us?"

"No. He needs you. This gig is right up your alley," Sierra claimed. Which meant it was totally social. Sierra handled the big corporate and studio events, the type of things that required juggling numbers, working with specific images or ground rules. In other words, the more traditional events that relied heavily on organization. Belle's specialty was the over-the-top hedonistic fantasies. And since she'd indulged in so many fantasies about Mitch Carter, the idea of having another shot at sharing a few with him sent her pulse racing.

"Spill," she demanded. She tried to ignore the excitement dancing in her stomach, making her edgy and impatient. This was crazy. Mitch hated her. He had to. But maybe, just maybe, this was her shot at making amends. At fixing the past and helping her father. And maybe, just maybe…at finally getting into his pants.

She'd blown it before, stumbling over that silly marriage idea. But she was older and much more experienced now. This time she'd be smarter. If she and Mitch did find common ground, all she wanted was sex. That, and help for her dad.

She took the file from Sierra with a smile of anticipation. Belle read the email. Then she read it again. The excitement curdled in her stomach.

"A resort grand opening? That's more your gig than

mine," Belle said, trying to ignore the disappointment that settled over her like an itchy wool blanket.

"That's what they say they want. But check out the details I found."

Knowing her friend's instincts were usually spot-on, Belle opened the file. It just took a glance, a quick flip through the papers and plans for her to see the perfect hook to turn his lush resort into the hottest, most exclusive getaway on the West Coast.

Mitch's background was in development. And he was damned good at it. But he was thinking too traditionally for this resort. It wasn't a run-of-the-mill hotel and shouldn't be treated that way. Given the remote beauty of the location, yet its easy access to L.A., it could be the nice luxury vacation place he had outlined. Or it could be the chicest spot for decadence in Southern California. Indulgent weekends, clandestine trysts, decadent fantasies. All there, for a price. All guaranteed to be unique, elite and, best of all, private.

Her blood heated, ideas flashing like strobe lights through her mind. Excitement buzzed, but she tried to tamp it down. There was nothing worse than getting all stirred up, only to be left flat. It was like foreplay with no orgasm. Amusing once or twice, but ultimately a rip-off.

"This email isn't from Mitch himself," she pointed out. "And his assistant isn't offering us the position, she's only checking availability."

"So? Since when have we waited for an engraved invitation to charm our way into a job?"

Good point. The two women had spent their first year in business clubbing and hitting every social event they could wiggle or charm their way into on the off chance of finding clients. Once at a fashion show someone had mentioned a director's wife with a penchant for poodles and Motown. The next day Belle contacted the director and suggested he throw his wife a surprise party, with the musical dog theme. Such ballsiness paid off both in contacts and jobs as they'd built Eventfully Yours.

But this was different. Mitch probably hated her. Then again, why would he be willing to work with her if he was holding a grudge? Belle sighed, not sure if her reasoning was sound or pure bullshit.

"We have an opportunity to kick ourselves to the next level with a job this exclusive," Sierra said quietly as she settled back in her chair. "Better yet, you have a chance here to settle up some past debts, get some of that fabled closure. Are you going to let semantics stop you?"

Was she? Belle glanced at Sierra, noting the assured confidence on her friend's angular face. Sierra wouldn't push unless she thought it was really important. She might be a relentless nag when it came to the success of Eventfully Yours, but she was a good friend and would never sacrifice Belle to snag a client. Even one as potentially huge as MC Development.

Belle had spent the past six years regretting her screwup. She should have faced Mitch herself instead of running like a wuss. Hell, she should never have agreed to marriage in the first place. She'd known better. Sex, as incredible as it might have been, was no reason to go off the deep end. But she'd been afraid to push the issue, then after the altar-ditch, too hurt and upset to face his anger.

Ever since, she'd tried to find a guy to replace him, both in her bed and her fantasies. None had stuck, though. Probably because she'd never actually had Mitch. This might be her chance to get over him, once and for all.

She glanced back at the files, the panoramic photo of the resort and its welcoming lakeside forest. She wanted to see it in person. Even more, she wanted to do Mitch, right there on the edge of that lake. Outdoor sex in the woods, like something out of a fairy tale. The orgasm she was imagining was probably mythical, too. But she didn't care. She wanted to find out.

Despite the nerves clawing at her, she set the file down, slipped her shoes on and grabbed her purse.

"Shopping?" Sierra asked, sliding her feet into her shoes, too.

"We'll start with lingerie. I heard about this new place called Twisted Knickers. The designs supposedly take provocative to a whole new level."

FOCUSED ON HIS CONVERSATION, Mitch strode past Diana's desk with his cell phone glued to his ear. His assistant waved her hand, trying to get his attention, but he held up one finger, then pointed to his office door. He'd talk to her when he was done.

"I don't want any more excuses," Mitch ordered his foreman. "The electrical has to be finished by the first of the month." This damned week had gone downhill fast. There'd been even more building delays, his designer had gone into labor two months early, and now electrical problems. To top it off, he'd talked to three event planners so far and none had come close to sparking his interest. He was wound so tight, he was ready to snap. "The plumbing is already three weeks behind. If we lose any more ground, we won't open on schedule. If that happens, we're screwed."

He listened to his foreman's justifications with half an ear as, still ignoring Diana's increasingly frantic gestures, he opened his office door. As always, the view of the lush green woods through the window beckoned him. Maybe he'd go for a run, shake off some of the tension. He'd rather have a long, sweaty roll in the sheets, but he couldn't afford the distraction. Not when everything was on the line.

One more step into his office and Mitch felt like he'd been hit in the face. Maybe it was sex on the brain, but even the air shifted, turning sultry and suggestive. He breathed in, his lungs filling with a musky floral scent.

Instant turn-on.

Seated as she was in the high-backed leather chair facing the window, all Mitch could see were long, sexy legs ending in strappy black do-me heels. He tried to swallow, but his mouth had gone dirt-dry. Those were wrap-around-the-shoulders-and-ride-'em-wild legs.

Damn. Talk about distraction.

Mitch flipped his phone closed, not sure if he'd said goodbye or even if his foreman was still talking. He stepped farther into the office, deliberately closing the door behind him. Two more steps into the room, and he could see around the high leather back of the chair.

Gorgeous. The impact was like getting kicked in the gut by a black belt on steroids. Swift, intense and indefensible. The first time he'd seen Belle, she'd been twenty-one. He'd thought then she couldn't possibly be more confident in her own sexual power. He'd obviously been wrong, since she was now a master of it. Or was that mistress? And why did that make him crave studded black leather shorts?

Six years had added layers of polish, maturity and assurance to her already powerful sexual charisma. Mitch's gaze reluctantly left those delicious legs to travel upward. He noted the flirty green skirt, the same shade as her eyes, ending a few inches above her knees. A wide leather belt accented her waist and emphasized her lush breasts in the gossamer-soft white blouse. Mitch let his eyes rest there for just a second, millions of regrets pounding in his head. He wished like hell that once, just once, he'd tasted their bounty.

He was sure if he had, he'd have easily kept her out of his mind. The only reason he'd never found another woman to replace her was that he'd blown the fantasy of sex between them all out of proportion.

He felt her amusement before he even looked at her face. Belle was used to being ogled, so he didn't waste time on embarrassment. He wondered briefly at giving her that much power this early in the game, but he couldn't seem to help himself. That there was a game afoot was implicit. The question wasn't who would win, either. It was how much it would cost him to play.

She arched one platinum brow, amused challenge clear in her eyes and the dimple that played at the corner of her full lips. Her hair was shorter now, angled to emphasize her rounded cheekbones and the sharp line of her jaw.

"Well, well," Mitch drawled, moving around to lean on his desk while he faced the biggest mistake of his life. "If it isn't my long-lost bride."

2

"LONG-LOST BRIDE-TO-BE, if you please," Belle corrected precisely.

She had to work to keep her smile in place. As much as she'd have preferred to avoid reference to their past, she'd known Mitch, for all his gentlemanly reputation, wouldn't sidestep the issue. She took a little breath before she lifted her chin. Since she had to deal with it, she'd face it head-on.

Or at least make him think she was dealing with it just long enough to flirt her way off the topic.

"Don't you look gorgeous," she commented with a wink. Since he'd made no attempt to hide his visual tour, she let her eyes take their own leisurely stroll, appreciating the view from head to toe.

Damn, he really had gotten better with age. His hair, still that deliciously rich auburn, was a little longer, a little less formal. His face was leaner, his shoulders broader. She was tempted to ask him to turn around so she could decide if his ass was any tighter. But it was awfully hard to beat perfection, so she doubted it.

"The years have definitely treated you well, Mitch."

Beneath her husky words and confident smile, her insides felt as though they were on a wobbly roller coaster. Despite that, she slid to her feet in one slow, sensual motion. His cinnamon-brown eyes blurred as she stepped forward. Heat flared between them, the same heat that had lured her from interested to obsessive so long ago.

Then, so quickly she wondered if she'd imagined the desire, he blinked and the look switched to simple curiosity. Belle had to fight to keep her smile in place. Damn him, that's how he'd always twisted her into knots. One second she'd been sure he was hot for her, the next he had total control.

Not this time.

Instead of the expected move, another step closer so she was in body-heat distance of him, Belle shifted her weight. Her hip to one side, she lifted a shoulder and gave a flutter of her lashes.

"Well?" she asked.

Mitch just arched one brow. His shoulders, she noted, were stiff, as though he was preparing himself. For what? she wondered. A handshake, a hug or, even worse, a big sloppy kiss.

She was tempted. But lurking behind that polite curiosity in his eyes was something edgier. Perhaps he was just waiting to verbally rip into her. Instead of intimidating her, that just added to the excitement.

"Well, what?"

Some insane impulse urged Belle to blurt out an apology. To tell him how sorry she was for the pain she must have caused. To confess her immaturity, her lack of consideration. Luckily, nerves trapped the words in her throat.

"Did you miss me?" she asked instead. Getting Mitch to deal with her, to give her the contract and with it the opening to butter him up so he'd help her father was going to be hard enough. Why throw fuel on the flames? Especially when she was much more interested in starting a whole new fire.

"About as much as I miss the Macarena," he shot back.

Belle snickered. Then, unable to help herself, she laid her hand on his forearm. "It is good to see you again."

Eyes narrowed, he glanced down at her hand, then back at her face. With a shrug, he gave a half smile and jerk of his chin. Only an optimist would call it a nod. Belle, being a glass-half-full kind of gal, took heart.

"Why are you here?"

"Right to the point, hmm?" Belle used the seconds it took her to return to her seat to take a deep breath. Control was crucial here. She had to play it just right.

With that in mind, she leaned back against the soft leather and gave Mitch a warm smile.

"I've got something you need," she told him.

"I'll pass," he responded instantly. "I tried to get it once before and look how that worked out."

Belle hid her wince. Whether the pain in her chest was from a singed ego or her bruised heart she didn't know.

"Maybe you were using the wrong inducement."

"Obviously," he said. Apparently resigned to the fact that she wasn't going to explain her presence until she was good and ready, he moved around his desk to take a seat.

"Oh, please. Let's be realistic. I was young and hot for you. For what I imagined would be incredible sex between the two of us. I wasn't looking for marriage, but that was the price you put on yourself." Talk about role reversal. She might be a jerk for her way of handling the situation, but he was a bigger jerk for being willing to use *her* lust to advance *his* career. But if she wasn't holding any grudges, why should he? "We'd have been much better off if you'd just gone for the kinky affair I was hoping for instead of insisting on milking the free cow."

"Why buy the cow if you can get the milk for free," he corrected.

"There you go," she said with a smile. "Except we were both after something other than milk, weren't we?"

She'd wanted sex, he'd wanted a foot up the career ladder. Neither one of them came off lily-pure, so she didn't bother pointing that out. Instead, she leaned down to pull a file out of her black leather portfolio.

"I understand you need an event planner."

Mitch's jaw tightened, but he just gave a dismissive shrug. His shirt rippled over arms that looked very intriguing. She'd bet there were some sweet biceps under that pristine cotton. Her teeth itched to take a nibble and see just how hard his muscle was.

"I might have considered a planner for the grand opening, but I'm not overly attached to the concept," he hedged.

Which meant he wanted one, he just didn't want it to be her. No problem. She'd change his mind.

"That's smart," she said, leaving the file in her lap instead of handing it to him. "Your grand opening should make a statement, of course. But you want that message to integrate with Lakeside's theme, its purpose."

"This isn't Disneyland," he pointed out, rolling his eyes.

"No, but you would do well to look at the success of theme parks like that. They have a clear message. A purpose that fulfills the guests' specific needs. Everything they offer, every single thing, supports that purpose."

"My resort has a purpose. You grew up in the hotel business, you already know this."

"But you're not trying to launch a hotel here, are you? You aren't targeting the average vacationer, honeymoon couple or getaway guest."

"I'm not?"

Even though he phrased it as a question, his tone was

pure let's-humor-the-airhead. She was used to people taking one look at her blond hair and sexy image and judging her by stereotypes. Since it usually worked to her advantage, Belle didn't mind. At least, she told herself she didn't. It wasn't like Mitch knew her well enough to understand her or anything. So she fell into her typical lure-'em-in-and-close-the-deal mode with a flutter of her lashes.

"Are you? What do you see this resort offering?" she asked offhandedly.

"Offering? What any resort offers, of course. First-class luxury accommodations. Relaxation and pampering. The perfect getaway."

"I can get luxury and pampering at my father's hotels for half the price," she pointed out.

His eyes flashed at the mention of her father. Uh-oh, not a good sign. But instead of commenting, he just pointed out the window.

"Not with this lavish view, prime location or decadent opulence. Lakeside is top-of-the-line. Luxurious suites, each with its own fireplace and bar. Three-hundred-count Egyptian sheets and down comforters, one-of-a-kind artwork and a stunning view from every room. We have the hottest golf course, three four-star restaurants, a ballroom, spa, designer shops."

Belle pressed her lips together to hide the smile brought on by his fervent recital of his resort's brochure. He sounded like a mama defending her baby against the crime of mediocrity. Good, that meant he was heavily invested in making Lakeside the biggest success possible.

"Let's cut to the chase, hmm?" she said once she was sure she could keep the triumph from her tone. "To really make your resort stand out, to make it a certifiable success, you need a hook. If you want the wealthy Southern California clientele to flock here like flaming moths you're going to need to offer something a little more exotic than nice sheets, a golf course and hot stone massages."

"Moths to a flame," he corrected.

"Exactly," she agreed with a wink. "And like those moths, the wealthy and famous will swarm here. With the right incentive, of course."

"What do you have in mind?" he asked, sounding reluctantly intrigued. His gaze fell to the papers in her lap.

She tapped one red-tipped fingernail on the file and smiled.

"To use that Disney analogy again, I'm talking about a theme park for adults. Wealthy adults. Or better yet, famous wealthy adults. Ones who are looking for a grown-up park to play in."

Belle leaned forward to put the file on his desk. Mitch's gaze dropped to her cleavage. From the heat in his eyes, the way they went dark and intense, she figured her Twisted Knickers leather-and-lace demi-bra had just paid off.

"You want to make this resort a standout, you need to cater to the rich and famous. If you want them lining up to get in here, you need to offer them the one thing they want more than anything else. The one thing they'd pay almost any price for."

Keeping his eyes locked on hers, Mitch used one finger to pull the file toward him. He didn't flip it open, but sat there with his hand over it as if considering whether it was even worth the effort.

"And that is?" he finally asked.

"Sex, of course."

MITCH'S JAW DROPPED. This was a multimillion dollar venture, prime real estate, and he had everything on the line—his money, his company and, even more important, his reputation.

"You're suggesting I turn my luxury resort into a sex club?"

He didn't know why the idea surprised him. Everything about Belle made him think of sex. It always had. From her husky voice to her bedroom eyes and on down that gorgeous body to her suckable toes.

But he'd screwed up his career once because he'd been obsessed with her. Blinded by the dream of having it all, he'd tossed aside his own plans to accommodate her and her father's wishes, and ended up with nothing. It'd taken him three years to rebuild his reputation, another two to regain lost ground. He wasn't about to screw up again.

"Actually, I doubt you'd be able to pull off the sex club," she replied with a long look that made it clear she'd love to see him try. "There are some fabulous ones around that make good money, of course, but that's not quite the niche I had in mind."

It took physical effort to keep himself from asking her just how familiar she was with these *fabulous* sex clubs. He managed, just barely, to smother the biting jealousy that clawed at his gut when he imagined her hitting those clubs with another man. Or, given the clubs, other *men*.

Dammit, six years ago, that ugly green monster had goaded him into proposing marriage instead of taking her up on the wild sexual affair she'd offered. He hated—not just disliked, but viciously rip-the-head-off-whoever-it-was hated—the idea of some other man touching Belle. She was the only woman in the world to inspire him to want to brand her. To make her his and his alone, in every way possible. For a man who considered himself evolved beyond caveman idiocy, it had been a blow to the ego. Not enough of a blow to stun the jealousy monster, though.

To distract himself from the images, and from the memory of her lush, lace-clad breasts, clearly visible when she'd leaned across to put the file in front of him, Mitch tilted his head in question.

"What exactly are you proposing?"

"Private sex," she said in the same tone she'd use to share a national secret.

"Huh?" He didn't get it. The rooms had locks. There were no video cameras around.

"The paparazzi and gossip hounds have declared open season on celebrities. They have no degree of privacy anymore. Not only actors and musicians, but any big name in the industry. Before you relocated here, you were based in New York, right?" At his nod, she continued, "You probably see it, or would if you paid attention, on the East Coast. But it's nothing like the insanity here in Southern California."

"What does that have to do with sex? Or, how did you put it? Private sex?"

Belle arched one brow. "Everything. Haven't you ever wanted some hot, wild getaway sex at a luxury resort?"

Hell, yeah. He wanted it now, as a matter of fact. Mitch did a quick mental tally of how many bedrooms were complete here at the resort. He could do Belle in fourteen hot, wild ways without using the same room twice. Even more if they went vertical. And that wasn't even counting the private cottages scattered around the resort grounds.

"Your rich and famous are welcome to come have sex here," he told her. "We're an equal-opportunity resort in that regard."

Her look made him laugh. Like a crack in her perfect image, she went from glossy sex kitten to cute and adorable in the wrinkle of her nose.

"I'm glad to know you have no restrictions on sex," she responded, her tone husky and blatantly interested. "I hope that applies to your personal life as well as your resort?"

"The only restriction I follow is to avoid trouble." His grin fell away as he remembered that Belle was pure trouble, inside and out.

She tut-tutted. "Safe sex? How boring is that? The only time those two words belong together is in reference to health precautions."

Images of swings, leather and handcuffs—without the cushy fur lining—flashed through his mind. His body stirred in instant reaction. Damn, maybe he needed to rethink this keeping-Belle-at-a-distance thing? After all, she was here, he was here. They had no commitment beyond the moment, were free to do as they liked. Maybe instead of cursing the past, he should take her up on the offer of pleasure so clear in her eyes.

Fourteen rooms.

Wild sex.

Handcuffs.

And then show her on her way.

"I take it you'd rather have unsafe sex?" he asked with a slow, teasing smile. Mentally watching his caution trampled by lust, Mitch waved goodbye to good sense and gave Belle a look that said just how unsafe he'd like sex to get between them.

Her expression didn't change, but a faint flush washed over her chest, letting him know she wasn't unaffected. His mouth watered to taste her there, just above the curve of her breasts. The rational, ambitious voice in his head warned him not to get dragged down by his dick. She was trouble. She'd proved that by almost ruining him when she'd walked out. His dick didn't give a damn.

"I like sex," she corrected, "without rules and restrictions."

"I like the sound of that. Tell me more."

"What I really want is a chance to show you."

Rock-hard and ready to sweep his desk clean for a hot, fast preview, Mitch bit back a groan. Principles fought lust. Need smothered angst.

Then Belle stood, took two short steps to his desk and leaned forward. One leg bent, she rested her knee and hip on the desk. Right there on the redwood surface where he'd just fantasized about stripping her bare.

Her scent, something that reminded him of a moonlit garden on a hot summer night, wrapped around him with long, delicate fingers. When she leaned closer, it was all he could do to keep from grabbing her. Better to let her make the move, he told himself. Less liability for going along than for doing the grabbing. He swallowed, his mouth ready to taste her, his tongue craving the feel of hers.

Inches away, she stopped. Mitch frowned. No kiss?

She arched one brow, then tilted her head to indicate the file lying on the desk between them. Of course. He snickered at himself, a mocking reminder that this woman was trouble.

A sardonic smile curving his lips, he took the hint and flipped open the file. Might as well give it a cursory glance so he could refuse her services before they got horizontal.

It didn't take long for Mitch to take in the file contents. Event outlines, yes. But more than just party ideas, the proposal included a general marketing plan and focus strategy.

A chill ran up his back when Mitch skimmed the vision statement. Either she was a hell of a lot savvier than he gave her credit for or she had an inside track to his company's information. Because this statement was the twin of his own, with a few tiny exceptions.

Vital exceptions in terms of marketing direction, focus. And, he had to admit, probable success.

Why couldn't she be just a pretty face and hot body? Her proposal was outstanding. The risk was minimal, the possible benefits innumerable. Damn. Mitch ground his teeth in frustration as the businessman in him overrode the horndog.

"This is a great plan," he reluctantly admitted. "By focusing on the paparazzi-hounded stars, we can provide the perfect getaway for the rich and famous. We'd amp up the security, spread the word that this is a photo-free zone." As ideas started to flow, Mitch grabbed a pen. "Special training for the staff, nondisclosure agreements, legal repercussions."

"Privacy is vital, but it's just one benefit," she cautioned. "Don't lose sight of the bigger picture. Yes, you want to bring in the Hollywood crowd. Once word gets out that you're offering a safe haven from the voracious press, combined with the buzz about how fab your resort is, I guarantee they'll be interested. But that's not going to be enough."

Mitch barely heard her, he was so focused on getting his flying thoughts on paper. Then Belle slid another folder on top of his notes.

He should have known. She was an event planner, and her initial plan hadn't mentioned a single party or gala. His eyes narrowed as he read the event outline.

"You do want to turn my resort into a sex club," he exclaimed in shock.

"Not exactly," she denied with a shrug that reminded him that her breasts were less than a foot from his mouth. Luckily her words were enough distraction. Almost.

"I'm suggesting you focus on indulgence of the most decadent kind. Couples' massages, chocolate baths, midnight champagne dinners by the lake. All romantic enough on their own, but you'll offer a few extras. I've got tons of ideas, and I'll share them if we go to contract on this. But basically, you'll have to take your standard resort offering and sex it up. Make it hot and inviting with just a hint of depravity. You do that and I guarantee you'll reel in the jaded Hollywood crowd."

"Depravity? Like what? On-call hookers and pole-dancing lessons?"

"There's nothing depraved about pole-dancing," she chided. "I do it and it's great exercise." She gave him a heavy-lidded look that promised all sorts of pulse-raising benefits. "Someday I'll show you."

Did nothing faze her? Mitch had to laugh.

"The difference between a high-class sex club and a luxury resort offering decadent indulgence is vast, Mitch." Her tone turned serious as all teasing flirtation left her face. "A sex club is cheap, base. It's all about the pickup, the kink, the instant satisfaction. You'd be offering a safe haven for your guests to indulge themselves in all ways, including their sexual fantasies. Masquerade balls, a menu that includes reputed aphrodisiacs, a lingerie shop in the lobby. Pure luxury in perfect keeping with the rest of your resort's offerings. Nothing tacky or low-class."

Decadent indulgence? She was right. That would definitely mesh with the extravagant luxury he'd planned to offer. As far as hooks went, it was certainly fresh. Definitely better than anything his marketing department had come up with.

But it meant focusing his business on sex. And working with Belle. Two things that he'd learned the hard way should never go hand in hand.

Mitch leaned back in his chair, both to show control and because he needed to put some distance between him and Belle's hypnotic scent. He glanced at the Eventfully

Yours contract, then gave her an assessing look through narrowed eyes.

"This plan has potential, I'll give you that," he acknowledged. "But I have to ask, what's to keep me from handing you back this contract, unsigned, and running with the plan on my own?"

"Ethics, of course." Belle's look was pure, pitying amusement. "You're one of the good guys, Mitch. You believe in helping others, not screwing them over."

He pulled a face. Yeah, she had him there.

"Besides," she continued as she studied her well-manicured nails, "you can't pull it off without my contacts. At least, not to the level necessary to be the kind of success you're looking for. And then there's the fact that if you do try without me, I'd take the plan to three hotels and resorts within driving distance and offer them the same idea. People are going to try to copy you down the road, but if you lose the exclusivity right out of the gate, you're guaranteed failure."

Damn. So she was hell on wheels as a businesswoman. Mitch knew he should be disgruntled, but he only felt an odd sort of admiring pride.

She read the frustration on his face and laughed. With a wicked look, she leaned forward and patted his cheek.

"Don't worry, you'll love working with me. I'm... fabulous," she purred. The innuendo made Mitch want to whimper.

"You realize if I give you this contract, sex between us is out of the question." He tossed the words out like a drowning man going down for the last time. *At least while they worked together,* he amended in his head. He wasn't stupid or delusional. He knew, sooner or later, they'd be doing the nasty. But he planned on calling the shots, and working together would make it much later than his body wanted.

"If that's the way you want it," she said agreeably. From the wattage of her smile, she was just as happy he'd issued the ultimatum. Damn her.

Mitch frowned, wondering if he'd miscalculated Belle. She came across as hot and sexy. Her nature, her demeanor and vibe were pure sensuality. Was it all an act? A hot front shielding a cold core? A tool to twist a guy by his dick so she could easily lead him around?

"You're fine with that," he clarified.

"Of course," she said, sliding off his desk. With a quick twitch of her hand, she straightened her skirt and made sure her blouse was tucked into the wide leather belt circling her tiny waist. He clenched his teeth to keep from drooling as she bent over to pick up her bag, and wished like hell he'd refused outright to work with her.

He forced his gaze from her ass to the folder, contents and plans spread over his desk blotter. No, he couldn't regret considering her for the job. Her take on the resort's events and focus was the most dynamic he'd ever seen.

He could wish they'd done the dirty on the desk first, though. Mitch stifled a sigh and came around to the front of his desk to escort her out.

Belle turned to give him a wide smile and held out her hand. Seal the deal with a handshake, he supposed.

When he took her delicate palm in his, she dropped their hands so, enfolded, they rested on her hip. Then she closed the distance between them until her breasts were a hairbreadth away from his chest. Mitch's erection returned, granite-hard.

Her gaze locked on his, Belle leaned forward. Up on her tiptoes, she used her breasts against his chest for balance.

She wrapped one hand around the back of his neck and gave a gentle tug, pulling his mouth down to meet hers.

Both fascinated and turned on, Mitch let her take the lead. She was the most sexually confident woman he'd ever met. Yet beneath it all, he sensed the same sweet vulnerability that had hooked him six years before. The sweetness, he knew, would be his downfall if he wasn't careful.

Not willing to show her how strong her power was, he held himself still as her lips pressed, soft and lush, against his. His hands itched to pull her close, to press her tight against his body so he could feel her curves surrendering.

Then her tongue, so soft and seductive, traced the line of his mouth. A quick flick to the corners, a soft slide across his lower lip. Blood roared through Mitch's head, drowning out all caution. When her teeth nipped, just a little, at his lip, he lost it.

His hands dove into her hair, holding her head still as his tongue took hers in a wild dance of pleasure. Slip, slide, intense and delicious, he gave way to the power of their kiss.

More, was all he could think. He had to have more.

He didn't know if it was that desperately needy thought or the sound of his groan that pulled him back to sanity. Unable to do otherwise, knowing it would likely be his last chance to taste her for God knew how long, Mitch slowly ended the kiss.

With a moan of approval, Belle stepped away. Her eyes, blurry with desire, stared into his as she ran her tongue over her bottom lip and gave a sigh. Then her mouth curved in a smile that screamed satisfaction.

"You'll give me the contract," she assured him, her

words a husky promise. "And we'll have incredible sex. And in the end, you'll be thanking your lucky stars you were smart enough to do both."

3

"I BLEW IT," Belle insisted, pacing her office. The plush carpet warmed her bare feet as she stomped from one end of the room to the other. "I got so caught up in the sexual game, in wanting to show Mitch what he'd lost by wanting some business deal more than me, I lost sight of why I was there."

"Chill," Sierra said, ensconced behind Belle's desk while working on a seating plan. "You haven't blown it. Mitch is a by-the-book kind of guy. When he's ready to reject both of your propositions he'll have his assistant email you."

Despite her anxiety, Belle snorted and gave a rueful shake of her head. No patty-cake from Sierra, nope. The brunette shot from the hip, to hell with the fatalities.

"You think he'll have his tidy little assistant send me a no-thanks-on-the-sex email?"

"Nah," Sierra said as she frowned at the sketch, then checked her guest list. "He'll make it all businesslike. You know, something like, 'I appreciate your time and creative proposal, but have decided it doesn't suit my needs. As clever and inventive as your suggestions are, I don't feel that's the right direction to take at this time. Oh, by the way, I'm not hiring you for the event gig, either.'"

The rejection sounded so realistic, Belle almost rushed to her laptop to see if Sierra was reading it verbatim.

"Did you hear something?" she asked suspiciously.

Sierra just rolled her eyes.

"We've been friends since training bras and boarding school, and in all these years, I've never seen you turn stupid over any guy but this one," Sierra pointed out. "Maybe we'd be better off if he does turn the deal down. I don't think he's good for you."

"He tasted good," Belle muttered. Tasted good, felt good, looked good. Her breath shuddered as she remembered how amazing his kiss had been. She'd only intended to prove a point, tease him a little. He'd been the one with the point, though. Hard and long, pressing into her thigh.

God, she was going crazy with wanting him.

"You're doing it again," Sierra reminded.

Belle glanced over at her friend, surprised to see she'd pushed aside her seating chart and was unwrapping a butterscotch candy. Sierra only resorted to sugar, and only in tiny amounts, when she was really stressed. Given the half-dozen unwrapped pieces in front of her, she was definitely worried.

"Doing what again?" Belle asked.

"Getting stupid," Sierra repeated. "It's like an automatic shutoff button gets flipped whenever you get near Mitch Carter. Your brain goes into hibernate mode."

Belle rolled her eyes and dropped into the chair opposite Sierra. "Don't be silly. I'm just hot for the guy. You've seen him, he's gorgeous. Sexy, smart and fun. That doesn't make me stupid, that makes me horny."

"I've seen you horny before. You don't blow business

deals over horny," Sierra said, chomping down on the candy with a loud crunch.

Belle winced at the sound. That had to hurt the teeth. Then her eyes went round as Sierra unwrapped another and popped it into her mouth.

Best friends since they were fourteen, the two women knew each other inside out. Belle had never considered anyone else to go into business with. Guilt trickled down her spine. And now she was stressing her friend into a sugar coma.

"I didn't blow it," Belle defended. At least, she didn't think she did. "I might have gotten a bit carried away, but a little flirting won't affect the deal. He loved my spiel. He was impressed with our ideas. Whether we get it or we don't will depend on whether he's open to the sexual angle or not. For the resort," she quickly added.

Sierra chewed up another hard candy without replying. She gave Belle a long, considering look, then unwrapped another piece.

The look was a familiar one. She'd worn it when she'd talked Belle into taking a chance on their business. She wore it when she told a client their request was over-the-top crazy. She always wore it when she told Belle her outfit sucked or her ideas were lame. It was her truth-at-all-costs look.

Belle hated that look.

For the good of her own ears and Sierra's dental bill, Belle reached over and scooped up the remaining candy.

"Belle, you barely knew this guy and you were willing to toss aside your principles and beliefs. For what? A piece of ass."

"I'm not some dumb tramp," Belle snapped back. "I might have been distracted during that meeting, but I'll be damned if I gave away a single principle and I sure as hell didn't ignore my beliefs."

Whatever that was supposed to mean, she fumed. God, if she didn't hate confrontation so much, she'd yell at her friend. Tell her to quit being so negative, so mistrusting. Instead she sucked in a deep, calming breath and reminded herself that this was just Sierra's way.

"I meant six years ago, when you agreed to marry the guy just so you could get in his pants," Sierra corrected with a roll of her eyes. "You weren't interested in happy-ever-after back then. But you gave in despite your better judgment. And look how that turned out."

Belle winced. She'd rather not think about it. "Please, do you think Mitch would be crazy enough to propose to me again? All he wanted was a leg up the ladder, and he doesn't need that any longer."

"You don't say anything about whether you'd be crazy enough to accept a proposal," Sierra pointed out.

"I didn't think I had to state the obvious. I gave up believing in fairy tales or happy-ever-after. I'm hot for the guy, okay? That's it. I know better than to risk anything other than a little time and some sexy lingerie."

"I hope so. I really, really hope so," Sierra said, her words dripping with doubt. "Because your history says otherwise."

A chime snagged her attention and Sierra glanced at the laptop. She clicked the mouse a couple times and heaved a sigh. Belle's stomach dropped to her toes at the look on her partner's face.

"Okay, here's the deal," the sleek brunette said in her no-nonsense tone. "If we get this contract, I need you to make me a promise."

Belle eyed the computer, her fingers itching to grab it and see what message had prompted Sierra's ultimatum.

"What's the promise?" Belle hedged. She wasn't about to agree to anything crazy, like keeping her hands off Mitch. Yes, she might lose a few brain cells around him. But she was an intelligent woman, she had extras.

Replaying those excuses through her head, Belle heaved a sigh and privately admitted they were bullshit. This job was huge, and not only to Eventfully Yours. If she pulled it off, made friendly—but not *that* friendly— with Mitch, there was a good chance he'd help her dad.

Belle thought back to the call she'd had that morning from her father's secretary. Her dad was stressed again, and even though he was supposed to be home recovering from his heart attack, he'd spent the past four days running to the office trying to find some way out of the mess he was in. Between a series of bad investments, the real estate crash and a sucky economy, Forsham Hotels was sinking fast. A wave of helpless frustration washed over her. She had to do something, anything, to get Mitch to talk to her dad.

Maybe Twisted Knickers lingerie carried chastity belts.

Sierra took a deep breath. Belle was nodding before her friend could even issue the request. Fine, no sex.

"As soon as you can, hell, the first day if possible, you haul Mitch Carter into the nearest closet and have wild monkey sex with him," Sierra commanded. "Have as much sex as possible. Do it as many times in as many ways as you can. Get it all out of your system. Do it on the ceiling if you have to. Use toys and kinky leather getups."

Belle's jaw dropped. She shook her head, sure her hearing was faulty.

"For the good of Eventfully Yours, for the good of your thought processes and, most of all, for the good of my sanity, I'm begging you—" Sierra placed both palms on the desk and leaned forward, her face intense "—do him. Immediately."

It took all Belle's strength to lift her chin off her chest. Sierra was a dyed-in-the-wool cynic, but she'd never been this…well, pragmatic about deliberately seducing someone.

Belle kind of liked it. Even if it was insane.

"You're kidding, right? I thought you were worried about my poor judgment with Mitch?"

"I'm worried about your judgment when your head is clouded with unrequited lust," Sierra shot back. "Once you've screwed his brains out a few times you'll be fine."

"Fine?"

"I've read studies that list all the ways sexual frustration hinders a person. This exact situation wasn't on the list, but I'm sure it qualifies. Once the sexual curiosity is sated, you'll be your normal, savvy self and kick butt with this deal."

"So this is for the good of our business?" Belle's tummy did a wicked somersault.

Shouldn't she feel excited instead of nervous? Sierra was the voice of reason, so her encouragement made the whole idea seem…well, weird.

"Sure," Sierra returned with a shrug.

"We got the deal?" Belle pointed to the computer and whatever message Sierra was hiding.

"We've got a shot at the deal. He wants a meeting to discuss it." She spun the laptop around so Belle could read the message from Mitch's assistant. Lunch meeting, tomorrow afternoon. Come prepared to negotiate.

Excitement buzzed through Belle's system like electricity. Her stomach tumbled, nerves and anticipation warning her to eat ahead of time. Yes. This was her chance, her shot at everything she wanted. She'd show him the fine art of negotiation…her way.

Belle gave a wicked laugh of delight. "Never let it be said I'm not willing to give my all for the cause."

While she didn't quite share Sierra's anxiety that she'd blow the deal or do something stupid, she wasn't about to turn down a direct order to hunt down the hottest guy she'd ever lusted after and screw his brains out.

As a waiter topped off his coffee, Mitch patted the pocket where he'd tucked the faded cocktail napkin with its gold foil inscription of his and Belle's names and their former wedding date. He'd spent two days dissecting Eventfully Yours's proposal with his management team, listening to their analysis and opinions. The unanimous belief was that of all the proposals, this was unquestionably the strongest. The best. And in Mitch's opinion, the biggest pain in the ass.

Not because the plan would be difficult to implement. All that meant was he had to work harder, smarter, than the average guy. Since he'd built his reputation doing just that, he never shied from difficult.

Proof positive was right here, he thought as he looked around Spago Restaurant. Airy, bright and lush, it was one of the top restaurants in L.A. He'd have had to save up for a month just to bring Belle to have a drink here when they were engaged. But not anymore. Six years and a driving need to prove himself to her, to everyone—including his former father-in-law-to-be—who'd thought he'd marry his way to success, had given him a much stronger edge.

So no, he didn't blink at taking on the difficult. But this plan came with his personal version of kryptonite: Belle Forsham. The one woman guaranteed not only to bring him to his knees, but to make sure he loved the hell out of being there.

Working with her could be a disaster. If he let himself get offtrack, the results would be ugly. He had everything on the line here. Not only the resort, but his investors' money and trust. To say nothing of his reputation. Sex with Belle wasn't worth risking all that. Which was why he was only agreeing to part of her proposal. The events, specifically.

As intriguing, and probably lucrative, as the sex themes had been, he didn't trust himself to deal with her on that level. She was simply too much temptation. He was afraid she'd use those themes to take that hot kiss one or two— or twenty steps further.

So—he fingered the napkin again—he'd keep her at arm's length. Business, pure and simple. Hell, he'd been burned once, he was a smart man. He knew how to keep his fingers—and other body parts—to himself. If he was otherwise tempted, he had his talisman as a reminder that Belle was off-limits.

Suddenly, as though someone had pushed a button, his body went on full alert. His senses flared as he glanced across the restaurant, not surprised to see Belle making her way toward him. Sleek and sexy in a simple spring dress of the palest pink, she sauntered between the linen-covered tables, her eyes never leaving his. Standing as she approached, Mitch eyed her half smile, the hint of naughty amusement igniting his body to instant lust.

His body would just have to get over it.

"Thanks for meeting me," he said as he gestured to the chair the waiter held out. "I'm sure you have a busy schedule."

Her green eyes narrowed as if she were trying to read

his tone, then Belle gave a little shrug and murmured her thanks to the waiter.

"My schedule's never too busy for you," she returned, spreading the napkin over her lap without releasing his gaze. "Unless, of course, you're planning a wedding or something. Then I might have to run."

Mitch's jaw sagged. The mischievous humor gleaming in her eyes assured him he hadn't heard wrong. Leave it to Belle to poke fun at something taboo. It wasn't just her smile that was naughty.

"I don't think you'll need your sneakers anytime soon," he deadpanned. "My tux is at the cleaner's."

Her laugh rang out, garnering a few indulgent smiles from other diners and sparking an irritatingly warm feeling in Mitch's belly.

"Whew. Good thing, since I don't even own a pair. Let's have lunch and talk business, instead. Okay?"

On cue, the waiter stepped over and handed Belle a menu. She barely glanced at it before ordering iced tea and salad. Interesting. Either she dined at four-star restaurants often enough to be blasé about the famous menu or she really was focused on business. Mitch wondered if she'd been here before, and what kind of men she dated. Irritated at his train of thought, he shoved aside the jealous curiosity and gave the waiter his order. The only thing he needed to know about her activities of the past six years was in reference to her business.

"Your assistant said you had questions, wanted to discuss Eventfully Yours's proposal in more depth?" she said, her tone professional. Her look, though, was pure sex. Glossy lips pursed, she let her gaze do a slow, appreciative slide over his face and chest. Mitch was grateful the table was between them, both preventing her from going any further and keeping his reaction hidden.

She arched a brow in query. The gleam in her eyes told him she knew she was sending mixed signals and was looking forward to seeing which ones he chose to pick up.

"I do have questions," Mitch said, his tone neutral. He wasn't going to play her game, but damned if he'd let her know that. Keeping her guessing was his only shot at maintaining the upper hand. And with Belle, he needed all the control he could get. She was like a wily dominatrix, luring him in with sugar and spice but hiding a whip and chain behind her back.

With that in mind, he pulled out his file of questions, suggestions and ideas. Through the rest of the meal he and Belle hammered out details for the grand opening, as well as a series of smaller pre-events that would build buzz for the resort. He was again impressed with her savvy suggestions, especially as she expanded on her proposal, filling in the crucial details that she'd held back initially.

Damn, she was good.

By dessert, she'd gone from good to mind-blowing.

"You're going to want to redesign the landscaping here and here," she said, poking at the sketch of the resort's property with one blunt fingernail. "If you bring in some fully mature trees, a few more bushes, you'll have a perfect sex-in-the-woods setting. Guests will love that, and if you set it up right they'll think it's their little secret."

Definitely mind-blowing. And thanks to comments like that, all he could think of were other things he'd like her to blow.

"You've obviously considered everything," he said. He wondered if keeping him in a constant state of arousal was planned, as well. Glancing at the amused awareness in her eyes, he figured it was. "Now, about your suggested themes…"

"I noticed you kept changing the subject when I brought

them up." There was no judgment in her eyes, only curiosity. "So, what? You're going to go vanilla?"

"Vanilla?"

"Safe and tame."

Ahh, there was the irritation. Mitch grinned in relief.

"Let's just say I don't think the two of us focusing on sex is a good idea," he returned.

"Chicken?"

"Prudent."

Belle rolled her eyes. "Safe sex again?"

He couldn't deny it. After all, the safest sex was abstinence.

"Because of our past association I think we should discuss our history and clear the air," he said instead. "I want us both to be on solid ground, which means we need to deal with any past resentments or issues."

For the first time in memory, Mitch watched Belle's expressive face close up. Like a door slamming, it simply went blank and unwelcoming. Then, so fast he wondered if he'd imagined it, she gave a roll of her eyes and flashed her sassy smile.

"The past is over, Mitch. I promise, I'm not bringing any old baggage to the table." She leaned forward, and for the first time since she'd waltzed out of his office two days earlier, touched him. A whisper-soft brush of her fingertips over the back of his hand. Gentle, teasing, easy. Heat flared, instant and hot, in his belly. "Any desire I have to chase you around is definitely fresh and new, not a leftover itch."

"You don't own sneakers, remember?" he snapped, equal parts irritated that she'd so easily closed the door to their past before he could find out why she'd really run off and relieved not to have to admit to his own part in their failed history. "So we'll just keep chasing off our list of things to do."

"Then what's the problem?"

"Like I said, given our history, I think it's wise to keep the sexual temptation to a minimum." He'd rehearsed and rehashed his next words multiple times since he'd decided to work with her, but Mitch still had trouble voicing them. "I've also written up the contracts event by event, rather than the job as a whole."

"Care to clarify that?" He'd had no idea her husky voice could turn to ice.

"I have everything riding on the success of this resort. That success will depend greatly on how well the events are handled. I have to depend on these events happening. As amazing as your proposal is, I can't afford to tie myself up for more than one event at a time given the circumstances of our last...association."

If he'd reached across the table and slapped her, she couldn't have looked more shocked. Mitch felt like a first-class bastard. Belle's luscious mouth parted as if to challenge him, her eyes sparkling with fury. Then, as if a switch had flipped, she sucked in her bottom lip and gave a jerky little shrug.

"No way. I'm sorry, but these mini-events are back to back, each one leading up to the grand opening. Eventfully Yours won't take the job without at least the pre- and grand opening events contracted." Her tone was pure business, her eyes shuttered.

The fairness of her words, spoken in that even, businesslike tone, made Mitch realize he was the one letting the past get in the way.

"That's fine," he agreed. "We'll contract for the five smaller events and the grand opening."

"Great. Unless there are any more grudges you're harboring, I'd say we're good to go."

"No grudges." At least, none he'd admit. "Like I said, just being prudent."

She rolled her eyes again, but the gesture didn't hide the hurt lurking in the sea-green depths. Mitch frowned, irritated that the sight made him feel like a jerk.

"Then we have a deal," she said, her tone making it clear she was glad to close the history book. Mitch was surprised, since most women were only too happy to discuss the past in all its gory details. "I'll be at the resort a week from Monday. Given the distance from L.A. and how much work is involved, I'll require a room on-site, of course. A suite would be best as I'll set up office there."

Belle opened a file, made and initialed a few adjustments on the contract to reflect his changes. With a flourish, she signed her name, then slid the papers back in the folder.

She handed it to him with a wink. Apparently she'd regained her good humor.

"I think I'll put you in one of the cottages," he returned. "Unlike the suites, they're already furnished and should suit you perfectly."

"How far are these cottages from your on-site office?"

"You can call me anytime you have questions," he assured her. And the distance would make him think twice about dropping in to visit.

Her brow creased, her eyes rounded. "You're starting to make me think you're harboring more issues, Mitch. Are you planning to avoid me the entire time I'm working with you?"

Not Belle, per se. Just sex with her. Mitch winced. There was no way he wouldn't sound like a pompous ass, but he had to make things clear.

"Please don't take this the wrong way, Belle. But I'm not going to sleep with you. We're doing business together, and business and pleasure just don't mix."

"Hmm, interesting. Too bad you didn't think that six years ago when you tried to mix your business with my daddy's and in the process ruined my pleasure."

He frowned, but before he could respond, she gave a quick shake of her head and a brittle, dismissive little laugh. "Now that does sound like I'm the one harboring some of those issues you're worried about. Let's start fresh, okay? I'm not the same person I was before and I'm betting you aren't, either."

He opened his mouth to retort, but closed it again. All of a sudden, he wanted to clear the air, to ask her the reasons behind her bridal dash. But to do so meant acknowledging emotions he'd locked away. Admitting mistakes he regretted. And worse, bridging the chasm of mistrust that the past kept firmly between them. As long as it was there, he knew they'd never have a shot at intimacy.

He slid his hand into his pocket and fingered the wedding napkin. Between his talisman and that chasm, he'd be safe from screwing up. He couldn't afford to lose again.

"I've changed a lot in six years" was all he said.

"So have I," she assured him as she laid one warm, smooth hand over his. Energy, mostly sexual but with a subtle layer of something else Mitch couldn't define, shot through his body at her touch. The most platonic connection, and he was hard, hot and horny. It boggled the mind to think what his response would be if they had full-body contact. Chasm and talisman, he reminded himself.

"I hope you're not upset," he said, telling himself it was guilt and not lust making him want to pull her onto his lap. "You're a gorgeous, sexy woman. You don't need to be chasing a guy."

"Who said I'd chase you?" she asked, her tone light and amused.

Mitch frowned. He knew he hadn't misunderstood her signal or her flirting words.

"Like you, I'm much smarter than I was six years ago. Smart enough to know better than to chase a man. Especially a man like you."

Mitch opened his mouth to deny that she'd chased him before, but she continued before he could get a single word out. "You say we won't have sex. I say we will. Simple difference of opinion and only time will tell which one of us is right. And if you're too uptight to do two things at once successfully, that's fine. I can wait."

"What the hell are you talking about?" he asked, watching nonplussed as she slid her folder into her briefcase and got to her feet. "What two things?"

"Rock your resort opening and have wild monkey sex with me," she shot back as she turned to leave. "When it happens, I won't have chased you to get it. You'll be the one doing the chasing…and the begging."

4

BELLE GLANCED OVER the guest list for the preopening event and added two more names. Actors, politicians, celebutants. She needed to scatter in some high-profile musicians, but she wanted to do a little more research first.

Almost two weeks had passed since her lunch with Mitch and she'd yet to spend any time alone with him. The first week was understandable. She'd been working from her office in L.A., finalizing things and tying up loose ends so she could spend the next few weeks here at Lakeside. The resort was a hundred miles from her office, and it was only practical that she work on-site for the duration. She'd figured the bonus would be seeing Mitch day in and day out for the next three weeks. Not only would she relish the sexual thrill, but she could drop a few hints and feel him out on the topic of her father.

But since she'd arrived to find her cozy cottage ready and waiting, he'd been avoiding her. And he wasn't even trying to hide the fact.

The perfect host, he'd had fresh flowers waiting in her room. But he'd sent his assistant to help her settle in. He'd remembered her preferences, making sure she had hot tea and a basket of muffins delivered each morning, but he'd avoided seeing her unless there were at least three other people in the room.

Today she was supposed to tour the grounds, the suites and the spa. And knowing Mitch, he'd send his rabbity assistant to do the honors.

She thought of her promise to Sierra. Do him. Fast, furious, as soon as possible. So far, she was failing dismally. Sexual frustration was never comfortable, but she was a big girl and could handle losing the game. But Mitch hadn't even manned up enough to play. She recalled his declaration that sex between them was off-limits. This must be his way of making sure she knew he was serious.

Well, so was she. And seduction wasn't going to work. It hadn't when they'd been engaged, it hadn't when they'd met again a couple of weeks ago. She obviously needed a new plan.

Nibbling on her second blueberry muffin, she punched a button on her cell phone, leaving it on speaker.

"Morning," Sierra answered cheerfully. "I take it you haven't died of sexual frustration yet?"

"I'm surviving," Belle said dryly. "Barely, though. I need your help."

"Sorry, sweets. You're not my type."

"Ha-ha. I need ideas, you dork. Mitch is running scared. He's avoiding me except for emails and the telephone. Try as I might I can't even get him to have phone sex with me."

"Shit," Sierra muttered. Belle heard the clink of glass against glass and knew her friend was topping off her coffee. Sierra always thought best when highly caffeinated.

"I need a plan," Belle said, stating the obvious.

"No kidding. Otherwise I'll be shopping for some ugly bridesmaid's dress again."

"Hey, the dress wasn't that ugly."

"Anything in Easter-egg pink is ugly and that's beside the point." Belle could hear the tap-tap-tapping of Sierra's nails against the coffee cup. "Give me a rundown of what you've done on the job while I think."

Belle thought best while lounging in a bubble bath or lazing in the sun, something that allowed her to relax and let the ideas flow. Sierra, though, was the opposite, needing noise and activity to find her solutions.

Pulling her notebook toward her, Belle went over the timeline and to-do list. On the off chance she managed to convince Mitch to consider the theme idea, she'd ordered sex-toy samples, sketched out three separate theme ideas and started the plans for the preopening event. To garner word-of-mouth buzz and set the tone for privacy, she'd suggested that Mitch hold a low-key non-advertised event before the media caught wind of the resort's offerings. It would offer that semblance of privacy while giving their potential guests a taste of just how special a stay at Lakeside would be.

"Quit flirting," Sierra said, interrupting Belle's recitation of the tentative guest list.

"I was reading in my most serious tone," Belle responded with a sniff. "I can't help it if my voice excites you."

"Ha. Seriously, though, your last encounter with Mitch, you tossed down the gauntlet. I don't blame you, of course, but still, the guy is definitely running scared."

Belle wrinkled her nose and pushed away what was left of her muffin. The idea of Mitch wanting nothing to do with her ruined her appetite.

"I told him I wouldn't chase him and I'm not," she defended, her tone stiff. "But is it asking too much that he meet with me without the chaperones?"

"You need to change tactics, lull him into complacency then reel him in."

"Lull him from afar?" Her pouty tone was only half-pretend.

"He's going to have to meet with you sooner or later," Sierra assured her. "Once he does, turn the tables. Play the professional card. You know, pretend you're there to work, to do a job."

This time Belle really did pout. "I *am* here to do a job."

"Yeah, yeah. But we both know you have ulterior motives. He's not stupid, so he probably suspects it, too. So confuse him."

"Professional?"

"More focus on the job, the reasons you're there. Including needing Mitch's help for your dad." Glass clinked as Sierra got even more coffee. "Less focus on how cute his ass is."

What, was she blind? Belle wanted to argue, but knew there was no point. Too much was at stake. Not only the job itself, but Eventfully Yours's reputation and her father's business. Mitch had made his disinterest plenty clear; she'd respect his decision.

"Have you talked to him any more about the theme program?" Sierra asked, obviously taking Belle's silence as agreement to her plan.

"I haven't seen him to pitch it any further," Belle reminded her.

Silence.

Belle sighed. "I'll send him an email. He seems to like those."

She and Sierra wrapped up a few more details then hung up, leaving Belle to feel like a total slacker. Sierra was right. She'd been so focused on her attraction to Mitch, she'd let her priorities slip. Well, no more. She grabbed her pen and started a list of what she needed to do to set things right.

Before she could write more than a few things, though, her cell phone chimed the "Boogie-Woogie Blues."

"Daddy," she greeted in answer. "How are you feeling?"

"I'm feeling sick and tired of being asked that question, princess," Franklin Forsham growled.

"People ask because they care, not out of some twisted desire to be irritating. You need to rest and give yourself time to recuperate. Quadruple bypass is nothing to blow off."

"I'm sitting on my ass instead of golfing, aren't I? That's recuperation enough." The pain of that was clear in his voice. Frank Forsham loved nothing more than a good game of golf. Belle glanced out the window at the gorgeous tree-studded view. Off in the distance the sun glinted, jewel-like, off the lake, and beyond that was what Diana had claimed to be a first-class golf course. Not big enough to bring in the major tournaments, but challenging enough to keep the guests entertained.

Her father would love it. Maybe after she got him and Mitch together, he'd come play a few rounds. She didn't consider it naive to believe it would happen any more than she considered herself overoptimistic to think she and Mitch would get together. Faith and hard work. She figured as long as she had both—and some hot lingerie—she was set.

"Of course, I wouldn't be able to golf anyway, given the state of things here," he grumbled, stealing her attention back from her idyllic imaginings. "Damned market is only getting worse. Forsham Hotels hasn't been hit this hard since the early seventies."

Belle listened to her father's description of the state of

his company. She knew enough about business to realize he was actually making light of how bad it was. Worse, though, was the tension she heard in his voice. He was supposed to be recovering, not working himself into another heart attack.

"It'll turn around and everything will be fine, Daddy," she said, even though they both knew it was an empty promise. But as always, Franklin didn't expect any real input or contribution from her, so he let the comment go unchallenged. She was his pretty little girl, no more, no less. Belle had long ago given up the idea of proving herself to him. But maybe, just maybe, he'd respect her a little if she saved his company?

"Come by tonight, we'll go to dinner," he ordered.

Belle glanced at her to-do list. Even if she rescheduled the tour, her plate was full. Added to that, it would take her an hour and a half to drive back to L.A., longer if she hit traffic. She flipped the page in her planner, noting an early breakfast meeting with the spa manager.

Then she thought of her dad, alone in that big rambling house.

"I'll be there at seven," she promised. "I wanted to talk to you anyway."

"About?"

"Um, I sort of ran into someone from the past and thought you'd like to hear about him."

"Him?"

She hated it when he did that. Single-word questions, then silence that made her feel as if she had to spill tons of details to fill the empty space.

"Mitch Carter," she said. Then she cringed and waited. But not for long.

"That cheating sonofabitch? I thought he'd run back to the East Coast where he belongs."

Belle winced. "Dad, I told you, Mitch didn't cheat."

"Harrumph."

"He didn't. Really. He just sort of misled me. I'm sure he thinks I did much worse, leaving him at the altar like that."

"He was a lucky man and he blew it."

Belle pressed her lips together. She had to get her dad to quit hating Mitch or there was no point in pushing Mitch to help him. Leave it to her to be stuck between two stubborn men.

"Let's talk about it over dinner, okay?"

"Let's not. I don't want to discuss the cheater or that debacle that was your wedding. Especially not when it's thanks to him that I invested in that damned property. His connections and contracting license were supposed to get us past the stupid zoning regulations. Thanks to his duplicity, I'm stuck. Can't build, can't sell."

Her father continued to mutter. Belle's stomach twisted. She'd told her father the day after the wedding that Mitch hadn't been with any other women, that she hadn't meant to imply anything like that. But her father had blown up at her, ranting about the humiliation and misplaced trust. Too horrified to ask if he meant his trust in Mitch or his trust in her, she'd gulped down her explanation and run from the room.

Her father's attitude didn't bode well for her little save-Forsham-Hotels plan. But she'd worry about convincing him later. For now, she needed to focus on getting Mitch to listen to her. That was enough of a challenge.

With that in mind, she bade her father an absentminded goodbye, promising to see him that evening. As soon as she hung up, she grabbed the cottage phone and dialed star-seven.

"Diana? Hey, I need to postpone the tour until tomorrow, okay?"

"Is there a problem?" Mitch's assistant asked in her hesitant tone.

"Not at all. I just have to run home for the evening. An offer came up that I couldn't refuse."

"Business?"

"No, dinner…" With her father? No, just in case Diana shared the excuse with Mitch, she didn't want to bring her father into the mix until she'd had time to butter them both up. "A dinner date."

"WHAT IN THE HELL DO you mean, the program crashed?"

The hotel manager winced, then he gave a helpless shrug. Tall, skinny and blond, Larry looked like a morose scarecrow. Mitch had handpicked him to run the resort because he handled the staff like a gifted choreographer and knew hotels inside out. And, theoretically, hotel computers. "We don't understand what happened. I've spent the morning on the phone with tech support—they're baffled, too."

The computerized reservation program was supposed to be bug-free, idiot-proof and have both on- and off-site backups. "You recovered the lost data, right?"

"We're working on it. The system has a backup, but somehow, well, the battery went dead."

Mitch closed his eyes and shook his head. Continual construction delays. The pipes had burst in the pool room, there was a gopher infestation on the golf course, and now this? Seriously, who had his voodoo doll and why the hell were they jabbing it so hard?

The only person he'd recently pissed off was Belle. And he couldn't see her going the voodoo route. She was too direct for that. She'd rather see him on his knees begging. Or maybe just on his knees.

"Get it fixed," he instructed tiredly. As soon as the manager left, Mitch lifted his phone and punched a button.

"Do you believe jobs can be cursed?" he asked as soon as Reece answered.

"Nah, that's the kind of thing suits like you come up with as an excuse for falling on their ass."

"Well, my ass is definitely getting bruised," Mitch acknowledged. "I'm starting to think it's more than a learning curve."

"You don't really believe that curse crap, do you? You want me to fly you out a witch doctor?"

"If I thought it'd make a difference, I'd have you hand-deliver one."

Reece laughed, although Mitch was only half joking. "Gotta hand it to you, cuz, you're the most hands-on guy I know. Guess that's why you're kicking butt. You stick your fingers in every pie you deal in, swinging a hammer as easily as you make those slick deals."

Not quite *every* pie. Mitch had been doing his damnedest to avoid the sweetie pie that was his ex. Not trusting himself around her, he'd justified his absence by putting Diana in charge of the events projects. And Belle was the Party Princess, after all. She didn't need his supervision to plan a successful event.

"Seriously, what's the deal?" Reece, or Cowboy, as Mitch's cousin and security guru was aptly nicknamed, sounded as concerned as he ever did. Which meant his drawl had slowed and the teasing humor had left his voice.

Mitch listed the resort's problems-du-jour, from construction to rodent infestation to computer crash. He was explaining about the staff issues when his cousin interrupted.

"Your event gal quit? Just like that? The hot little red-head who loved to party? What happened?"

"She's in rehab."

"No shit? What're you going to do about that opening weekend party you were so hot to have?"

"If I can't stop this streak of bad luck, there won't be an opening," Mitch hedged, not wanting to mention Belle's involvement in the resort. Since Reece had been his best man, he had a pretty vivid memory of her. "I'm willing to accept a few problems here and there, but not this level of misfortune."

"Sabotage?"

"That sounds so paranoid."

"It ain't paranoia if they're out to get you," Reece pointed out.

"Right."

The two men were silent for a minute, then Mitch heard Reece shuffling some papers. That his bronc-riding cousin was working in an office amused Mitch. A go-getter Kentucky cowboy, Reece was more suited to riding horseback than riding a desk. Rather than putting his military time to use in law enforcement, he'd opened his own security firm.

"Did you get the note I sent you about new requirements for the resort?" Mitch asked.

"Something about catering to the fancy-ass folks there in Hollywood?"

"That's it. Why don't you send a guy out early? He can start assessing for the upgrades, and poke around a little at the same time."

"Two birds with one stone. Good plan."

They nailed down the details, then hung up. Mitch let his head fall back on the chair, his eyes, as always, going to the view.

Ever since he was a kid, he'd dreamed of a place like this. Oh, not the rich and fancy angle, but of owning something huge, something major. He'd wanted to make his mark, to be special. An only child, he'd been one of seventeen cousins. The last words his dad had spoken to him before he'd died were to tell him to be the man, to take care of his mom and show the world what he was made of. Even at five, Mitch had taken those words to heart.

They'd sparked his desperate need to prove himself. To be important.

Starting out in construction as a teen, he'd worked his way up the ranks in his stepdad's company by the time he'd entered college. He'd graduated with a degree in business and been left the construction firm when his mom and stepdad had died just before his twenty-third birthday. Like Reece said, he'd worked every aspect of his business, from swinging the hammer to marketing property to making deals. Within five years he'd launched his development company and figured he was well on his way to the big time.

But he'd wanted more. Enter Forsham Hotels and the biggest mistake of his life.

Which reminded him…

Mitch pushed away from his desk and strode into Diana's office. As soon as she saw him, the mousy brunette held out a sheaf of papers.

"Larry sent these up," she said.

"Obviously his team hasn't figured out the problem yet," he observed, flipping through the pages of technospeak as if he had a clue what they said. With a shrug, he tossed the report back on Diana's desk and asked, "Did Belle have a list of suggestions after her tour?"

"Um, not yet." Diana busied herself with shuffling the tech report, then clipping the pages just so.

"She's writing it up?"

"No, I don't think she is."

Mitch's earlier irritation, still bubbling away just below the surface, threatened to erupt.

"I suppose there's a good reason why she hasn't done what I specifically asked?"

"Well, maybe because she had to cancel," his assistant mumbled, bending low to put the tech report in the bottom filing-cabinet drawer.

"Why the hell did she cancel the tour?"

"She had a, well, a date," Diana said, her face almost buried in her keyboard.

Either she'd figured out how irritated he got when people wasted his time on the job or she was still afraid to look him in the face when she gave him bad news. Either way, her timidity pissed him off even more.

"Get her on the phone," he snapped. When Diana winced, Mitch sighed, feeling like he'd kicked a puppy. "Please."

"She's already left the resort. She said since she had to drive into L.A. anyway, she'd leave early and go into town to meet some vendors, store owners and suppliers to look into possible liaisons for the resort."

If Diana's face got any closer to the keyboard, she'd smash her nose on the *H* key. Mitch swallowed a growl and tried to remember all the organizational qualities that made her a great assistant. Maybe he'd better take to carrying a list in his pocket?

"Get her on her cell, then," he barked, this time not bothering to temper his tone. Diana was just going to have to get over her fear, because he didn't have time to baby her. And damned if he hadn't been right about Belle being a flake. Less than a week here at the resort and she was already slacking off.

Date. Fury bolted through him like lightning. Fast, furious, deadly. It was because she was screwing off, he assured himself. Not because she might be screwing some guy other than him.

Reece was right. Mitch had built his success by taking part in every aspect of his business. Every single thing. Which obviously needed to include his luscious ex-fiancée. This hands-off approach wasn't working. Not for the resort, and definitely not for his resort's event planner.

"Her phone goes direct to voice mail," Diana said, dread clear in her tone.

Images of Belle and some faceless guy sent that bolt of fury right through him again, ripping a hole in Mitch's gut.

"I'll deal with Ms. Forsham and the tour tomorrow," he decided. "No more of this letting her do things her way. I'm stepping in and showing her who's boss. From now on, she'll answer to me."

5

HUMMING HER FAVORITE pop star's latest song, Belle strode through the resort lobby with a swing in her hips and a smile on her lips. Her heels tapped a pleasing counter-beat as she crossed the polished marble and breathed in the rich scent of fresh flowers from the atrium.

Gorgeous morning. It was weird how good she felt waking up in the enchanted forest, as she'd taken to calling the wooded view outside her bedroom window. Throw in tea and muffins on the tiny, private deck, and she'd managed to shove aside all her worries about her father and grab a positive attitude.

After all, she was a smart woman. A talented woman. A woman on a mission. And she'd succeed. Although it would be a lot easier if she could get Mitch to face her instead of pretending she didn't exist. Maybe her email would help? As soon as she'd gotten back to the resort last night she'd drafted an outline of her pitch, detailing the many reasons why this resort should be themed to cater to the sexual needs of its guests.

Now to see if he responded.

Of course, there were advantages to not dealing with Mitch face-to-face. One of which was wearing jeans and a tank top instead of dressing like a fancy professional. She still wore a crystal-trimmed satin bra under the turquoise silk tank, though. Nothing overt, just a flirty hint of femininity. Her pep talk with Sierra fresh in her mind, she had a solid game plan. Professional and polite, all flirting—except lingerie-style hints—were now off-limits.

That reminder firmly in her head, she gave the manager a finger wave and winked at his trainees as she passed behind the check-in counter to make her way back to Diana's office.

And even though she knew she shouldn't, she gave a little prayer of thanks for her fancy bra when she saw the delicious treat awaiting her.

The only thing better than seeing Mitch Carter first thing in the morning would have been seeing him a little sooner. Like as soon as she'd opened her eyes.

Like her, he wore jeans with his T-shirt. Belle had noticed early on that while the rest of the staff dressed upscale casual, Mitch didn't bother with the upscale part. His rich auburn hair, shoved back off his face, was just past the need-for-a-haircut stage and curling toward his collar.

Her fingers twitched with the desire to touch that hair, to feel it beneath her palms and see if it was as silky and warm as she remembered.

"Mitch," she greeted him with a smile. "This must be my lucky morning."

"Following your lucky night, I suppose."

Belle frowned at the angry snap in his tone, but just shrugged.

"It could have been luckier, of course," she returned, since she'd have much preferred to spend it with him than driving back from L.A. at midnight. "But I had a great time."

"I'll bet."

She made a show of looking around the room, empty but for the two of them. "Just us? I was starting to think that was against the rules or something."

As soon as the words were out, she winced. So much for professional. But, she realized, looking at his stormy face, she was a little hurt at Mitch's blatant avoidance of her, even if he was a total grump-butt in the morning. Someone must have missed his caffeine fix. Belle couldn't recall ever seeing Mitch so out of sorts. It would have been endearing if she didn't feel as if she was blindly stepping into the path of a natural disaster.

"Rules? Don't you just ignore those? Things like showing up to work, agreements and contracts? What, too much like a wedding ceremony for you?"

Anger blasted Belle's amused confusion to bits. She had to grind her teeth to keep from snapping back at him. Lips pressed tightly together, she glared. How dare he?

Mitch arched a brow, challenging her to defend herself.

Belle opened her mouth to yell back, then closed it again, swallowing hard. She hated ugliness and fights. Her parents had fought constantly. Right up until her mother was diagnosed with cancer, every little thing had been an argument. She knew better now, but in third grade, she'd been sure her mama had been argued to death.

Mitch was pissed, most likely because she'd left yesterday. She debated telling him she'd gone to see her father, but didn't see how making him angrier would help anything.

Instead she plastered on her social smile and, with a wink, wiggled her sandal-shod foot toward him. "No sneakers, remember?"

She took his twitching lips as a good sign and opened the leather portfolio she had tucked under her arm. She pulled out the list of local recommendations she'd come up with, along with an outline of the mini-events. And, with another glance at the lurking fury in his cinnamon eyes, she steeled her spine and added the theme-pitch outline, as well.

"Although both our agreement and contract show these reports due next week," she said, handing them to him, "they're almost complete now and I'd like your input before I go any further. Maybe we can sit down and hammer out some details?"

"I've scheduled the morning to give you the tour you blew off yesterday," he returned.

His words were short, but the curt edge had left his tone. Hearing it gone, Belle felt some of the tension melt from her shoulders.

"Then let's tour," she agreed. "I'm sure I'll have more questions when we're through and we can handle them all at once."

Jaw tight, Mitch gave a stiff nod. Belle hid a sigh. No wonder he and her father had once considered partnership. They were both grumpy SOBs when they wanted to be. Another shock, since she'd have sworn during their engagement that Mitch was the most affable guy in the world. Just went to show how blind she'd been.

"I'll tell Diana we're going" was all he said. But he took the papers with him as he strode into his assistant's office.

Her body tight from the stress of not yelling at his bad-tempered self, Belle dropped into one of the plush chairs outside the main office and heaved a huge sigh. She didn't know which was worse: the way Mitch's irritation pushed her to face her fear of confrontation, or the fact that he was even sexier when he got all intense and uptight like that.

Either way, the man was bad for her control. Part of her wished hard for a pair of sneakers. The other part, the mature businesswoman, steeled her spine and gave

thanks that she and Sierra had agreed that professional
was the new plan.

An hour later, she was recalling the sports store in town
and wondering if sneakers came in pink. Since they'd arrived in the dining room, she'd spent more time sketch-
ing pictures of Mitch's butt in her notebook than making
notes of the menu plans, rotation of celebrity chefs and
floral arrangements.

"Are you getting all of this?" he asked, his words right-
fully suspicious. "You look a little distracted."

"The meals I've had since I arrived are excellent, so obviously your chefs are top-notch," she said as if she'd been
paying full attention, "but I agree having guest chefs and
rotating your menu will keep things fresh. I think, too, that
you might want to incorporate some type of theme that
works with each chef. For instance, when you bring in the
latest Italian wonder, integrate a taste of Italy into the entire month at the resort. Decor, events, that kind of thing."

Mitch's eyes lit up at her suggestion, but he didn't comment. Instead he gestured toward the door and the next
stop on their tour. Belle didn't mind, though. She knew
she was getting through to him. This was how she liked
to do business. Face-to-face. Or, she thought with a tiny
sigh as he strode ahead to open the heavy oak door for
her, face-to-butt.

God, she wanted him. It was killing her to hold back
the flirtation. Instead she kept dropping subtle suggestions and hints that supported her idea to slant the entire resort toward a sexual theme. She wished she could
blame her lusty awareness on that, but she knew all the
credit went to Mitch.

She reached the door and was surprised, after all his
careful avoidance, that Mitch had barely opened it. She

had to brush against him to get through. As she did, her eyes met his and she raised a brow.

"The door's stuck," he muttered. "I've got a carpenter coming to look at the hinges."

"Mmm" was all she said. That was the fifth problem they'd encountered so far on the tour. Slipshod construction, a computer failure, a missing stove and, if she hadn't been mistaken, a few too many holes on the golf green.

For a brand-new resort set to open to the public in four weeks, it was a little disconcerting. She knew the hotel business inside out and a few start-up problems here and there were normal. These seemed excessive.

As they made their way out of the restaurant and toward the spa and gym, Belle slanted Mitch a sideways glance. She'd thought he was the best. Her daddy had thought so, too, as did everyone she'd talked with. Everybody couldn't be wrong. Could they?

"Do you usually take such a personal hand in your developments, Mitch?" Like the rest of the resort, the mosaic-covered walkway was a combination of art deco and lush greenery. Plants, perhaps echoing the woods beyond the resort, were tucked in every corner, graced every curve. The decor was rich, intense, reminiscent of the Erté statues she'd seen in the foyer.

"My name is on the project, my money is invested in it," he said simply. "I'm going to be involved from the ground up."

Admirable. And, she frowned as she noticed wilting trellis roses, a little concerning. Mitch, who seemed to notice the browned roses at the same time, swore.

"My nana swears that a little water fixes that particular rose problem," Belle joked.

Mitch glared, then pointed to the ground beneath the

roses. Belle saw the broken sprinkler heads. Brow furrowed, she stepped closer.

"They look like someone kicked them." A few times, she noted, taking in the destroyed plants surrounding the black plastic. Her first thought was kids, but there were no kids around Lakeside. "Vandals?"

"Maybe. The gardeners keep finding this type of destruction. All minor stuff, just enough to be a pain in the ass."

"This isn't the first vandalism problem?" Construction problems, personnel issues and now vandalism? What was going on? Sure, one or two could be blamed on start-up woes. But all three? Who had Mitch pissed off?

"There've been a few similar landscape issues, along with some missing supplies. The linen shipment disappeared from the laundry room, showed up a week later in the generator shed." The frustration in Mitch's tone was echoed in the cold anger in his eyes. Belle was glad that look wasn't aimed at her. "Nothing I can take to the police as proof there is an actual problem."

"You don't have video out here, right? I remember that being one of the things that factored into my idea to run with the sex theme. You offer so much privacy, it's a shame not to use it. Then again—" she waved her hand at the poor roses and wrinkled her nose "—if you're going to waste my plan anyway, maybe you should put in some kind of security measures."

"You have quite a few ideas for someone who can't tear herself away from her hot sex life to do her job," he snapped. "Why don't you focus on not screwing up these events and let me worry about handling my resort."

Belle gasped. Fury such as she'd never felt before flashed hot and bright. She didn't even think to temper it, instead giving in to the wave of anger. "How dare you? Who the hell are you to question my work?"

Normal restraint disappeared, leaving Belle freer than she'd ever felt before. She threw her notebook to the ground, the slap of leather against tile ringing out like a gauntlet.

Two steps was all it took to put her up close and personal with Mitch. Her sandaled toes butted up against his work boots. She glared into his shocked face.

"I'm damned good at my job and have never screwed up a single event. Can you say the same? No," she plowed on before he could respond, "I don't think so. If you have an issue with my work, just say so. Although how you'd have a freaking clue is baffling since all you've done for the last week is hide."

"I—"

She swung her arm up in an arrogant, speak-to-the-hand gesture she'd never thought she'd use and cut him off. Anything he said was only going to piss her off more.

"And for your information, my sex life currently sucks." She slapped her palm against his chest to push him out of her way. She knew it was shock that made him step back, not her strength. She didn't care, as long as he moved. "Just so you know, I blame you for that, too."

MITCH'S MIND REELED between regret at his unfair accusation to astonishment at Belle's reaction. But as she shot that final slap, both physical and verbal, his jaw dropped.

His fault? The hell it was.

Her hair was a silken wave that hit him smack in the face as she spun around to leave. Before she could take more than a step, Mitch grabbed her arm and pulled her back.

Anger, frustration and a pounding desire all beat at

him. All the practical excuses and sane reasons he'd taken to reciting daily in an effort to avoid temptation flamed to cinders when he met the fury in her stormy sea-green eyes.

"We need to talk," he said in a low growl. With a quick look at the deserted landscape, he decided it was still too exposed for the chat he had in mind. So, his hand still gripping the soft skin of her arm, he pulled her with him toward the pool's linen room.

"We don't have jack to discuss," she snarled, trying to tug free. "I don't want to talk to you and I guarantee you don't want to hear what I have to say."

"On the contrary," he snapped, pushing the door open and pulling Belle with him into the dimly lit room. It was the size of a small shed. Neatly folded towels filled the shelf-lined walls and the air was warm with the scent of laundry detergent and sunshine. "We obviously have a lot to say to each other."

Belle tugged her arm free and glared. Her breath shuddered in and out, drawing his eyes to the lush bounty he'd been trying to ignore beneath her silky tank top. Mitch's gaze traced the curve of her breasts to the sweet indention of her waist, emphasized by a jeweled belt before the silk gave way to denim.

All week, hell, for the past six years he'd dreamed of her long legs wrapped around him. Of those hips welcoming him. Caution screamed in his head, a blaring warning that he was treading on thin ice. He'd promised that he'd keep his hands off her as long as she worked for him. Too much was at stake.

Apparently unaware of Mitch's inner struggle between desire and his vow to stay the hell out of her pants, Belle planted her fists on her hips, tugging the silk tighter against her breasts in a way that showed a narrow strip of her bra. Sparkling jewels caught the faint light like a treasure.beckoning.

"What the hell is your problem?" she asked, her tone as angry as the look on her gorgeous face. "When did you turn into a caveman?"

"We needed to talk," he repeated. "We both have jobs to do. Given all the problems I've had, the last thing I need is you stomping off in a snit."

"Snit?" She actually hissed the word.

Getting turned on by her anger was probably a bad sign.

"Look, I overreacted, okay? But I promised myself I'd keep my hands off you. Which isn't easy with all your blatant flirting and come-ons, I'll have you know."

From the sneer she shot him, it was a piss-poor explanation.

"Want to remind me of when I begged you to put those hands on me?" she asked. She gave him a long, slow, up-and-down look that jacked his already cranked-up libido into full gear. "Did I touch you? A little pat on the ass? Flirty suggestions or come-do-me looks?"

Mitch arched a brow, about to remind her of their first meetings two weeks before. Catching the look, Belle rolled her eyes and flicked her hand toward him. "Bullshit. Anything that happened before we signed our contract doesn't count. You said the only way you'd be comfortable with us working together was if it was all business. I complied."

He hated that she was right. She'd been totally professional. At least she had until she'd blown off the previous day's tour to go on a date. Mitch mentally winced. Was that the real reason for his anger? Was he jealous? Pitiful, especially since he had no right to be.

Mitch's brow furrowed. Damn. It was one thing to be pitiful, but he had no right to take his anger out on her.

He ground his teeth and tried to shove the emotion aside. He owed Belle an apology.

Ramming his hands into his pockets, Mitch stiffened his shoulders, battled down the fury and opened his mouth to offer up his apology. Before he could say a word, though, she was off and running again.

"Just because you're too sexually uptight to handle a hot relationship doesn't mean you should take your attitude out on me," she snapped, stabbing at him with her finger.

Mitch's apology turned into a glare but she just rolled her eyes.

"Oh, please. Even if we accept your silly excuse about our past and your business being too touchy to allow anything to happen between us, there's still the rest of it," she scoffed. "Admit it, you're too uptight to consider an incredibly innovative and exciting proposal that would guarantee your resort's success."

He'd had enough. Enough of her accusations. Enough of the sexual frustration that kept him churned up and crazy. Enough of being practical and self-sacrificing for the good of the many.

Screw it all, he was sick and tired of denying himself. For once, he was taking what he wanted.

He gave a low growl. Belle gasped. Before she could do more than blink, he moved, grabbing both her wrists and pinning her, arms overhead, to the smooth wall of the linen shed.

Heat, lust, anger all tangled in his system as he pressed his body close to hers. Like a drug addict grabbing for his fix, he closed his eyes in ecstasy even as he hated himself for giving in to the need.

But damn, it felt good.

Mitch didn't wait for Belle to recover. Instead he took her mouth in an intense, wild kiss. Passion flamed hot and furious between them as she opened her lips to his seeking tongue. Her welcoming moan sent a shaft of desire through him. His downfall felt deliciously decadent.

SHOCK FADED AS BELLE gave over to the power of Mitch's kiss. She had no idea what had incited the move, but she loved it. Loved the feel of his lips, soft and slick as they moved over hers. The power of his tongue as it tangled and wove, inviting hers to join him in the sensual dance.

Her breath came in pants now. Between the heat of his kiss and the wild excitement of feeling trapped by his hands holding hers prisoner, her panties were damp. She'd never gone for the submission thing, but Mitch holding her captive made her wild to let him have his way with her.

She squirmed a little, needing Mitch to hurry, to do something to relieve the building tension in her belly.

"More," she murmured against his mouth.

"Wait," he murmured back.

She groaned as he slid his lips from hers, already missing the hot dance of his tongue. She sucked in her lower lip, wanting, needing, to taste him.

Mitch traced kisses, hot, wet and exciting, down her throat. Belle groaned when he reached that spot, just there where her neck met her shoulder, and nibbled.

She tugged at her hands, needing to touch him. To feel his shoulders under her fingers, his chest and biceps. She just wanted to grab him and hold on while he took her for a wild ride.

Mitch wouldn't let go. Instead, he shifted so he held both her hands in one of his. Belle thought briefly of how large his hand must be to wrap so neatly around her wrists. The realization made her grin, then, unable to help herself, she pressed her hips closer to his, a quick undulation to check out the myth.

Yummy. If the very hard, very large length pressing against her thigh was any indication, that myth was based on reality. A reality she wanted to see, to feel and get to know up close and personal.

"More," she demanded again. The need in her belly was getting tighter, more urgent. "Quit playing and show me what you've got, big boy."

Mitch chuckled, as she'd hoped he would. But even better, he used his free hand to test the weight of her breast, then in a swift move he released her hands to tug her tank top and bra straps down one shoulder.

Belle's breath caught, her gaze locked on his face. She'd never worried about being judged before, but Mitch was different. She felt she'd wanted him, just like this, all her life. Lust and pure masculine appreciation were clear on his face. That look was as much a turn-on as the feel of his dick, hard and throbbing against her thigh. Tension fled, leaving only desire and need as he met her eyes. Their gazes locked as Mitch traced his finger over her areola, then flicked her hardening nipple.

She gasped.

His gaze dropped to her chest, color heating his cheeks. He bent and touched just the top of his tongue to the aching tip of her breast. Belle wanted to cry at the torment.

But she'd be damned if she'd beg again. Instead she shifted, wrapping one leg around his hip so she could press her wet, hot core against his thigh. The move lifted her breast higher. Mitch showed his appreciation by taking her nipple in his mouth, sucking, licking and nibbling.

Belle whimpered, her breath coming in pants now. Her head fell back against the wall, eyes closed to the dim light as she gave herself over to the wonderful feelings Mitch's mouth was inspiring. She didn't even notice that he'd let go of her wrists until she felt one hand under her butt. That hand lifted, controlled her undulations as he pressed her closer. The other tugged the second set of straps down to bare both breasts.

His mouth still tormenting one nipple, he worked the other with his fingers. Belle groaned her approval, pressing tight enough that the seam of her jeans added to the spiraling pleasure.

Mitch released his grip on her butt, shifting just a little so Belle could wrap both legs around his hips, his dick pressed against her throbbing core. The denim between them only added to her wild excitement.

Holding a breast in each large hand, he pressed them together. His thumbs worked her nipples as his mouth moved, wet and wild, first tormenting the left, then the right. Belle's hips jerked. She pressed closer, her ankles grabbing tight to his butt.

Heaven. When he nipped, teeth sharp yet gentle, at her wet nipple, she cried out in pleasure and lost control.

Gasping for breath, she came hard and fast. Lights exploded behind her eyes, her body melted with the power of the orgasm.

"Ohmygod, ohmygod, ohmygod," she chanted as she rode the wave. Mitch kept her up there, his tongue still working, his hand back beneath her butt to support her as she collapsed in delight.

Tension—hell, all feeling—fled her body as she sank into the afterglow of a first-class orgasm. Her legs numb, she dropped her feet to either side of Mitch's, but didn't shift away from the throbbing power of his dick where it pressed against her belly.

It took her a minute to realize he'd stopped his torment of her breasts. When she did, she lifted her head and opened her eyes to meet his.

She had to laugh. His grin was pure male ego.

Then it faded. Belle heard voices outside and realized his crew had probably shown up to fix the sprinkler problem.

Seeing she'd regained control, Mitch stepped away, visibly working to regulate his breathing. Belle stared through foggy eyes, satisfaction throbbing in her belly, between her legs. Damn, she felt great.

"Your turn?" she asked, her voice husky with pleasure.

She watched him swallow, then glance out the narrow window.

"The last thing I need my gardeners seeing is my bare ass," he said with a grimace.

Belle smirked. The chances of the gardeners peeking in were slim at best, but she didn't bother calling him on the flimsy excuse.

"I'm not uptight," he insisted. Belle kept silent, letting her arched brow speak volumes.

Well, he hadn't *felt* uptight, that was for sure. But then, he hadn't dropped his drawers, either. Rather than giving him the agreement he so obviously wanted, she just shrugged and adjusted her clothing, again not saying anything.

She hid her grin when she heard his teeth grinding from across the tiny shed.

"I'll read your proposal again," he suddenly promised. Shocked, Belle met his eyes. "If it's as solid as I remember, I'll submit it to my management team."

She didn't want a job—any job—based on sex, or in Mitch's case, unrequited sexual need. But she did want a chance.

"Why?" she asked.

"Because you're right. The idea is solid, it meshes with what I'm trying to do here. So it's worth considering."

"And if your team agrees?"

"We'll modify your contracts."

Belle nodded. Then she moved forward, close enough to feel the assurance that he was still hot, hard and excited. "And what about us?"

Mitch winced. "It'd be stupid to screw up a business deal over sex."

"It doesn't have to be like that," she returned, noticing he didn't say they wouldn't have sex. "Think of it this way. My proposal for your resort is based on sexual thrills. Don't you owe it to your clientele to try them all first?"

Mitch's eyes went round, then crinkled with laughter. "Why don't we see how the proposal goes first?"

Belle grimaced, thinking of what the last proposal between them had cost her. But she was smarter this time and definitely nowhere near as naive.

With that in mind, she gave Mitch her most wicked grin and stepped closer, letting the back of her fingers brush over his still-straining erection.

"You take me up on my proposal—business, pleasure or both—and I promise, you won't regret it."

With that and a quick butterfly kiss, she turned to saunter away. She felt the heat of his gaze on her swaying hips and let her grin fall away. Now she'd better figure out how to make damned sure *she* didn't regret it, either.

6

"WHAT KIND OF SEXY food did you have in mind for the room-service menu?" Mitch asked the people around the board table. This was their first group brainstorming session on the resort's new theme and he wasn't doing so well. It was a struggle to use the same tone he'd employ to discuss the type of artwork they'd carry in the lobby or how many brands of scotch the bar should have on hand. In other words, to keep this discussion at the level of pure business.

Damned hard, too, seeing the woman sitting across from him who had cried out as he brought her to an orgasm in a towel closet three days before. The look she was giving him, pure flirtatious amusement, told him she was waiting for a repeat performance.

"Probably just two or three items," Belle said, her delight at the conversation, and probably at his apparent discomfort, clear in her tone. "The trick is going to be choosing the right ones. You might want to tie into your revolving-guest-chef theme with these. Keep a standard on the menu at all times, say oysters, since their reputation is so tried in food."

Mitch exchanged confused frowns with his manager, then asked, "Tried and true?"

"Exactly." She shot him a grin before leaning over to dig through her satchel and pull out files for everyone at the table. Their current discourse on sexual turn-ons was being shared with two of his managers, his head chef, Jacques, and Miles, the resort's head of security. A nice, intimate group with which to brainstorm kink.

Belle had put them all at their ease, though. From the minute she'd walked into the room in her demure black skirt and red sleeveless turtleneck, she'd had his staff in the palm of her delectable little hand. A couple of jokes, a personal comment to each guy to let him know she'd done her research and appreciated the job he did, and they'd all relaxed.

And, given the topic, relaxation was key. At first, nobody had wanted to jump in with an opinion, so it'd been just Mitch and Belle talking sex. But after a quarter of an hour or so, the group hadn't been able to hold back. Now the opinions and ideas were flowing fast and furious, which gave Mitch time to sit back and watch Belle at work.

He glanced at the list she'd handed out. Title: Aphrodisiacs. He couldn't help but laugh. Belle winked at him.

"The room-service menu should otherwise be standard, of course." She glanced around the table and all the men nodded in agreement. Mitch suspected they'd have nodded if she'd suggested adding popcorn and Popsicles to the menu, they were so equally fascinated and out of their element. "But for the restaurant menu we can get more creative. Maybe cultural or thematic—Mexican chocolate, oysters Rockefeller, Greek honey cakes. That kind of thing."

"Graphic desserts?" offered Larry.

"Too bachelorette partyesque," Belle rejected with a

grimace. "Think classier. Something that convinces people this isn't a gimmick, that it will really work."

"Asparagus and arugula salad?" he offered.

"There you go," she said, pointing her pen at him in approval before making note of his suggestion.

Mitch snickered when Larry preened as though he'd just been given a gold star.

Damn, she was good. She definitely knew what she was doing. Her society-princess title had been well earned. She orchestrated the meeting like a cocktail party, introducing this idea and that, making sure everyone had a chance to interject their comments before rearranging and serving the concepts back to them on a platter.

Who knew watching a sexy woman using her brain to work a room could be such a turn-on. Mitch wasn't a chauvinist pig; he respected women for more than their bodies. But he'd had no idea Belle had so much more going on.

He thought back to their engagement. He'd never seen her as a real person, just a princess to be won. And then there was their towel-closet encounter. While she'd obviously enjoyed the end results, he doubted she was impressed with his finesse and gentlemanly behavior.

Mitch grimaced. Maybe he was a pig.

"Now that we've covered the menu, let's see if we can nail a few of the special amenity details," Belle suggested, launching the discussion in a whole different direction.

Since most of those details were sexually explicit, Mitch had to work to keep his expression neutral.

"Do you really think handcuffs are necessary?" he asked as Diana brought in a tray of coffee and snacks. Apparently Belle had left word that she needed a midafternoon pick-me-up and his assistant was only too happy to oblige. Mitch couldn't say he blamed Diana, since he'd willingly do quite a few things, most cheap and kinky, to see Belle's smile of gratitude flash his way.

"Of course you need handcuffs," Belle said, her green eyes flashing wicked delight at odds with her matter-of-fact tone. "The key to having this work is to keep the sexual offerings classy by making them a standard amenity. If a guest has to call down to the concierge and ask for sex toys, it ruins the spontaneity."

From the bemused looks on the faces of his staff as Belle passed around a tray of cookies, Mitch figured they were as speechless at that image as he was.

"And our goal is spontaneous sex?" he finally asked, giving up all pretense that he wasn't completely out of his element.

"That is precisely our goal," Belle said, her eyes hot and intense as she nibbled at a chocolate cookie. "The more spontaneous, and the more sex, the better."

Mitch went from intrigued to rock-hard in two seconds flat.

"You'll need to specially train your front desk and your concierge," Belle continued, talking to Larry. "Given the target demographic, you want to support the high-end thrill and excitement of a sexual getaway. Few people looking for the privacy to indulge their sexual fantasies care to explain to a concierge whether they prefer their handcuffs fur-lined or solid metal."

"Good point." Mitch frowned as he made a note on his report and muttered, "Apparently I'm going to need to find a supplier of kinky toys."

Belle pulled a paper from her file and handed him a complete list of companies, color-coded by fetish.

Helpless to do otherwise, Mitch snorted with laughter. Damn, she was good. Belle shot him an impish smile that said she knew what he was thinking and looked forward to proving just how good she could be.

BELLE LEFT MITCH'S BOARDROOM, doing a little happy dance as soon as the door swung shut behind her.

"That went well, I take it?" Diana asked, a hint of something Belle didn't understand in her tone.

"It was fabulous," Belle returned, too curious about the other woman to feel embarrassed. "I think this is going to rock. Everyone had great ideas. It's got success written all over it."

From Diana's grimace-faking-it-as-a-smile, Belle figured the other woman might have some issues with the sex stuff. Leave it to Mitch to hire a prude as his assistant, Belle thought affectionately. But she'd brought him around, and she was sure she could bring Diana to accept the concept, as well.

With that in mind, she pulled a chair up close to the woman's desk and leaned forward with her friendliest look.

"This must be fascinating," she said conversationally. "Being in on the ground floor of opening such a great place. I mean, you're surrounded by luxury, an incredible view and a hot boss. And once the place is open, it'll be like free cable. The inside scoop on famous people and clandestine sex. Not a bad job, huh?"

Diana looked at her as if she was a two-headed dog and both sides were missing a brain. Uptight *and* no sense of humor? Poor Mitch.

"Or not," Belle muttered, wondering if she had any common ground with this woman. She surveyed Diana's polyester blouse, navy slacks and flat pleather sandals. Probably not.

Belle glanced at her watch and sighed. How much longer was Mitch going to be?

"So tell me, Diana, how's the resort shaping up?" she asked after a few minutes of miserably uncomfortable silence. She didn't really care about the answer but was desperate for some conversation.

"Falling apart is more like it," the other woman mumbled into her computer screen.

"Beg pardon?"

Diana slanted her a sideways look and shrugged. "You know, it's just one problem after another. I've never been in on the—how did you say it?—ground floor of a resort opening before. But I'd imagined it'd be a little smoother, if you know what I mean."

Belle's brows shot up. "You mean things like the sprinklers and construction hitches?"

Diana winced. "Sure, those and the gophers and the computer crashes and the laundry mix-up and the lost supplies and, well, I could keep going but you get my drift."

Funny how the woman lost her quiet reserve when she was reciting all the resort's issues. Belle frowned and gave a one-shouldered shrug. "I'm sure that's all part and parcel to opening a new venue."

At least, she assumed it was. Her father's hotels had never hit so many hitches, but then he'd been at it a long time. This was Mitch's first hospitality venue, so maybe he just hadn't found his stride yet?

"Maybe," Diana agreed doubtfully. "I mean, I've heard such amazing things about Mr. Carter. He's got a reputation for being such an expert."

Diana's tone made it clear that she wasn't buying the rep any longer. Doubt washed over Belle. Was Mitch the guy to help her dad? She'd been so sure. As Diana said, he had a stellar reputation for being Mr. Amazing when it came to business. She frowned. Was that rep wrong?

"Can you excuse me for a minute?" she asked Diana. "If Mitch comes out, just let him know I had a call I forgot I have to make."

"You can make it here," Diana said, pointing to the phone.

"Um, no, thanks." Belle waved her cell phone and gestured toward the hallway. "It's...private."

The other woman gave her an ohhh-one-of-those-calls look and shrugged.

Once alone, Belle punched a button and paced impatiently while waiting for Sierra to pick up.

"We might need to rethink a few things," she said as soon as her partner answered.

"Which few?"

Belle explained the resort issues she'd discovered, both on her own and the ones Diana had shared. "So now I'm wondering if Mitch is really the right guy to help daddy."

"What about the Eventually Yours gig? Do we need to pull out?"

Pull out? Belle considered the question. They couldn't. They'd tied up a lot of time and energy in this project. If it went belly-up, they would definitely hurt. But not enough for her to consider ditching Mitch. He believed in the resort and had so much more at stake. She wanted to give him her support, even if he didn't realize it. The only thing she was risking was her time and energy. Yes, Eventfully Yours might take a hit, but as long as she came up with some other idea to help her dad, she could handle it.

"I gave my word, I can't back out." Her fear of failure faded a little as she made the statement.

At Sierra's snort she pulled the phone away from her ear and rolled her eyes.

"I've matured," she claimed, talking into the speaker again.

"Matured my ass. You just want to get in his pants."

"That's beside the point," Belle mumbled. So what if she did? Was that the only reason she wanted to stick with the job? No, of course not. She believed in it. She'd had a great time in their brainstorming session and the ideas they'd all come up with were awesome.

With that in mind, she squared her shoulders, shook off her nerves and claimed, "This is business and we signed a contract. Besides, I really haven't seen any hard evidence to make me believe Mitch isn't all his reputation says. Just little things that could easily be chalked up to normal start-up woes."

"You wouldn't have called me if you weren't worried."

"Not worried. Cautiously concerned about the big picture, you know?" And she hadn't wanted to voice her doubts about Mitch's success aloud. It seemed so disloyal.

"You mean you don't want to let your lust for this guy blind you a second time."

Belle pulled a face and, feeling like a slug, mumbled, "I'd rather just depend on us, if you know what I mean. As long as you're okay with the decision."

Sierra was silent for a second. Belle heard the cellophane crinkle of a candy wrapper. Then, "Eventfully Yours can handle whatever happens. The real question is, what do you want to do about your dad? Find someone else to help him? Like who? You're the one with all the hotel experience."

Blinking away tears of relief at her friend's understanding and support, Belle paced and considered. "Let's just see what we can come up with ourselves, okay? I don't want to make any decisions yet. I just, you know, needed a sounding board and to get your brain in on the action."

"What are you going to do while my brain works?"

Mitch strode out of his office just then. Unlike the businessmen her daddy worked with, who always did the suit-and-tie thing, Mitch seemed to have left that phase behind him. Other than their meeting at the restaurant when they'd signed the contracts, he always wore jeans.

As Mitch turned to respond to something Diana had said, Belle sighed. Damn, she loved a guy in jeans.

"Continue with plan A," Belle said as her eyes met Mitch's when he turned around.

"Jump his bones?" Sierra confirmed.

"You know it." With that, Belle pushed the disconnect button and slid her phone into her bag.

"Ready?" Mitch asked, referring to their plans to tour the golf course and wooded picnic area.

"I need to change," she said, waving her high-heeled sandal-clad foot his way. "Let's stop by my room and I'll get some flats, okay?"

They headed outside toward her cottage.

"I don't think I ever saw you in jeans when we were dating or engaged," she commented.

Mitch's look of surprise must be due to her bringing up the past, Belle figured. But while she wasn't about to play the blame game, it was silly to pretend they didn't have a past. Maybe if they melted the ice with easy chit-chat, she'd be able to work up the nerve to apologize for abandoning him at the altar before her job here was done.

"Six years ago I had too much to prove to let myself wear jeans," Mitch finally said.

Intriguing. "And did you?"

"Did I what?"

"Prove your point? And what was it? That denim makes your ass look great, but you wanted to be taken seriously so you denied the world the sweet sight?"

He snorted and shook his head. They'd reached her cottage, so he gestured for her to precede him to the door. Belle glanced back to see if he was going to answer and caught him checking out *her* ass. She grinned. Well, tit for tat and all that.

"Hardly," he said, shrugging an apology for the ogling. Belle just winked back to let him know she didn't mind. "I wanted to play with the big boys. Hotels, entertainment. I figured nobody would take a hammer-swinging kid seriously so I went the businessman route."

"Trying to be a wolf with silk ears?"

He frowned, then after a second corrected, "Wolf in sheep's clothing? Or silk purse out of a sow's ear?"

"Both." She smiled up at him as she pushed open the door. "But I heard talk before you showed up in those fancy suits. Nobody thought of you as a kid or as less than a driving force. They were looking forward to working with you. You had a great rep."

At least he had before she got ahold of him. Belle winced and, before he could respond by pointing out that exact fact, she gestured to the bowl of fruit on the small kitchenette table. "Help yourself to a snack while I change, hmm?"

And off she scurried, like a scared little mouse, guilt pounding at her like a sledgehammer on speed. In the bedroom, she dropped to her bed and stared at the ceiling while reciting all the reasons she'd screwed up and why he had the right to hold them against her. Then, once they were out of her system, she shot up and tugged open the plantation-style closet doors to grab a denim skirt and casual blouse for their tour.

MITCH BLINKED AT THE closed door, wondering what the hell had just happened. One second he and Belle had been having a friendly jaunt into the past. The next she was offering him a banana and running away.

Apparently that was the theme of their relationship, that running thing.

He sighed and glanced around the cottage. *California casual* was the term the decorator had used—light woods, soft fabric, bare tile floors. The space was open and airy with a few plants here and there to make it welcoming. As comfortable as it had started out, in less than a week, Belle had made it her own.

Colorful scarves over the chairs added rich splashes of green and turquoise. A wooden bowl filled with engraved stones sat on the coffee table. Mitch walked over to pick one out. *Perseverance,* he read. Motivational sayings? Belle?

He noticed a small framed poster on the wall. Stone in hand, he stepped closer to read about the ABCs to Achieve Your Dreams.

Wild. He frowned at the closed door and tried to adjust his image of her, a flighty sexpot with great planning skills, with the idea that she bought, let alone used, motivational tools.

It was then that he saw it. A small, fluffy, pink, stuffed bunny rabbit. As spotless as the day he'd won it for her at a corporate fund-raising carnival, it sat in the rocking chair looking fat and content.

Mitch grinned at the sight and, tossing the stone back in the bowl, lifted the bunny for a closer look.

"Don't mess with Mr. Winkles," Belle said, coming out of the bedroom. Her tone was light, but there was still a lingering frown around her eyes.

"I can't believe you still have this," he said with a laugh, holding up the stuffed animal. "I never took you for the sentimental type." He considered, then added, "I never thought our time together was something worthy of sentiment, to tell you the truth."

As soon as the words were out, Mitch winced. He sounded like an ass. But, well, the truth was, he'd never allowed himself to think about their time together as anything but a business deal gone bad. It hurt less that way.

She gave him the glare of death, but in a blink, the look was gone. Had he imagined it? Maybe.

Then she snatched the toy from his hands as if he'd stolen it. That's when it hit him.

"Are you embarrassed?" he asked with a grin. "There's no reason to be. I think it's sweet."

Her porcelain skin flushed crimson and the death glare returned in full force. She gripped one hand so tightly around the rabbit's neck, it'd be stew meat if it wasn't a stuffed toy. Mitch winced. From the look on her face, she was imagining his throat between her fingers.

"Sweet, my ass," she shot back. "I'm not sentimental over our time together. Believe me, the last thing I need is a constant reminder of my mistake."

Mitch's spine snapped straight, his amusement fleeing at that one word. *Mistake*.

Oh, yeah, there had been mistakes. But they were his. It'd taken him six years to make up for the business ones, and damned if he needed his personal ones thrown in his face by the woman at fault for all of them.

"Mistake? Care to clarify that?" he asked, his tone the one he reserved for embezzlers, liars and cheats. Icy-cold and precise.

"Oh, please, like you don't know." Her sneer was a work of art. Angry, but still disdainful enough to hide the hurt he'd glimpsed earlier. And he'd called her sentimental? "You can pretend all you want that we're business buddies here, but we both know damned well what happened."

"Us and a couple of hundred guests," he shot back.

Belle rolled her eyes. "That's your own damned fault," she declared. "If you hadn't put such an insane price on your body, we'd never have ended up in that mess."

Mitch had fallen off a fifth-story girder once, his safety rope keeping him from serious injury. That was the only time he recalled ever being this close to speechless. He stared, mouth open. "My body?"

"I wanted sex," she declared, pointing the bunny at him like a pistol. "Simple, uncomplicated sex. But no, you had to turn it into something else. Complicate it. You ruined everything, and for what? Ambition?" Disdain dripped from her words like battery acid, burning Mitch.

He clenched his jaw, struggling to find a response. Anger pounded at his temples: fury at the past and at the woman in front of him for reminding him that he'd never measured up.

He'd spent his entire career trying to prove himself. To prove he was man enough to take care of his mother after his dad had died. To prove he was worthy of the trust his stepfather had later showed in him. And then to prove that he wasn't going to fall apart when he'd been left with the responsibility of his stepdad's construction company.

And then he finally thought he'd found his perfect woman. The one he'd seen as proof that he was man enough for anything. And she'd walked out on him.

Mitch had never admitted, not to anyone but himself in the dark hours when it was just him and his thoughts, his fears that Belle had found him lacking. That she'd decided he wasn't rich enough, wasn't talented enough, wasn't worthy enough.

It was the last one that really grated. All he'd wanted from the moment he'd set eyes on the sassy blonde was to sweep her off her feet.

Mitch glared at her, all grown up now and just as sassily sexy. He should have swept when he had a chance. Maybe if he'd knocked her feet out from under her she wouldn't have run away.

Well, he'd blown his chance once. He wasn't stupid enough to blow it twice.

"You wanted sex?" he ground out, anger and lust sharp and jagged in his system. "Fine, I'll give you sex."

Two steps was all it took to pin her between the hard, needy length of his body and the wall. Belle's shocked gasp was lost against his mouth. Her sea-green eyes glared into his as she gave a low growl. Being a smart man, Mitch kept his tongue out of the game just yet. But he used his lips to full effect.

And his hands. Because, if he did say so himself, he was damned good with his hands. He skimmed them over her hair, a gentle glide down her shoulders then a quick, barely there flick along the sides of her full breasts, crushed against his chest. He gripped the gentle curve of her waist for just a second, then gave in to the need and scooped his hands under the sweet curve of her ass.

Mitch groaned as the move pressed her tighter to the throbbing length of his dick. God, he wanted her.

Tossing off all restraint, all the rules he'd tried so hard to live by, he let himself go. His hands gripped Belle's butt, squeezing her soft curves one more time before he pulled her between his thighs. One hand slid up to cup the back of her neck, holding her head in place when she tried to jerk away from his kiss.

Feeling her heart pounding in her throat, he told himself it was passion and, desperately needing to taste her, he risked it all and slid his tongue along the seam of her full, soft lips.

Her shuddered gasp was barely discernable, but he felt

it. Both against his mouth, and in the way she pressed herself tighter against his erection. Her wiggle was a tiny thing, but damn, it felt great. His grin was fast and triumphant before he took her mouth in a wild ride. Tongues dueled and tangled in a dance of passion. Quick, deep kisses that hinted at dark pleasures and intense emotion. He gave over to the power of tasting her, feeling her. Belle, the one obsession he'd never been able to shake.

A voice whispered in the back of his head to slow down. Mitch told the voice to shut the hell up. In pure defiance he shifted her, one quick move, to straddle his hips and gave a guttural groan when she wrapped those long, delicious legs around him. Mitch pressed, once, twice. Belle mimicked his rhythm, taking on the slow, intense undulation.

Desperate now, he released her hip and neck to cup her breasts. The heated warmth filled his palm. Her soft whimper turned to a moan when he flicked his thumbs over her pebbled nipples.

Need pounded now, a heavy dark beat. Mitch gave in to it, releasing her mouth as he pulled her blouse over her head. Seconds before he lost himself in the lush bounty of her breasts, he met her eyes. Head supported by the wall, her blond hair a cloudy pillow behind her, Belle stared back. Desire, power, pleasure all shone in her gaze.

Mitch's ultimate dream, here in his hands, the taste of her rich on his tongue. The image he had of him and Belle—the poor kid in patched jeans and the princess— flashed through his head. *You've come a long way, baby,* that voice said. But, he vowed, not nearly as long as he planned to make Belle come.

7

WHO KNEW CONFRONTATION could feel so good? Belle's breath trembled, the wall a hard pillow behind her head, and she closed her eyes and let the delicious sensations wash over her in powerful, throbbing waves.

Her fingers slid, caressing their way through Mitch's hair as she pressed his face closer to her breasts. The contrast of his mouth, so soft and moist and warm, and his cheek, roughening just hours after his morning shave, drove her nuts.

Fingers stroked, squeezed, in rhythm with her movements. Belle hitched just a little so her skirt shifted up higher, out of the way. Ahhh, she pressed closer, her silk panties moist and hot. They added to the intensity of his rough jeans against her swollen nether lips.

She wanted to squirm, to ratchet up the power. She wanted hard and fast and intense blood-pounding sex against the wall.

But Mitch was in charge, and despite the wall and the absolute control he'd grabbed early on, he was taking it slow. Damn him.

With deliberate care, he scraped his teeth over her aching nipples. Belle gasped and gripped his hair tighter, needing more. His tongue swirled, taunted and teased the tip of one breast, then switched to the other to continue the torment. Belle ground herself against the hard length of him.

"More," she moaned.

"Soon," he said, his breath hot against her damp flesh. Belle squirmed again, losing the rhythm. Her frantic movement made Mitch groan, the smooth stroke of his tongue turning to an almost desperate sucking motion.

Oh, yeah. Heat, fast and furious, shot through her body like a bolt of lightning. Pleasure bordered on pain as his mouth ravaged her breast, his hand gripping the other in a heated caress. Yeah, that's what she wanted. Her head fell back again, her eyes closed as she gave herself over to the sensations. Her panties were soaked now as she rode up and down the rigid length of his turgid, zipper-covered dick.

"I'm not doing this alone—again," she panted. "This time I want you with me."

"I'm right here."

"Naked," she insisted. She'd spent six-plus years wanting to get her hands on his naked body and she didn't want to wait a second more. "I want to see you. Touch you. Taste you."

He groaned and gave a little shudder, but didn't stop.

"After," he said.

After?

Mitch shifted, bringing one hand down between their bodies while the other still caressed the nipple he wasn't sucking. His fingers stroked the wet silk between her legs, sending a jolt of pleasure through her. Belle gasped, her thighs trembling as he worked her swollen clitoris through the fabric.

He played her body like a virtuoso, bringing her higher

and higher with every flick of his tongue, brush of his fingers. As her climax built, she knew which "after" he was referring to.

Then he slid the fabric of her panties out of the way. He danced his fingers over her slick folds, pressing, sliding, driving her crazy. Stars danced behind Belle's closed eyes, her body on overload. Mitch's tongue teased her nipple, then sucked it deep into his mouth as he worked her with his fingers.

One finger in, then out, was all it took. Belle exploded. Her thighs tightened, her fingers grabbed Mitch's shoulders as the orgasm shook her body. Spirals of pleasure danced through her system, spinning higher, wilder as she flew over the edge.

She slowly floated back to earth, her breath soft pants as she became aware of Mitch again. His mouth pressed into the curve of her throat, he held her tight against his body. As her thoughts coalesced, she felt the tension and strain in his shoulders, the bunched muscles of his back. And, she realized, that ever so deliciously hard muscle throbbing behind his zipper.

Twice now he'd made her come with all her clothes on, not taking anything in return. While she wouldn't deny the thrill of being taken against the wall—twice she still wanted a little more active role in screwing Mitch's brains out.

With that in mind, as soon as she thought they'd hold her, she let her legs slide down Mitch's hard thighs, sighing at the sensation of denim against bare flesh. Feet on the floor, she felt her knees try to buckle, making Belle grateful to be sandwiched between the wall and Mitch's body.

Time to upgrade this event to a couples theme…

"Off," Belle purred, needing to feel skin. Years. She'd waited years for this opportunity and she'd be damned if she was going to waste a single second of it. Not even to bask in the afterglow of a rockin' orgasm.

Her hands slid up his forearms, the soft hair tickling her palms. As she passed over the rolled-up chambray sleeves, she paused to squeeze his rock-solid biceps. She wanted to see those muscles. Now. She pulled at Mitch's shirt to get it out of her way. Buttons flew everywhere. She didn't care. Her eyes were focused on the prize, on the broad planes of his smooth, golden chest.

"Mmm," she murmured as she took in the sight. She let Mitch deal with getting the shirt off his arms. She was busy appreciating the view. Golden skin stretched over the nicest set of pecs she'd seen since ogling the big screen. Like the first fall leaves, a dusting of mahogany hair trailed down his chest. Belle swallowed, her eyes landing on the very large, very hard package pressing against the worn denim of his jeans. Yowza and come to mama. She placed one hand against his hard chest while she smoothed the other over his shoulder, down those biceps again. Mitch wrapped his hands around her waist, but she barely noticed his caress, so focused was she on the tactile wonderland of his body.

She leaned forward, pressing her face to the warmth of his chest, breathing in his cologne, then turned her head just a little to flick her tongue over his flat nipple. He swiftly sucked in his breath, his abs going concave.

Belle grinned her appreciation before letting her head fall back to look into his face.

"You're gorgeous," she told him. "Sexy, buff and delicious. I plan to taste every single inch of you."

His eyes seemed to lose their focus at her words. Releasing her waist, he shoved his hands into her hair, fingers gripping the back of her scalp. He pulled her up to meet his mouth. Hot and wild, his tongue ravaged hers.

Belle wasn't about to give up control, though, so she met him thrust for thrust, then sucked his tongue into her mouth in a way that made him groan and reach for her naked breasts.

"No," she gasped, moving away before he could work his magic and distract her again. "My turn."

And she made the most of it. In little, nibbling bites and long wet kisses, she worked her way over his chest and down his belly.

Dropping to her knees, she pressed her cheek against the bulge in his jeans and, glancing up to give him a wicked grin, reached around to squeeze his butt. Mitch's laugh eased her tension, and with an answering wink she released the catch on his pants and eased his zipper down.

A quick shove was all it took to bare his straining dick, right there at mouth level. She sighed in appreciation at the sight, sure that very tasty treat was going to bring her untold hours of pleasure.

Like a yummy lollipop, she ran her tongue up the length of his shaft and grinned when he grabbed her shoulders and groaned. Oh, yeah, she was definitely going to enjoy this. With a sigh of pleasure, she wrapped her lips around the smooth cap, and after a couple of teasing swirls of her tongue, quit playing and gave him the best head she could.

After a couple minutes of service, Mitch's fingers dug into her shoulders in a gentle signal that he was reaching his limit. She briefly considered pushing him over that limit, sending him right off the cliff, but then realized there were so many more delights to be had. Why rush things?

With a smooth slurping motion, she released him and leaned back on her hands. Mitch watched her like a man possessed, waiting to see what her next move would be, a wicked grin playing at the corner of his mouth.

"How're you at numbers?" she asked, her breath shuddering as the spiraling heat reignited in her belly. Pressing her fingers against her damp, aching mound, she pulled them away to show him the wet evidence of her desire.

"You mean like sixty-nine?" At her nod, Mitch reached down and took her hand, dropping to his knees as well and sucking her fingers into his mouth. Belle whimpered at the action, the tension between her legs ratcheting even higher. "I'm damned good, as you're about to find out," he promised.

"Do that again," she instructed, "just, you know, somewhere else."

Mitch's grin flashed. In a quick move, he kicked off his shoes, tugged his socks and jeans off, too. Naked, he lay back on the floor and gestured.

"Gimme," he said. "But get naked first."

Belle glanced down at herself—on her knees, her blouse long gone, her bra scooped under her breasts, pressing them up and together in a way that made them look much larger than they actually were. Her skirt was bunched around her waist like a belt, and her panties but a tattered memory of silk and lace.

She stood, placing one foot on either side of Mitch's hips and giving him a clear view of her wet, pink folds. Like a magnet, his eyes flew to the sight and his grin fell away. He reached for her but she shook her head, so he settled on running his hands up and down her calves, accented by the high heels she still wore.

She smoothed her skirt back in place. He frowned, then watched as she flipped the hook and zipper open. Belle shimmied, her breasts swaying with the movement. Mitch's eyes went opaque. She pushed the tight skirt down her hips, and bending one knee to bring her legs together, she dropped the skirt to the floor, then kicked it away.

Almost naked now and loving Mitch's full attention, Belle stood, legs spread, and gently scraped her nails up her thighs. She passed her hand over the damp curls between her legs, pausing to flick one finger over her clit. The movement made Mitch's dick jump as though it was jealous. She loved his eyes on her. It was almost as good as his hands, although not nearly as sweet as his mouth. She felt like a sex goddess, the way he looked at her. She slid her hands up her torso, cupping her breasts and squeezing them. Head falling back, she closed her eyes and let the sensation, hot, intense and powerful, wash over her.

Her fingers tweaked her aching, turgid nipples, amping up her desire, preparing her for the thrust of Mitch's tongue. As if he heard her thoughts, suddenly his mouth was between her legs. Belle gasped, then gave a keening cry as he skipped all the preliminaries and thrust his tongue inside her.

Her knees buckled again, but his hands were there on her ass to hold her up. She looked down and almost came at the sight. Her nails teased and circled the pointy pink tips of her nipples, and there below Mitch half sat, half lay, his eyes staring into hers as he used his tongue to drive her crazy.

She wanted to come. Two more seconds and she would. But she'd promised herself the next time she'd be taking him down with her. Calling on a willpower she'd have sworn didn't exist, she stepped away from the best tongue job she'd ever had and pointed to the floor. Mitch frowned. Belle arched her brow. Not bothering to take off her shoes, she gestured to the floor again and ran her hands over her breasts in promise.

Mitch lay back, his dick as rigid as a redwood, waiting for her. As gracefully as possible, Belle dropped down, one knee on either side of his hips. Her wet bush rubbed against his dick, tempting her to simply shift and take him inside her. But she wanted more, she wanted to drive him so crazy he never forgot her. She wanted him to want her so bad, she became the most important thing in his life. Even if it was only for the moment.

Needing the connection, she let herself fall forward so her hands braced on either side of his head, and kissed him. Dark and drugging, the kiss tasted like musky sex.

With one last bite at his lower lip, she sat upright, then swung her legs around so she faced backward. Falling forward to brace her elbows on the floor on either side of his hips, she wrapped one hand around the base of his straining dick and, knowing he was waiting, feeling the tension in him building, swirled her tongue over the silky head. Mitch groaned and grabbed her hips, his fingers digging erotically into the soft flesh. She swirled again, then pulled just the head into her mouth, sucking it like a lollipop. He got even harder and she felt him groan, a warm gust of air between her thighs. Then his mouth was on her. He licked, then sucked her clit into his mouth, causing Belle to shudder.

Determined to make him come first, and hanging on to her control by the thinnest thread, she poured everything she had into giving him the best, the hottest and sexiest blow job of her life. Lips, teeth and tongue worked magic as she sucked and swirled, taking him deeper. His tongue mimicked lovemaking, spearing her in then out, as his finger massaged her swollen lips.

Belle couldn't take much more. While still sucking, she scraped her teeth, gentle as could be, up the length of him. Mitch stiffened and grabbed her hips. She did it again. His fingers tightened, then proving those rock-hard biceps were well-deserved, he lifted and flipped her around so she faced him.

He reached up and wrapped his hand around the back of her neck, pulling her mouth down to meet his. Wet, sliding, open-mouth kisses added to the intense, needy ache in her belly. While driving her crazy, Mitch reached over to pull his jeans to him and grabbed a condom out of his pocket.

Releasing her mouth, he let his head fall back to the carpet and handed her the foil packet. "Ride me," he demanded.

In quick moves made jerky by impatience and need, she sheathed his straining erection in the ribbed-for-her-pleasure condom and rose to her knees.

One leg on either side of his hips, she locked eyes with Mitch. Excruciatingly slowly, she lowered herself one delicious inch at a time on his rock-hard cock until she'd taken all of him inside her.

With a shuddering moan, she ran her hands up the sides of her body, her skin so sensitized the barely there move made her want to scream with pleasure. She slid her hands over her breasts and up her throat, then speared them through her hair. Lifting her arms overhead, she gave silent thanks for the delicious treat she was about to enjoy.

Then she set out to pleasure the hell out of herself. Riding him, slowly at first and with ever-increasing strokes, she let the tension build. Tighter, deeper, need coiled low in her belly. Belle's gaze stayed locked on Mitch's, watching his eyes to gauge his pleasure. Fingers meshed as they held hands, their focus completely, totally on the sensations building in both of them as Belle rode him.

Her climax just a breath away, her body started to shake as she tried to hold off. She needed to see him come first. Had to know she could give him as much pleasure as he gave her. With that in mind, trying as hard as she could to hold off the pounding orgasmic waves, she swirled her hips, adding a deep undulating move to each thrust.

Mitch's eyes went dark, then closed for a second as he fought for control. Belle's breath hitched and she did it again. He hissed, his gaze meeting hers once more.

She licked her lips and, their hands still entwined, raised one of his to scrape her teeth along his knuckles, to run her tongue over his palm.

Mitch exploded. His guttural cry of pleasure set hers free. Belle felt the power of his climax, her own body shuddered with wave after wave of the most incredible sensations.

Panting, she dropped onto his chest. Mitch's arms wrapped around her in a hug that was more emotional than sexual and brought tears to Belle's eyes. Just orgasm overload, she assured herself as she struggled to catch her breath.

"Now aren't you sorry you didn't take me up on my offer earlier?" she teased, trying to lighten the mood.

"Better late than never," he said with a laugh, his own breath sounding labored. "And keep in mind, I only get better with age."

Didn't that image simply boggle the mind? Belle shifted her legs so they lay alongside Mitch and hummed at the mini-climax she felt at the move.

"Tell you what, gorgeous. If you only improve with age, you're going to be off the charts by the time you're forty."

Mitch snickered but Belle fell silent, realizing she wouldn't know. She'd be nowhere around in eight years when Mitch hit that milestone. Some other woman would likely be reaping the rewards of his age-improved sexual games. But not Belle. She'd thrown away—or rather, run away from—the right to know.

The idea made her miserable. Her stomach pitched and

her eyes filled. Blaming it on emotional overload brought on by four orgasms in a row, Belle sniffed and rolled away to hide her tears. What now? Did she pat him on the ass, hand him his jeans and get back to business? It sounded so cold when all she wanted was to curl up in his arms and be held.

"Getting that good takes a lot of practice," Mitch mused, wrapping his arms around her from behind and tugging her back against his hot, naked body. "I have a few ideas I've wanted to try out on you, with you."

The painful tension eased from Belle's body, only to be replaced by tension of the sexual kind. Much happier with horny over weepy, she turned in Mitch's arms and grinned. "Do tell. I'm always intrigued by self-improvement programs."

He laughed and in a single move stood and scooped her up in his arms. Belle linked her hands behind his head and cuddled, a soft glow of joy settling in her chest.

"We need a mattress for what I have in mind," he told her, heading for the bedroom. "Something soft and comfortable, since next time I want you on the bottom."

"Sounds prosaic," she teased as he dropped her on the bed.

"Prosaic, my ass," he growled, kneeling at the bottom of the bed to take hold of her foot, still shod in her strappy sandal. A few quick flicks of his fingers and he'd unstrapped first one, then the other. Sliding his hands up her body in a way that left yummy tingles, he reached her mouth and planted a quick, hard kiss on her lips.

Before Belle could respond, he rolled away and shot a swift glance around the room. Her open closet apparently offered exactly what he was looking for, because he leaped from the bed and grabbed two belts and a silk scarf.

Belle's jaw dropped when he grabbed her wrist and, using a soft suede belt, tied it to the headboard.

"You're kidding," she breathed, scared, intrigued and totally turned on, all at the same time.

He didn't answer, instead holding out his hand and waiting. With a silent gulp, her breath coming a little faster as her body heated, Belle put the fingers of her free hand into his. Mitch tied it to the headboard as well, then lay on the bed next to her.

His gaze moved over her captive body like a caress. Her nipples peaked at his look, damp heat pooling between her legs. He stared for so long, she started to squirm.

Meeting her gaze, Mitch's eyes were hot and intense, filled with sexual promises. Belle pressed her lips together to keep from whimpering.

"I've wanted to tie you up for what feels like forever," he said softly. "Keep you here, at my mercy where you can't run or hide. Now that I have you, I'm going to touch you, kiss you, taste you." He ran the length of silk fabric between his fingers, then trailed it along her hip, over her quivering belly, and draped it gently over her aching breasts. "I'm going to use my tongue and my fingers. I'm going to drive you crazy."

Then he shifted, pulling the fabric from her breasts so the silky texture teased her nipples. Belle gasped and pressed her thighs together to ease the building pressure.

"And I'm going to do it all while you're blindfolded," he told her. Belle's gasp was lost in his mouth as he kissed her senseless while wrapping the jade-green silk over her eyes and tying it gently behind her head.

Belle planted her bare feet on the mattress, raising her pelvis in supplication. Mitch moved so he was between her widespread legs, his hard dick brushing against her aching center, but not relieving any tension, not entering her. She felt him lean forward, the mattress dipping on either side of her as he supported himself.

Holding her breath, she waited. Damp and hot, his tongue licked one nipple, then the other. A gentle gust of air teased the already hard peaks into aching stiffness. Belle couldn't hold back her whimper now. She needed something, anything.

"Do me," she begged.

"My way."

His way was killing her.

Still keeping that delicious pressure against her clit, he shifted. His hands cupped her breasts, pressing them together, his thumbs working her nipples as his mouth worked them in turn. Sucking, nibbling, licking. Teeth and tongue, just rough enough to make her crazy with need.

Oh, man. She was going to come before he even reached her aching center. She just knew it. And, she realized as the orgasm exploded behind her eyes, she just loved it.

Later, much, *much* later, wrapped in plush towels warmed by the heated towel bar, Belle and Mitch fell to her bed in a state of exhausted pleasure. Her eyelids drooping, she glanced at the clock and yawned. Five hours ago, they'd stopped off here so she could change her clothes for the tour.

And now she was floating on a cloud of sensual satisfaction like nothing she'd ever felt before. A tiny frown, all she had the energy for, creased her brow. If she hadn't messed up, she could have been floating like this for years. At least a few, she told herself, knowing the trophy-bride role wouldn't have worked for long.

Her thoughts ran like a snag in a favorite sweater, irritating and ugly, ruining her mood. If she'd been a trophy then, what was she now? Why was Mitch with her? Sudden lust? Tension seeped down her spine. What if she fell for him again? It'd hurt badly enough before, when she'd known it was only infatuation. What if this time, now that they'd had the incredible sex and she was able to deal with him on a one-on-one adult level, she really fell hard? What if he broke her heart?

Panic tightened the muscles across her back, her breath starting to hitch.

Mitch's hand curved around her waist, pulling her closer. His warm breath on her back was all it took to melt the icy fear. Determined not to ruin what had been the best sex of her life, she shoved her fears aside and let her mind empty.

"We missed exploring the grounds," she murmured sleepily.

Ever the gentleman, Mitch tugged the blankets over them before curling up behind her and draping one arm around her waist.

"Tomorrow," he said, his voice sounding as worn-out as she felt.

Tomorrow. They had tomorrow. Belle drifted off to sleep, the satisfied smile on her face due more to that promise than the fact that she'd just had the most incredible sex of her life.

8

"It was...incredible. Totally amazing," Belle rhapsodized over the phone. Her mind was still filled with the memory of her and Mitch, naked. Two hours had passed since he'd left her bed after a hot bout of early-morning delight and she could still taste him. She shifted, just a little, and her unused-to-such-wild-sex body felt the reminder of him inside her.

"But, I don't get it—when I'm with Mitch, I totally lose control," she admitted to her best friend from the very bed where she'd had that wild sex. Now, though, it was man-less as she carefully applied a second coat of blushing burgundy to her toenails.

"Well, good sex will do that to a gal. I thought you'd have realized that by now," Sierra returned grumpily. Belle felt a surge of guilt at the worry she was causing her partner.

Not enough to drop the subject, though.

"Ha-ha," Belle deadpanned, capping the polish and setting it on the bedside table. "I mean, I keep..." She trailed off, needing to talk about it but realizing how stupid she'd sound.

"Keep what? Having premature orgasms? Screaming in

ecstasy loud enough to bring the gardeners running? Welcoming your climax with a litany of filthy porn words?"

Belle's jaw dropped. Not at the words, but at the tart tone. She pulled the phone away from her ear to stare at it in shock, then flipped over on the bed so she lay on her stomach.

"Something's wrong," she decided aloud. "Is there a problem with Eventfully Yours? Are you okay? What's going on?"

Silence. Then she actually heard Sierra shrug, the fabric of whatever she was wearing brushing against the phone. "No problems. Nothing's going on. Company is fine."

Shorthand for Sierra didn't want to talk about it.

One of the cornerstones of their lifelong friendship was knowing when to push the other and when to back off and let her stew. Belle's telltale clue to leave Sierra alone had always been how many millimeters her lower lip stuck out. A champion pouter, Sierra was open to commiserating if she had the lip out. But if she'd sucked it in, concentration-style, she was off-limits.

Belle silently cursed the distance between them and tried to figure out what to do.

"What lipstick are you wearing?" she asked.

"What kind of question is that?" When Belle didn't say anything, Sierra admitted, "I'm not wearing any right now."

Chewed it all off. Definitely off-limits. Automatically backing away from the confrontation, Belle shifted back to the original topic. "I feel like an idiot," she admitted, "but I keep losing my temper with Mitch. You know me, I don't get angry. This is so bizarre."

"You do, too, get angry," Sierra pointed out. "You just don't allow yourself to express it. You'll end up with ulcers if you don't learn to let go of some of that, you know."

"Apparently I've found my release valve."

"Sex'll work every time," her partner agreed. "But since I'm not getting any, I'd rather talk about something else, okay?"

Sierra would never be in danger of ulcers. Despite her unwillingness to share whatever was bothering her, she never bottled up her emotions. Why bother, she usually said, when it was so much more fun to let them spew all over like a well-shaken bottle of soda.

Except now, when she seemed to be holding them in even better than Belle ever had.

"Okay, so, um, did you get my notes about the sex-themed ideas?" Belle asked, obediently changing the topic. "I'm going to need additional staff to help set up for the pre-events. I think Mitch said something about his security team running checks on everyone to guarantee a complete media blackout."

"We've got two dozen independent contractors on file who've passed top security screenings. That should be enough, shouldn't it?"

Belle glanced at her leather portfolio, flipping pages with the pad of her finger so as not to smudge her fresh polish. "That should work, in addition to Lakeside's serving staff."

The two of them went over details for the upcoming opening, plus ideas for possible follow-up contracts, such as holiday-themed sex and weddings à la kink.

"I talked to a couple of bigwigs when I was handling the CEO gig last week," Sierra said after they'd wound up business. "You know, just a few questions about who they think the top developers are, what they'd do in today's real estate climate and economy, that kind of chitchatty thing."

Belle sat up and drew her knees to her chest. She glanced at the tab in her notebook titled *Dad* and grimaced. She'd been so busy getting mad at, then getting on top of, Mitch, she'd forgotten the most important reason she was here.

"And?"

"Things just suck right now. They all said the same thing your dad did. It's not the time to build. In their opinion, anyone sitting on a big fat piece of land is stuck with it for the next little while."

"The next little while will bankrupt Daddy."

Sierra gave a sympathetic sigh. "I know."

Out of the blue, Belle thought back to the contract she'd seen on Diana's desk. There was a luxury spa in the resort lobby—fancy and very upscale. And oddly enough, it was not owned by the hotel but was leasing the space from Lakeside. Was that an option for her dad's hotels? An additional income? It was worth looking into.

"Let me talk to a couple of people," she told Sierra. "I thought of something earlier, but I need to get some details to figure out if it even makes sense."

Belle stared out the window at the gorgeous golf course. Morning sun washed it in gentle light. Lush, green and exclusive. Her father's hotels were lovely, but not in the same category as Lakeside. This resort would cater to an elite clientele, whereas Forsham's catered to upscale business travelers, wedding parties and couples looking for indulgent getaways.

Maybe the spa angle was the answer to increasing the cash flow until the real estate market turned around and her father could sell the properties without losing everything. She watched the gardeners putter along the green in a golf cart, stopping every ten feet or so to check on the bizarre gopher population explosion, and sighed.

"I'm going to dinner with Mitch tonight," she said. "I'll see if I can get some hypothetical advice or something."

Sierra made a sound that could be taken as agreement, then said, "Just be sure you ask him before you throw your next fit."

"What? Why would I throw a fit?"

"I thought temper tantrums were your new foreplay."

"Ha." Belle started to laugh as she hung up, then stopped. What if he was only interested in her when she was pissy? Did he only want her because she was a challenge now? Unlike before when she'd tried to serve herself up on a platter?

She told herself she was being silly. But still, her initial reaction was to pick a fight as soon as she saw him. That wasn't fair, though. She had to know. Which meant she'd be an absolute doll all night, flirt to her heart's content with nary a hint of anger or confrontation, and see how it went.

Hell no, she wasn't going to take the easy way out. Belle gathered all the confidence she could and squared her shoulders. She'd have him begging for sex again and she'd do it with a smile on her face.

"Reece?" Mitch frowned as he crossed the lobby to greet the tall guy in the cowboy hat. "What're you doing here?"

Unselfconsciously, he gave Reece a quick man hug, the arm-around-the-shoulder kind that he knew wouldn't embarrass his ex–Green Beret cousin.

"I thought I'd drop in, check the place out," Reece said in his slow drawl.

"Check up on your investment, you mean?" Mitch asked, referring to the fact that all the family members were stockholders on the MC Board of Directors.

"Nah, just wanted to see what kind of trouble your sorry ass has been getting up to." Reece made a show of looking around. Mitch followed his gaze, taking in the towering potted plants, the glossy marble-inlaid floor and ornate rosewood check-in desk. Reece gave a nod. "Long way from home, cuz."

"Ain't that the truth." Mitch pulled back his shoulders and grinned with pride. "You think the whole family will turn out for the grand opening blowout event?"

Reece pulled a face and gave a slow shrug. "Not so sure about that. I mean, if I read your reports right, you're shifting focus from a ritzy resort to a sexually charged amusement park for the rich and famous. Might be a little racy for Grammy Lynn, if ya know what I mean."

Mitch snickered. "Grammy Lynn sent me a list of suggestions to make sure we were offering enough sexy options."

"I shoulda known." Like everything else about him, Reece's grin was slow and easy. That smile deceived the enemy into thinking he was slow, women into thinking he was easy. They soon found out they were wrong. He was also loyal, tenacious and brilliant, but few people outside the family knew that, since Reece had a habit of keeping everyone at arm's length.

Mitch stood visiting with his cousin, feeling on top of the world. Family, success and hot sex. What more could a man want? The image of Belle as he'd last seen her, naked except for a very satisfied smile, flashed through his mind. Mitch shoved it right back out, figuring a hard-on while discussing the resort's sex themes might give the wrong message. Besides, he was still trying to sort through how he felt about last night. Awesome sex aside—and damned if it hadn't been the most awesome of his life—his mind was a mess. He ricocheted between sexual satisfaction, concern over being led around by his dick, and terror that it'd meant nothing to her. Hell, he felt like a teenage girl PMSing.

For the twentieth time since leaving Belle that morning, Mitch shoved the worries aside and forced himself to focus on the here and now.

So he asked about Reece's business. His cousin had opened a security firm after leaving the service. While he consulted and supervised security for MC Development, there was definitely not enough business in Mitch's little world to keep a man like Reece busy. Instead he kept his wits sharp working as a for-hire bodyguard, defense trainer and, as Mitch liked to rib him, all-round spy.

"Seriously," he asked when he'd been brought up-to-date on everything, "what're you doing out here? You didn't say anything about a visit when we talked the other day."

"I had some stuff to go over with you, wanted to take a look around. Maybe meet your planner and discuss the security list you sent on her behalf."

Well, shit. Mitch hummed. He'd known his family would have questions once they found out Belle was his new planner, but he'd figured he had plenty of time to come up with a reasonable explanation. And more important, plenty of time to get used to—and over—the wild sexual intensity that flamed between them before he was faced with the threat of it being extinguished by the past.

Maybe he could keep Reece and Belle apart? Tell her he'd meet her later, have Larry haul his cousin around for a tour?

Keeping his smile in place, Mitch felt his mind race with possibilities. Despite the mind games he was playing with himself, things were going too well right now. He wasn't ready to give this pleasure up. He'd dreamed of being with Belle for years, wanted her for what felt like forever. Bottom line, he wasn't letting reality—in any form—intrude on this time with her.

Not even his cousin.

BELLE WALKED OUT OF THE spa into the resort's lobby, a satisfied smile on her face and three pages of notes in her portfolio. Apparently, MC Development rented space to all the little boutiques in the resort. Which not only cut back on their overhead, but brought in a tidy little income, as well.

With a purr of pleasure, she raised her hand to her nose and sniffed the rich, floral fragrance on her silky smooth skin. Smelled good, felt great. The owner, Kiki, was a savvy businesswoman with an eye for success.

Belle had a feeling they'd get along great, and she'd know for sure the next day when they had lunch together. That was enough time to run her idea past Sierra, work up an outline and make a quick phone call to Daddy.

And, she thought as she spied Mitch across the lobby, even more important, time for that couples' massage and chocolate bath she'd talked the spa owner into booking for them, despite the spa not being open yet.

With that in mind, she sauntered toward Mitch, her heels making a snappy sound as she crossed the marble floor. She focused on his jean-encased butt, so sweet and tempting, and wondered how long it'd be before she could bite it. Again.

For now, she settled on a pat when she reached him. "How'd you like to get naked and play in chocolate?" she asked, coming up behind him.

Mitch spun around, a look of appalled bewilderment on his face. Quick as lightning, he grabbed her hand off his ass and, with a gentle squeeze, shook it as if they were distant business acquaintances.

Hurt and confused, Belle tried to figure out what his problem was.

The sound of male laughter clued her in. She glanced around Mitch's shoulder and saw a lanky, Southern hunk seated on the white-leather couch and realized she'd embarrassed Mitch. At least she hoped that look had been embarrassment and not distaste for her suggestion.

Putting on her best society-princess smile, she stepped around Mitch and held out her hand in greeting. As the guy got to his feet, she gave a mental frown and tried to place him. He looked vaguely familiar.

"I'm Belle Forsham, and I'm afraid I've reached my limit of naughty offers for the day, but I hope we can be friends anyway?" she greeted in a light, joking tone.

"Reece Carter. It's a pleasure to meet you." It wasn't the touch of his large hand engulfing hers that clued Belle in. It was Mitch's supportive one grazing the small of her back. "Again."

A buzzing rang in Belle's ears, and her breath stuck somewhere in her chest. Carter. Mitch's cousin. The cousin, she remembered, that Mitch considered his best friend and had asked to be his best man. That's why he looked so familiar. He'd attended their kiboshed wedding and probably thought, with good reason, that she was a flaky bitch from hell.

Gathering what little nerve she had and taking strength from Mitch's warmth, she looked into Reece's midnight-blue eyes, but she saw no trace of judgment. Just an odd sort of waiting. The steady gaze made her stomach hurt. Maybe censure would have been better?

Mitch's cell phone rang and he excused himself, stepping away to take the call. She didn't know why, but Belle wanted to grab his belt loop and follow him to safety.

She offered Reece a hesitant smile. He didn't return it. Instead he gave her a long, intimidating stare that let her know without words that yes, he definitely remembered what she'd done and flaky bitch from hell was the nicest way he could think of her.

Belle wondered how fast she could run in these heels.

"I hear your naughty suggestions are going to be the highlight of this resort," Reece finally said.

Oh, fun, talking sex with a guy who completely hated her. She'd rather take her chances with her heels, but for Mitch's sake, she knew she couldn't.

Belle swallowed twice, trying to wet her tongue. She stretched her lips into a smile. "They'll make Lakeside the go-to playground of the rich and famous. I'm not sure how much Mitch has shared, but we have some great ideas that I know will lay a solid promotional foundation."

Realizing she was babbling, Belle stopped and pressed her lips together. She barely heard Mitch rejoin them and take over the description of their plans for the resort. She wanted, no needed, to leave. Now.

"Gentlemen, I'm so sorry, but I have to run," she interrupted.

Mitch frowned at her. "I thought we were having lunch." He looked at his watch, then gestured to his cousin. "Reece'll join us. We can go now if you're hungry."

She'd really been looking forward to eating with Mitch. Lunch and a little footsie, some flirting and maybe a quickie nooner for dessert.

"Um, I can't. I'm sorry, but I forgot I need to run by your office and talk to Diana about a few things. I need to use her fax to send off some contracts, too."

Belle knew she was a rotten liar and now apparently so did the men standing in front of her. Mitch gave her an angry look that slowly shifted to suspicion, staring at her as if she was an intriguing puzzle with a few vital pieces missing.

"We'll do dinner instead, then," he said after a few moments. He used his business voice. The one that let her know he was speaking as the guy signing her contract, not the guy who'd done her doggy-style before breakfast.

"I'll look forward to it," she lied before turning to make her way across the marble foyer toward the questionable refuge of Mitch's office. It had been a stupid lie, since the men could easily and justifiably follow her, but her brain had stalled. When she saw them head toward the restaurant, she heaved a sigh of relief.

Not willing to be proved the liar she was, she decided to go visit Diana anyway. Just CYA.

She scurried down the hallway and into Mitch's assistant's office. Except Diana wasn't there. Belle gave a huff of frustration and debated her options. She could just go to her cottage, but that meant losing her witness. She could wait for Diana, but, well, she really didn't like the gal enough to waste who knew how long twiddling her thumbs.

Or, she eyed the fax machine, she could send a fax as she'd said she would. That would turn her lie into a truth and make it all right. She grinned at her twisted justification and, flipping open her portfolio, grabbed the specs from the spa and penned a quick note to Sierra to outline her idea. She'd planned to email them all, but hey, faxing meant she didn't have to type up all the specs since she didn't have a scanner.

She rolled her eyes at the continual justification.

"Hey, Belle."

She turned and saw Larry in the doorway and grinned. Perfect. "Hey, Larry, how's it going?"

"I'm glad I found you. I pitched an idea to Mitch about bringing in a live band each month and he said to get together with you to expand on it."

They chitchatted as she set her stuff on the armoire housing the office equipment and slid her papers into the fax machine's paper feed. Punching in Eventfully Yours's number, she listened to the manager's ideas and considered tasteful ways to integrate the sex themes.

Before she could offer any feedback, Larry glanced at his watch and shrugged. "Lunch over, I've gotta run. I'll send you a memo about this, okay?"

She nodded and said goodbye as she gathered the faxed papers from the tray.

Well, that had worked out nicely. Despite being bummed at being cheated out of her lunchtime sexual romp, and very nervous over the arrival of Mitch's cousin, Belle was feeling pretty good as she sorted the specs to put back in her portfolio.

As she filed them, she noticed a crumpled ball of paper stuck under the fax tray. She tugged the wad out and, about to toss it in the trash, noticed the word *gopher*. Had Mitch found a way to get rid of the pests? She smoothed the page flat and glanced at it. A memo typed on Lakeside's stationery.

Then she read it from beginning to end.

Confused, she turned it over, looking for what she didn't know.

Was someone deliberately causing damage to Mitch's resort? She looked at the typed to-do list.

Damage sprinklers, reroute laundry, break bench slats. The list went on and on. Brow furrowed, a sick feeling in her stomach, she scanned the rest. And right there, gophers on the golf course.

She bit her lip and wondered briefly where the hell one imported gophers from, then shook her head. Did it matter? Someone was doing all of this deliberately. Messing with Mitch's property, trying to screw up or ruin the launch of the resort. She flipped to the second page and noticed a handwritten note. Her stomach sank as her vision wavered in shock.

Keep up the good work. This is exactly what Mitch asked for. Inflict as much damage as possible before the end of the month.

It was signed with the initials L.N.

"You DIDN'T MENTION your event planner was the little blonde who turned your world upside down a few years back."

"Belle?" Mitch grimaced and took a drink of his coffee to buy time. "I sent the specs on Eventfully Yours. I'm sure you read her qualifications."

"Glowing. And nary a mention that she'd once planned the event that left you doing a solo act at the altar." Typically, Reece's voice held no judgment. Just a musing sort of curiosity.

"She's the best planner on the West Coast. Her company is perfect for what I want here, and she's already proved her worth by coming up with the theme idea that you yourself claimed was brilliant," Mitch defended. When Reece just stared, Mitch rolled his eyes and shrugged. "Let's face it, she was right to call it quits six years ago. Getting married was insane. I was the one in the wrong, marrying her to seal that deal with old man Forsham."

And to prove to everyone, including himself, that he was enough of a hotshot to score the boss's princess daughter. Mitch might admit that to himself, but he wasn't about to tell his cousin. Not that, nor the fact that he'd straight up used Belle's desire, their sexual attraction for each other to manipulate her into the engagement.

"You trust her?" was all Reece said.

Mitch shrugged. "In business, sure." In bed, too. "I'd think twice if it involved rings or ministers, though."

Their waiter arrived with lunch and both men fell silent.

Hoping the topic was over, Mitch picked up his knife and fork and cut into his Baja grilled chicken. Reece lifted his Angus burger, but before taking a bite he gestured with it and claimed, "Your girl's nervous about something. Might be the past. Might be more. I'm going to do a little checking."

"Don't bother," Mitch said, his brow furrowing. "I trust Belle, okay?"

"Glad to hear it. Trust always makes the sex hotter, I'm sure." Reece's grin was quick, wicked and knowing. "But someone's deliberately screwing with you and this resort, cuz. And I find it mighty curious that you're having all these unexplained problems right about the same time your ex shows up. Can't hurt to poke around."

All Mitch heard was *deliberately*.

"You're sure it's sabotage?" he asked, all defensiveness over his past mistakes forgotten.

"Looks like."

"Check everyone." Fury flashed like a strobe light behind Mitch's eyes. *Deliberately.* He'd worked his ass off to get this far and someone was trying to ruin him. He clenched his fist, anger burning in his gut. He'd be damned if they'd get away with it. "I want whoever is behind this caught and strung up."

"And if it's the pretty blonde?"

Frowning, Mitch thought of Belle. Her smile, the laughter and fun she had teasing him. Mr. Winkles and the vulnerability she tried so hard to hide. The sexy way she walked across the room and the mewling sound she made when she came.

"It's not her," he declared, trying to shrug off the idea.

"But before you tell me it's your job to check everyone thoroughly, I'm saying go ahead. Just don't be surprised to find out you're wrong."

Worry pounded at his temples until Mitch forced himself to think the situation through. Once he did, he was able to relax a little. After all, Belle might be a lot of things. A little flaky, impulsive and quick to react without thinking. Sexy, flirtatious and sweet, definitely. But the one thing he was positive about was that she wasn't a liar.

9

"You still haven't explained why we're here instead of your cottage." Mitch asked for the third time as he followed her down the short hall to one of the guest suites the next evening.

Belle glanced back at him, a thrill of excitement flashing at the sight of his version of evening casual. Jeans, a black button-up shirt and, her gaze dropped to his feet, dress shoes. He looked so good, even better now that she'd seen him naked. She sighed. The man was simply delicious.

And, she glanced at his face, so not the kind of guy who'd play some elaborate scam to screw over his own company. She'd asked him to trust her to make dinner arrangements, and had been gratified—and a little shocked—when he'd readily agreed. She figured this was the perfect time to do some subtle questioning, just to assure herself he was as innocent as she thought.

It had to be her own doubts that had her imagining the suspicion in his voice. Belle tried to shrug off the weird feeling, telling herself it was paranoia brought on by Reece's surprise arrival and the papers she'd found in Diana's office.

"It's a surprise," she told him again. With a deep breath, she reached into her purse to pull out the room card. Her tummy spun with nerves and she missed twice before she could get the flimsy card into the lock. She'd never been this nervous to present an event or theme to a client before.

Of course, she'd never planned to get the client naked before, either. She didn't know if it was that, or nerves over playing Mata Hari on a quest for secrets that made her feel so intimidated.

It definitely wasn't because they'd had the most intensely wild, passionate sex of her life or that it left her feeling emotionally naked and vulnerable. Worrying about that would be ridiculous, especially since she couldn't do anything about the vulnerability unless she was willing to stop having the incredible sex. And that was out of the question.

She told herself for at least the hundredth time since yesterday to quit obsessing. And while she was at it, just to put Reece-the-intimidating out of her mind and forget about the note and the suggestion that Mitch had asked for damage to be done to Lakeside. It just didn't make sense for him to ruin his own resort.

Belle shook her head as if she could knock the thoughts out of it. With a deep breath, she focused instead on the previous night, the great sex, and the hot lovin' she had planned for tonight. Whew, much better.

With a deep breath and a little wiggle of anticipation for what she hoped was about to come—namely her—Belle pushed open the heavy door.

"We're doing dinner here tonight," she said as she entered the dimly lit room. Hurrying before Mitch could get a good look around, she grabbed the lighter and lit the bank of candles on the dresser. "I thought we'd have a preview of what your guests can expect when they stay."

"Really?" Excitement, curiosity and a hint of naughty pleasure were all packed into that one word.

His tone instantly settled her nerves. Belle pasted on a seductive smile and turned to face Mitch. Leaning one hip on the dresser, she gestured to the room.

"What you see before you is a typical, luxurious resort suite. Comfortable seating, antique furnishings, good art. Quality all the way, which your guests will expect." She tilted her head toward the table in the corner, set up to her specifications. "A delicious private dinner for two, wine and a decadent and one-of-a-kind dessert. Yummy by any standard, but we're hinting at something more. Something, dare I say it, sexy?"

Mitch's lips twitched but he kept his expression intrigued instead of amused. "Sexy?"

"Just a hint," she demurred, stepping to the table and curving her fingers around the handles of the domed silver covers she'd instructed the kitchen to find. She wanted that movie-star ambience. Lifting the covers, she set them aside and gestured again, this time toward the love seat next to the table.

Oysters, asparagus, lobster and a spice-encrusted steak. This time Mitch didn't bother to hide his grin. Instead he stepped forward, and after a quick glance at the table pulled her into his arms for a kiss that put the ninety-dollar-a-plate meal behind them to shame.

Belle gave herself over to the kiss, needing it in a way she couldn't even explain to herself. Maybe because it was the first one since he'd left her curled up naked in her sheets, or maybe it was just the nerves, but as soon as his lips touched hers, her entire body relaxed in one huge sigh of relief. She was silly to suspect him.

A kiss and a grope later, Belle peeled her fingers off

his ass and they settled on the plushly cushioned love seat for their meal.

"This is fabulous," he said after a few bites of his steak. "Not just the private dinner, but the whole setup. The candlelight and roses, the view—" he gestured to the open balcony window and the moonlit copse of trees "—it all adds to the romantic ambience."

Pleased, Belle glanced around the room that worked perfectly with her theme. Romance went hand in hand with sexual fantasies.

But the theme would be pointless if whoever made that list hit their goal and Lakeside went belly-up before the end of the year. Belle squared her shoulders, remembering her private mission for the evening. Dig.

"So, how's it all coming for the resort's opening?" she asked as they ate. "It's just a week until the first party, three weeks until the doors open to the public. Is everything ready to go on your end?"

A tiny frown came and went, but Mitch just shrugged and nodded. "It's coming along. Things will move a little smoother now that Reece is here."

Was that because Reece was Mr. Security? Did Mitch know who was behind the problems and had brought his cousin out to catch them? Or was Reece here to stop any further incidents? For about the hundredth time, Belle considered showing Mitch the list. But, as always, she recalled the comment about the damage being something he'd requested and held back.

"You've run security checks on all the resort employees, haven't you? Including management?" That memo had definitely been sent by someone who wouldn't be questioned hanging out in Diana's office.

"Sure, a check is standard and we sent around those confidentiality agreements you wanted, too." The look he gave her, curious and just a little suspicious, let her know it was time to change the subject.

"Wait till you see dessert," Belle said, shifting so her thigh slid along his. The move pulled the hem of her dress higher, leaving bare thigh pressed to the rough fabric of his jeans. "Since I thought it'd be better to postpone the chocolate spa treatment until, um, later—" like, after Reece had left "—I came up with a fun after-dinner treat that has a similar effect."

Tearing his eyes from her silky thigh and its hint of the naked delight barely hidden by her dress, Mitch looked at her and frowned. "Chocolate spa treatment? What's that?"

"I met with your spa owner to discuss some ideas I had." Like finding out if Kiki, who was looking to launch two more spas, might want to consider renting space in a Forsham Hotel. But that wasn't her point. "She and I came up with a dozen or so sexy-themed services she'll offer and I booked us to try the couples' chocolate spa treatment."

Belle had also noted that none of the "accidents" had affected the spa or any of the other privately owned businesses. Only Mitch's direct holdings.

"Sounds…intriguing," he said with a grin. Setting his fork down, Mitch rested his hand on her knee. His warm fingers sent a tingle of excitement up her bare thigh all the way to the heated core between her legs. She wanted to shift, to encourage him to slide his hand higher and discover for himself that she was commando under her slinky black dress. But she was on a mission. Besides, part of the fun was anticipation, so she forced herself to be still.

"Why'd you cancel the appointment?" he asked.

"I…" She'd been so distracted by Reece's appearance, and then her discovery that someone was deliberately trying to tank the resort, she'd forgotten to confirm a time. Belle tried to come up with a decent excuse, but his fingers were making a slow, hot trip north and she couldn't think straight. "Um, you have family here."

Mitch's jaw dropped. Belle frowned. She didn't so much mind shocking him, but she did mind that his fingers stopped their delicious journey.

"What?" she asked when he started laughing, not sure why she felt so self-conscious all of a sudden. It wasn't as though she'd confessed that she'd spent months practicing her signature as Mrs. Belle Carter.

"I'm just surprised," he admitted. "I mean, I would have sworn you didn't have a shy bone in your body."

"I don't," Belle snapped, offended.

"And yet now that we're not having anonymous, hotel-employees-are-totally-discreet sex, you're taking it into hiding?"

"Did you want to ask your cousin to come watch?" Belle shot back without thinking. "Or maybe videotape us doing it in the shower to show at the next family reunion?"

"Most of the family will be here for the pre-event next week," Mitch mused. "We can show it then. Really kick off this sex theme with a big bang."

She stared in slack-jawed shock, irritated embarrassment forgotten.

"You'd actually show your family sex tapes?" She couldn't even read romance novels in the presence of her father, he was so uptight about the topic.

"Nah, I was teasing. They don't want to see my naked butt move to some porn sound track." Mitch grinned and gave a rueful shake of his head. "But they are amazing, especially my grandma. She pretty much raised all my cousins and me."

"And your sister?" Remembering Mitch's snotty sister from their abandoned wedding, Belle hid her grimace in a fake smile. She'd spent months regretting not letting Sierra kick her rude ass.

"Sister?" He frowned, then his face cleared and he shook his head again. "Lena? We lived in the same house for a year or so when my mom first married her dad, but then she left for college. After our parents died, we grew apart. We reconnected right before I went to work for your dad. I'd decided to merge her late father John's construction company with MC Development and I needed her signature."

Belle remembered the bland woman's taunts as if it were yesterday. Of course, she'd replayed her "runaway" reel in her head a million times, so that actually felt like yesterday, too. Lena had been so cocky about her knowledge of Mitch's character.

"Most of my family is on the board of MC Development, except her. I offered her a chair, but she had other things going on. Other than Lena, who never really hung out much, the family is really tight. When I was growing up, my grandma was the family babysitter. Even after she remarried, my mom was a working woman. All my aunts were, too."

The love he had for his family was clear in his voice. Belle felt a twinge of jealousy. Sure, she loved her dad, but they weren't tight like Mitch's family seemed to be. Would she have been welcomed in if they'd gotten married? The thought of what she might have had made her want to cry, so she gestured to Mitch to keep talking.

"The family all lived within four blocks of each other so instead of after-school care, my cousins and I went to Gram's house." Mitch went on to describe his childhood and random details about what various cousins and family members were doing now. From the sound of it, each and every one would be arriving at the resort the following week.

Belle felt like throwing up her perfectly delicious lobster. All of them. Here. Knowing exactly what she'd done to Mitch, how she'd run away on their wedding day. Wouldn't parading naked down Rodeo Drive be easier?

"So that's why you canceled the chocolate and sex massage?" Mitch asked as he finished the last of his dinner. "Because you didn't want my cousin to know we're practicing what you preach?"

Embarrassed heat washed over Belle from the top of her forehead to the edge of her bra. She hated when she blushed. The color totally clashed with her hair.

Trying to save face, she just shrugged and pointed out, "This is what your clientele would be dealing with, you know? They want to have wild, uncensored sex and the oddest things cause inhibition. You might want to talk to your cousin about making sure the resort's security is solid. That'll be crucial if you want to pull this off."

Mitch's arched brow told her he hadn't missed her blatant avoidance of an answer, but he let it pass. "I've set up a meeting between you and Reece for tomorrow," he said.

Belle licked her lips. Meet with Reece? Alone? Um, no. Even though he'd been perfectly cordial through dinner the previous evening, she hadn't forgotten that threatening look he'd given her when they'd first met. He obviously had it in for her, and while he might be willing to play nice in front of his cousin, she had no doubt the gloves would come off in private.

"Can we make it the day after?" she asked, buying time as she stood and made her way over to the second room in the suite. Time for dessert. Or at least a change of topic.

Mitch just shrugged in answer. His attention, she realized, was on the bedroom. The bedroom containing her pièce de résistance, the culmination of her sex-themed evening. Her nerves returned. Fingers laced together, she tried to keep herself from bouncing in her high heels as she waited for his reaction.

MITCH FELT LIKE HE'D died and gone to heaven. A delicious dinner, Belle and, from the look of the bedroom and glimpse of the bath he could see from the doorway, a very hot night yet to come.

Like the romantic dinner, the dimly lit bedroom screamed romance. A midnight-red trail of rose petals lay strewn over the floor and across the cool, white expanse of the turned-down bed. Every surface held candles waiting to be lit. He squinted, trying to see the array of items displayed on the silver tray on the nightstand. The thick, knobby curve on one of the things worried him a little. Belle had talked about sex toys for the guests, but he wasn't sure he was ready to play hide the dildo with her. The light glanced off something metal—handcuffs, he realized. He'd just have to cuff her to the bed before she hauled out the Rabbit vibrator.

He glanced at Belle, who was trying to read his reaction. The moonlight shone through the window, casting a glow of pearls over her skin and blond hair, tousled and sexy for their date. But the luminescent beauty that tugged at his heart was all hers.

She nibbled her sweet lower lip between her teeth, brows raised in question. Mitch could see the nerves in her sea-green eyes, that underlying worry he'd been so surprised to find in such a confident woman. He supposed that was why she was so good at what she did. She cared, really cared, about her clients loving her work.

Not that he saw this as being about business, of course. What was between them was all personal. No matter how she tried to wrap it up as justifying her contract. Or how much Reece tried to argue that Belle was only after some weird revenge by sabotaging his resort.

"I take it this is phase two of our evening?" he asked.

"The dessert phase," she responded seriously.

Mitch glanced around again, but didn't see anything resembling food. "I take it we're each other's treat?"

Which suited him perfectly. Feasting on the sweetness of Belle's body was an ideal ending to a delicious dinner.

Her eyes danced in delight as she giggled, but Belle shook her head. "No, no. I wouldn't cheat you out of a yummy ending to such a special dinner. Dessert is waiting."

Mitch followed her gesture toward the bathroom, then glanced back at her in question. Hardly his idea of the ideal eating place.

"I need a couple of minutes to get everything ready," she said, sounding a little breathless. He hoped it was anticipation and not amusement. "While I'm preparing the surprise, why don't you think about preparing yourself for a little fun?"

He looked over at the dildo, even bigger now that he could see it clearly, and arched his brow. She followed his gaze and laughed aloud. "No, no, that's just a sampling for the guests. You don't want to judge what they might indulge in. You just want to give them plenty to choose from."

"And your choice is?"

"You," she said, the laughter fading as she stepped close and pressed her hands against his chest. He automatically reached up to curve his fingers over her breasts so lovingly encased in filmy black fabric. Her nipples perked under his palms, her breath hitched just a little as she stepped up on tiptoe to meet his lips.

Mitch tasted the rich lobster, butter and the sweetness that was all Belle as he sank into the kiss. Tongues danced a slow, wicked waltz, making him painfully aware that the bed was waiting just a few feet away.

Needing more, he curved one hand behind her neck and felt the hooks that held her halter dress together. With a flick of his fingers, the fabric loosened and skimmed down her body.

"We'll call this a taste of what's to come," she purred with a satisfied look on her face. Belle stepped away, wearing nothing but a strappy pair of black sandals and gorgeous smile. "While I get the next course ready, why don't you undress? I hate to be the only naked body enjoying the treat."

Screw the treat. Mitch wanted her. Now. He reached out to grab her but Belle danced away, surprisingly nimble in such high spiked heels.

"No, not yet. Go undress." She gave a little wave of her fingers toward the other side of the room. "I want to do this for you, okay? For you, with you. You'll love it."

With that and the mouthwatering view of her naked ass as she scurried from the room, she was gone.

Mitch sighed and, after a quick recitation of the first twenty U.S. presidents, managed to return the blood from his throbbing dick back to his brain.

Deciding she was right and naked would get him inside her hot, wet body sooner, he stripped. From the bathroom and dressing area he heard the rush of water in the tub, the clinking of glass and, at one excruciating point, her moan of delight.

"She'd better not be starting without me," he muttered as he left his jeans in a pile with the rest of his clothes.

Naked and rock-hard, Mitch strode across the room. When he reached the suite's dressing area, he noticed the carved, tufted rosewood dressing bench had been covered in thick towels. Next to it was a small glass table, a bowl and two spoons. The bowl was filled with what looked like ice cream and some kind of topping, making Mitch's mouth water as he thought about eating the treat off Belle's naked belly.

Steam poured from the open bathroom door, the scent of peaches and heat filling the room. Like a dream, Belle stepped out of the steam naked. Droplets of water dotted her bare flesh, one trailing a wet caress to the tip of her right breast.

Mesmerized, Mitch walked across the room, not breathing until he reached her. He bent down and sipped at her wet nipple, making her mewl like a kitten begging to be petted.

His hands moved easily over her damp skin, up and down the planes of her back twice before he pressed his fingers into the curve at the base of her spine to bring her tight against his body. His sips now turned to nibbles. One hand slid around her waist and down between their bodies to cup her damp and, he realized in shock, very bare sex.

Mitch pulled back from his feast to see the discovery his fingers had made.

"Well, well," he said with a grin.

Belle giggled, then arched one brow in a vampy look. "A smooth surface was better for what I have in mind."

"Later," he dismissed, wanting to run his fingers and tongue over that silky expanse of bare flesh.

"Uh-uh," she corrected, stepping back. "Keep your hand on your bird and not in my bush."

"A bird in the hand is worth two in a bush," he corrected absently, shooting her a grin. "Besides, you're bushless now."

Belle's giggle made Mitch feel like a million bucks. The

simple fact that here she was, the princess of his dreams, naked, laughing and totally focused on him— Well, it blew his mind. Mitch recalled how excited he'd been to buy the resort, to see what he'd thought of as his dream actually come true.

But he looked at the woman staring up at him, amusement and happiness clear on her face, and realized this was his real dream come true.

"Come see why naked is better." Oblivious to the shocked realization that'd just kicked Mitch in the face, Belle grabbed his hand and pulled him back to the dressing area, where she'd set up the towel-covered settee and dessert.

Telling himself he'd overreacted and to focus on the naked woman and incredible sex in store for him, Mitch shoved aside the emotional bomb and watched Belle. His mouth watered both at the richly sweet scent filling the air and the sight of her naked ass as she swayed across the room, still wearing those sexy do-me heels.

Wiggling her brows at Mitch and giving him a look that was a combination of flirtation and amusement, Belle sat in demure nudity on the cushioned bench. She lifted a crystal bowl filled with ice cream, peaches and what looked like a caramel sauce.

"Freshly made vanilla-bean ice cream, brandied peaches and caramel," she told him as she held out the bowl for him to see. Then she puffed out her lip in an exaggerated pout and gave a tiny shrug. "But it's so rude to eat out of the serving bowl, isn't it? So you'll be my dessert plate and I'll eat off you, hmm?"

His cock jumped at the image of her eating dessert off his body and it was all Mitch could do not to grab the bowl and pour the sweet confection over himself.

"What about my dessert?" he asked, the gentlemanly

part of him struggling to overcome the powerful urging of his dick.

"You'll get to eat all you want later," she promised. When he started to protest, she made a tut-tutting noise and shook her head. "Ladies first, remember."

He told himself it was manners that stifled his protest, but they both knew it was the fact that she took his hands and pulled him forward so his dick was level with her breasts.

Visions and ideas flashed through his head, each one more erotic than the last. But before he could act on any, Belle shook her head again and dropped to her knees so he was now level with her mouth. She lifted the bowl and with a wink she blew him a kiss and poured.

Mitch groaned at the sensation of cold ice cream and warm caramel sauce sliding over his straining head. Then Belle added her hot mouth to the mix. His hips bucked, and unable to help himself, Mitch tunneled his fingers through her hair and held on as she blew him and his control all to hell.

His orgasm hit hard, fast and intense, and Mitch growled with pleasure when Belle didn't stop sucking, licking or nibbling away at her dessert. Everything went black, his knees almost buckling as he gave over to the pleasure pumping out of his body.

It took him a solid minute to regain his senses. When he came back to earth, he realized Belle had stopped sucking and had laid her head against his belly and was giving him a hug, her arms wrapped around his thighs.

He smoothed a caress down the back of her tousled hair, causing Belle to pull back and grin up at him.

"Now, that was a tasty dessert," she purred. "Shall we follow it up with a relaxing bath and wash off the stray peaches?"

"What about mine?" he asked, wanting nothing more than to taste her juices mixed with hot caramel.

"Help yourself," Belle said with a wink.

Mitch noted a peach stuck to her shoulder and grinned. He scooped it up with one finger and popped it into his mouth, then proceeded to enjoy the clean, smooth pleasure of peaches, Brazilian style.

Ten minutes later Mitch sighed with pleasure as he held her back against his chest and sipped champagne in the huge spa tub.

"So what do you think of this particular theme?" she asked, her face still flushed from her climax.

"It's perfect. Traditional yet just kinky enough to appeal to the average guest," he assured her. "Like everything else you've come up with, it's perfect."

"Wait till you see the setup for the kinkier guests. You know the ones—seen it all, done it all." He felt her laugh as her shoulders shifted against his chest. "The leather goods, floor-to-ceiling poles and edgier sex toys arrived this afternoon."

"I can't wait to try them out," he assured her before taking a drink. The explosion of bubbles, alcohol and peaches filled his taste buds and Mitch sighed. Damn, life was good.

"Hmm, I think that means I deserve a reward," she mused. Wicked humor lit her green eyes, but before she could take charge of their lovemaking again, Mitch set down the champagne flute and grabbed her hips.

A quick move and he had her pressed against the opposite side of the tub, her breasts just above water level and her butt up in the air.

His fingers went to work on her nipples as Mitch sucked and licked the trail of water up her spine until he reached the back of her neck.

His body holding her in place, he slipped into the glorious wet pleasure of her body from behind. Belle's moan was breathy, lost in her soft pants of delight.

The steamy heat, the slickness of the water added another level of decadence to their lovemaking. Mitch took his time, building her pleasure with long, even strokes countered by tiny flicks of his fingers over her wet, turgid nipples.

When Belle couldn't handle it anymore, her pants becoming whimpers and her body pressing tighter against him, he pulled out, turned her in one swift move and pulled her right back down on his throbbing dick. The move, so hard and fast, sent him over the edge and his explosion of pleasure brought her right along. His mouth took hers as they came together. Belle's gasping cry of his name added an emotional edge to his orgasm.

He scooped her slippery slick body out of the frothy bubbles and, still kissing her, carried Belle into the other room. Uncaring that they soaked the sheets, he dropped to the bed, pulling her with him. He couldn't release his hold on her, not even to grab a towel, to pull up the blankets. He didn't want to let go of Belle.

Ever.

His last thought before sleep wound its way through his sexual haze was that he couldn't wait to introduce Belle to his grandma. Six years ago, he'd used the excuse of their rushed wedding as his reason for not bringing her into his family circle. The truth was, he'd been afraid of losing her.

This time, he knew it'd work out.

This time was forever.

10

"Knock it off, Reece," Mitch snapped the next afternoon. His glare should have slain the man in his tracks, but his damned cousin was made of tougher stuff. "I don't want to hear this crap. It's bullshit, you're wasting my time."

"Cuz, I know you don't want to hear bad about your ladyfriend, but you have to face facts. Someone is screwing you over and everything is pointing in her direction."

"Belle isn't behind the sabotage. It was happening long before she signed on. There's no reason to suspect her." He slammed his fist on his desk. Mitch's vision blurred as fury filled his brain. "What's your problem with her, Reece? Are you holding on to a grudge on my behalf? Do you hate blondes? Is Belle just too much for you? What exactly is the problem here?"

The fury did a slow burn as his cousin just sat there calmly, staring in silence. The contrast of his own anger and Reece's composure only added fuel to Mitch's frustration.

Then, stretching his jaw to either side, Reece pulled off his cowboy hat and contemplated the curve of the brim before setting it back on his head. Preparing for battle.

Mitch recognized the move and steeled himself to win. Because there was no way in hell he was backing down.

"Look, I know you're into the gal and I'm not saying I have a personal issue with her." At Mitch's glare, Reece shrugged and admitted, "Well, other than the whole screwing-you-over-and-leaving-you-standing-there-with-your-dick-in-your-hand thing, I don't have a personal issue with her."

Mitch thought about defending his dick-holding practices as his business, but realized it'd be a waste of time. Family defended family, end of story.

"But you have to be realistic. Your resort is seeing problems and this gal has a history of problems. She also knows the hotel business inside out. She's the daughter of a guy who thinks you screwed him royally. And, well, bottom line, she's female."

Mitch squinted. "Care to justify that last one?"

"She's a woman. Women do the strangest things. Who knows, she might have spent the past half-dozen years stewing over whatever it was that pissed her off enough to leave you at the altar and is just now implementing her revenge."

The flames of his fury were doused as if they'd been hit by a deluge of water. Mitch just shook his head in pity. "You still reeling from your divorce, cuz?"

"Nah, I'm over the hangover now." Reece shot him a grin that Mitch had seen turn women from disinterested divas into panting groupies. Mitch was probably the only person who knew that grin was hiding a pained heart. Not broken, but bruised. Even Reece would be surprised at the news.

"Shawna aside, since she was in a class by herself, I just don't get what goes through their pretty little heads sometimes," Reece continued with a shrug.

Mitch didn't comment. There wasn't much to say since he'd never cared two damns about what went on in a woman's head until Belle had showed up—this time, he forced himself to acknowledge. Their first round, his only interest had been in proving himself, in snagging the biggest prize in the game.

"You said you wanted me to investigate." Reece's grin fell away as he leaned forward to rest his elbows on his knees. The look he speared Mitch with was all business. "That means man up and listen to the results of that investigation, regardless of what your dick wants to hear."

Mitch set his jaw and with a jerk of his head indicated his cousin offer up those results.

Reece stared for another few seconds, then lifted a file folder from the seat next to him. He held it up for Mitch to see, then without opening it tossed it on the desk.

"You've had a series of emails coming out of the resort. Not unusual," he said before Mitch could scoff, "except that each one is going to the same IP address and each one is deleted from your server. A few a week, sometimes more, never less."

Mitch frowned and laid his palm on the file.

"Interviewing the staff and repair crew involved in each incidence, I think it's clear the problems the resort's faced in the past month have all been deliberate. The lost linens, the destruction of property, even the gophers."

Mitch pulled his head back in shock. How the hell did someone come up with that many gophers?

"The gophers, by the way," Reece continued, pointing a finger at the file folder under Mitch's hand, "were actually shipped direct to the resort. Ballsy move, that."

Mitch pulled the folder toward him but didn't open it.

"From what I've gathered, the person behind it is a woman."

Mitch glared, but waited for the justification he knew was coming.

"I say that because all of the destruction was small-ish, things easily broken by someone of a slight stature." He went on to list the items to support his supposition. While he listened, Mitch flipped open the file folder and scanned the reports of property damage. With each one, his anger and frustration mounted.

"You really think all that is definitive evidence it's a woman behind the problems?" Mitch asked, his tone dismissive. He had small guys on the crew and in his management team. He was sure it could have been any of them.

"Nah, that's all circumstantial." Reece leaned out of his chair and across the desk to flip the pages in Mitch's hand to a manifest. "That the gophers were delivered to and signed for by a woman is definitive."

Mitch stared at the loopy and decidedly feminine scrawl on the delivery manifest. Two dozen gophers, signed for by Janie Doe. He hated that his brain was scrambling to remember Belle's signature. He glanced at the date on the invoice. The same as the date of her first visit to talk him into hiring her. Mitch felt sick, but told himself it wasn't her. His gut knew it wasn't, but there weren't many women at the resort yet, especially not ones with enough authority to commandeer a direct delivery without being questioned.

"This doesn't point to Belle," he stated unequivocally, tossing the folder down. The pages fanned over his desk but he and Reece both ignored them.

"Her old man is in trouble—financially sinking and the cause is pretty much your fault," Reece said, his voice quiet with resignation. Mitch knew his cousin figured he'd just delivered the death knell to Mitch's relationship and felt rotten about it. "That deal the two of you cooked up, then you bailed on when your princess ran off has him tied up financially, and with real estate tanking, he's screwed with no way out."

"That sucks." And it did. Hugely. Mitch hadn't heard a whisper about it, but he wasn't surprised. Franklin Forsham was good at keeping things hush-hush. Regret washed over Mitch in a heavy wave. He'd been an asshole to leave Franklin in a lurch like that. Sure, he'd been humiliated and feeling justified in slapping out at anyone named Forsham, but the bottom line was it'd been bad business. He considered the current real estate climate, the tightened zoning laws in California and the probable debt Franklin had incurred holding the property all this time and winced.

"That totally sucks," he repeated. "But how does that make Belle the culprit in Lakeside's sabotage? In the first place, the problems started before she got here. Second and more significantly, she's under contract with me. The success of her business hinges on the success of my resort."

"Maybe. Or maybe she's more interested in her daddy's business right now." Reece grimaced, then pulled some more papers from that damned file. "I was chatting with Kiki, the gal who runs the spa here." In other words, flirting and looking for a good time. "Turns out Belle made her a very interesting proposition."

Mitch's mouth watered as he remembered the Brazilian treat he'd enjoyed the night before. "So?" he asked.

"It seems she's trying to lure Kiki away from your resort." Mitch's smile dropped away as Reece continued. "She's offering her gigs at her daddy's hotels. Same deal you have, but a few extra perks."

"That doesn't put her behind my resort issues."

"True," Reece agreed. Then he handed Mitch the papers he'd been holding. "Copies of the emails sent through the resort server from Belle to her partner."

Mitch started to point out how wrong it was to invade her emails when the words caught his eye.

The plan is in motion. Daddy will be thrilled.
Check timing of all of this. Can't let the cat out of the closet or Mitch will know.

Cat out of the closet. It was totally Belle-esque. His stomach fisted at the idea of her screwing him over with such calculation.

She'd walked out on him once without giving him the benefit of the doubt, not caring that she left him looking like an idiot. She was clever enough and resourceful enough to pull off revenge at this level and confident enough not to bat one long, mink eyelash.

But despite all the proof Reece was pitching, regardless of how many papers he stuffed in that file pointing the finger at Belle, Mitch wasn't going for it.

With a smile at odds with the subject, he settled back in his chair and finally identified the feeling he'd been struggling with since he'd walked into this office and seen his past waiting for him. He was in love with Belle. He had been six years ago, although he'd called it ambition. He was now, although he'd been trying to tell himself it was lust.

Love. Mitch shifted his gaze out the window to stare at the expanse of trees and gopher-infested lawn. Who knew it would feel so confusing?

But confusing or not, he loved her. Which meant, bottom line, he trusted her.

She might only be in this for the sex. She might still run away at any time, Mitch realized as his heart sank a little. He swallowed the bitter taste of fear at the possibility and told himself he'd deal with it later. The truth was, he wasn't blind to Belle's issues. But he knew screwing him at the same time she was screwing him over wasn't one of them.

"You're meeting with Belle tomorrow to talk security for the grand opening," he told Reece. "If you need to ask questions to make you feel like you're doing your job, go ahead. She's clean. But keep digging because the real culprit needs to be stopped before they do any more damage to my resort."

"You're gone, cuz." Reece shook his head in a pitying, you're-so-stupid kind of way.

"Totally gone," Mitch acknowledged, shoving aside the doubts. "And I'm loving every minute of it."

"I'VE GOT IT, THE ANSWER to our problem," Belle claimed in her daily phone call to Sierra. She tucked the cell between her chin and shoulder as she sliced a peach. They were now officially her favorite fruit.

"A blow-up doll with remote-control hands?" Sierra shot back.

Belle rolled her eyes at the phone. "Hardly. If we're using remote control I plan on operating something much more interesting than hands."

"Right. So what's our problem and then what's the answer?"

Sierra was usually so on top of things, but she'd been distracted during their last few phone calls, forgetting to send papers and contracts, just sort of disconnected from everything as far as Belle could tell.

Taking her snack to the table, Belle frowned in frustration. Questions were pointless. Sierra answered them all with annoying assurances that everything was just fine.

"Kiki's in," Belle explained. "She's really excited to take her spa to the next level and sees aligning with Forsham Hotels as the way to do it. Besides all the info I already sent you, I just found out she's courting a contract with one of the big-name beauty suppliers for an exclusive label."

"Do you think that's enough to help your dad?"

"I hope so. She'll pay top dollar for the square footage, but she'll also bring in a huge clientele. Between the label and her own promotion, they're going to skyrocket." Belle considered. "I have to convince Daddy, but if it works, he'll be able to switch all his on-site boutiques and stores. Rather than entities he runs and assumes the business expenses for, he can let his tenant take on the employee, inventory and liability risks. He'll cut his own expenses by at least an eighth."

Belle nibbled on her peach as they went on to brainstorm a few more ideas and kick around ways to pitch the proposal to her father. Finally deciding Belle would do it over Sunday brunch the next weekend, they wound up the topic.

"What about Lakeside?" Sierra asked. "Have you talked to Mitch about borrowing Kiki?"

"No," she said slowly. "I just didn't think it was a good idea until we'd worked out all the particulars."

"In other words, you don't want to rock the nookie boat until you're sure your dad's on board."

Belle was glad her shamed flush couldn't be seen over the phone.

"Kiki doesn't have an exclusivity contract," she defended.

"Doesn't mean Mitch expects her to be stolen away by his bed buddy."

"She's not being stolen. After she set things up here, she planned on leaving a manager in charge anyway. Besides," Belle justified, "it's good insurance for her. If someone really is playing some game here and the resort is going to suffer, she needs a safety net."

"Speaking of which, what'd you find out?" Sierra asked.

Glad to change the subject, Belle thought of the list she'd copied from Diana's office the day before. Someone was deliberately trying to ruin the resort. Was it Mitch? Despite the note, she couldn't believe it.

"It's not Mitch," she declared. "Why would he ruin his own venture? There just isn't anything in it for him. His board of directors is made up entirely of family. It's a family-held corporation, even."

"So?"

"So, nothing means more to him than family. This guy has a total *Brady Bunch* mind-set."

"Are you sure you're not just trying to rationalize the fact that you're not done playing in his pants?" Sierra asked.

Pulling a face, Belle dropped to the couch and huffed out a breath. "Do you really think sex is that important that I'd risk everything for it?"

"You did before."

Belle frowned. It wasn't sex, she wanted to say. It was Mitch. Just Mitch. Sex with him was her only excuse to intimacy, she realized. And didn't that make her a pitiful love-struck idiot?

"Look, I need your input then. How'd you like to see the resort firsthand?" she asked after tucking her notes into her portfolio. "Come out, get a feel for the place, see Mitch in person and give me your opinion on what's what."

"You want me to come out there? Why? What'd you do?"

Belle rolled her eyes and made a huffing sound of irritation. "I didn't do anything. At least, nothing I need you to come fix. You have doubts about Mitch, I want your feedback. And I thought you'd enjoy getting the lay of the land, so to speak, before we kick into high gear next week preparing for the first event."

"Well, I'm grateful you don't want me to come fix your sex life," Sierra said with a laugh. "And you've already got a solid lay, so to speak, so I doubt you need me there."

"An upside-down head needs twice the help," Belle pointed out.

"Two heads are better than one," Sierra corrected with a sigh.

That she was desperate for Sierra to pinch-hit for her in the security meeting wasn't going to fly as a reason, even if it was pure truth. She was totally freaked to face Reece alone. Even worse, she was terrified he'd ruin what she'd found with Mitch.

But she wasn't telling Sierra that.

"I'd love to have your take on who's tanking the resort, and maybe while you're here you can see if there's anything I could add for the first party, the one for Mitch's family and board, next week," Belle claimed instead. "I'm just a little nervous about pulling this off given that someone is trying to screw things up. It'd help to have a second set of eyes."

It was a flimsy ploy and she knew it. Belle orchestrated events for thousands on her own and never needed hand-holding. She cringed, waiting for her partner to call her on it and trying to figure out how to get out of dealing with Reece. Pretend to be sick? Really get sick? Family emergency and run home? She had to do something, anything. She so did not want to deal with the hot cowboy. Not when she knew he was just waiting to get her alone and confront her about the past.

"Okay, I can be there tomorrow morning," Sierra agreed after a long silence.

Belle kept her squeal of triumph to herself. "You can?"

"Sure. You want my help, I'll come give it. Why the shock? We're partners. That's what we do, help each other and tell each other crap."

Interesting theory, since Belle knew damned well Sierra was keeping *crap* from her. But confronting her friend was pointless, so Belle kept that a silent observation.

"Great." Never one to ruin a miracle by asking too many questions, Belle rushed on, "Since you'll be here anyway, you can take the meeting with the head of security and go over all the details, okay?"

"I should have known there was a catch." Sierra laughed. "Fine, I'll take the meeting."

Noting a movement out of the corner of her eye, Belle glanced out the window at the golf course. Mitch and Reece strode across the green expanse. Although both wore jeans and work shirts, the two men couldn't look more different. Yet they seemed to be solid friends in addition to having that family connection that was so important to Mitch.

Family. Since it was just her and her dad, Belle didn't quite get the whole clan feeling Mitch seemed to embrace. But she definitely knew how important it was to take care of her loved ones. Worrying over her father was proof of that.

Belle gave herself a second to appreciate Mitch's gorgeous ass, encased lovingly in denim, before she glanced at his leggy cowboy cousin. A sneaky plan formed in her head.

Six years ago she'd thought Sierra and Reece looked great together. Both tall, dark and gorgeous, they'd been striking at the pre-wedding festivities. If Reece had Sierra to distract him, it would keep him off Belle's back while she tried to figure out who was behind the dirty deeds at Mitch's resort.

It had nothing to do with the fact that Belle was so far gone over Mitch that she wanted everyone to experience the wonders of coupledom. Or if it did, she forced herself to admit, it was only because good sex was something her best friend deserved.

"Great," she told Sierra. "You're so much better at those details than I am and this security guy is hot. You'll have fun."

She figured Sierra was due for a hot, wild fling and Reece Carter was the perfect man to show her friend a sexy time. Belle couldn't wait to watch the sparks fly.

SPARKS, HELL. IT WAS like watching an inferno. Belle gaped as Sierra and Reece did everything but get naked and duke it out on the boardroom table.

"The resort has enough staff to handle the opening," Reece said in his long, slow drawl. "We don't need to bring in outside help and deal with more of those damned confidentiality agreements and clearances. Besides, how many people does it really take to serve a plate of mini hot dogs and tacos?"

"Don't worry about those mini hot dogs, cowboy," Sierra said with a wicked smile. "Nobody's going to hold yours against you. Besides, we figure the guests will have a little more refined taste. That means gourmet food, circulated while it's hot and fresh. And then there's the resort's theme—"

"Waste of time and money," he muttered, scrawling something over his notes. "People don't need silly games to have a good time."

Belle started to defend the themes and Mitch shifted his chair, leaning forward at the same time to comment.

But before either could utter a word, Sierra gave a deep, patently fake sigh and shook her head.

With a pitying look, she tossed her long, dark hair over her shoulder and made a tut-tutting noise. "Are you afraid of games in sex, cowboy? Or is it the idea of other people coloring outside the lines that bothers you?"

"I'm all for a good time," he said with a look that made it clear to everyone in the room just how good a time he'd like to show Sierra. "It's when the good time veers out of easy and into complicated that I see it as a problem. Nobody should have to work for fun. Games just mess it all up."

Belle had the feeling she was missing half the conversation. The best half, if Sierra's breathless little laugh was anything to go by.

"As long as nobody's trying to slap handcuffs or nipple clips on you, what do you care?" Sierra asked. Then she gave him a taunting look. "Or are you afraid to play?"

"Sweetheart, I wrote the book on how to play. And," he said slowly, leaning across the table with a wicked grin, "how to win. You want a peek at a few pages, you just let me know."

"I'm trying to cut back on my fiction," Sierra told him with a wink.

Belle glanced at Mitch. He was staring, jaw slack, at the battle of verbal foreplay.

"So," Belle said bravely, breaking in to what should have been a simple security discussion, "I can see the two of you have this in hand so I'm going to take Mitch and do a walk-through of the weekend plans."

They ignored her.

Belle offered Mitch a helpless shrug. With one last look at the warring pair, now standing and facing off on either side of the table, she grabbed Mitch's hand and pulled him from the conference room.

As the door thudded shut behind them, Mitch started to ask a question. Before he could do more than mutter "oh, my God," they noticed Diana standing at the fax machine, her eyes huge.

"Guess you heard that," Belle said with a wince.

"Is everything okay?" the assistant asked quietly. "I needed your signature on some orders, Mitch, but it was so loud in there I figured I should wait."

"Security is a touchy issue," Mitch quipped as he strode over to take the file and pen from her.

Belle laughed and sat on the edge of Diana's desk to wait. She tried to think of something to say that would calm the other woman, who was visibly agitated, but all she could come up with were dirty jokes. Trying to get control of herself, she glanced away. Her gaze dropped to the computer monitor, where bubbles bounced across the screen.

Across the bottom of the open Word files was one with a stylized header. Belle noted how pretty the gold MC lettering was as the purple bubble shifted to turquoise. MC? Mitch's logo wasn't that girly, was it?

Before she could ask, he handed Diana back the papers and pen. "Stay out of the boardroom," he instructed his assistant as Belle joined him at the door. "If you hear furniture breaking, call the cops."

"But only furniture," Belle cautioned. "Groans, yells or screams should be ignored."

They were halfway down the hall before Mitch glanced at her in question. "Groans?"

"Oh, please, they're so going to be doing it up against the wall before the day is over."

She'd taken another two steps before she realized he'd stopped cold.

"Doing it?" he asked blankly.

"*It.* The vertical vibration. The dirty deed. Riding the wild stallion. Bumping uglies." He still stared. Belle laughed and grabbed his hand to get him moving again. "Jeez, Mitch. What'd you think that was in there?"

"I thought it was hate at first sight," he muttered.

"With all that sexual innuendo? Hardly." They stopped at the front desk and Belle offered her thanks and a smile to Larry, who handed her a large picnic basket. Mitch took it from her and gestured for her to precede him out the door.

She waited until they were in the golf cart on their way to the woods to continue sharing her theory. "Heck, the sexual sparks and tension were so heavy back there I was getting turned on just being in the room."

"Are you sure that was them and not me?" he asked, glancing over as he steered the machine toward the trees. "I'd like to think you get hot and horny just being in the same room."

"You'd like to think that, hmm?" Belle laughed and patted his thigh before getting out of the now-stopped cart. "I admit, you do have a way of turning my thoughts to sexual escapades, whether you're in the room or not."

She reached for the basket, but he beat her to it. With a wink and a quick kiss, he gestured for her to step back and let him set up their lunch like the gentleman he was.

Belle settled against a tree trunk and looked out over the clearing, her entire being filled with a sense of peace and happiness she'd never felt before. She didn't know if it was the result of a week of incredible sex, her feelings for Mitch or the utter beauty of the woods. Whatever it was, she felt great.

She was curious, though.

"Is your family going to have a problem with the sex angle?" she asked, watching him spread the thick red blanket over the lawn, then place the picnic basket on the corner before kicking off his shoes.

He laughed and held out his arm. Belle slipped off her sandals and settled on the blanket, where Mitch immediately grabbed her and rolled so she lay flat on top of him. He bunched the blanket up as a pillow and settled his hands on her waist with a sigh of contented pleasure.

"Believe me, my family has no issues with sex. From my youngest cousin to my gram, they're all pretty open-minded. Remember that list of sex-theme ideas I gave you? Those were straight from my family. Including this picnic, which was decidedly the tamest."

"Yeah," she said, her attention more focused on tracing his lips with her fingernail and reveling at the sweetness of the moment than their discussion. "There were some good ideas there. I tend to think a little bigger, and Sierra a little kinkier, so those were a nice balance."

"Kinkier? We left kinkier with my cousin?"

Delighted, Belle met his gaze and grinned. She was so in love, she realized. And even though it could be the biggest mistake of her life, right at this moment, she didn't care. She wanted to jump up, scream from the treetops how incredible Mitch was. Equal parts happiness and terror made her light-headed. Okay, she realized as the ringing in her ears turned to a buzz, maybe the terror had an edge over the happiness.

There were so many reasons why this was insane. Why falling for Mitch was a horribly bad idea. Their history alone made believing they had a shot at happy-ever-after a total fairy tale.

But for right now, just this moment in time, she didn't

care. She was giving happiness free rein and wringing every drop of joy from this interlude. And since joy translated so easily to sexual energy between them, she wiggled her hips a little. Mitch's body reacted instantly.

She melted at the humor in his cinnamon-sweet eyes and leaned closer. "That's okay. I've got bigger here with me," she said, referring back to his concern over his cousin being left with a kinky Sierra.

The humor left and Mitch's gaze went dark with desire. One hand slipped from Belle's waist down to cup her butt and press her tighter to him. The other combed through her hair.

"Why don't we see how much bigger we can get?" he said as he pulled her mouth to his.

Just before their lips met, Belle whispered, "And when we're done, I have a whole basket of aphrodisiacs there to prep you for the next round."

11

BELLE TRIED TO STOP her hands from shaking as she carefully lowered herself into Diana's office chair.

"It's not booby-trapped, you know," Sierra hissed from the door where she was standing lookout. "Just sit down and get to it."

Belle rolled her eyes at her partner in crime. Her exasperation was more calming than the deep-breathing exercise she'd been trying since they'd decided to break into Mitch's assistant's office.

Her stomach constricted again.

No, *break in* was the wrong term. It was business hours. Broad daylight. Just because Belle had carefully timed her visit to coincide with Mitch's trip to the airport and had arranged for Diana to pick up a special order that suddenly couldn't be delivered didn't mean it was wrong.

"Get on with it," Sierra snapped. "We don't have that much time."

Belle glared, but before she could say anything, her lookout did a hurry-up motion with her hand. Figuring finger gestures were next, Belle bit the bullet and, with a cringe, started peeking into file folders.

"You're positive she's the dirty dog who's screwing

Mitch over?" Sierra asked as Belle carefully repositioned the laundry invoices in their file.

"No," Belle shot back. "I already told you, I'm not positive. But every bit of evidence I've found has been right here in her office. And since I refuse to believe it's Mitch himself, that leaves her. Now stop bugging me and keep watch."

Finished with the folders on the desk and not brave enough to start on drawers, Belle moved the mouse beside Diana's computer. The floating bubble screen saver cleared and her gaze flew to the bottom of the screen. Of course, there was no incriminating document open today. Clueless but determined, she randomly opened and scanned document files. While she did, she considered the question. At least Sierra had stopped arguing that it might be Mitch. After meeting him again, spending the past few days in his company, she'd been totally won over.

The same couldn't be said for her opinion of Reece, Belle had noticed. After that first explosive meeting four days ago, they'd retreated behind a wall of polite iciness. So much for sexual tension. Instead of being engulfed in heat, they'd straight up frozen each other out. When she'd tried asking Sierra about it, her friend had claimed instant irritation as the culprit and stated she was taking the high road and ignoring the idiot.

Frustration built as the seconds ticked and Belle came up empty-handed. Sierra hissed. Terror slapped Belle and her gaze flew to the door. Instead of a bust, though, Sierra made another hurry-up gesture. Belle opened her mouth to retort but Sierra put her finger to her lip for silence and raised both brows. She was having way too much fun with this covert crap.

With a curl of her lip, Belle mentally flipped her friend off, then went back to her snooping. Her silent cuss-fest halted when she found the recycling bin and stabbed the mouse button to open it.

Gobbledygook. Most of the files had recognizable names, but a few were weird combinations of numbers and symbols. All had the current date. Did that mean Diana emptied the recycle bin daily? The extent of Belle's computer knowledge ended when she hit Send on her email, so she had no clue. She clenched her teeth in a silent scream of frustration. She should have let Sierra check the computer, but if one of them was going to get caught, Belle needed to take responsibility.

Helpless to do anything else, she started opening random files.

And found what she was looking for in her third gobbledygook.

"Holy shit," she whispered as she read.

"What?"

Belle waved Sierra to silence as she right-clicked, trying to find the print command.

"Belle," Sierra muttered.

"I'll tell you in a second," she said, brows furrowed as she tried to find the print icon. She hated this new operating system, she had no idea where anything was.

Aha. She clicked.

"No." Sierra's words had gone from a hiss to full-out panic. "Now—you have to move now."

"What?" Panic was a stifling blanket of intense black heat as it poured over Belle. Her gaze flew to the printer, spewing pages, and back to Sierra's freaked-out face.

"That damned cowboy is coming up the hall," Sierra hissed, her eyes flitting around for someplace to hide.

"Damn."

Belle stood so fast the chair flew back and hit the wall. But the move didn't make the printer spew any faster. How long was that file? She gnawed at her lip, dancing in place. Did she hit Stop and leave it in the queue, tipping Diana off? Did she grab and run? Did she...

She caught herself actually wringing her hands and gave a little scream of frustration at the printer.

"Hold him off," she ordered.

"What? You're crazy."

She glared at Sierra and pointed toward the hallway. "Now. Get his attention, drag him off to look at a horse or something. I don't give a damn what you do, but keep him out of here."

Sierra huffed and glared. But Belle watched thankfully as she turned on her heel and with a quick shake of her shoulders sashayed down the hall. As the door swung shut behind her, Belle sent up a brief prayer for the cowboy's virtue and cleared the files from the computer screen. Finally, the last page printed. She grabbed the stack of papers, folded them and then looked down. A-line skirt, camp shirt, sassy heels. No purse, no pockets, no hiding place.

She glanced at her breasts. Too small, shirt too tight not to notice the sharp angle of folded pages. Oh, to be a C-cup and have hiding room.

With another glance at the door and knowing that as good as Sierra was, if he wanted in this office, Reece would be storming in any moment, she slid the pages into the waistband of her skirt right at the small of her back. Tucking her shirt over the top of them, she winced and realized she'd have to walk sideways down the hall to keep them hidden. Of all the times to forget her portfolio.

But a girl had to do what a girl had to do. So she smoothed a shaking hand over her hair, pasted her biggest fake smile on and headed for the door. Opening it just a smidge, she peeked out.

Nothing. No Sierra, no Reece. Belle frowned and tried to angle herself to peek the other way. Still nothing.

Had Sierra really dragged him off to see a horse?

Did she care? Nope, Belle just heaved a sigh of relief, and with a quick grab for an empty file folder on the cabinet, retrieved the pages from her skirt, tucked them in and opened the door.

She couldn't wait to get back to her cottage to see who was behind the dirty deeds. Belle grinned, gave a finger wave at the concierge and practically skipped through the foyer. Wouldn't Mitch love her when he realized she'd saved him, too? Hey, she'd take any way she could to get into his heart.

MITCH WATCHED THE RUSH of bodies hurrying through Lakeside's foyer in satisfaction. Waitstaff bringing food to the registration desk for the guests. At the concierge station, uniformed men were polishing the brass of the luggage carts. Housekeeping was running a damp mop over the marble and berating the waiter for dropping a crumb. Mitch grinned. Crazy busy preparation for the party that night. He loved it.

"What do you think?" he asked Larry, who was checking items off some list in a frantic way. The only person Mitch knew who was more list-obsessed was Belle. Totally beyond his comprehension, but he was damned grateful for the results.

"Timing, check. Food, check. Housekeeping, check. Flowers…where are the flowers?" Larry asked in a panicked tone.

Mitch nudged him, then pointed to the bouquets flanking the registration desk and the three people setting other arrangements around the foyer. His manager's lips moved as he counted them. Then he nodded and made a mark on his clipboard.

Assured that things were under control, Mitch grinned and slapped Larry on the shoulder before heading over to the desk to sample the appetizers.

Before he could eat more than one brie-stuffed mushroom, Reece strode up, his face set in hard lines. He reminded Mitch of a gunfighter taking his stance to draw.

"What's wrong?" Mitch asked when his cousin came closer. "Did you have a row with one of the cousins already?"

The investors, aka their entire family, had been arriving all day for tonight's event. He'd been fielding congratulations and backslaps all afternoon and he was loving it.

"We need to talk."

Mitch's smile didn't falter. He was in too good a mood to be worried about his cousin's recent doom-and-gloom attitude.

"So talk."

"Privately."

"Look, I don't have time for a covert exchange of information. I've got a lot going on here, in case you didn't notice. The entire family flew in. I picked Grammy Lynn up at the airport a couple hours ago. She's up in her room now laughing over the sex toys. The party is in three hours, so you should think about getting yourself ready."

In other words, Mitch didn't want to deal with this shit now. His focus was the party, a small-scale practice run for the special invitation to the press and A-listers grand opening starting the next week. They were still serving an aphrodisiac-inspired menu, hiring a live band for dancing and inviting couples to participate in the sex-themed offerings. But as much as he loved them, Mitch didn't think his family would appreciate caviar and Cristal. Not when they knew the costs came out of their investment.

"Belle was in your office," Reece said in a low voice.

"So?"

"Snooping around, using the computer." Reece's tone changed. "Her and that high-maintenance friend of hers."

Mitch sighed. "Again with Sierra? You don't have to maintain her, so what's the problem."

"No woman is worth the energy it'd take to maintain that one," Reece mused. He rocked back on his heels and shoved his hands into the front pockets of his jeans while he contemplated the idea. "Although she's one helluva short, sweet ride."

"Giddyap," Mitch muttered as he took the clipboard from Larry. After glancing at the liquor-delivery invoice, he signed his name and returned it with a nod of thanks. "You said *is?*"

Pulled out of his reverie, Reece stared blankly. "Huh?"

"*Is* a wild ride. Not *would be*, not *seems like*. *Is*. Care to fill me in?"

His cousin stood stock-still, no expression on his usually affable face. Then he shrugged.

"That's not the point," Reece stated. "Those women had no reason to be in there. I think they were up to something."

Mitch sighed.

"Look," Reece said, stepping around so he was face-to-face with Mitch. "You don't want to believe it, that's fine. But security is my job. Let me do it my way."

"Do what your way? Giddyap?"

Reece's eyes flashed rare anger. Mitch braced himself, even though he knew the punch wasn't coming. His cousin never lost his temper.

"Mitch," called a woman's voice.

Both men glanced over to watch a stunning, heavy-set woman cross the foyer in khaki capris and a white military-style shirt.

"Lena, you made it," Mitch greeted, glad to see his stepsister. They exchanged a hug before she turned to Reece and, a hand on his biceps, pulled him close for a half hug.

"Royce, how are you?" she asked. She tossed her dark hair behind her shoulder and gave him a toothy smile.

"It's Reece, and I'm doing pretty good. It's nice to see you again."

Mitch doubted that. Reece had complained more than once about Lena back when Mitch's stepdad and mom had been alive. The two families hadn't blended well, though not for lack of trying on the adults' part. But Lena hadn't ever quite fit with Mitch's bevy of cousins. Reece in particular had developed a tendency to leave the room as soon as she entered. Probably because she'd thought he was—how'd she put it? Mitch frowned then remembered. The bomb.

He gave a silent laugh and watched her pour the charm on his cousin and realized that whatever was bugging Reece must be major, since he wasn't excusing himself to leave.

Apparently Reece's monosyllabic responses outweighed his appeal as the bomb, so, after a minute of attempting to catch up, Lena turned her attention back to Mitch.

"I'm so excited for you. I just took myself on a tour around the grounds and, wow, Mitch. This is one gorgeous property."

"Thanks."

They discussed the resort's amenities while Reece loomed like a silent nag behind them. Since she wasn't an actual investor or on the board, Mitch hadn't considered Lena when he'd told Diana to arrange for his entire family to come out. He rarely saw the other woman, but since he'd loved her father and the old man had always been there for him, he'd readily approved her addition to the guest list.

"It's so great to see you both," Lena gushed again. "But I'm going to go ahead and pretend I'm a posh guest here and do the registration thing, then relax a little bit before the fancy soiree this evening."

The men offered their goodbyes, and, as Lena turned to leave, she tossed an invitation over her shoulder. "Reece, you be sure and save me a dance. I'd love to revisit old times."

"Old times?" Mitch teased under his breath as she left.

"Whatever," he muttered back.

Mitch laughed in delight. This was going to be one helluva fun evening.

"You need to let me do my job," Reece said when they were alone again.

Mitch shrugged. "We've been through this already. Go ahead, do your job. But don't screw with my event and don't be making any unfounded accusations. You nail someone, you better be damned sure you have the right person and enough proof to make a case."

"You'll have your proof by the end of the night," Reece assured him.

The words were right, but the feeling in Mitch's stomach was all kinds of wrong.

BELLE DISCONNECTED HER cell phone and was just tossing it in her evening bag when Sierra came into the cottage.

"What took you so long?" she asked. "We're due on-site in five minutes."

She spent ten seconds admiring her partner's vintage

Vera Wang dress before she glanced at Sierra's face. Belle frowned.

"You're chewing on your lip," she mumbled.

"So?"

The brunette's tone was not only confrontational, it had do-not-disturb vibes all around it. Belle wanted to know what had happened that afternoon, where Sierra had hauled Reece off to, that kind of thing. But it didn't take a half-assed Sherlock Holmes like herself to put two and two together and realize wherever it was, whatever they'd done, Sierra wasn't happy about it.

"So, nothing," Belle said, backing down. No point in starting a fight. "Do you want to see what I found?"

Sierra took one eager step forward then grimaced and shook her head. "We don't have time. Give me the summary."

"The file was a detailed list of instructions on how to cause trouble for the resort. Everything from those animals in the golf course to the canceled meat order are listed there."

"Diana typed up a list?" Sierra's tone made it clear how dumb she thought that was.

"No, they're instructions from the person she works for." Belle checked her hair in the mirror one last time and adjusted the strap of her ice-blue evening dress. Bias-cut silk, it hugged her curves in ways she hoped Mitch appreciated. "Apparently she's supposed to delete any files from the computer each day, too. Thanks for the idea to send her on that wild-goose chase to pick up the replacement supplies. Otherwise she'd have emptied the recycle bin and I wouldn't have proof."

"Who's behind it?"

Belle paused, still trying to believe it herself. Then

she shrugged and said with a frown, "L.N. Larry Nelson. Mitch's manager."

"No," Sierra breathed, her blue eyes wide with shock. "He seems so geeky and devoted. Are you sure?"

Belle cringed at the question. She felt so defensive even making the accusation. Like a traitorous bitch.

"I don't have proof positive," she defended. "But his name is mentioned here and these are his initials. He's also on the access list and was involved with the computer crash."

"That's pretty sketchy," Sierra pointed out with a grimace. "Remember at one point you thought it might be Mitch based on that first note?"

"I never believed it was Mitch," Belle defended angrily.

"Right, I know. But it looked like it. All I'm saying is this isn't enough to hold up in court, if you know what I mean."

"I know." Belle's defensiveness dropped away. She thought of the list. Only half the items on it had been crossed off. Some looked like they were supposed to take place after the grand opening. The ones about contacting the paparazzi would ruin the resort.

She shoved a hand through her curls and tried to think straight. They were silent for a few seconds, Belle trying to figure out how to tell Mitch what she'd found and wondering how angry he'd be with her for snooping, Sierra undoubtedly imagining how this was going to affect their contract.

"Have you told him yet?"

"Told Mitch?" Belle's stomach tensed again, fear dulling her anger. She swallowed twice before answering. "No, I haven't had a chance yet."

"But you're going to, right? As soon as you see him?" Sierra's face set in stubborn lines.

"I'll tell him later," Belle hedged. Her friend glared. "What? I'm supposed to grab him just before the party he's throwing for his entire family and tell him to turn around so I can point out the knives two of his most trusted employees shoved in his back? Warned is unarmed, as they say."

"Forewarned is forearmed," Sierra said with a roll of her eyes. "That's stupid. You're sidestepping the confrontation. Just talk to the man, Belle. You get naked and eat fruit off each other, for God's sake. You can tell him."

"I was talking to my dad just before you came in," Belle said, changing the subject. Sierra sighed, but didn't say anything. Belle ignored her blatant disapproval. She wasn't going to push for a confrontation at the party. That'd be crazy. She'd wait until tomorrow, sit down with Mitch and show him the proof. She took two deep breaths to calm her nausea and focused on distracting Sierra.

"He met with Kiki and they're good to go. He's offered her space in two of his hotels for her spa and he took your suggestion to make the same offer to some boutiques. He even has a meeting on Monday with Cartier and Tiffany's to bring in some bling."

Sierra paused in reapplying her lipstick to grin, genuine pleasure edging out the disapproval in her bright blue eyes. "That rocks. It sounds like he figures this is the right track?"

"His people crunched some numbers and estimate the changes will keep things afloat until the real estate market levels and he can get out from under that property."

"And…" Sierra shot her a long, narrow look. "You're nervous about something. Is he okay?"

Belle bit her own lip now and pressed her hand to her stomach to calm the flutters. "I invited him to the main event."

"Here?" Her eyes huge, Sierra gave a silent whistle. "Did you tell him whose resort you're opening? Aren't you afraid of an ugly public blowup?"

"I told him. He was…" *Ugly* would be the best word. But Belle had stood up to him. She'd almost puked, but she'd stood her ground. "I told him I'm serious about Mitch and they need to mend the fence I kicked down. He agreed to go to dinner with Mitch and me next week."

Sierra dropped her lipstick into her beaded black purse and the two women made their way out the door. "Mitch is cool with this?"

Belle wrinkled her nose. "I hope. I'll ask him over whipped cream."

The two women walked through the garden, lit with fairy lights, past the fountain with its cushioned benches and into the ballroom.

Staff was putting last-minute touches on the flowers and lighting candles at the small tables around the room. The bar staff was setting up the champagne fountain while two bartenders organized their stations on either side of the room.

"You need to tell him," Sierra said as they stood in the entrance.

"You need to back off," Belle shot back. "If we're going to play show-and-tell, maybe you could fill me in on the cowboy?"

Silence.

Then her friend shrugged and shook out the skirt of her dress.

"It looks good, everything is on schedule," Sierra said with a glance at her watch. "An hour till showtime?"

"Yep," Belle agreed. "You're in charge of keeping an eye on Larry."

Sierra wrinkled her nose, but nodded. "Let's rock this party."

And later tonight, after a vigorous bout of hot, sweaty sex, Belle would tell Mitch his assistant was in cahoots with his manager to destroy his resort.

12

"LADIES AND GENTLEMEN, welcome to Lakeside," Belle said from the raised dais, the microphone carrying her words to the glittering corners of the ballroom. "You're all going to enjoy an incredible stay at this gorgeous luxury resort, and for you couples here, you're in for one wild time."

Mitch watched the nudges spread around the room and grinned. Belle was like a sexy fairy up there on stage, wooing and entertaining his family and friends. She described the features of the resort and the quote-unquote "normal" special events they had planned for the next three days.

"And for those, shall we say, more adventurous among you," she added, her tone changing from charming to flirtatious, "we've got a few special treats."

Her emphasis on *special* had the room laughing. "As you know, Lakeside is going to be much more than a posh vacation spot for the rich and famous. Only at Lakeside can paparazzi-weary A-listers come for complete and total privacy. For relaxation. For romance. And best of all, for great sex."

At her last words, the entire room broke into applause. Belle waited for the wave of chatter to die down before going on to describe some of the more exotic extras the resort would offer. She also listed a choice a few of the guests would be able to sample for themselves tonight.

Mitch's grandma elbowed him in the side and lifted her champagne flute. "Good job, sweetie. She's got style."

"She came up with a great plan for the success of the resort," he said, unable to take his eyes off Belle as she descended from the stage and stopped to speak to Larry, then to Sierra, who for some bizarre reason had been clinging to the manager all evening. Mitch liked Larry well enough, but wondered if he should warn him about Belle's business partner. If Reece couldn't handle the giddyap kink of that sultry brunette, there was no way Larry could.

Belle, looking serious and intense, was speaking to some guy Mitch didn't recognize. Must be one of her people, he guessed. Mitch's gaze slid over her tousled blond curls and he sighed. Damn, even in a room filled with glitz and glitter, she still sparkled.

"She's caught your eye again, that's for sure," Grammy Lynn noted.

Mitch just shrugged. Why deny the obvious? He tore his gaze from Belle to look around for Reece. His cousin was at the far end of the room talking to one of the security guys. Mitch frowned. Had something else gone wrong? He caught Reece's eye and raised a brow in question. Reece gave an infinitesimal shake of his head and nodded toward the lake, visible outside the open French doors.

Good. Preparation for the tour details. The tension left Mitch's shoulders as he returned the nod. Just then, Belle sauntered over, a gorgeous smile lighting her face.

"Phase one complete," she said, sounding happy. A tiny purse dangled from her wrist and Mitch had to wonder if she had one of her infamous lists all folded up in there.

She offered his grandmother a warm smile and said hello, reminding Mitch that he was being rude.

He reintroduced the two women, feeling a little ashamed about the last time they'd met—the nonevent of their wedding.

"I was just complimenting my grandson on how well you've put this all together," his grandmother told Belle after the introductions. "When he first mentioned this to the board, I was worried it'd be tacky. You know, like that penis confetti at my niece Jenny's twenty-first birthday party."

He grinned at Belle's wince when Grammy Lynn said *penis*. For such a sexually adventurous woman, Belle was oddly prim in some situations. Satisfaction and happiness settled around him like a comfy blanket as Mitch watched his grandmother and Belle fall into an enthusiastic discussion. In five minutes, they covered parties, the perfect cake and, as Belle's initial inhibitions faded, the right way to display condoms.

Before they could start exchanging sex tips, he laid a hand on Belle's forearm and gave his grandmother a warm smile.

"We need to start the tour," he told his ladies. *His ladies.* He liked the sound of that. Knowing the message it'd give, he slid his hand down Belle's arm to wrap his fingers around hers. She shot him a panicked look and subtly tried to shake his hand off, but he didn't let go.

"So it's like that, is it?" his grandmother said in satisfaction.

"No."

"Yes."

They answered at the same time, then Belle gave him one of those what-are-you-doing-are-you-crazy? looks. Before he could say anything else, she unwrapped his fingers from hers so she could put her hand out to shake Grammy's.

"I'm not… We're just…" She glared at Mitch. He just rocked back on his heels and grinned. "It was a pleasure talking with you, Lynn. I'd love to have brunch tomorrow and hear more of your ideas."

With that and one last searing glance at Mitch, she gathered the silky fabric of her skirt in her hand and swept away.

"You gonna make it to the vows this time?" Grammy asked.

Belle subtly crooked her finger at a waiter, who immediately approached her, carrying a large crystal dish on a tray. Mitch watched her hand each set of guests who'd signed up for the sex-theme tour an envelope. She spent a few minutes with each couple, chatting, putting them at ease with her jokes and natural warmth. Damn, she worked the room as easily as she'd worked his heart.

"You bet," he said, his gaze still locked on the sweet sway of Belle's hips as she moved between couples. "I'm a lot smarter this time."

HER SMILE LARGE ENOUGH that she figured her cheeks would ache in the morning, Belle handed the second-to-last envelope to one of Mitch's cousins and his very pregnant wife.

"I've been looking forward to this weekend for months," the petite redhead told her as her husband tore into the envelope. "But when Jase told me about this little sideline, I'll admit, I went into impatience overload."

She leaned closer and dropped her voice to a whisper. "This last trimester has me so horny, Jase is going to have to go on early paternity leave to keep up with me."

"I had no idea pregnancy had such a stimulating side effect," Belle said, intrigued. Before she could decide if she wanted more details or not, Jase showed his wife the invitation. From the looks of it, they'd drawn the rose garden adventure. Pure fairy-tale fantasy, complete with a rose bower and fairy lights. Belle gave a silent sigh of relief. As horny as she seemed, Belle doubted a ride in a golf cart over a gopher-ravaged golf course at night was good foreplay for a pregnant lady.

With a giggle and a promise to chat the next day, the couple hurried out of the ballroom. Belle smiled and gave a rueful shake of her head. She felt like a madam sending her couples off for a night of decadent debauchery.

This whole evening was incredible. She loved Mitch's family. Fun, easygoing and interesting, they'd all welcomed her as if the wedding fiasco six years ago had never happened. Well, all except that one weird guy who'd tried to get her to agree to meet him for a private talk when she'd left the dais.

One last envelope to go. She had no idea what the sexual treat hidden in the heavy card stock was, but she couldn't wait to find out. She saw Sierra across the room holding court among the single guys, including Larry, and headed that way.

She'd made it halfway when she came face-to-face with her worst nightmare. Belle's vision wavered as fury hit. The woman who'd ruined her wedding. Belle wanted to scratch her eyes out.

Pleasant and distant, she told herself. This wasn't the time or place to tell Mitch's stepsister what a nasty, rotten bitch she was. Belle clenched her teeth so tightly she thought they'd crack and forced a smile on her face.

"Well, well," drawled the stocky brunette. "I'd heard you were in charge of this little sexcapade, but I thought it was the family's idea of a joke. What kind of kinky things did you have to do to con Mitch into trusting you?"

"Lena," Belle said, her voice pure ice in an attempt to smother the fiery anger. "I'm surprised to see you here. You have an odd habit of showing up at Mitch's celebrations with an eye toward ruining them."

The other woman gave her a toothy grin and looked around the room with a disdainful shrug that shifted her blue beaded evening dress in unattractive ways.

"This party is already doomed. Why would I waste energy?"

"Doomed, is it?" Unable to help herself, Belle stepped forward until she was close enough to smell Lena's oversweet perfume. "Why would you say that?"

Lena's brown eyes narrowed and she flipped her hair over her shoulder with a look of disgust. "It's a no-brainer, isn't it? You're in charge." She arched her brow. "Things are bound to be unfinished. Did you plan to escape before or after the champagne runs dry?"

Belle hissed.

"Ladies, dessert is being served," Sierra said, her tone dulcet. The hand on Belle's waist squeezed in warning. "Lena, why don't you go on in? I'm afraid I need Belle's help for just a second."

After a ten-second stare-down, the woman shrugged and left. It was all Belle could do to keep herself from going after her.

"Well, this is a fine turnaround," Sierra said with a tense laugh as Lena flounced away. "You looking like you were going to kick her ass and me being the voice of reason."

"Scary," Belle agreed as she tried to shake off her anger.

"You can't go after her," Sierra cautioned. "You're too emotional. If you blow up, it'll make you look like a fool and ruin the event." Sierra's voice trailed off and she gave a quick glance around. Nobody was paying any attention to them, so she just shrugged and said, "You have a fit and you'll play right into her hands. You've won over Mitch's family, and that's saying a lot considering they all thought you should have been strung up for leaving him. Don't ruin that. Just avoid her."

Mitch.

Belle took a deep breath and smoothed a hand over her silk-covered hip. With a second deep breath she looked around to find him in conversation with Reece. She pressed her lips together to try to keep from growling and forced the anger aside.

"Escape, my ass," she muttered, clenching the envelope in her fist. She gave Sierra an angry shrug and instructed, "Cover the dessert reception, please."

Then she stormed across the room to get her man.

"Belle, no," Sierra warned, hurrying to keep up with her. "Do not ruin this event. You'll regret it."

Belle kept going.

"Don't let her win. Again."

Belle stopped so fast she was surprised there wasn't smoke coming off her Manolos. "She ruined my wedding."

"No." Sierra stepped around Belle so they were face-to-face and gave her a long, serious look. Her voice was low and apologetic. "She didn't. She pushed the buttons, but the problems were already there. You know that."

Belle was about to protest, but when her friend just raised a brow, she dropped her gaze to the marble floor. Sierra was right. Belle didn't want her to be, but she was. Belle had ruined her own wedding, pure and simple. Shame washed over her as she blinked to clear the tears from her eyes. She wanted to leave, to go to her cottage, curl up under a blanket with Mr. Winkles and pout. But she couldn't. This wasn't the time or place to have a girly breakdown. Mitch was counting on her, and she was counting on herself.

"Okay, you're right. She didn't do anything," Belle finally conceded.

Sierra's arched brows drew together over angry blue eyes. "Oh, no, I didn't say that. She's a selfish, conniving bitch and we're going to haul her out to the woods and kick her ass when this is all over."

Belle's surprised laugh faded as she watched Lena and Diana greet each other like long-lost friends. A quick hug and the two women put their heads together, talking at the same time. She'd had no idea they even knew each other. Were she and Sierra the only ones in the room not family or close friends?

Before Belle could speculate, a hand curved over her hip and someone dropped a kiss on the side of her neck. With a gasp of surprise, she spun around. It was Mitch, of course. Who else would it be? she asked herself as she tried to calm her racing heart.

"What?" he said with a laugh. "You two look all guilty. Like you're planning to rob a bank. Or…" He glanced around the room, then noted the envelope in Belle's hand. He reached out so they held it together. "…talking sex."

"Definitely sex," Sierra agreed with a nod. She puffed out a little breath, her only sign of nerves, and gave Mitch a warm smile. "And speaking of sex, if you'll excuse me, there's a man I'm interested in."

Belle wanted to grab Sierra back and force her to stay with them until she'd got her thoughts under control. Between worrying that Diana and company had some trap planned for the evening and the shock of seeing Lena the bitch again, Belle's nerves were shot.

"Care to share?" Mitch said in a low, sexy tone as he leaned closer.

"Um, share what?"

He laughed again and moved her hand. She glanced at the envelope and grimaced. As hot as Mitch was in a tux, for the first time since she'd set eyes on him, she wasn't interested in having sex with him.

"You know, it's probably tacky for the host and the event planner to sneak off and have nookie," she said, giving him a wide-eyed look.

"It's a nookie kind of night," he pointed out. He slid an appreciative look up and down the length of her body. Belle felt as if he'd stripped her naked and licked his way down to her toes. Hot, damp excitement sparked inside her. "And there are no peaches on the dessert menu."

Unable to say no when he gave her that cute, little-boy grin, Belle giggled and released her hold on the envelope. "You're going to have to give other fruits a chance, you know."

"Nah, why mess with perfection? Besides, I have a bowl of peaches waiting in my room for later," he promised, his attention on ripping open the envelope. When he read the card inside, a huge grin split his face. "The lake? In a boat? Right on."

So in love it hurt, Belle burst into laughter, and even though she knew she should suggest they go to his office and talk, she let him whisk her out of the room.

MITCH FELT DAMNED GOOD. He'd impressed the hell out of his family with the resort. The party had rocked. And now he was taking his woman out to play water games. Life didn't get much better than this.

"Wow," he said as they approached the lake. The long, wooden dock was lined on either side with jars, each one containing a flickering candle. Rather than a motorboat, she'd gone the safer route and had a large rowboat tied to the end of the dock. As they got closer, Mitch could see there was a bottle of champagne chilling, glasses and what looked like some kind of dessert.

"Peaches?" he asked hopefully.

Belle grinned and shook her head. "Chocolate-covered strawberries."

Mitch watched her balance on one foot, her hand on his arm as she slipped off one shoe, then the other, before stepping onto the grass. He took the strappy sandals from her and, dangling them from one finger, clasped her hand in his and led the way to paradise.

He wasn't sure if she was tired after all her work on the party or if someone had upset her, but Belle seemed a little distant and disconnected, as though she didn't mind humoring him, but would rather be anywhere else but here.

Wanting to help her relax, he dropped her shoes in the grass and wrapped his arms around her. One kiss turned into two, deepening as Mitch lost himself in the glory of her mouth. He felt the tension leave her body as Belle relaxed and leaned into him, her tongue dancing around his in sensual delight.

Mitch's hands curved over the smooth fabric of her dress, smoothing his way down her hips and over her butt. She drove him crazy. He pulled her close to grind his hardening dick against her silky warmth.

Releasing her mouth, he trailed wet kisses over her jaw, down her throat. When he reached the curve of her neck, Mitch buried his face there and breathed in the delicious scent of her.

He slipped the tiny straps of her dress off her shoulders, his mouth giving the delicious peak of her breast a nibble. Before he could do the same to the other breast, he was blinded by a flashing light.

"Do her on the grass," a male voice yelled. Insults and degrading suggestions flew through the air.

More lights. Click and whir. Belle screamed. Mitch pulled away, pushing her behind him as he tried to see into the dark woods. Fists clenched, he ran forward to find out what was going on. Before he could take more than three steps, a golf cart flew across the lawn, grass flying behind it as it suddenly braked.

Wrapping a protective arm around a shaking Belle, Mitch watched his cousin Reece leap from the cart and grab someone at the edge of the woods.

"Oh, my God," Belle breathed as they watched him do some intense martial arts move and kick an object from the guy's hand. Then with a flying leap, he sent the other person flying backward, where he smacked into a tree with a loud thud.

Two more golf carts flew by, security staff jumping out to grab the guy and haul him over to Mitch. Reece sauntered over, scooping up his dropped cowboy hat on the way and smacking the dirt off it before putting it back on his head.

Mitch almost laughed at his cousin's nonchalant attitude, then he caught sight of the creep being held by the scruff of his jacket.

"Who the hell are you?" Mitch demanded. He wanted to haul off and punch the guy in the face, but the idiot was still dazed and bleeding from his lip, thanks to Reece's roundhouse kick.

Dammit, his cousin got to have all the fun. Mitch consoled himself with the promise that he'd have one hell of a time prosecuting the guy.

"Don't worry about that," Reece said. "The question isn't so much who he is but who called him out here."

"Paparazzi?" Belle asked in a small voice, sounding

shaken by the lightning-fast change from passion to violence. God, Mitch thought, if the guy had shown up ten minutes later, his shots would have been X-rated.

Obviously thinking the same thing, Belle took a deep breath and seemed to be fighting the need to cry. She gave Mitch a watery smile. "At least he didn't get any incriminating shots, right?"

Mitch frowned, but before he could reply, his cousin stepped between them.

"What if it had been someone else? This is exactly what you're promising your guests they'll be protected from, isn't it?" Reece stepped close and dangled the broken camera pieces from his index finger. "This could have been any one of our family members. While I'm sure cousin Jenny's lakeside frolics wouldn't make headlines like some movie star's, it'd be pure misery for her to see them splashed across a gossip rag."

"This is what security was supposed to prevent," Belle snapped. "All those meetings, all our discussions. Confidentiality agreements, key codes, alarms. And yet this dirtbag still managed to get in here? This entire plan hinged on the guarantee of privacy. What the hell happened?"

"Someone tipped him off," Mitch accused. Fury blurred his vision at the betrayal. He stepped forward and grabbed the guy's collar.

"Who the hell hired you?" he growled.

The guy muttered through swollen lips, "The party gal."

Shocked, Mitch almost dropped him. "Belle?"

"Don't know her name. Just had the phone call that this was some big fancy A-lister gig with a lot of money shots. Sex, partying. I was told to come on out. She put my name on the guest list, texted me to tell me where to hide."

No. Mitch reeled at the words. Reece grabbed the guy from his slack hands and wheeled him around.

"Bullshit," Reece claimed. "You're saying Belle Forsham hired you? Tipped you off? What?"

"Don't know her name. Just that she's the gal in charge of the party," the guy snapped defiantly. "We talked by phone, email. I never saw her before."

"He's lying," Belle called out. Horror filled her voice, tears glistening on her cheeks.

"Why would he lie?" Reece wondered aloud.

"I don't know," Belle cried. "Why don't you ask him?"

"I don't think we need to ask anyone except you, Ms. Forsham." Reece's words were quiet, bland. But his accusation hung in the air.

"Me? Why the hell would I do this?" Anger snapped in her eyes.

"You could be working to discredit the resort," Reece said in his slow drawl. "Your dad's hurting, needs money. You might have thought putting Mitch out of business would keep away some competition."

Belle shook her head. "You might want to go back to security school, cowboy. So far you're batting zip. First you let that camera-toting idiot in here, despite all the supposed precautions. Then you accuse me of something impossibly far-fetched. This resort is no competition to my father."

"Sure it isn't," muttered someone behind Mitch. "She screwed him over once, she's obviously doing it again. This time she's getting pictures, too."

Belle gasped, her eyes filling. But instead of letting the tears fall, she lifted her chin and faced the crowd that had formed around them.

Shaking off the feeling of fury and betrayal, Mitch followed her gaze and saw her glare at Lena. Mitch frowned.

He glanced at his stepsister, whose grin looked evil in the glinting moonlight. Belle opened her mouth as if to say something, then she shrugged and turned to leave.

"Where do you think you're going?" he asked.

"Away." He could hear it in her voice, the need to escape. To get away from the whispers and judgmental eyes.

"This isn't settled, Belle."

She gave him a dirty look. "What's to settle? Did you want to wait for one of your kinfolk to go grab a rope from the golf cart so you can hang me?"

"You're overreacting," Reece said quietly. "This isn't a lynch mob."

"Could have fooled me," she shot back.

Mitch realized that his family and friends were all looking pissed enough to justify her accusation.

He took Belle's arm and pulled her away from the crowd, up toward the ninth hole where they could talk without all the commentary.

"Belle, tell me what's going on," he asked when they reached some semblance of privacy. "The truth this time."

"I told you the truth. You're choosing to believe that guy over me." She gestured to the photographer Reece was tossing into the golf cart. "You're so busy obsessing over your image, over your need to prove yourself perfect that you won't even consider that you're wrong."

Mitch bristled at the accusation. To hell with that. He wasn't trying to prove a damned thing. He was just protecting his investment. He recalled her reluctance to come down to the lake earlier. Had she been having second thoughts? Or had it been because her plans were derailed when they'd gotten the lakeside envelope? God, he was the world's biggest idiot.

"Is that what you think?" he asked. "That I'm obsessed with image? Well, if I am, you sure blew it all to hell with this little stunt. Again," he accused. Mitch spared a glance at his family, here to watch another of his dreams smashed to hell.

Belle gave a bitter laugh and shook his hand off her arm. She took a step backward as if she couldn't stand to be close to him. Mitch wanted to grab her and yell that he wasn't the guilty party here. He'd be damned if she'd make him feel bad that she'd been busted at her own game.

"You go ahead and believe that," she said. "It's easier for you to blame me than figure out the truth." She gave a wave of her hand toward the crowd and swallowed, her jaw working and eyes blinking rapidly. "I thought I could trust you this time. I thought you were different. My God, I was such an idiot."

Spying her shoes on the grass, she leaned over and snatched them up, then tilted her chin at him. "There is no advantage to me ruining my own business reputation. There is no point in busting my ass to make this event, this entire themed resort, come together perfectly if I was going to just screw it all up in the end."

She stepped closer and punched her index finger into his chest. "Someone is fucking you over and it's not me. Why don't you grow up and quit flexing your dick and go find out who it really is?"

With that, she stomped up the hill toward the golf carts parked haphazardly all over the ninth hole.

Her words echoed in his head. His family's voices faded into background noise.

Brow furrowed, Mitch watched Belle slam the golf cart into gear and drive away. Part of him wanted to yell to her to wait. He wanted to run after her and fix things. But his family was all standing around. And they'd just seen Belle make him look like a loser idiot in front of them. Again.

He let her go. Confusion and pain clawed at his gut. Belle had used him, used this event, all for publicity?

Once again, he'd lost the princess. And once again, he'd lost face in front of his entire family as she screwed him over.

Mitch tried to console himself that at least this time he'd had a whole bunch of hot, wild, kinky sex. But all that did was remind him of what he'd lost. Of what he'd never actually had.

Wasn't he a pitiful chump?

13

BELLE STUMBLED INTO her cottage, tears streaming down her face. She stopped cold when she was hit with a faceful of bright light and heavy metal music.

Damn. She'd forgotten Sierra would be there.

"You're back early," her friend yelled over Black Sabbath. "What happened? All that rocking the boat make you seasick?" She was one to tease, given that she was twisted around like a pretzel with her ass in the air.

"Paparazzi," Belle said shortly, not able to find her usual razz about Sierra being the only person in the world who practiced yoga to Ozzie. She scrubbed the tears off her face with the back of her hand.

Sierra fell sideways with a crash. "What?" she asked, rubbing her shoulder. She finally took a look at Belle's face and jumped up to slap the stereo off. "Oh, my God, what's wrong?"

"Paparazzi," Belle repeated, throwing her shoes across the room so hard they knocked a teacup off the table, sending it to a shattered death on the tile floor.

She glared at the mess, and not even caring that she was barefoot, stormed over to the couch. She dropped to the cushions, drew her knees up for comfort and waited.

She didn't have to wait long. Two seconds later and Sierra was right there, wrapping her arms around Belle. Belle took a shuddering breath, but before she could spill the details of the horrible encounter and Mitch's betrayal, someone pounded on her door.

"Belle, I want to talk to you."

Her body went numb at the sound of Mitch's voice. Sierra stood to answer the door but Belle grabbed her damp T-shirt and gave a shake of her head.

He pounded again.

"Now."

Her chin flew up and anger, drowned out earlier by her tears, rekindled.

Sierra took one look at her face and yelled back, "Get lost."

Silence.

Sierra gave a satisfied smirk, but Belle knew better. Ten seconds later the pounding started again. Confused, angry and hurt beyond belief, she still knew she had to face him. But not yet.

She went to the door and, after flicking off the overhead light to help hide her ravaged face, she set the security chain, then opened the door.

Mitch's fury was clear through the small opening. It was all she could do not to start crying again at the sight. Determined to cling to some form of dignity, she took a deep breath. Before he could say a word, she held up her hand. "I'll discuss the situation with you in a half hour," she told him. "I'm not dressed for this and I'm not prepared to talk to you yet."

"You're not negotiating a contract, Belle." The disdain in his voice was so sharp, she wondered if she'd be left with a scar.

She inclined her head toward him and gave a one-shouldered shrug. "No, but this is business, isn't it? If you want to talk tonight, I'll come up to your office in a half hour. Otherwise it will wait until tomorrow."

She watched his jaw work and knew he was struggling for control. His anger, so clear in the set of his shoulders and furious glare, shouldn't turn her on. But, sicko that she was, it did, just a little. Her heart whimpered at the uselessness of the realization.

"Fifteen minutes," he finally said.

"Thirty," she repeated.

He snarled and lifted his fist as if he were going to pound it through the door. But he didn't. Instead he growled, "Fine."

Belle didn't wait for him to leave. She shut the door and, knowing it would only add to his fury, flipped the locks with a loud snick.

She turned to see Sierra staring, the shock in her blue eyes echoed in her slack jaw.

"What?"

"Just wondering where you're hiding those brass balls. Your dress is awfully revealing."

Belle gave a watery laugh and collapsed against the door. Her fury-induced adrenaline washed away, leaving her limp and miserable.

"We're just getting hot and heavy on the dock and out jumps a blood-sucking photographer snapping pictures, calling dirty suggestions." Belle shivered at the memory. "It was horrible. Then, before I could take that in, up squeals Reece like the cavalry, grabbing the guy and beating the hell out of him."

Sierra's fascinated curiosity turned to derision and she shook her head. "Leave it to him to get all macho," she muttered. Then she glanced at the clock, grabbed Belle's arm and tugged her toward the bedroom.

"Talk while you're changing. We have twenty-five minutes."

"The paparazzi said it was me, the party girl," Belle whispered. "He said I'd hired him. Arranged all this."

Sierra sucked in a sharp breath. Then she let out a low, vicious growl that would do a mama cat proud. "Someone's setting you up."

Belle shrugged and started changing.

"And there was that smug-faced bitch, Lena Carter, just gloating over the whole ugly mess," Belle summed up as she finished recounting the horrible scene while reapplying foundation to cover her blotchy, tearstained skin.

"Lena Norris," Sierra corrected, her voice muffled by the sweater she was pulling over her head.

Belle lowered the makeup brush and stared at her friend's reflection. "What?"

Sierra settled the black cashmere sweater in place and pulled her hair free, then met Belle's eyes in the mirror. "Norris. She's not one of the Carter clan. I found out tonight when I read the guest list over Larry's shoulder."

She and Belle exchanged a long, comprehending stare.

"L.N.," they said together.

Stunned, Belle dropped her makeup brush on the counter and sank onto the wide edge of the spa tub. That nasty vindictive woman was behind all this?

"What a bitch." Sierra gave a little growl and shook her head. "I can't believe it. I thought she had it in for you, but it's actually her own brother she's been trying to screw over all these years."

Belle tugged on her short suede boots and considered the idea. God, she'd been a gullible idiot.

Six years ago she'd scurried away at the first sign of conflict instead of talking to Mitch or her father. As always, she'd been so sure she'd be rejected if she confronted the issue. Shame washed over her. Apparently she was a wimp as well as an idiot.

But not this time. She sucked in a deep, fortifying breath and squared her shoulders, trying to find courage. Hell, Mitch had already rejected her, so she had nothing left to lose. And one hell of a lot to gain by outing that obnoxious bitch, Lena.

"She's planning on ruining more than a wedding this time," Belle pointed out, anger making her hand shake as she tried to apply lip gloss. "Mitch's business is her goal this round."

Belle tried to focus on that, but she couldn't quite get over the indignity of being so easily manipulated. She wanted to beat the hell out of Lena. And not some girly slap-fight, either. She wanted to gut-punch the other woman.

"What a dirty sneak," she muttered.

"Exactly."

Belle let the fury of it all propel her out of the room. "C'mon," she called back to Sierra, who was hopping from foot to foot trying to put on her platforms. "I have to tell Mitch. As soon as he hears this, we can sit back and watch him deal with that duplicitous bitch."

Belle had never been one to contemplate revenge before, but suddenly the idea filled her with a grim satisfaction. She couldn't wait to see Lena pay for everything she'd done. To Mitch, to the resort. To Belle.

Five minutes early, Belle stormed into Mitch's office, Sierra hot on her heels. It was like walking into an ice-filled courtroom. Belle shivered, her momentum stalled at the implacable coldness on Mitch's face. Like a judge, he sat behind his desk, the position of power loud and clear.

There was a movement by the window and Belle's gaze shot to the prosecutor du-jour. The fiery anger in Reece's glare was the only heat in the room. Nerves snapped and snarled in her stomach, the little voice in the back of her head warning her to give it up and run. Get the hell out of there before they verbally shredded her.

She'd actually taken a step back before she realized what she was doing. No. Belle squared her shoulders and forced herself to stand still. They wanted to judge, that was fine. She was here for justice.

Knowing the only way she'd get through this was to block Reece's intimidating presence out of her mind, Belle focused on Mitch. It took her two deep belly breaths to get the nerve, then she stomped over to his desk and slapped her hands on the surface.

It was a good indication of how angry he was when he kept his gaze locked on hers instead of letting it drop to the view highlighted by her low-cut blouse. *Okay, fine.* She told herself she wasn't worried that her one real weapon had already proved ineffective.

"Look, I know who's behind all your problems," she said quietly. His blank stare didn't change, but Belle pressed on. "Just hear me out and we'll get to the truth of this whole mess."

"Truth?" Mitch snapped. She winced as his frigid tone sliced at her. "Or excuses?"

Tears threatened again, but Belle blinked them away. She felt Sierra come up behind her. Her friend didn't say anything, just stood a little behind and off to the side, giving silent support. It was all Belle needed. With a deep breath, she handed Mitch the papers she'd found in Diana's office. He didn't look at them, just slid them aside and kept his eyes on hers. With a quick glance at Sierra, who nodded, she went on to describe how they'd searched through Diana's computer files.

Through it all, the men said nothing. Mitch just sat

there, his hands steepled as he stared at her emotionlessly. Reece lounged against the windowsill, one cowboy boot tapping impatiently.

Finally, Reese straightened and walked toward the door. "You're accusing Diana?" he asked as he passed her.

"I found the information in her office," Belle shot back, her tone pissy and defensive. It was like they hadn't even heard what she said. She gave Reece the evil eye, to which he only raised a brow.

"We talked to her," Mitch said quietly. Belle glanced back at him. His face was still blank. Her fingers twitched nervously. She couldn't read him at all and it was starting to scare her. "Turns out you're right."

Belle opened her mouth to argue with him, then closed it. "Right?"

"She's not the mastermind, obviously. Diana's just a very good, very efficient assistant." She knew him well enough to recognize the betrayed hurt beneath his bitter words.

"Mitch, I'm sorry," Belle murmured.

Instead of accepting her sympathy, he just gave a snort of disbelief.

Belle's brows drew together.

Before she could say anything else, though, Reece opened the side door to the boardroom and gestured to a security guard on the other side.

Suddenly nervous but not sure why, Belle looked at Sierra. Her friend shot the security guard and his big gun a concerned look and rubbed a quick hand over the small of Belle's back in support.

But the only person to enter the room was unarmed. And, from the look of her, totally broken. Diana's hair, styled so carefully for the party, hung in a stringy curtain around her tear-ravaged face. She shot Belle a fearful look, then took the farthest seat away from everyone.

Reece sat opposite her, his long legs kicked out in front of him in a pose so relaxed it was a total insult to the situation. Belle wanted to beat him upside the cowboy hat with Mitch's desk blotter.

"Diana, you go ahead and repeat what you told Mitch and me earlier."

"I'd rather not," she mumbled into her lap.

"That's too bad," Mitch said shortly. "It's talk to us or talk to the cops. Take your pick."

She gave a deep, shuddering sort of sigh, then, twisting her hands together in a way that was painful to watch, started in a hesitant voice, "I told you already, I admit to helping sabotage Lakeside."

"On whose orders?" Mitch demanded.

The tension in Belle's shoulders loosened, anticipation and a weird sort of vindication surging through her. Yes, now Lena would get what was coming to her.

"Hers," Diana mumbled, the word so quiet they all had to lean forward to hear it.

Sierra and Belle exchanged confused looks.

"You mean Belle?" Reece asked in a low, empty tone.

"What?" Belle couldn't believe the question.

"Yes," Diana whispered.

The room tilted just a little and Belle felt her stomach pitch. "You're so lying. I didn't do a damned thing."

Diana just shrugged. Reece took off his cowboy hat and ran the brim through his fingers before putting it back on. Belle's gaze, filled with confusion and panic, flew to Mitch. He didn't believe this crap, did he?

He stared back at her, his eyes steady and furious.

Apparently he found the crap perfectly believable.

Her heart cracked, tiny tentacles of pain radiating

through her system. She should have known. She never should have let herself feel anything for him. Tears burned the backs of her eyes as she tried to figure out why Diana would tell such lies. And more important, how Mitch could so easily believe them.

"Since when did you start taking orders from Belle?" Sierra snapped.

Diana gave a helpless little shrug, her gaze locked on her toes. "Since she offered me a job with her father's hotels."

Belle's gasp drowned out Sierra's hiss at the lie.

Showing the first spark since she'd come slinking into the room, Diana ignored them and threw an accusing look at Mitch before continuing. "She promised me her father runs a normal office. I'd be managing a successful hotel, not ordering disgusting sex toys."

Belle narrowed her eyes. "The sabotage was happening long before I showed up with my disgusting sex ideas."

Diana gave a tiny smirk and inclined her head. "That was the plan, wasn't it? And why I pushed your business so hard when you lured away the last event planner."

Belle stared in shock. "Oh, my God, you don't really think they're going to believe this, do you? You are sitting there telling straight-up lies and you think you can get away with it?"

"Why would I lie?" Diana countered. The look in her eyes made Belle realize that this little mouse had sharp teeth and deadly claws. "I'm already being brought up on charges. I've lost my job, my reputation and, since you blew it, I'm sure I've lost all the recompense you promised me, too."

"I didn't promise you a damned thing," Belle growled, her hands fisted on her hips.

"Did you have contact with Diana before you came to Lakeside?" Reece asked.

"Of course." Before she could explain that it had been Diana who'd contacted Eventfully Yours for the job, Reece continued.

"Did you come to Lakeside for any purpose other than to secure a job contract?"

How could she answer that? If she admitted she'd come for her father, they'd only see it as more guilt. But she couldn't lie, either. Belle wet her lips.

"Did you?" Mitch asked quietly.

"I, well, yes, I had other reasons. Mitch and I had a history. I wanted to see him again."

Reece's passive demeanor cracked just a little, showing a hint of derision. "Really? The man you left at the altar? You had a sudden hankering to what? Stroll down memory lane?"

"Of course not," Belle said with a scowl. "We had unfinished business. I wanted to see Mitch," she looked at her ex-fiancé and shrugged. "I tried to see you a couple of times before, but never got past first base. We had stuff to talk about, a past to deal with."

Belle tried to find the words to apologize for running off on him, for the humiliation and devastation of leaving him at the altar. But there were too many people in the room, too much nastiness going on. Instead she just shrugged.

"So you admit it," Reece said. "You had motive, means and opportunity before you showed up here."

"Oh. My. God," Sierra snapped. "What is this, a bad Sherlock Holmes novel? Get a magnifying glass or get over yourself."

"I had an apology to make," Belle said softly. She saw Mitch's eyes widen in surprise and wanted to scream with frustration. What? Did he think her so much a bitch that she'd have no regret about what had happened?

Belle pressed her lips together. With every fiber of her being, she wanted to throw her hands in the air and say screw it. To walk—no run—out of the office and escape this nasty scene. Then her gaze fell on Mitch. Beneath the palpable fury emanating from him she saw something else. Pain.

Tears, so easily held at bay for herself, welled up for him. Regardless of how she felt about the unfounded accusations, the ugly mistrust and rotten character assessment, the bottom line was he was the one being hurt.

And she was the one being used to hurt him. She needed to focus on that, to let it excuse his actions. But as much as she tried, she couldn't. The truth was he didn't trust her. And without trust, they were nothing but fuck buddies.

"This is the second accusation thrown at me tonight," she said quietly through the pain of her realization. "Both of them are complete and total bullshit. If you knew me at all, if the past few weeks we've spent together had meant a damned thing to you, you'd know they were bullshit."

Belle stepped away from the desk and, because she was suddenly freezing, wrapped her arms around herself and shook her head at Mitch. "But you're too busy worrying about your image. The only thing that matters to you is that people think you're Mr. Perfect, that your family holds you on some stupid pedestal."

His fist clenched on the desk, Mitch didn't say anything.

Fury driving her words, Belle continued to spew uncontrollably. "The fact that it makes no sense doesn't seem to matter to you and your vigilante cowboy here. If I wanted to screw you over, there are a dozen ways. None of them include busting my butt to create and implement a creative and unique hook to help you succeed."

Belle shoved a hand through her hair and saw it was shaking. Hell, her entire body was shaking, she was so upset. Her breath came in gasps now, her vision blurred around the edges.

"If you want to blame me, you have a good ol' time with it. But the person you should be looking at is your sister." Even through her pain, Belle winced at the raw delivery and its effect on Mitch. His face paled, his mouth dropped open. All in all, he looked as though she'd just kicked him in the 'nads.

Oh, God, look what confrontation got her. A big fat lot of pain and misery. She hadn't changed their minds about a damned thing, and now she'd hurt him. Belle pressed her hand to her mouth to hold back a scream of frustration and shook her head.

"I can't do this. You go ahead and believe whatever you want. If it helps to make me the culprit here, go ahead. I'll send you my lawyer's name. We'll deal with it that way." She had to get out of the room. She could barely breathe through all the tension and pain pounding in her chest.

She felt Sierra's arm on her shoulder and leaned in, needing the support of at least one person in the room. She drew strength from her friend, then straightened and gave Mitch a long, clear look.

"You're right, though. I wasn't completely honest with you. I did show up here hoping for more than a contract from you. I came here hoping you'd talk with my father. Give him some advice and ideas." She felt like a traitor admitting her self-serving motivation, but figured the truth couldn't be anywhere near as debilitating as the crap they were making up.

"But once I got here, once I got to know you again—

no," she corrected, "got to know you period, then my reasons changed. All I wanted was to see you succeed, Mitch. To see the resort succeed."

Behind her, Diana gave a watery snort. Belle spun around, not sure if she was going to scream at the bitch or beat the hell out of her. Before she could do either, though, Sierra launched herself past Belle, claws outstretched.

Diana squealed and jumped back, lifting her feet onto the seat with her as she tried to curl up in a ball.

Reece grabbed Sierra around the waist and swung her away from the whimpering traitor.

Belle's nerves were jangling and raw at the violence, both in the room, and churning inside her.

Mitch just sat there watching, his face impassive.

"You don't believe her, do you?" she asked, her words barely discernible as Sierra screamed obscenities at Diana and Reece tried to calm her.

"I don't like being used," Mitch finally said as Reece's and Sierra's swearing died down.

The implied accusation tore her heart in two.

"You're one to talk," Belle sobbed. Finally unable to hold back the one ugly truth that had eaten at her heart for more than six years, she said, "When have you done anything but use me?"

Saying the words aloud was like opening Pandora's box. Pain, misery and a million and one self-doubts all came flying out at her. Vicious and biting, they ripped at her. The look on Mitch's face, judgmental and angry, proved that she'd never stood a chance.

Belle tried to speak, but her throat was constricted with tears. She just shook her head and turned away.

It wasn't until Reece handed her a handkerchief on her way out the door that she realized she had tears dripping off her chin.

14

MITCH WATCHED REECE escort Belle into the foyer of the hotel, his heart stuttering a little at how gorgeous she was in the morning light. Apparently she took the phrase *dress to kill* seriously. A short, fitted skirt hugged hips his fingers itched to hold and her blouse wrapped around her torso enticingly, highlighting her cleavage. Power heels in a kick-your-ass-red completed the look.

Her face was set, like a beautiful ice carving. Her eyes, though, sparkled with fiery anger. God, he loved her. His gut hurt at the idea of how much pain he'd caused her last night. As soon as she'd left, he'd told Reece it was a setup. He was sure of it. Despite the mountain of proof Diana had offered—emails, faxes, Belle's signature on everything, he knew she hadn't done it.

Starting with the papers Belle had left him, they'd spent the entire night digging for the answer. An answer that had hurt like crazy but one that Mitch knew was true.

Now all he had to find out was why. And that, he figured, Belle had a right to know, too.

As they reached him, he murmured his thanks to Reece, who nodded and tilted his head to indicate that he'd be waiting in the restaurant.

"How fun. We've gone from unsubstantiated accusations to goon patrol?" Belle commented, giving him a dirty look. "Am I so worthless that you can't just come talk to me directly? You need to send your big security chief to fetch my criminal butt?"

Mitch opened his mouth to explain, but one of his aunts walked past just then and yelled an enthusiastic hello. He grimaced and shut his mouth again. He'd almost blown it. This was too important to screw up with a lame explanation. He had to show her. To show her and his entire family that Belle was innocent.

Belle frowned in confusion when he didn't say anything. Then she glanced at his departing aunt and got one of those you-are-such-a-pig looks on her face. "Ooh, I get it. I have cooties. You need to distance yourself from me so you don't tilt any further off that precarious pedestal you're perched on."

Even though he knew he was being a jerk and that she had every right to be angry, Mitch couldn't stop from giving her a narrow-eyed look and asking, "Alliteration so early in the day?"

Anger spat from her sea-green eyes and her mouth thinned. She looked like she was going to slug him. Mitch realized he was a sick puppy when the idea turned him on. God, he had it bad when any sign of passion from her, even nonsexual, got him all hot and horny.

"Let's walk," he suggested.

"Let's not," she returned. "You were too rude to talk to me privately before I'm escorted off the premises, so you can tell me what you want right here."

Mitch grinned and took her arm to pull her to his side. Yeah, she was one helluva turn-on. "C'mon, I'll show you."

Her fury was clear in the snap of her heels against the

floor and the stiff set of her shoulders. Of course, the sharp elbow in his gut was a good indicator, too.

But she didn't pull away as he escorted her into the packed restaurant. She hesitated in the entrance, her step hitching just a little. Realizing she must think he was furthering that public-lynching thing she'd accused him of last night, Mitch shifted his hold, releasing her arm to wrap his hand around her waist.

Her accusation about him using her echoed in his head. Had been echoing through the long night. She was right and he hated himself for that. He'd hoped that publicly vindicating her would start to make up for his previous dicklessness, but once again, he'd miscalculated.

"It'll be fine," he whispered. He knew Reece wanted the element of surprise on their side. That for the trap to work hinged on Belle's unscripted reactions. But he couldn't stand seeing her suffer. If it meant only that he, Reece and the culprit knew the real truth, that was fine. He realized he didn't want the public vindication at the cost of Belle's feelings.

"Look, let's go to my office," he said softly, watching the nerves play over her features at the sight of his entire clan gathered in the dining room. The need to protect her overwhelmed him. Whispers carried around the room, fingers pointed and angry looks flew at Belle. Mitch shot a blanket glare at everyone.

He'd been a total idiot to give in to Reece's plan. All he'd thought of was to publicly prove Belle's innocence. To push Lena to admit in front of everyone here that she was behind the problems. Not to vindicate himself, but so nobody, ever, could doubt Belle again. He hadn't thought the scheme through enough to realize what she'd have to endure in the process, though.

"Let's go," he repeated. "We'll talk there."

Some of the tension left her body as she leaned into him just a bit. She started to nod. Then something, or someone, caught her eye and she went steel-straight again and gave a little growl under her breath.

"That *bitch* is eating my afterglow special?" she asked.

Mitch followed her gaze and pulled a face. He glanced at Reece, seated across the room at the table next to the afterglow special, and grimaced.

Guess the show was still on. Belle pulled away with a hiss and stalked across the dining room. Yep, show on, whether he wanted it to be or not. He shoved his hands into his pockets and, body tensing for battle, followed her across the room.

Belle, apparently the consummate hostess even when blinded by spitting fury, sidestepped his family's snide comments and rude questions graciously. But she didn't slow down.

Thankfully his legs were longer, so, by the time she reached Lena's table, Mitch had caught up. Mitch joined her as she sat, uninvited, at the damask-covered table.

"Lena," he greeted quietly. He watched his stepsister's eyes, knowing they gave the only clue to what was really going on behind that wide forehead of hers. They showed curiosity. He had to admire her. She was so damned sure she'd won, she didn't feel a speck of fear.

"I realize it's a public restaurant, so to speak," Lena said in a haughty tone, "but I think I have the right to enjoy my breakfast without being interrupted by a traitorous sex-peddler."

Mitch glanced out the dining room window at the gorgeous view of his beloved woods. The woods that had made him buy this property. The ones that made him feel like he'd finally made it. The woods where he'd been made to look like a loser idiot. And not, he knew, turning his gaze to Belle, by the woman he loved.

No, he had family to thank for that.

"I'll give you sex—" Belle started to rage, leaning across the table.

"Really, Lena?" he interrupted, laying a hand on Belle's knee. She shot him a furious look. Her anger turned to confusion when his eyes asked her to trust him. He was asking for the moon, he knew. That, the sun and a few planets, given that all he'd ever done was betray her.

But damned if she didn't give it anyway. With a tiny furrow of her brow, she gave an infinitesimal nod and released her breath.

"I'm surprised you can sit there eating like you haven't a care in the world," he continued, gesturing to her almost-empty plate as well as the two side dishes she'd apparently enjoyed. "Are you so sure of yourself that you aren't the least bit worried?"

Lena scooped up a bite of strawberry mousse and gestured with her spoon. "I haven't done anything wrong. Although I've been hearing whispers from your staff, one of your cute security guys to be precise, that the same can't be said for everyone at this table."

Belle looked positively feral and Mitch decided he didn't want to play the game. Unable to keep the hurt and anger from his voice, he leaned across the table and asked quietly, "Why'd you do it, Lena? Why'd you try and sabotage my resort?"

At Belle's loud gasp, the few people that weren't already watching the tableau looked their way. Her hand covered his where it lay on her knee and squeezed. Satisfaction and a spark of hope that she might forgive him sprang to life in Mitch's heart.

"What'd she do, screw you stupid?" Lena shot back.

Belle surged out of her chair so fast, it toppled over. But she wasn't as fast as Mitch or Reece.

Mitch was around the table before Belle's chair hit the floor, grabbing his stepsister by the arm and pulling her to her feet. Reece put his hand on Belle's arm, probably worried she'd resort to the same type of violence Sierra had tried the night before.

"As always, she's a public embarrassment to you, isn't she, Mitch?" Lena mocked.

"Kiss my ass," Belle suggested sweetly. But Mitch could see the pain the comment had caused in Belle's eyes.

"Oh, please," Lena snapped. "I don't know what kind of game she's playing, but this is ridiculous. She's making a fool of you with your entire family as witnesses. Again. Keep this up and nobody's going to have to wonder if they should doubt your judgment or not. They'll know you've let them all down."

He had to hand it to her, she definitely knew where to twist the knife. Mitch saw a movement out of the corner of his eye and winced when he recognized the straw purse. Grammy Lynn had joined them. Good. He didn't want one single person missing the proof that Belle was innocent.

"You know, the funny thing about computer messages is that even though you can fake an email address, you can't fake an IP address," Mitch said quietly. "And that paparazzi you hired? He's the kind of guy who ignores orders to delete phone records. You—or Diana—covered your asses when you made the calls from the resort. But those text messages you sent him last night? They traced right back to your cell phone, Lena. It was a clever plan. But not clever enough."

His stepsister hissed and wrenched her arm away. With a glare of hatred, she said, "You're just Mr. Golden Boy, aren't you? You think you're so perfect. Everything just falls into your lap. You deserve all these problems. These and more."

"You're such a nasty bitch," Belle accused in a shocked whisper.

"And you're an interfering one. I was this close," she spat, holding her fingers in front of Belle's face, "to winning. You just lucked out, that's all."

Mitch gave Reece a look, and in an instant his cousin had switched places with him. Now Reece had Lena cornered, leaving Mitch free to put his arm around Belle's shoulder.

"No. Even without proof, I knew Belle wasn't behind this."

"How?" Belle asked quietly beside him.

He looked down into her face, her beautiful green eyes glistening with tears and happiness. Mitch's heart shifted, all the worries and fear dropping away as he leaned down to brush a soft kiss over her full lips.

"Because I trust you."

"I WANTED TO SMACK you silly when I first saw you this morning," Belle murmured to Mitch an hour later. After the big show and resulting fallout, she and Sierra had watched gleefully from the sidelines as Lena was hauled off the property by the cops.

Now, an hour later, she and Mitch had escaped to the serenity of the woods for a "picnic" and a talk. She'd rather picnic than talk, but he'd told her to keep her clothes on until he'd said his piece.

Then he'd proceeded to pull her down on the blanket and kiss her silly instead of talking.

"I could tell you were eyeing me like a punching bag," he acknowledged against her hair. His chest shook as he laughed silently. "Don't actually hit me when I tell you this, but it was a total turn-on seeing you that pissed. I wanted to strip you naked and do you on the registration desk."

She pulled back to look at his face and laugh, then she shook her head. "Crazy. You're absolutely crazy."

"I can't help it. It drives me nuts when you get all confrontational."

Belle ducked her head back onto his chest to hide her tears. The one thing she'd always been so afraid of and Mitch loved it. A bubbling kind of joy burst inside her, sending sparks of happiness through her system. Belle wanted to laugh and cry and dance around wildly. She swallowed, not willing to cry all over him again. Apparently she was free to hit him, though.

A beautiful sense of peace washed over her. She had no idea where they were going from here, especially since her contract with the resort would be fulfilled by the end of the month. But she did know she was holding tight to Mitch, and hey, if she wanted to get in his face about any issues that came up, she'd just been green-lighted.

Still giggling at the idea of her aggression being a turn-on, she wondered if the registration area was ever completely private. Belle snuggled deeper into his arms and sighed as she watched the breeze dance through the canopy of leaves overhead.

After a few more idyllic minutes in his arms, though, Belle started squirming. All this cuddling stuff was sweet, but she wanted her picnic.

"I'm still waiting to hear your *piece,*" she finally reminded him. "If you'd get on with it, we could move on with this afternoon's entertainment."

Mitch laughed and hugged her even tighter.

"Why'd she do it?" she asked quietly, afraid to ruin the tranquility of the moment but needing to know.

"Money. Apparently she was livid that her father willed his company to me. He'd left her a small fortune, but she thought she should have gotten more. She saw his leaving me anything as a betrayal. She said that's why she refused to sit on the board, to have anything to do with me. She's partnered up with a rival developer and I guess she figured when I tanked here, she'd swoop in and buy the place cheap."

"Crazy," Belle breathed. "She really thought that would work?"

Mitch's shirt rubbed softly against her cheek as he shrugged. "She had the financial backing. Real estate is plummeting and she's got the inside track. Hell, if her plan had worked instead of us…you…catching her, I'd have probably thanked Lena for bailing me out."

"That's like saying if pigs could fly then Manolos would fall from the sky," Belle scoffed. Mitch's brows drew together as he tried to decipher that, but she kept going before he could ask. "Her plan couldn't have worked. At best, it was an annoyance. A pain in your butt and a crash test in 'what could go wrong' for the resort."

"Sure, now," he agreed. "But you read the list. Hell, you found it. She was saving the big guns for after the resort was actually open to the public."

"What's going to happen to her?" Belle asked quietly.

"We'll press charges. I don't want her jailed or anything, but Reece pointed out that we need to take legal steps just in case she tries something in the future."

She could tell he was beating himself up over it all. Determined not to let Lena leave a nasty aftertaste, Belle pushed the issue.

"You didn't do anything wrong. You're a success for a good reason, Mitch. You bust your ass, you're a brilliant strategist and, like my daddy always said, you have the touch. She couldn't have hurt the resort. Not really."

Belle bit her lip after saying that. While she thought of his hurt as having to do with business, maybe Mitch was suffering emotionally. After all, family was everything to him. "I'm sorry she hurt you, though," Belle added softly.

Mitch's eyes, so hard and irritated a second ago, melted to that soft, sexy cinnamon that she loved so much. He shook his head and grimaced. "She didn't hurt me so much as she slapped at my pride." He took a deep breath that made his chest do yummy things against Belle's breasts and shrugged. "It was bad enough her gunning for me. I mean, yes, her thinking was twisted, but there is some justification in her anger that I took her father's business and not only made it mine but brought my entire family on board and left her out in the cold."

"A cold she chose." Belle repeated what Reece had told her earlier. "You offered her a board position. She's the one who turned her nose up as if it wasn't good enough for her."

As Mitch considered her words, some of the tension left his shoulders. Then he nodded and told her, "She never really connected with my family. Grammy Lynn said it was because she was a snob and we weren't upscale enough. I just figured she felt left out."

Then his expression hardened. "But as much as I might try to understand her reasons for aiming at me, there is no excuse for her trying to incriminate you."

Belle searched herself, but there wasn't any anger left. The sight of Lena's arrogant ass being hauled off in hand-cuffs had satisfied her need for revenge. Not wanting to waste any more time on Lena or her twisted motives, Belle shifted just a little so her breasts brushed Mitch's chest. Smart man that he was, he slid one hand inside her blouse to cup her, his fingers doing a soft, easy swirl around her hardening nipple.

"No matter, it's done," Belle said, angling her bent leg over Mitch's thighs so she could feel his erection hardening. "She doesn't matter, she's finished. We're not, though."

"And that's what counts," Mitch said with satisfaction.

Their lips met in a kiss that scared the hell out of Belle. Not because of the intensity of it, but because of the sweetness. She could so get addicted to this kind of kissing. It felt like the promise of forever.

"By the way," Mitch said as he curled his fingers through hers and lifted her hand to his lips, "I talked to your father this morning."

Nothing said *cold shower* on an intimate moment louder than the mention of a parent. Belle automatically tugged her blouse into place and shifted just a little so she wasn't pressed against his erection.

"Daddy?" she asked with a confused frown. "Why?"

"I didn't realize until Reece did some digging that your father was in a financial mess, in part because of that property we'd planned to develop. Although he did say that you'd done a fine job of bailing him out of most of his problems."

Belle blushed at the impressed smile he gave her, but didn't say anything. She wanted to know why he'd called her father. More important, she wanted to know how the two most important men in her life had gotten along.

"Your dad and I are meeting next week. Apparently we already have a dinner date," he said, giving her a teasing look. "We're going to go ahead with our original plans and develop that property."

Belle had to forcibly refrain from clapping her hands and cheering. She did grin, though, and gave Mitch a tight hug. When she pulled back, she noticed a look in his cinnamon-brown eyes. Dark, intense, direct. It scared the hell out of her. She swallowed. She'd promised herself the days of avoidance were a thing of the past, so instead of distracting him with sex, she asked, "What else? You look like there's something important you want to say."

He gave a snort of laughter and nodded. Then, her hand still in his, he kissed her palm and held their entwined hands against his heart.

"Through everything that's happened, you've believed in me, Belle. I've spent most of my life trying to prove myself, wanting to impress people. But you never needed proof and were impressed despite my mistakes." He looked deep into her eyes and sighed.

"Belle, I love you. I've always loved you, even if I wasn't smart enough to know it. I wanted to marry you six years ago for a million reasons. But love was definitely one of them."

Joy spun through her system so fast she was dizzy with it. Her laughter rang through the trees as she pulled her hand free so she could hug him close. Her body pressed against his, Belle could feel the beat of his heart and gave a giddy thanks, knowing it belonged to her.

"I love you, too," she said softly, pulling back to smile into his eyes. "I love everything about you. Your ambition and drive, your integrity, your devotion to your family. I love your sense of humor and how freaking incredible you are in bed. I just love you, Mitch."

He gave her a huge grin. "Good. Then you'll say yes."

"Sure," she agreed. Then her brows drew together and she shook her head. "Yes to what?"

He carefully rolled aside and reached around to the picnic basket. Pulling a medium-size package out, he handed the festively wrapped box to her and motioned that she should open it.

Lecturing herself for wishing it was a smaller, jewelry-sized box, Belle leaned on one elbow and tugged at the bow. With an excited laugh and a questioning glance, she pulled the lid off the box.

Her jaw dropped as tears filled her eyes.

"Oh, Mitch," she breathed.

Blinking furiously, she pulled out a pair of tennis shoes.

"I want to make sure you have a choice. Six years ago, I wanted to marry you for a million reasons," he repeated. "This time, I only want to marry you for one. The only reason that matters. I love you."

Belle wiped away the tears. She'd be damned if she'd be a weepy mess for the most incredible moment of her life. The man she'd been dreaming of forever, her perfect hero, was being all gushy and she wanted to enjoy every wonderful moment of it.

"Forever?" she asked.

"Forever."

With a cheek-splitting grin, she handed him back the tennis shoes and shook her head. "Then I won't be needing these, will I?"

* * * * *

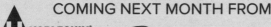

COMING NEXT MONTH FROM

HARLEQUIN *Blaze*®

Available May 21, 2013

#751 I CROSS MY HEART • *Sons of Chance*
by Vicki Lewis Thompson

When Last Chance cowhand Nash Bledsoe goes to investigate smoke at a neighboring ranch, the last thing he expects to find is a super sexy woman. But he hasn't got time for a relationship, especially with *this* female. Still, where there's smoke, there's fire....

#752 ALL THE RIGHT MOVES • *Uniformly Hot!*
by Jo Leigh

Whether it's behind the wheel of a sports car or in the cockpit of a fighter jet—or in bed!—John "Devil" Devlin has never faced a challenge like gorgeous spitfire Cassie O'Brien. Challenge accepted!

#753 FROM THIS MOMENT ON
Made in Montana • by Debbi Rawlins

Every time gorgeous cowboy Trace McAllister flashes his signature smile, the ladies come running. But street-smart Nikki Flores won't let another handsome charmer derail her future...which is definitely not in Blackfoot Falls.

#754 NO STRINGS...
by Janelle Denison

Chloe Reiss wants Aiden Landry, badly! But because of a no-fraternization rule at work, the only way they can indulge their passions is to do it in secret. Unfortunately, even the best-kept secrets don't always stay that way....

YOU CAN FIND MORE INFORMATION ON UPCOMING HARLEQUIN® TITLES, FREE EXCERPTS AND MORE AT WWW.HARLEQUIN.COM.

HBCNM0513

Love the Harlequin book you just read?

Your opinion matters.

Review this book on your favorite book site, review site, blog or your own social media properties and share your opinion with other readers!

Be sure to connect with us at:
Harlequin.com/Newsletters
Facebook.com/HarlequinBooks
Twitter.com/HarlequinBooks

HREVIEWS

REQUEST YOUR FREE BOOKS!
2 FREE NOVELS PLUS 2 FREE GIFTS!

red-hot reads!

YES! Please send me 2 FREE Harlequin® Blaze™ novels and my 2 FREE gifts (gifts are worth about $10). After receiving them, if I don't wish to receive any more books, I can return the shipping statement marked "cancel." If I don't cancel, I will receive 4 brand-new novels every month and be billed just $4.74 per book in the U.S. or $4.96 per book in Canada. That's a savings of at least 14% off the cover price. It's quite a bargain. Shipping and handling is just 50¢ per book in the U.S. and 75¢ per book in Canada.* I understand that accepting the 2 free books and gifts places me under no obligation to buy anything. I can always return a shipment and cancel at any time. Even if I never buy another book, the two free books and gifts are mine to keep forever.

150/350 HDN F4WC

Name	(PLEASE PRINT)
Address	Apt. #
City	State/Prov.	Zip/Postal Code

Signature (if under 18, a parent or guardian must sign)

Mail to the **Harlequin® Reader Service:**
IN U.S.A.: P.O. Box 1867, Buffalo, NY 14240-1867
IN CANADA: P.O. Box 609, Fort Erie, Ontario L2A 5X3

Want to try two free books from another line?
Call 1-800-873-8635 or visit www.ReaderService.com.

Terms and prices subject to change without notice. Prices do not include applicable taxes. Sales tax applicable in N.Y. Canadian residents will be charged applicable taxes. Offer not valid in Quebec. This offer is limited to one order per household. Not valid for current subscribers to Harlequin Blaze books. All orders subject to credit approval. Credit or debit balances in a customer's account(s) may be offset by any other outstanding balance owed by or to the customer. Please allow 4 to 6 weeks for delivery. Offer available while quantities last.

Your Privacy—The Harlequin® Reader Service is committed to protecting your privacy. Our Privacy Policy is available online at www.ReaderService.com or upon request from the Harlequin Reader Service.

We make a portion of our mailing list available to reputable third parties that offer products we believe may interest you. If you prefer that we not exchange your name with third parties, or if you wish to clarify or modify your communication preferences, please visit us at www.ReaderService.com/consumerschoice or write to us at Harlequin Reader Service Preference Service, P.O. Box 9062, Buffalo, NY 14269. Include your complete name and address.

SPECIAL EXCERPT FROM

HARLEQUIN®

Blaze®

New York Times bestselling author
Vicki Lewis Thompson is back with three new,
steamy titles from her bestselling miniseries
Sons of Chance.

I Cross My Heart

"Do *you* like an audience?" Bethany asked.

If he did, that would help cool her off. She wasn't into that. Of course, she wasn't supposed to be feeling hot in the first place.

"I prefer privacy when I'm making love to a woman." Nash's voice had lowered to a sexy drawl and his blue gaze held hers. "I don't like the idea of being interrupted."

Oh, Lordy. She could hardly breathe from wanting him. "Me, either."

She took another hefty swallow of wine, for courage. "I have a confession to make. You know when I claimed that this nice dinner wasn't supposed to be romantic?"

"Yeah."

"I lied."

"Oh, really?" His blue eyes darkened to navy. "Care to elaborate?"

"See, back when we were in high school, you were this out-of-reach senior and I was a nerdy freshman. So when you showed up today, I thought about flirting with you because now I actually have the confidence to do that. But when you offered to help repair the place, flirting with you didn't seem like such a good idea. But I still thought you were really hot." She took another sip of wine. "We shouldn't have sex, though. At least, I didn't think so this morning, but then I fixed up the dining room, and I admit I thought about you while I did that. So I think, secretly, I wanted it to be romantic. But I—"

"Do you always talk this much after two glasses of wine?" He'd moved even closer, barely inches away.

She could smell his shaving lotion. Then she realized what that meant. He'd shaved before coming over here. That was significant. "I didn't have two full glasses."

"I think you did."

She glanced at her wineglass, which was now empty. Apparently she'd been babbling and drinking at the same time. "You poured me a second glass." When he started to respond, she stopped him. "But that's okay, because if I hadn't had a second glass, I wouldn't be admitting to you that I want you so much that I almost can't stand it, and you wouldn't be looking at me as if you actually might be considering the idea of…"

"Of what?" He was within kissing distance.

"This." She grabbed his face in both hands and planted one on that smiling mouth of his. And oh, it was glorious. Nash Bledsoe had the best mouth of any man she'd kissed so far. Once she'd made the initial contact, he took over, and before she quite realized it, he'd pulled her out of her chair and was drawing her away from the table.

Ah, he was good, this guy. And she had a feeling she was about to find out just *how* good….

**Pick up I CROSS MY HEART by
Vicki Lewis Thompson, on sale May 21,
wherever Blaze books are sold.**

Copyright © 2013 by Vicki Lewis Thompson

HBEXP79755

They don't call him the "Devil" for nothing.

Air force captain John Devlin, the "Devil," lives for high-risk maneuvers, both in the cockpit *and* in the bedroom! A flyboy—even a wickedly hot one!—is the last thing Cassie O'Brien needs. Between the bar, grad school and her troubled brother, she is stretched to her limit. Yet the scorch and sizzle between them proves to be too much temptation. And when she gives in to this devil, she'll get more than she *ever* bargained for....

Pick up

All The Right Moves

by *Jo Leigh*,

on sale May 21 wherever you buy Harlequin Blaze books.

Red-Hot Reads

www.Harlequin.com

HB79756